Praise for
Joyce Weatherford and *Heart of the Beast*

"This sweeping modern Western . . . is hard to put down."

—Danise Hoover, *Booklist*

"*Heart of the Beast* brings to life part of the history of the Northwest, blows it up in full detail, and forces readers to think about how the West was won—all in a way that sandblasts the glossy trimmings off of the traditional Western. There are no cowboys here—only real people forced to deal with incredible hardship."

—D. J. Morel, *The Seattle Times*

"This is not a book, but a spell, an act of magic. Joyce Weatherford writes with a ruthless, fearless intelligence like Plath. She's an alchemist of language. Fueled by ferocious intensity and a glittering love of danger and risk, Weatherford has composed a brilliant, daring work."

—Kate Braverman, author of *Palm Latitudes*

"*Heart of the Beast* is an alarmingly beautiful book. I am sure we will all be reading Joyce Weatherford for a long time."

—Jim Harrison, author of *Legends of the Fall*

"A gripping novel of the dark American West . . . Weatherford's understanding of the violent hunger for ownership of land and the rich details of its working is nothing short of miraculous."

—Janet Fitch, author of *White Oleander*

"Joyce Weatherford's *Heart of the Beast* earns my highest praise. In crystalline language, Weatherford relates a fresh, new story of farming life in Eastern Oregon, the harm wreaked in the name of family, while also providing a unique slant on Native-American issues. Weatherford knows what it means to survive the above, and how to evoke necessary change in the constantly evolving New West. Her voice is strong and unflinching; her story is poignant and heartfelt."

—Jo-Ann Mapson, author of
Hank & Chloe, The Wilder Sisters, and *Bad Girl Creek*

"A moving portrait of an unforgiving yet beautiful land and the toughness needed to survive in it."

—Karen Anderson, *Library Journal*

"Pioneers who settled the intermountain West were a hard, restless, and ambitious lot. But only the hardest and most ambitious survived. *Heart of the Beast* is the tough-hearted story of such a family, a fierce book about fierce, privileged, overweening people. Joyce Weatherford knows her scene and her emotional territory cold, and she pulls no punches. This one will keep you up in the night."

—William Kittredge, author of *The Nature of Generosity*

Heart
of
the
Beast

JOYCE WEATHERFORD

SCRIBNER PAPERBACK FICTION
Published by Simon & Schuster
New York London Toronto Sydney Singapore

SCRIBNER PAPERBACK FICTION
Simon & Schuster, Inc.
Rockefeller Center
1230 Avenue of the Americas
New York, NY 10020

First Scribner Paperback Fiction edition 2002
SCRIBNER PAPERBACK FICTION and design are trademarks of
Macmillan Library Reference USA, Inc., used under license by
Simon & Schuster, the publisher of this work.
For information regarding special discounts for bulk purchases,
please contact Simon & Schuster Special Sales at 1-800-456-6798 or
business@simonandschuster.com

Designed by Kyoko Watanabe

Manufactured in the United States of America

1 3 5 7 9 10 8 6 4 2

The Library of Congress has cataloged the Scribner edition as follows:
Weatherford, Joyce.
Heart of the Beast / Joyce Weatherford.
p. cm.
1. Inheritance and succession—Fiction. 2. Women ranchers—Fiction.
3. Young women—Fiction. 4. Oregon—Fiction. I. Title.

PS3623.E38 H4 2001
813'.6—dc21 2001020662

ISBN 0-7432-1179-0
0-7432-1180-4 (Pbk)

part one

1

THE HARVEST WAS COMPLETE IN THE MORNING, AND THAT evening my mother died. I went to bed late that night, full of the raw ending of crop and life, and dreamed about the Nez Perce children, their shiny black hair cut short and falling smoothly to the side. They ran to my house screaming, chanting; but it wasn't for money, *kitchway*, like my mother described. I walked outside and saw the bodies of the children's parents cut into pieces, bound oddly back together. A wide-eyed head coupled with a foot, a hand joined a stomach, red and messy; it was a bloody totem. No matter how carved up they were, I could still see it was their mothers and fathers. I knew then, I could have killed my parents for what they had done.

I didn't grow up where my mother did. Elise Steele flourished in the cattle country of the Wallowa Mountains of Oregon, on the ranch Chief Joseph of the Nez Perce called Heart of the Beast. I was my father's daughter, born twenty-eight years ago at his homestead alongside the Columbia River. I was what occurred two centuries after Lewis and Clark sailed down our river eating dogs and writing history.

On that last day of harvest, the full moon passed. My pioneer family had always farmed by the cycles of the moon, and I was no different, cultivating the way my father taught me. The waning period, when the pull of the moon releases, is the time to reap, to plant, and to dig. It is when the ground lies vulnerable, carvable, and pliant. Ike Steele was my father, and he told me how things would go in the end. Life pours out from the downward horns of the moon.

Only twenty acres remained of the bright-colored wheat, a half day's cutting. As I walked out to my combine, all around me unfolded the darker auburn of harvested stubble, tinted by the minerals of the soil. My mother was so sick now, I could barely stand to leave her in the house alone. But a farmer had to finish reaping. It was as simple as that.

I fired up the combine, and waited while the engine smoothed out. That Indian summer morning, a soft breeze blew across my ear like the whisper of a beloved. I inched forward past the truck parked next to me, and made my way out to the last land. The sickle zigzagged into the standing grain, mowing the rustling carpet of bounty. The combine eased into the endless pattern of tracks that lay down platinum against the burnished spent stalks, the nourishment gone to seed.

Even after two months of harvest, I fell under its spell, watching the waving awns shake as the glinting bat of the header laid them over the blades. I sliced them forever still. The smell of wheat filled the cab as the cutting began, and sometime later gold grain rushed into the bin the way a mother's milk comes in a while after a baby is born.

The sun warmed the earth quickly, hardening the wheat. Most mornings went slowly because dew made the stalks cut and thresh poorly. It was my father who taught me how to cut grain, and how to seed land. My mother taught me never to let go of it.

With the thirty-foot header, I worked the long rectangular piece down and down, trimming away its edges and shortening the ends. Finally, all that remained were the small triangular patches where I made my corners. I cut up one side, completed them on the return; and I was finished. The end of harvest was the termination of the land's and my twelve months of labor, simultaneously the birth of the seed and the death of the crop. I loved and feared that time—loved it because the cycle of guessing, hoping, and shepherding the stand was finally over. I feared it because a person could never tell what would come next. Fire, floods, disease, drought. These were the things that could get in the way.

For a moment, I turned the combine loose, not bothering to drive anywhere while the wheat threshed completely out. Unloading at the truck, I slipped the machine into fourth gear for the sprint home. In the past, there was a tradition of pulling the headers up and racing them back to the ranch. The run home wasn't as exciting now that I was the only one there. But still, charging over the completely cut fields from twenty feet above was the best part of the year.

It was the course of things to wash the machines afterward, to blow the awns of wheat from the pulleys, flush the last bits of grain from steeled and twirling augers. But instead I left it by the compressor and steam cleaner, and started into the house to see how my mother was doing. I took off my bandanna, shaking the dust from my hair. I hadn't washed it for days, but it still glowed white blond, the color of flax. By now, my hair had lost the green tint that came in the spring. After the long chill of winter was over, I always felt the sun in my feet and the urge to swim in the emerald Columbia. Every spring, the water turned my hair the lightest shade of green, the color of newly sprouted wheat.

My mother's sickness was why I had stopped reaping three days before, an unconscionable act for a farmer. I was compelled to take her to the mineral baths one last time. In May, the doctors at Hanford Regional Health Center in Richland had told me she had advanced brain cancer.

"Your mother probably doesn't have more than a couple months, Iris," said Dr. Groves, the oncologist. "We see a lot of this lately," he added, placing his hand on my back. His fingers were drawn together like a feeding sea anemone.

I imagined he was reading my bones, deciphering a braille X ray.

"Lefort was the first to study the head," he whispered, as if he were sharing a great secret. "Before any of them. Such humble beginnings," he said, making soft clicking noises with his tongue.

I drew away. I resented his authoritarian manner. "I've never heard of Lefort," I told him.

"He took guillotined heads of the French Revolution and smashed them," he said, staring down the hospital hall.

"Smashed them how?" I asked nervously.

Groves shrugged. "With boards. Cracked them with rocks. Dropped them on the ground. He wanted to see how the breakdown happened."

I nodded. There was an uncomfortable silence. I thought it was odd what doctors thought about when faced with death.

"It's brilliant the way Lefort discovered how things fall apart in the head," he said finally. "Don't you think?"

At home, my mother sat during the day in the green parlor room filled with her sister's art—the busts of the family Hanna had done long ago. At eight o'clock every night, she went to bed. I stayed up later, long enough to help her when she called because she had wet her sheets. She was always cold and had a permanent chill in those bones that I had once come from. They stuck out now and were barely covered by her skin of wet tissue paper. Her snow-colored hair floated around her as the tide pulls and sways in ocean forests. My mother had always been stunning, but when she was dying, she was as beautiful as anyone I had ever seen. She had the violet eyes of fate, and the loss of weight made the bones in her face stand out like I imagined Helen of Troy's—the beautiful destroyer of two worlds.

Before the end of harvest, my mother had told me she wanted to go to the mineral baths. She loved Carson Springs; and like her parents and grandparents before her, she went to the waters with religious regularity. Mother worshiped her family, especially her father, the horse trader, who successfully bargained the Nez Perce out of their best Appaloosas. They were some of the finest horses in the world, so tough they were exported for the military campaigns in North Africa and the Bosphorus.

When my mother's family first came to the state of Oregon, my great-grandparents went to sit in the caves along the Columbia River. They placed satchels of camphor around their necks to ward off disease, drank fossil water, and twined copper bracelets around their wrists, curing themselves of rheumatism that laced their bones into stone. For days, they lay thin and naked to the numbing cold night, strengthening their movement and will through the alchemy of mountains. The ranges of the great Northwest were made of strange erupting volcanoes that healed even the clear-cuts.

"It's my baptism," Mother said to me. She touched the bone of her wrist to her half-closed eyes as I lifted her into the Blazer. "It's time for me to go under the water."

For two months, she had been closing down, sleeping constantly. She napped even while drinking her coffee, spilling it on herself. I could not get her fine clothing clean, and trips to the dry cleaners in Pendleton were impossible until after harvest. She wore her designer clothes daily, refusing my offers of T-shirts and sweats. Mother sat remote and spotted with sepia like the photographs of our family generations ago.

Together we drove out to the Columbia River Gorge, and that empty feeling came back, the way it did every year near the end of harvest and before seeding the new crop. I felt as if I'd been lifted up by my flanks and thrown to the ground hard, had the wind knocked out of me like our calves, caught in the chute and waiting to be branded. I would catch my breath for a minute before the air was pushed out again by the weight of the glowing red brand, twisted and fashioned into the shape of my family name—the Bar S. The Steele bars.

When I drove out to the river, I understood why Meriwether Lewis killed himself after navigating it. A melancholy came over a person there. It was ironic that this river would call forth the migration that created our country. My ancestors had planted trees to shelter themselves from what they called the immensity of the land. Even back then, they tried to escape from the wind sickness that plagued our family and caused the jangle of nerves. They used to call it shell shock. Where we live is like that, so vast that a person feels unnecessary, where everything without snarl and tangle is blown away.

I blamed the melancholy on the colored winds of the Indian summer, blamed it on anything. We drove through them there at the water, the white blasts that came at dusk generated from the current charging through the turbines of the Columbia's dams. I loathed that wind, thought it would poison me, take me as my mother's generation had been taken. So, I sped under the power lines, the unending metal tributaries that came running like rain off the water dams. Even energy was harvested in fall; the river filled again, and California would be ready to buy its power once more.

Flowing over the white gales of the river was the wind of the west, a deep shade of crimson. The farmers in the Willamette Valley grew clingy crops like pole beans, grass seed, and other tender yields dependent on rain and caring hands. The scarlet of their field-burning smoke blows over us, as every autumn they light their lands on fire to kill the diseases harbored from reproduction. We never did that; we always let disease go.

Driving to the mineral baths, I glanced over at my mother. She was slumped down to the side with her head drooping. It was a long-held terror of mine that my mother's features would someday run together and there would be nothing to remember her by. There, with her head forward, I saw her mouth part and let escape a glistening line of saliva. I thought then she had given up her complex thoughts to the wind.

We rode on west, under the blowing wire harnesses with the sun setting over Mt. Hood, mauve and pink, colored like a cathedral. There was a righteousness in Oregon that annoyed me. We passed it along the gorge: the truck drivers that haul garbage from Portland and Seattle to the largest landfill in the Northwest, out here in eastern Oregon.

The people in the cities were righteous as well, those who made all that garbage and dumped it here. They were the same ones who complained about the farm subsidy program when they bought cheap food at the grocery store. They said we didn't care about the land, our mother they called it. Said farmers just robbed it, cut it up, and poisoned it with pesticides.

The truckers didn't bother with philosophical arguments. They figured there was no one but themselves to enforce any law, and their rules were naturally the best ones. They drove in tandem down the highway so you couldn't go speeding by them. Plastic chickens danced out of their windows, and they fired starting pistols at cars they thought were going too fast. They made for treacherous road.

I mostly ignored them, the self-appointed freeway constabulary. I sped by them on any side of the highway I pleased, and hoped that when I passed, a rock would fly up and dent their shiny tractors—to the truckers, that was like damaging their jewels. So I gave the garbage haulers the finger and blew past because we had Ike's old Blazer with a Hearst gearshift and a 454 engine, quicker than those trucks'. The hood rose up and down from the rattle and hum of the motor, and we sailed on down that highway as though we were surfing on the big river itself.

When we passed over the Bridge of the Gods, a trucker yelled out his window at me. I slowed down and drove alongside him. My mother had slumped over even more, and with her relaxed face and open mouth, she looked handicapped. I kept her by the trucker's window for miles; I wanted him to feel as trapped as I did. He quit bothering me then. Maybe he thought I was on my way to a hospital and he figured that's why I was driving so fast.

"It'd be an insane asylum," I said to myself. I'd go to Dammasch, the same one she took her sister, Hanna, to, and drop her off there for good, just like what my mother had done.

My first memory of my mother was of her singing. She said it was the same song since the day I was born. In the evening air that breathed with the saw of crickets, she rocked out on the screened-in porch, waiting deep into the night for my father to come in from the fields. "My bonnie lies over the ocean, my bonnie lies over the sea," she crooned softly, and swayed in the Shaker rocking chair.

"Your bonnie is right here, Mom," I interrupted her, hoping for some attention.

"Oh, bring back," she sang on, and then stopped. She walked inside the house, over to the wall next to the washer and dryer, and hit her forehead against it three times. It sounded deep, funereal, the toll of a bell. "You can never get away from your blood," she told the old flower-papered house.

I knew she was right; I couldn't cut her loose, especially now that she was about to die. If I did, I knew, out of retribution, I'd get all the same diseases and problems she had, and her mother had had, and on and on. So I kept her with me by my side, and we went out to the mineral springs instead. I should have slowed up but the sun had gone down and that meant no one was on the road but us. I wondered why she hated sunsets so much; I've always liked them better than the sunrise.

We rented a cabin for three days. It was made of pioneer wood that talked all evening as if it had found a long-lost friend in the wind. It didn't matter because my mother had fun that night waking me up every hour to go to the bathroom. It was her Norwegian philosophy that if she was paying for my lodging, she deserved to get something out of the deal. I had to help her sit down and get up from the toilet, and if I didn't get there fast enough she screamed from her room, and gave me a dirty look when I came running. I knew it was difficult for her. It was as if all her bodily functions were developing personalities of their own and disagreeing with her about the timing of their use. But I became angry anyway. She told me to pour warm water between her legs to help her urinate. I was embarrassed by the sight of the trickle running down her small and unprotected white crotch.

She delighted in the reversal of roles, called me her little nurse-maid. It occurred to me then that she had once done this to my body. I was mortified that I had ever been so small and helpless that I had to depend on her for such fundamental things as voids and sustenance.

As the nights at the springs drew on, we commerced in health. I watched her fall into sleep, hypnotized by the black spiders dancing on her eyes, those things caused by the cancer. I began napping like her in the day and sleeping restlessly as she did at night. We sojourned on at the baths, gaming like sinners of Babylon.

In the mornings after her massage, I gave her showers. Though it would have been smarter and easier for me to take one with her, I refused. It became hard for me to undress around my mother. I avoided her envious eyes. I washed her standing in the shower with my shorts on, like I was washing a dog. I became entirely wet as I cleaned the places that scared me—her armpits, her breasts, her stomach that pouched out and looked perpetually pregnant. She told me it was the price she paid for my having invaded her body for nine months.

I pulled up her arms while steadying her, soaping those armpits, the endless hollows. I reached my fist into her body there, like she was a puppet waiting for a hand to take her over. If I could have invaded my mother, I would have captured her idols and held them ransom. I would have massaged her heart to make it beat more sweetly.

The laws of the earth talked to me as I labored my way down her body. Gravity had pulled everything into that immensity of belly. Her torso was thin and witchlike, and her legs came out of her like crooked wood. I wet towels, soaped them, and cleaned between her legs. I rinsed them out and washed her again, worrying whether all the soap had been removed or whether she might contract a bladder infection. I wondered if it ever crossed her mind whether she had left me clean.

"Your father abandoned me when you came. That's why we never had any more children. We were happy before," she said. "And now all I have left is you." I noticed she was smiling.

"He abandoned you before I came. He did it when Jake was born," I replied. I couldn't stand anything being blamed on me when I could just as well blame someone else, especially when that someone happened to be my brother.

"When you were born was when I stopped practicing law," she mused.

"You were having so much fun at home you couldn't stand to leave us?"

She smiled and closed her eyes. "Yes," she said. "That's right."

"People make choices," I replied.

"Ike never talked to me after you were born," she added.

"That's because he was so busy telling me what to do," I said, smiling back at her. "And anyway, isn't that what happens to people when they have children?"

"I never heard that one," she whispered hoarsely.

"It's what everyone says," I responded. " 'Kids ruin everything.' " I rinsed the washcloth. "I would have known," I said. "I always know how things will turn out."

The truth was my parents survived together as long as they each had an enemy. My father's was his son. My mother's was her daughter.

"Everything would have been different if you had been another boy," she said. "You can't be as strong," she told me. "And there is the name. Ranchers need to keep their legacy."

"Do you wish you were born a boy, Mother?" I had asked.

"Not for one second," she responded.

I think my mother felt she had contributed, had rendered something that my father could use in the fields. But everything beyond what my father worked, my blood, muscle, bones, and the turning to stone of my tongue, I knew belonged to her.

We soaked in the lithium pools together. In the ultrabuoyant water, I anchored a circular life preserver at her neck, two around her knees, and she floated. She laid her head back in the water nature had given Vikings like us to make up for our deficiencies of mood. I watched her while I sat immersed down deep in lithium. I inhaled the sweet smell, drank the soft water, and felt dizziness, gnawing euphoria. The skin on my fingers puckered and curled into miniature mountain ranges. The water floated my hands up, holding her near me as she slept. She looked peaceful, and I smiled at her before she dozed off. In that sleep, her body flowed into me. She pushed me over toward the hard rock edge.

It was on the third night of our stay that I murmured, "We need to finish the harvest."

"Yes, it's time," Mother answered, stirring from sleep.

Sitting on the side of her bed, I rubbed my palm on the white satin sheets I'd brought so her weak body could move more easily while she slept. I was infatuated with those heavy sheets that draped like a river over me. I had begun to sleep with my mother; we shared her bed, and I lay back next to her and thought of my great-grandparents. They were the ones to slap their soles to the Oregon Trail, the ones who claimed the earth. I wondered if I would ever be different, if I would ever be free of them.

My mother talked to me as we lay there. "They say, if you want to learn about yourself, study your mother." Her head shook from loss of muscle control.

I found myself thinking she was nodding like she was an expert on the subject. I responded with silence.

"Do you want to know what you will look like," she went on, "when you die?"

I watched the bones in her head move as she spoke from above the shimmering satin. "You," I whispered. "I'll look like you." She frightened me. If she had said jump off the Bridge of the Gods, I would have done it for her. At that moment, I would have done anything.

"And what will you know when you die?" she asked me.

I searched her eyes for the answer. But she didn't look at me. She never looked at me. "What?" I asked.

After a long pause, she growled in a fresh rush of pain.

"Tell me," I insisted softly, leaning over and placing my ear to her lips.

"Water will never rise above its source," she said, closing her eyes and drifting off to sleep.

I stared at my mother for the rest of the night, didn't fall asleep until almost daylight, when even the rhythm of my breathing matched hers.

2

As we left the mineral springs the next day, I looked in the rearview mirror, and there in the heat, vast swirls of purple stretched out for miles behind us like the glimmering tail of a serpent.

Where we lived, driving was as constant as the drying wind. Our food, correspondence, machine parts, everything we needed was at least as far as Lona, fifteen miles from the Bar S. When Mother and I returned home, I drove to town for the mail; the letter arrived on the day before she died.

It was one of those glaring afternoons. The sun turned the stubble to magnetized golden filings and pulled them west with its afternoon decline. The dust of a neighbor's plow rose to the sky like a great finger dragging a line through something finished.

I walked into the post office and opened box 3. Noel the postmaster came to the teller window and leaned out. He was one of the Pankits, the notorious family of bad debts and laments.

"Parcel from a lawyer," he said, slapping a manila envelope on the counter and placing his hand over it. "Need to sign."

I set my bundle of letters down and grabbed the pen. Since we didn't retrieve the mail more than once a week, our box was always crammed. Co-op bills, farm service letters, and agricultural journals spilled down the counter like a fan of cards. The pile stopped at a poster announcing the stamp series commemorating the family farm.

"Anything juicy?" I asked, knowing he had probably read every word that my registered mail contained. Small towns. I signed the yellow slip. "Thanks," I said, reaching for the envelope.

"I wouldn't thank me just yet." He paused. "It's heavy. Lawyers don't send out books like this for the fun of it."

I wanted to leave because Noel would tell our business all over town. He was a professional crier at the Baptist church in Kamania. Noel loved his job at the post office because he often received the heads up on tragedies even before the victims did. He sniffed them out like a rat-killing dog.

"How's your mother?" he asked.

"Still my mother." I nodded, looking level at him.

"Not for long," he said, shaking his head with pity. Noel licked his lips and squinted hopefully at me. "Everyone comes in and asks if I know how Elise Steele's doin'."

"Kind of them. Lot of concern around here," I replied, taking the envelope from under Noel's hand.

"Thought that one might have been from your mother's sister," he said, pointing at one of my letters. "Folks here wonderin' when she's comin' home."

"Not in thirty-one years. No reason to now," I said, as I left the building.

I drove out the same way I came in; there was only one road to town. Lona was a begrudging little place. It looked like its name, which came from the legend of a baby abandoned by his mother. Turn-of-the-century houses decayed in the back skirts of town, and there was one lone restaurant. The motto danced on a sign perched on the rooftop, Only Two Places to Eat, Here and Home. A tavern with a bleary red Budweiser beacon crowded next to the chemical depot.

I always shopped the grocery store in Lona even if it was expensive. The next supermarket was sixty miles away in Pendleton. There wasn't much else to Lona—a grade school, high school, grain elevator, parts store, two churches, and a soda fountain called Hasty Freeze. The H in Hasty had broken long ago and it read nasty Freeze.

Grabbing at the letter in the mound of mail on the passenger seat, I drove the Blazer sloppily with one hand. The air smelled of perfume from an advertisement in a Nordstrom catalog. The registered mail was from our attorney, Miles Emmerett. Miles's letters were never good: long five-pagers about estate taxes, land values, depreciation and loss. I threw the letter back on the seat. I could see why people out here turned to the land. It was the only thing that never died.

The fall universe spread out before me like an infinite lover. It made a person want to be alone with the sky billowing out in a soft sheet. The land turned tender and became a refuge in the fall. Colors intensified into Halloween shades. Russian thistles changed into deep crimson with brick-colored tips, and yarrow yellowed into the setting sun. Clouds burned orange and purple, every sunset a bonfire. My family had covered this land like a cartographer's map, turning it fertile in search of Eden, and I was no different.

When I arrived home, I read the letter sitting in the Blazer. It felt safe in there, and I wanted to stay all day, the doors closed, the wind shut out, the sun caressing me softly through the windows. But I slid out finally with the thought that my mother might have fallen, and headed inside our old white ranch house.

I stared at the wide-jawed porch that looked as if it could eat a person. Our home unfolded from the peaked attic as if it were an elongated barn. The dark green front door centered below the roof's apex. To the right, the parlor room opened onto a patio.

Mother would be sitting in there on her rocking chair, pillows cushioning her fragile bones. The rocker sat permanently pushed up against the wall, so she could get into it alone, and the runners made black marks there when she sat in it. She spent her days in that chair and lived in the past, talking about harvest crews from years ago. To the left, off the kitchen, lay the screened porch where twenty ranch hands used to eat dinner in the hot summer nights of harvest. Rawhide-laced chairs still cluttered the wooden floor where the crews relaxed after a fourteen-hour workday, eating the plentiful but tough beef that came from our own slaughtered cattle.

"Mother?"

She opened her eyes and nodded. I wondered if on the verge of her death she would finally come clean with me about Heart of the Beast.

"Do you know anything special about the upper place?" I asked.

The air smelled of fall foxtail, dry and ready for combustion. It reminded me of riding the range with the sagebrush bruising my knees and the yellow color of my horse Jade's silver bit when she ate yarrow mixed with the wild wheat grass.

"Like what?" she answered slowly. She closed her eyes again and slid down in her chair; she was a drifting mutiny.

"Just what I said. Do you know what's on it?" I was impatient.

"No," she replied in that innocent lawyer's way that meant, "Show your hand and I'll trump you."

Her game of possum tested me. "What is on it," I said, "has to do with the Nez Perce."

She was silent, sphinxlike.

"Want some water?" I asked. I wanted a drink—of something that would numb me.

"No, thank you. I'm fine," my mother said. She was radiant, the way people get before they die.

In the kitchen, I placed my feet on the cracked tile, imagining I was walking down a giant razor edge. When I was young I used to play a game with my brother called risk. He'd ask me, "Would you rather slide down a razor's edge into a pool of alcohol or would you rather have married Dad?"

I went to the liquor cabinet and took out the bottle of vodka. I grabbed a tumbler from the cupboard and sent the door back with a push. Standing there, I imagined all of the possibilities I could hold in my hand: her sleeping pills, rat poison, pesticide, violet-colored diesel, anhydrous ammonia, the sickle of a combine, the rope my brother used on the cat he hung from the rafters of the tack room. I poured myself a glassful of vodka, no ice.

"The Nez Perce tribe this time. Not the government. They're suing you, they want your land," I announced when I returned.

I knew this information would piss her off. My mother had graduated from Lewis and Clark Law School. She practiced law, ran the ranches and my father's estate after he died, and paid the inheritance taxes with the seven-figure insurance policy my father had bought with his life. After spending two-thirds the cost of the whole ranch, she saw how the government wasted her money, investing millions in fish ladders that caused more damage than they spared when the floods came.

"What do they want with it?" she asked hoarsely.

"They say it's sacred," I said.

"It's nothing but a bunch of rocks out there," she stated. I could hear her labored breathing.

I was silent for a moment as I thought about what I had read in the letter. It claimed the Nez Perce creation happened on her land. It was a simple hill up on her ranch, one hundred miles east in the Wallowa Mountains where we pastured our cattle in the summer. I used to go hunting for arrowheads there.

"You never noticed anything unusual about it?" I took another drink.

"Peo Peo Tholekt and his band used to camp up there. My father would talk to him, and Hanna would sit on his lap," she said disgustedly. She hadn't spoken the name of her sister in years.

"For some reason, it's addressed to both you and Hanna," I said quietly, looking at her.

"It's not hers anymore," my mother replied, fiercely. "We owned it together. Inherited it together, but I bought her out. I bought her out of everything. So she could have money to leave." My mother grimaced. "The artist."

The room remained silent; she refused to elaborate much, just like any good lawyer. "Who was Peo Peo Tholekt?" I asked finally.

"Chief Joseph's nephew," she said. "It wasn't just him. Lots of Nez Perce came 'round."

"Do you know why?"

She shrugged. "They went everywhere. Like Gypsies. When we took the cattle up we always saw the Indians," she said, waving her hand. I noticed she had removed her wedding band.

I took a sip of vodka. I heard Carl, the hired hand, in the crawler coming back from the 1600; the low hum of the diesel engine worked the house over like ragged wind. He would have just finished preparing the fallow land for winter seeding. We needed rain and there had been none.

"The letter," I said, holding it up for her to see. "Says a lot about the place you were born, Heart of the Beast. The Nez Perce claim there's a legend that goes with your property. Have you heard it?" I asked casually.

"I know where I was born," she snapped at me. She gripped the rests of the rocker. Her arms shook as she tried to pull herself back up in the chair. "Do you think I care about that? Now?" She closed her eyes and inhaled deep and hard.

"They say their people were created from your land." I took another drink. My boots splayed to the side of my chair, the silver of the Bar S brand stitched into the heels.

"Created from my land? Ha. They were created from Africa. We all were."

I went on reading from the letter. The pages were thick and white. Bankers bond from a lawyer. "They call themselves the Nimiipuu, the People."

"It's Nez Perce," she said, putting a finger on her temple, her hand holding her head up. "Lewis misunderstood Sacagawea. He thought she called them pierced nose, Nez Perce. That's the way things go. Tough shit, Nimipo," she rhymed.

"They say the land was taken illegally. Is this true?"

"God damn them all," my mother said. "Always the same. Pitching their tepees outside our house, demanding bonuses from my father. *Scio kitchway.* That's Nez Perce as you can get. 'I need money.' Been that way since my grandfather settled the place."

"They don't want money now. They want your land," I said. "The Nez Perce want justice from you." I watched her carefully. "You didn't answer my question."

"A day late," she growled.

"No," I replied looking at her. There was something about it all that pleased me immensely. "They got us at the exact right time."

"What are you smiling about?" she asked. "It's your land now. Your problem."

"I'll just give it to them," I lied. I wanted to infuriate her, get back at her for doing such a bad job of everything, then dying and leaving me.

She paused, staring straight ahead in disbelief. "I never understood it," she said, narrowing her eyes.

I saw the icy fluttering of cataracts in her black pupils. She had had them removed but they came back. Her eyes looked like frozen lakes. I thought of the story of the blind man led by his daughter and wondered if Oedipus was possible in the age of technology. Sure it was, I decided. "Understood what?"

"You're nothing without this," she said, waving her hand again. "What you are and what you have didn't appear out of thin air." Her body began moving in small convulsions as if she were serving herself blows. "Stolen land," my mother said angrily. "So what? We all live on stolen land. The Indians weren't here first. It was the land. It was here before they all migrated over it. Before Columbus. Before horses, before farmers, before agribusiness, and before the trash company used it for the toxic waste dump. Besides"—her voice cracked—"they didn't want land, they wanted fish."

"Sure, they didn't want land." I nodded as if I agreed with her. "It was just their home."

"It's not just land," she said abruptly. "It's you. It's your home."

"No," I said. "It's not me."

She stopped and looked across the room at the clay statues. The heads. The room was full of them, all of my family there, except me. The twelve of them lined the walls and competed with the living for air. They were overwhelming, with their pioneer personalities of grit, determination, and perversion.

They were the busts that my aunt Hanna had created before she went into the mental institution. My mother told me of the hours she spent sitting for her sister. My father never sat still long enough to be sculpted. She did him anyway, from memory. It was supposed to be her masterpiece, some kind of personal quest of hers that she utterly failed. None of them were ever cast in bronze. They remained mired in clay like Agrippa, deteriorating and bolted on their earth-spattered wooden stands. Arranged by generation, they rested on pedestals of redwood, oak, granite, and twirled marble, like a Roman gallery of patrician busts. It was embarrassing sometimes, and it certainly took people aback, especially my friends, when they came to our house.

I seldom went into this room. I couldn't stand it. No matter where I stood, the heads never looked at me. Especially when I gazed into my mother's eyes, hers stared past me, as if I weren't important enough to be recognized.

Since my mother's illness, the green room had become her favorite place. It gave her comfort to be with the people who had gone before her when she was about to cross over herself. For that reason, I had a mind to take them all to the dump after she died. They scared me, the way they kept a decomposing vigil. Because I wasn't there, I felt like they demanded I tend them, care for them.

My mother looked intently at her husband's likeness. "The land is yours," she said. "It has already scarred you with its thirst."

I balanced the glass on my thigh and began to think my mother had become altogether too lucid.

"Stupid," she announced. "You're stupid if you give it up. The Indians didn't. Never let it go until they died. No one just gives up a chunk of his heart." My mother's death-colored cheeks flushed red.

"Well. Let me be the first." I leered at her like a drunken bride. "What about your sister? She gave it up."

"She left," my mother said sharply. "It's not a part of her." I heard the pump jack begin drawing water to the reservoir, the low heartbeat of the house.

"The only sane one of us," I retorted. For the first time, the room appeared beautiful to me, the way ugly things begin to look lovely and gain texture when the brain sponges up alcohol. I lost my sense of smell. I no longer breathed the leather in our house—the hide-bound lawyer chair, the giant painting of Chief Joseph on the stretched antelope skin.

"Weak. She was the only weak one."

"She wasn't weak; she was strong," I declared, tapping my drink on the armrest.

"I never understood it," my mother said again, shaking her head.

"What?" I demanded, curling my lip. "What don't you understand?"

"Why Ike liked you so much."

"Now we're getting it. How much did he like me, Mother?"

"Pipsqueak," she blurted. "I always thought of you as a pipsqueak. That you wouldn't amount to much." She shifted in her chair. "All of this was supposed to be for Jake. Ike was the one who demanded we have more children in case one of you died." She shook her head back and forth, like a horse fighting a bit.

I stared at her in disbelief, and the heat began rising. "Self-fulfilling prophecy, wasn't it?"

"I lost everything when my baby boy left me," my mother went on.

My mother blathering about her lost son made me want to kill her. Not with pills or easy methods. I had in mind bringing her to the top of the elevator and kicking her out the door. "That beautiful boy," I replied through tight lips. "Do you want to know what I think about him?"

"He was everything to me," she said. Beyond her illness, she suddenly looked weak and vulnerable, as if she were a twenty-year-old describing the death of her betrothed.

"He wasn't anything to anybody else," I seethed. "He never worked, he was always angry and mean." My eyes began to water, stinging tears. "He left."

"Ike was too hard on him."

"And it was okay for Ike to be hard on me?" I said, striking my thigh and spilling my drink.

"The one you love the most. You beat the most. Haven't you heard that? It's an old Scandinavian saying."

I had had it with her. It was over. It was war. "Do you want to know what Ike said to me before he died?"

"I know," she lied.

"No you don't," I blurted. "You didn't see our accident. You never saw what happened to him." I took a deep fast drink.

She was silent for a moment. "Carl told me," she lied again.

I regarded my mother. Carl wouldn't have said anything, was mute when it came to family matters. I took another drink. The glass felt as if it would stay in my hand. It was the sea bell of a mermaid. I was underwater again; the vodka held my hand as the arms of a harbor hold tranquil ocean. "Ike said I was the most beautiful woman in the world." I drew my words out slowly, elongating them into freshwater pearls and savoring her reaction.

In that next second, I saw a change. Ever so slightly, my mother cocked her head and took a breath. "You think you're so smart," she said. "Think you know it all." She had a pure look in her as if all the possibilities of water in her body had frozen and turned into white light.

Suddenly I was afraid of her. I had not won. The world was made up of my mother and me, and we both knew I was not the most beautiful woman in our world. She was. She would always be everything I wasn't. I looked at her, and for a moment, I wanted to retreat. I imagined she had beaten her disease, slipped her skin, and recovered from the brain cancer. A little girl was in control of me, and I wanted my mother back.

"Why do you think I never said anything?" she snapped, her face lighting up with the joy of battle. "You working like that? Twelve years old. Driving combine for fourteen hours a day. Always driving. Driving cattle from one ranch to another. Across two counties. Do you think I didn't notice you were raw from one knee to the other?" She paused. "You think you're so smart."

"I learned from the master," I told her.

"Goddammit," she said loudly. "I gave you to him."

I let go of my glass, dropped it on the floor, the sound of it shattering like ice breaking over plowshares. I sat back in the long arcs of the rocker. It rolled over some dirt, some broken glass. There were shards everywhere. There was silence.

3

THE MORNING AFTER OUR FIGHT, AS I WALKED OUT TO
finish harvest, my boots sank into the earth like thin knives, gathered
dirt, and turned permanently brown. The heat in the air dried up my
body, and I wasn't able to sweat. My clothes clung dumbly to me and
white rolls of skin on my stomach stubbornly pushed out my belly button so it could be seen through my T-shirt. I despised it because it was
an outie. It rose up and poked out over the top of my Levi's. I had tried
covering it with a Band-Aid, the way pregnant women do, to hide it.
But that didn't work; nothing would bury it, that little onion head in
the middle of my stomach.

I lashed around in a crimson state of tantrum, kicking my dogs out
of the way when they came to meet me after I returned from harvesting. Instead of going into the house to see my mother, I had parked the
combine and grabbed my rifle out of the pickup, looking to shoot the
feral cat. It was then I remembered the Angus yearling ready to calve.
Hiking out to check on her, I took the gun with me. I had half a mind
to shoot her too, just for the trouble she caused.

We had recently sold most of the cattle, but twenty head or so still
roamed loose on the range around the Bar S. The yearling had been
one of these. She waited to drop her calf out in the airstrip—a long
uphill pasture covered by bunchgrass where my father used to leave
the earth in his red Super Cub. I stepped over the ropes cemented in

the ground, tethers to hold the plane back from the wind by its weak wings.

The yearling languished at the far corner, as far away from humans as she could get. I heard the noise before I saw her. A low, growling bellow shook her lungs. Even from far away, I could see she was rocking, moving her legs and trying to get up. Immobilized on the ground, she lay in a deformed black ball. Only the rounded mass of her belly poked up off the land.

I hurried back to the ranch for the pickup and Carl, and placed the rifle in the rack. Carl was the Norwegian bachelor who had been a hired hand for my family for thirty-seven years. He didn't do much anymore except work on the equipment, but I was glad to have him stay on. Decent hands were nearly impossible to find. The younger ones always tried to get me to fall in love with them, hoping they could marry me and get my ranch.

We backed the pickup down into the corral and to the barn. The equipment for calving was mostly in the tack room. The smell of dirty leather, horse sweat, hay, and rolled oats permeated the room. Saddles, from ancient to brand-new, were lined up, placed on thick planks anchored to the wall. The smallest, my father's first one, was only a foot long and barely came down below a horse's withers. The old black stock seats came from the turn of the last century, with their high cantles and pommel rolls for bucking, tiny wrapped horns for roping, and latigo straps for lariats. The new saddles sat to the right, with padded seats, soft caramel-colored leather, larger saddlehorns, and tailored tapaderas. I loved everything about the tack room. Before I was old enough to ride, I played in there. I crawled up into the huge saddle seats and pretended I was riding Peruvian Paso parade horses.

In one messy corner we kept the branding iron, old yokes for oxen, the materials for the calving season. The stories of calving are gruesome. The worst case was when my father had to cut up a calf inside the mother to get it out. Carl loaded the calf puller, a big winch that sits on the haunches of a cow and hooks into the calf and pulls the head out. I remembered the time my father had botched a delivery, had gotten the tongs in the eyes of a calf. If that happened, I'd get the whole mess over with: take the .22 to the mother, then pop her in the stomach to end both their suffering.

"We should shoot her if she gets into trouble," I told Carl as I climbed into the driver's seat and started the engine. I hated myself for being such a coward in front of him. In the worldview of a ranch hand, the boss's daughter was useless, especially when the boss was dead.

"We'll have to see," Carl said, as I drove away from the barn. He rubbed the pearly snaps of his denim sleeve over his forehead. Carl spoke slowly and practiced great pauses before articulating his ideas. "Don't want to"—he hesitated—"lose them both." His elbow bumped on the window frame, as the pickup beat itself over sagebrush and bunchgrass. The rain-colored cowboy hat slid toward me on the sunken seats, and we breathed dust and the smell of empty grease gun canisters.

When we approached the yearling, she tried to get up again. Her hindquarters, partially paralyzed, dragged along the ground. I parked and we walked up slowly. The forelegs of the calf stuck out from behind like two devil legs, cloven and black. Carl pushed on her dull belly to see where the calf was. There was ammonia in the air around her.

"It's down already," he said.

"That's good," I replied, looking out toward the Columbia River. I hoped we wouldn't have to poke the forceps in the calf to pull it out.

The afternoon heated her breath into heaves. Long sticky straws of mucus fluttered out of her blue nose. We waited on her, and waited. The longer it took the more nervous I became. The idea of their never being free of each other turned me hot and sick. Helplessly watching the yearling frustrated me. I preferred violence. Violence usually worked.

"We're gonna use the muscle relaxer," I asked as much as said, grabbing the bottle from the red ice chest along with the needle and the syringe. We had to keep the cattle medicines cold. At the house, the refrigerator still brimmed with combiotic and vaccinations.

Carl didn't reply. I walked behind the yearling and placed my knee on her spine. She threw her head back at me the way they do to get rid of flies. I held the hypodermic in my right hand, and slapped her haunch hard three times with my left. On the fourth strike, I stabbed in the needle. Angus skin is blue-black, the same as a Kenworth tire. Giving cattle shots is like breaking something; there are occasions when the needle doesn't come out whole.

"It's gonna take a half hour to cure," Carl said.

I placed the syringe back in the cooler. "Twenty minutes," I countered, and walked over to the reservoir to wait under the aspen trees. I hated the waiting.

Already the fall leaves shook down brown; they no longer sparkled in the sun like the shoulder bangles on decorated soldiers. Winter calving was worse than this, I decided. If you didn't get the calves up right away they'd freeze to the ground. I'd take them in the house when it became cold like that, save the afterbirth to smear on them later. The mother always recognized a part of herself, even if she didn't know her calf.

The yearling shouldn't have been bred in the first place. Though she appeared mature enough, she was too young. You can never really discover the truth about something unless you look long and hard at it. I learned that lesson when Carl and I made the mistake of thinking the yearling was a breeder.

We never culled her out back during the sorting process, a day's worth of separating the cattle into categories: calves, yearlings, steers, cows, and bulls. When spring had come, the cows lay down and began calving again. The yearling was dry, a scab, and I decided to sell her. As summer came on, it scorched the earth. The wind blew through the sagebrush and cheat, the sound of it like a ghost walking through the grass.

It was too hot for the cattle to eat, so we took salt blocks out to them; they lived on salt licks and water. We saw the yearling then, bred late and huge, pregnant with the shelf of calf jutting out on her right side. She walked lopsided, out of tune, like the unbalanced Sherman, who rode his horse with his left arm in the air.

I went out with Jade, my blue roan Appaloosa, and brought her in slowly. We kept the yearling around the house, grazing on my father's old airstrip, away from the rest of them.

As we waited for the drug to take effect, I kicked the roots of a Russian thistle with my cowboy boot. Those weeds appeared during the years of the Cold War. Everybody liked to say that the Russians had sent a rocket full of them over to get back at us for coming up with the bomb first. The Communists were well known then to be general disrupters of the internal harmony of the farm. In reality the weeds came from the big grain corporations buying cheap seed wheat in Russia. They sold it to American farmers and didn't tell them where it came from.

I blew on my arm hairs; the air cooled my skin. That year the heat and wind were as unrelenting as the harvest, which had stretched a month late into the end of September. The red gales of the Indian summer had already blown in, a sign of more trouble, a dry, flame-filled fall.

Already, lightning fires ignited the countryside. They filled the air with blood-colored smoke and ate what was left of the harvested fields. The seasons never simply lay down and allowed themselves to die; they loved their prime too much. My mother was like that; after all, it was her family's name—Winter.

Out here, the seasons conquered one another violently. Fall was the most dangerous, sweeping in with adolescent energy like fire. It took over summer's spent and furious force of reproduction, the way chaos and carpetbaggers come in after a war. Winter killed, had the most power. Its arsenal froze, fogged, flooded, starved, and set in with a hopelessness that took all the rest down with it. But spring was my favorite. Spring had wiles. If it had a name, it would have been Odysseus or Artemis. It came not so much with the might of the others, but sweetly and irresistibly like a pang of guilt for winter's ruin. I placed my money on spring.

The weather is the most important element of a farmer's life. Everything on a wheat and cattle ranch divided out along the lines of the seasons. Spring and fall were for planting, plowing, pregnancy, and birth. The summer was for the reaping. Winter was for those things left unfinished.

I watched the thistle roll over in the breeze, becoming a tumbleweed as it went. The smell of my clothing drifted up. It reeked of burlap and caught the rough edges of the wind—errant pieces of dying crop. The hot air made it difficult to breathe. I imagined it was like the nerve and mustard gas left over from the world wars, stored out along the Columbia. What you can't see is always the most dangerous; the trouble with my family and me was like that, like what happened at Hanford when they let all the radiation out.

After we had waited on the yearling twenty minutes, I looked over at Carl. He was as tall as my father had been, and had to take his hat off to fit indoors and inside vehicles. He sat in the pickup, working on a U-joint; a long Levi'd leg stretched to the ground.

"They're both going to die if we leave them stuck together," I hollered to Carl as I walked over to the pickup.

I would have called the vet in winter calving season. He worked continuously, traveling from ranch to ranch. But during the rest of the year, the forty miles to our place was too far for a house call. The vet worked magic, pulled on his long plastic glove and slid his hand into a cow that was calving, or a horse with colic. He was the one-armed man of a tarot reading, with the healing hand hidden inside the hind end of an animal. Sometimes, and for colic especially, the arm disappeared all the way to his shoulders. Reaching into things and rearranging them was the realm of witchcraft, but you had to know what you were doing.

I unhooked the tailgate and yanked out the calf puller. It was made out of an aluminumlike material, and I could manage it myself. But the truth was, I had never used the calf puller before. I'd only watched my father, and was afraid of repeating his mistakes—like gouging out that calf's eyes.

I had seen many blind animals, though most often it was moon blindness. The disease that caused it had a legend, an old wives' tale. It was a madness that made animals stare too long at a full moon. Their eyes turned a milky white. The colts, calves, and kittens spent the rest of their lives following their mothers, as if their noses were attached to their mothers' haunches. They smelled shit all their lives, and I refused to do that to an animal.

The long brace fit poorly on the yearling's hips, but I unloosed the winch anyway, and pulled out the tongs until I had play. Carl watched silently. Even if he disagreed with me, he wouldn't say it until much later. It was the Norwegian in him—that was why we got on so well. I found a burlap seed sack in the back of the pickup. Oil had stained it where it poked into a half-used Pennzoil can. The yearling sweated and shuddered. She'd given up pushing. But still, I avoided those back legs as I squatted down behind her. It was a mess back there, where she had successfully forced everything out of her body but the stubborn, unborn calf.

I grabbed the calf's front legs between my fingers; the filmy hide had dried into curly clumps. First wrapping the seed sack around the legs, I then wound the tongs and cable over it. Only the tiny front hooves showed, the color of onyx.

Balancing the brace against her hipbones and the other end on the ground, I cranked slowly. The cow bellowed, her body convulsed. She lifted her tail and slapped it on the ground. As I wound tighter, her cries changed. The loudness shocked me—rapid, high-throated wails. It was as if she were calling to her calf, telling it to come out. Nothing happened. I sat there helpless; I didn't have anything to soothe her, no medicine but antibiotic for hoof infections and iodine for the eyes of the calf. Every so often, the yearling still bucked on the ground, trying to get rid of the mean trap attached to her uterus. I wasn't close to shooting her yet, but I knew we had to try something else. We were all sweating. The sun dropped down in the sky, the clouds burned off smoke as it touched them near the horizon.

Carl handed me a hammer and I knocked the lock off the winch. The crank spun out of control with a nasty buzz. The cable went slack, and the yearling twisted again, trying to get up.

The forelegs of the half-born wiggled in the opening of her haunches from the writhing. They were grotesqueries of nature—as if the yearling had eaten the calf and now was having trouble passing it. She kicked again with her hind legs and struck me below the knee.

"Motherfuckin' sumbitch anyway," I screamed. I thought she had broken my shinbone. And then I backed up the pickup. I wrapped that calf's front hooves in the burlap seed sack again and wound the tow chain around them and then around the hitch of the truck.

"Give me the signal when it's out," I ordered.

"Not going to be much," Carl said gravely, looking at the cow.

"Better than nothing," I snapped.

Watching for hand signals from Carl, I yanked the pickup into second gear, so I wouldn't pop the clutch. I rode that pedal out like a surgeon. As I felt the grab of the synchromesh, I remembered one of the calving stories my father had told me. Twenty years ago, when he had to feed the cattle because of the snow, he backed over a newborn's hindquarters, cleaving it in half. He had to shoot it with the coyote rifle because he couldn't stand what he'd done.

I didn't even feel the chain tighten or catch before Carl closed his fist up and signaled me to stop. Shutting the engine off right there, I left it in gear so it wouldn't roll backward. I slid out of the cab wondering whether I'd find a pair of ripped-off legs. I forced myself to look at it.

It was the entire calf. Lying there stretched on the ground, its head still twisted back as it had been in the birth canal. There were pieces of meat-looking things trailing out of the cow, still attached to the calf. I saw it was shuddering, its thin wet neck shaking in the dusk air. I took the burlap from its shiny, glasslike legs and closed it around the nose and mouth to clean the mucus out. It was then I thought about pressing my hand tighter, just to end its misery. I don't know why I didn't.

Carl loaded the puller. He threw the hammer back in the pickup's toolbox. I heard it clank as it landed against the box-head wrenches. The lid slammed down.

The calf trembled beneath me, warm and sticky. A silvery white caul draped up over its shoulders. Of all things I had stuck my hands into—chemical barrels, grease, oil, gas, diesel, manure, wheat, weeds, torn tin, running machinery—this was the worst. I searched the pickup for my gloves. I owned twenty or so pairs. I never bothered to carry them with me; they just slopped around in all the vehicles and all the machines. This time I couldn't find any.

"Use your knife?" I asked Carl.

He pulled out his mother-of-pearl pocketknife. It had a big bowie blade; Carl liked to hunt, to skin things.

I crouched down next to the calf in the mess of the afterbirth. Once the calf finally came, the rest spit out easily, a jellylike mass. I pulled off the caul, an eerie sticky membrane, which stretched back to the cow. The superstitions of the pioneers still traversed the lips of farmers; they said a child born with a caul over it would in later life have the gift of second sight. If the child carried it with him, he was supposed to be exempt from misery and adversity. I threw it on the ground.

"She has to get up," said Carl, looking at the yearling. "Otherwise she dies." He took hold of the cow's tail and twisted it around her, pulling her forward. "Come on," he yelled, kicking her with his cowboy boot. "Get up. Hyeah!"

I cut short the cord of the baby, put KRS on the bloody end, and scrubbed her with burlap. There were a number of pioneer superstitions, like the lithium pools for improving mood. My favorite was sin eating, where the sins of a person recently deceased are transferred to another through the consumption of bread passed over the dead. It was the good old-fashioned Scandinavian theme of the sins of the fathers visited on the children, just like in *Ghosts* and *Dance of Death*. My mother loved the Scandinavian artists. She would take me down to Portland to see any play of Ibsen or Strindberg showing at the Artists' Repertory Theater. When she came out of the theater she would say, "Now, I call that real drama."

"It was tragedy, Mother," I would reply.

"It's the only thing worth watching," she would say as she slid into the car and we began the three-hour journey home.

There were plenty more superstitions. The hair of a dog placed over its bite for healing. Mirrors sheeted in lightning storms. Photos turned to the wall in the presence of death. The pioneers used whatever they could to survive amidst the fevers, the cholera, the weather, and the Indians.

I dried the calf. She wasn't clean, and the hair still clumped together with the thickness of the insides of the mother. I bundled her into my arms, lifting her to stand. The lightness surprised me. Everything in my world was heavy and hard. She didn't want to be on her feet; her legs plowed under. I spread the legs out and held the calf aloft again. She stood wobbling, unsure of how to operate herself. She moved one leg with huge effort.

Carl hadn't raised the yearling. He was still pulling on her tail. She showed no interest in the calf, didn't even bother to look at it. They usually do immediately. The mother turns her head to sniff at her baby, and the smell imprints in them.

It's only when something goes wrong that the mother doesn't look for her child. One time I saw a cow drop a calf and thought it was going to be the easiest delivery I had ever witnessed. They both heaved themselves to their feet. The still weak calf hunched over its spindly legs as if it were a spider. But the mother stood up and ran away from the calf. She knocked him down hard on his side in her rush to get by. She never even looked back.

I took care of that calf, fed it from a bucket with a nipple attached to the bottom, every day, twice a day, until one morning I went down to the corral and found it dead. It was like that cow had known her calf was going to die and had killed off her maternal instinct to spare herself the grief.

Now, in front of me in the smoky dusk air, the two of them struggled in the dying day.

"She's not going to get up," Carl said, letting go of the tail.

I picked up the calf and carried her over to the yearling. "Rope those back legs," I told him. The calf stood below me, barely coming up to my knees; we both stared at her panting mother.

Carl looped a grease-blackened rope around the hind legs of the yearling and hitched them to the pickup.

The calf and I slid up to her belly. I folded her legs so she lay on the ground like a cat. She smelled her mother and poked her nose forward. The yearling tried to kick us but the rope caught her hooves. I grabbed a black swollen teat and aimed it at the calf's nose; she needed the colostrum to survive. The dust from where the cow had thrashed about hung in the air. The calf finally found her mother's breast and sucked, but I couldn't tell if she drank anything.

We left them there, untied the cow's hooves, and went. I did move the calf a little ways forward so she wouldn't be kicked. I figured by tomorrow we'd know who was the survivor.

4

Heat lightning started over on the Washington side of the gorge as Carl and I made our way back to the house. He took his cowboy hat off, the marks of the sweatband rimming his silvered crew cut. We had glassfuls of Early Times, just the way he and my dad used to do. The liquor burned my throat and empty stomach. I sat sideways in my mother's rocker, holding hard on to the armrest. Carl chose my grandfather's lawyer chair, the both of us silent as we finished our drinks.

Carl stood up. "I'll get here early tomorrow," he said. Carl lived at the Creek Ranch, eight miles up from the river. "To check on them. I'll take care of what has to be done."

I listened as the pickup churned out the gravel drive, and then went in to see my mother. Her arms were up; her hands held her head. My mother's eyes were closed. They were always shut now. I stood over her and leaned my head down to her face. I felt as if I were robbing her of oxygen standing over the Biedermeier bed. I waited with her, and whispered to her. I breathed in her exhale for the hour before she died.

I touched her neck, felt the cool loose folds in her aged skin. I remembered how Mother and I had said good-bye to Ike, and wondered if she'd remember too. We stood over his bed for days and said, "Time to get up now, Dad." We pleaded with him to open his eyes; we recounted the jobs left undone, the land still unseeded.

Ike never looked, and my mother didn't either. It wasn't scary anymore. One minute, she was alive, the person I had most loved in my life. The next, she was dead. But she wasn't gone. Same woman. Same body. Same memory. For months, I had been terrified, wondering whether I would cover my eyes and not look at her because she was dead. But she smelled the same, felt the same. I looked for signs of trauma magically appearing. There was nothing; it was as if she had drowned, her white skin an Ophelia shade, the deep-set eyes closed and peaceful, her lips perfect. I thought she looked even prettier because she didn't have to do the work of breathing. Effortless beauty. She would have loved that, I thought, smiling. She had etched herself in my memory as unattainable beauty. She had won.

In the autumn of deaths and letters, I made the closing telephone calls. I phoned the hospital, called the police so they wouldn't come out. I listened to Bruce Springsteen's "Mr. State Trooper" and "Wreck on the Highway" and drank more Early Times bourbon. I hated state troopers. They always lost their way when coming out to our place. They were incompetent, tried to be tough, but when it came to strange deaths or informing a family that a beloved son or daughter had died on the highway somewhere, they were chickenshit. I wanted them nowhere near.

I had known my aunt Hanna only from embarrassed conversations with my mother. Her telephone number was in my mother's files. She kept her sister on an index card covered with scratchy writing that looked like twigs. Room 211. Dammasch Psychiatric Hospital.

Hanna had always been different from the rest of my family. She was the wanderer, the passionate one, so opposite from our atavistic nature. She went with the itinerant wind instead of rooting herself to fight against it like the rest of us. I never knew much about her except for what my mother had told me, how she had left when she was twenty and traveled to Spain to study with Serra. It surprised me that my mother talked about her sister before she died. She hadn't spoken her name in years. I kept telling her, Hanna can't come to see you. She's in Dammasch, where she's always been.

When Hanna had come home from Spain, she became obsessed with re-creating the family in bronze. She worked on them in the bunkhouse with her tarps laid down over the plank floor. Her bales of clay were delivered on the train. As soon as a sculpture was finished, she started on another, twelve of them total.

My mother told me sculpting was all Hanna could do. She hated to be touched. Something had happened to her in Spain; she had married a count, a doctor, who had performed abortions in defiance of Franco. She never completely recovered from hiding for over a year in fear of torture. When she finally returned, she spent fifteen months with my parents working on her strange masterpiece, the heads of my family, the pioneers. But she never finished them. Something sent her over the edge and down that wide black fog-covered river.

A young woman's voice answered the telephone. I asked to speak with Miss Hanna Winter. I heard her cover the telephone receiver, and a muffled conversation ensued. There was a pause when she said the name of my aunt to her superior.

"Why not?" I heard in the background. The voice sounded tired, coppery.

"Just one minute," she said. There was another pause. "Who's calling please?"

"Iris Steele," I said. "Her niece."

The receptionist placed me on hold. I imagined what went on in mental institutions. Nurse Ratched with a ring of keys walking down a rusted iodine-smelling hall. I hurt my ear holding the receiver too tightly.

I began to get angry at the cost of the long-distance bill. Dammasch was down in the Willamette Valley, a hundred and fifty miles away from where we lived on the Columbia River. I switched the receiver to the other ear as I walked into my mother's room. Besides the heads, a few other pieces cluttered our house. Hanna's paintings lined the walls of my mother's room. My mother said they were mental patients, the people in the hospital with Hanna. "Just like Goya," she had said. "That one is John." She had pointed to a queer-looking man with second sight in his eyes. "Estrella," she continued, pointing to the painting that frightened me most. "It means star in Spanish."

When I was little I studied Estrella. It looked as if there were a cyclone in this woman, somewhere in her blue eye on the dark side of her face. Yellow light on her forehead warmed her brain, kept it company like a nest of eggs.

My mother had told me Hanna was having electroshock therapy. She said it was helping Hanna to get better. I knew that was not right; when I looked into Estrella's eyes, they bored into me, they didn't blink. I thought of the nurses placing the electrodes to the head, the medication, the heat, the fire, and the explosion. I imagined her mind separating from her body, flying to the ceiling, into the corner, under the bed.

The painted air looked hot by her head and cooled down by her body. She had no hair, only a scarf tied at the base of her neck crazily like a jester's knot. Estrella held her hand delicately to her cheekbone, but it turned into a crustacean. Her fingers appeared like a lobster claw ready to be cracked, the tenderest part sucked out and eaten. She morphed into orange and yellow, and moved sideways, like the tide pulled in by the moon. She was at the bottom of the blue whirlpools of her eyes. Hanna's art terrified me.

"Hello." Hanna's voice was high and frail. Her salutation resonated as if she had opened the door of a cavernous mansion to a thief. I pictured her standing in the doorway with nothing but a knit cardigan sweater to protect herself. I imagined her thin shoulders.

I wasn't expecting it; she sounded similar to my mother on the telephone. What I couldn't stand most was that she was so alone. I thought there were echoes in the line. I began wondering if there was an afterlife for my mother, a place for her to be, or whether she was just lost and cold.

"Hanna?" I tried to sound cheerful but only managed hopeful. "This is Iris Steele. Your niece." My voice was condescending, the way it started up high and came down with a lilt as if I was trying to sell her a vacation home.

"Yes. How are you, Iris? How are you surviving?"

Her question caught me off guard. I suddenly wondered if she was joking. "Fine," I said, and stopped myself. "Well, not so good, actually. My mother passed away. Elise. Your sister." I had always been bad on the telephone, and I was nervous because I expected Hanna to start shrieking or something. I looked out the window, down the canyon to the river. Two more lightning strikes hit the Washington bluffs; the storm was in full force now.

"I'm sorry," she whispered. "The funeral?"

"Saturday."

"Of course," she said. "Never start anything on Friday."

"That's right."

"How are you? Alone out there," she repeated. I thought it was an odd question, but the way she said it sounded so natural.

"Okay," I lied. Drinking since three months ago when my mother started losing weight and the diagnosis of the brain cancer that followed. It was then I began wine and whiskey with the ease of a veteran greased elbow.

"I've been thinking about you," said Hanna. "Wanting to come out there. It's time now. Isn't it?"

"I didn't think you could come. I mean get out." I was embarrassed to be talking about her institutionalization.

"I can check myself out anytime I want," she said.

Oh sure, I thought. She's been there thirty years and can just check out anytime she pleases. "I'm doing okay, Hanna," I said. "I don't have time to come get you. It's best you stay put." I spoke to her as if she were very susceptible to suggestion—as if she were crazy.

"I've been thinking about this for thirty-one years," she said, breathing into the telephone. "Unfinished business," she went on, "that's like a life wasted."

"What do you mean?"

"The heads."

"The heads are done," I said, dismissing her.

There was silence on the other end of the telephone. "Iris," she said slowly. She was surprisingly calm. "I need to place your head, together with the rest of them."

"Nobody's touching my head." I felt hysterical all of a sudden, trying not to laugh at her absurd ideas.

"You'll understand when we have them cast, when we watch the bronze poured. Their faces will appear before us. You'll know why."

"Sounds like a ghost dance," I said, going along with her. She was crazy and I was drunk. "Like the Indians held before the cavalry mas-

sacred 'em all." I walked to the back window. It was a magnificent lightning storm. I wanted to be out in it. Maybe I could be struck by lightning. "Another thing that will add up to nothing," I told her.

"It won't go away like the ghost dances," she said. "I've located a
foundry. Near Heart of the Beast."

"Did Miles send you a copy too?"

"A copy?" she asked.

"The letter from the Nez Perce tribe," I said indignantly. I looked at
the letter. It was on the phone desk off the kitchen; I hadn't yet moved
it to the office and computer room opposite the pantry. Now that the
death of my mother had sunk in, the letter had come to annoy me
immensely. I knew more than anyone, we had paid for that land. My
family paid for coming out on the Oregon Trail, with as much blood as
could be twisted out of their dry ruthless hearts. It was no good coming back now.

"My business goes to Mr. Emmerett," Hanna said.

"The Nez Perce want Heart of the Beast back," I said, grabbing the
letter.

"More of my unfinished business," she whispered.

"It doesn't have anything to do with you," I said. "It's not your business anymore." The lights flickered from the storm. The refrigerator
buzzed back on. I wanted to get off the phone and wade into the bathtub. In a lightning storm, you could be electrocuted in the bath if a bolt
touched the house. I was in the mood for accidents.

I thought of an argument my mother and I had had about the heads.
She wanted to have them cast and made permanent before she died.
Someone might want them, she said, looking at me sadly from her chair
full of sickness. *To remember us.*

Who would that be? I had asked icily. I declined to be saddled with
sustaining my parents' memory, especially when I felt my parents were
never squarely burdened with me. I floated behind them, always in
their wake. An afterthought that ate.

I heard Hanna's breath through the phone. I began to get panicky
the way some indigenous people do when tourists take their pictures.
I thought talking any longer would put the evil eye on me. I didn't need
any more bad luck.

"I'm coming out there," she said.

"How can you come back here now?" I interrupted her angrily. "After all that happened? You ran away."

"Can't run anymore. Maybe you can."

"You don't want to finish those sculptures," I reminded her slowly. "They're what sent you to Dammasch in the first place." She wouldn't be able to get out of the institution, let alone all the way out here.

"You'll never get away from them. I never could."

"I'll get away from them all right," I said roughly.

Hanna remained silent.

"I just thought you'd want to know about Elise, that's all." I took a drink of the Early Times. "Good-bye," I said, and hung up.

Afterward I walked to the Civil War chest in the green room and took out the pictures of my mother and her family. On the Winter homestead, Heart of the Beast, I looked at my mother's past. I studied her parents and sister. As I set the photos out on the kitchen counter, I noticed one with Hanna on the knees of a man with a tall, open-crown raven-black hat, the color of his eyes. From his skin, his dark clothes, and blanket, I knew he was a Nez Perce, probably Chief Joseph's nephew, Peo Peo Tholekt. My mother had said long ago that he was the first one who noticed Hanna was an artist. "He was the one," she said, narrowing her eyes and nodding.

I had forgotten things about my aunt, the way my parents used to talk about her and the word *insane* in the same breath. When Mother said she was having electroshock therapy, I imagined it was something like what we used on the cattle to prod them in the right direction.

I remembered seeing my aunt only once. I was six years old when we visited her at the institution. My mother, Jake, Hanna, and I were out on the great sloped back lawn that was bordered by the ominous Douglas firs known to scare patients with their fierce silhouettes so that they did not escape. Mother and Hanna sat in the Adirondack chairs talking about their parents' ranch.

They spoke of their childhood and their mother, remembering how she had hated having the Nez Perce wandering around so close to the family, camping in their tepees outside the house, asking for money.

Their father, Willy, had liked them coming; he spoke some Nez Perce——just enough to buy their horses.

When Willy died, my father took over operation of Heart of the Beast. It was then he began running both places, hauling cattle back and forth, spreading himself thin and too thin again.

The first thing my father did was to run the Indians off. He said they were breathing down his back. He despised them, he said all they did with their money was get drunk. He became watchful of what I ate, because big women reminded him of all the lazy fat Nez Perce squaws. He assumed people were overweight because they were lazy.

I found another photo of my mother and my aunt, taken when they were about eight and twelve. They were riding two leopard Appaloosas on the meadow of Heart of the Beast. My mother was standing on top of her saddle, holding the reins by their tips. Hanna, more timid, stayed glued to the seat, grimly smiling at her sister.

The one good thing my father did was to bring those horses down to the Bar S for us to break. The herd was dwindling in the hard winters of the Heart of the Beast hills. A wrangler had come by and told my father that the animals needed to be sent for glue or hamburger. I loved my father when he gave me those Appaloosas.

I cherished everything about them—especially the way they looked, as if they were half clothed in hide. The coloring of the Nez Perce horses was of combustion, as if there had been an explosion in them that caused the savage marks on their skin. Violent mixtures of black, white, brown, and red rippled across their pelts. The white markings on their faces and legs weren't orderly and clear, starlike or blazelike. They tore across their faces and fetlocks as if cut by barbed wire. And those Appaloosas had wild eyes, white around the sides of the brown like humans'.

The Nez Perce knew what they were doing when they perfected their horses. They loved their herds like a band of Gypsies, ragged, exotic, and figuring all the wealth in the world lay in the hide of a good horse and the arch of an arrow. The horses were bred for toughness, agility. Their color camouflaged them with a mixture as brutal as the land they came from. But more than anything, they were indomitable because of their will. Jade came out of that herd. I was riding her on the last cattle drive when I finally confronted my father, and I've seen his shocked face every day since then. I picked up my father's glasses afterward, and never had a chance to give them back to him.

I began packing Hanna's photos, figuring the least I could do was send them to her. I remembered how my mother and Hanna had talked that day at Dammasch about murder and lynchings, things that went on in their hometown. I noticed Hanna's glasses had electrical tape binding them across the bridge of the nose and on the left wing. She had been breaking them, one of the attendants told Mother. He was always repairing them, he said. Hanna just wouldn't look at her life.

I wanted to play hide-and-seek with my brother and another patient's kid, but they said I was too young. Said I'd cheat. Jake was right. I would do anything to beat my brother. He was four years older than I and had an unbearable advantage in everything. Hoping to get him in trouble, I started crying, next to the free tree of the hide-and-seek game. It was a great weeping willow in the middle of the lawn.

It was then my aunt walked up to me. I stopped crying to look at her face, and it had changed. It was as if the wind were blowing through it. The branches of the tree above me stretched out over my head and the breeze rustled them on the roots of my hair.

Hanna placed her hands across my eyes and screamed out to my brother, "One," and started to count. As she counted, I began to see the colors. I remember thinking to myself, Why am I not seeing black? The colors changed depending on which of Hanna's fingers were pushing against my eyes. They were not colors I had seen before, because there were thoughts with them. It started out like a weepy stain of corrugated tin, and then dull purple, the tongue color of a chow dog; it turned absinthe green like liqueur, and red like the pillows of sultans and scarlet-throated birds. When she finished counting, I was standing there looking at the bronze color that everything turns before you faint. And then she took her hands away, and it was black again.

I remember opening my eyes, and walking straight to where my brother was hiding because I knew exactly where to find him. I turned around to run back to the free tree and stopped when I saw Hanna clinging to that willow. She was standing there holding on so tight it looked as if she were afraid she'd fall a million miles if she let go. I wanted to know what it was that Hanna had inside her hands. And I wondered, the way little kids do, if that tree was seeing colors, too.

5

Iknew I couldn't sleep that night, so I decided to search the attic, gathering more of Hanna's things to send to her at Dammasch. I found buckets of dried red dirt, and crooked-finger metal pieces anchored into wood plates. All of this was covered by a plaster-spattered drop cloth that smelled of moldy canvas like that of an old burlap water bag.

But when I found the old law books, I forgot about the red dirt. Spread about in the middle of the room were a thousand or so books, leather-bound, caramel-colored, and rain-stained. I picked one up, it felt alive. The skin of its covering was as strokable as a pelt. Faded gold bindings lined all of them—holding vellum pages with purple ink blotches from the wayward drip of a quill pen. When I opened them, I imagined they spoke to me.

They were the laws of the country, my great-grandfather's, grandfather's, and mother's legal books: *Federal Reporters* from the 1800s, *Northwest Reports*, Elliot's debates on the Constitution. There were pages full of the addresses of John Jay, Patrick Henry, and James Madison. I found pale purple dried flowers among the debates between Henry and Madison at the convention of the Commonwealth of Virginia, amidst the discussion of slavery. There was a book entitled simply *Murder*, suede-bound copies of the works of Thackeray and Twain, and a copy of the Gettysburg Address.

In one of the dark trunks with bronze locks, I discovered the Indian wars. They contained the books on the Indian campaigns written by my grandfather, the colonel: *The Bannack-Paiute War, The Sahaptian War, The Yakama and Flathead Wars.*

The colonel was Mark Steele, my father's father. After he retired from the war to end all wars, he missed combat. To make himself feel better, he continued wearing his military dress until he died. He practiced law as his father had, and wrote books on the Indian wars, long boring ones full of military campaigns, pyrrhic victories, and racism. I had never read them. My father told me about them once; they described how the Indians fought, laying waste to the land in the summer. They fired the grass and burned the country. They isolated the infantries with a lake of flames before them and decimated land behind. The soldiers were forced to feed on their horses, and pack supplies on their own backs. I hesitantly picked up the Curtis photograph of Chief Joseph and looked at the books, wondering if I had the heart to read them. I thought about the month of Cat-skinning that fall, all the while looking out over the Columbia toward Hanford, where Joseph had deteriorated on a reservation, reduced to asking only for a horse. I placed the books and photo back in the trunk and closed the lid.

Though my father had always done upsetting things, I tried to avoid blaming him. I placed the fault on his father, the colonel. He had become so hardened from his experience in the First World War that he never seemed to have thought twice about all those sons of his that died at birth. But I think in the end, the guilt overcame him. He knew he was killing them off one by one, by his pure will. Until my father came, the colonel's children died right there on the hospital table next to their mother. They never uttered a cry, nor ever competed with him for the undivided attention of his wife.

It all started with his picking one of those thin-lipped women who wasn't uppity enough to mind the suffering that went on out on a ranch. One who wouldn't be bothered when three of her four children died, and then gave up her life for the fourth child, my father. I noticed that there was no sign of her in the attic. No embroidery, quilts, or needlepoint. There were none of her clothes, nothing at all left of her person except the dust on a pot where she had cooked food for the men, and an old delicate watch with a diamond placed at midnight.

Everything changed when my father was born alive, I thought, sitting there in the attic. Ike must have always felt he had killed his mother. But I already knew, judging from my mother and me, that women and children never worked out in a place like this.

The colonel took up smoking Romeo and Julietta cigars, which in the end drew the black line through him and placed that old man down in his grave. He liked to blow the blue smoke into my father's crib until once when my father was old enough he reached out and grabbed the burning end, branding his palm.

I imagined my grandfather then noticed the thumb of his baby boy. It was thick and short and had an impossibly small nail that was taken up and shaped entirely by the milky half-moon of lunule. Ike's irregularity scared the colonel. He named Ike a different name from all of his other children—Mark Jr., Marky, and Marcus, and then he banished my father from the house to grow up with the hired hands in the bunkhouse. To survive if he dared. But I think he was afraid of my father; he left Ike, just like the king of Thebes who ordered his baby abandoned on the rock with a spike thrust through his feet.

Everything Ike did the colonel bettered. In my family, it was as if each generation tried to outdo the previous and the following. One hundred and fifty years ago, when the colonel's father, Ingram Steele, came to the state, he abandoned his wife and her only child one winter after the crop was planted. He left for the capital, Oregon City, to read the law and to become an attorney. Some of these books had been his. He journeyed there with his drooping Missouri eye, his walrus mustache and high white forehead. Ingram started the first law practice in the state and became the Speaker of the House of Representatives. It wasn't hard back then; there weren't many people to run against. He left the work of the ranch to his wife and her only son, my grandfather.

The men in my family had always practiced law and agriculture, the things of great societies. But there was a price for progress. My grandfather survived his father's neglect, but he made sure to pass on the favor to the next in line. After Ike's birth, the colonel bought off all the judges in Illian, Horrow, Lynn, and Baron counties, so he won every case in his law career. And he made sure my father lost most of his battles.

He sent Ike out on endless tasks of walking the fields with a hoe and gave the honor of driving the first diesel Caterpillar in the West to a hired hand, a man the same age as my father. The colonel made my father almost blind by forcing him to read by candlelight and sent him off, lying about his age, to World War II and the South Pacific, where, he hoped, the misery of the weather and the impossibility of advances would be worse for him than dying at Normandy. My grandfather taught Ike how to treat my brother, Jake.

My father avenged himself in various ways. He married a woman who was a lawyer. He knew the colonel couldn't stand to admit a woman to his practice, and that he would have to see his legacy die out from his own prejudice. I think the colonel's prejudice had something to do with my father's treating me no different from my brother. It was rare. Extremely rare for a farmer to respect a daughter as much as a son, inasmuch as Ike respected anything.

I tried not to hate my dad when he screamed at me for not retrieving the right wrench in the jumble of tools, or when he dragged me backward by my wrist and threw me onto the barbed wire fence that I had spliced by looping the wires instead of twisting them. It annoyed him that I was a maniacal reader of books. I think he thought it was a sign of laziness. I always thought it meant something that he did not name Jake after himself. But that generational war started all over again anyway. In the end, I guess my father won, though Jake used some of our father's tactics just as skillfully. Of those two, Ike was the last man standing, before I took him down.

That night of my mother's death, in the Michelangelo thunder of an Indian summer storm, I left the attic and walked west out to the reservoir. At dusk, the hill we lived under reached far up into the sky. The curve of the horizon was giant and rounded black; the twilight shone past 9 P.M. at the fiery edge so perfectly marked and distinct it looked like a lunar eclipse of the sun.

I went into the night with the jug of red wine I lived on. Red was the color of blood and reunion, and tonight, I decided, I was going home too. I gazed out into the vast sky that matched the miles of chaparral and stubble fields, thinking about the land. A blessing and a curse—it was what brought us here and kept us here. It was astoundingly beautiful.

To the south, the sky loomed dark and sticky, and ran together with the wine like candy apples. Stars fell in and apart with a blur of my shuddering breath. Up north and across the river, lightning punished the earth. Thunder sounded in the distance as if it were anger incarnate. Fire burned uncontrolled on the Hanford reservation, seventeen thousand acres already incinerated. The flames illuminated the smoke as it billowed up white, blood colored, and then black like the Birth of Venus.

I walked out the road of the eclipse, my boots on the gravel driveway sounding like the closing of a thousand boxes. Everything hurt. The heels, worn down and buckled under, poked into my arches. My back ached from driving the combine; it felt like fire. The muscles on the side of my neck were streaked with pain as if I'd been gashed with a blunt knife.

I heard the sound of Jade's coughing float out into the stillness. We were all waiting for water. Winter had withheld everything; there had been no rain that year. The horses stood with their tails to the breeze, their heads down, concentrating on breathing. Jade choked deep dry heaves that threatened to knock her to her listless knees when they rattled through her lungs. The sound resonated, as hollow and forlorn as the drumming of powwows.

There was something unusual in this never-ending harvest. With each day, I felt the dirt in handfuls landing on top of me. I was disappearing; the land was taking me over. I began to look like it, my skin turned dull like earth, my fingerprints rubbed out, obscured by dust. Even in the soft bathwater, I could not coax the whorls of my fingers back.

Rising in the east, the white light of the moon lit the landscape like soothing particles of ether. My family had always lived by the moon, not just planting and harvesting by it, but when the moon was full, they followed it west with sundown madness, as it traveled around the earth. My family journeyed here pulled in the wake of the moon.

When my father's grandfather Ingram Steele came west, he settled a place that lay in the lee of the wind. Four thousand acres unfolded to the Columbia River like a potlatch blanket. Ike told me that his family had come to Oregon because they were hunters. Land and animals defined worth; purpose was getting and keeping them. If you could, it was sweetest to get them out of someone else's hide.

My mother's grandparents, Iris and John Winter, trekked out next. She was my namesake: everyone in the family was named after a dead person, whom they orbited like a lasso until eventually they crawled down beside them in their graves. John and Iris had walked at the side of the wagons wearing their shoe soles thin to save the oxen the added burden of their weight on the wagon. They were constantly on the lookout for buffalo, because they had heard those wild beasts had the ability to stir the blood of their more placid relatives, the oxen, into madness. It was their first lesson on the power of nature.

My mother told me the stampede happened near the Applegate cut-off. The oxen pawed and bellowed when they smelled the buffalo. The green hands believed they could stop the oxen with reins thick and wide as slabs of bacon. But my family knew something about the reason oxen ran themselves to death, about the uselessness of riders running alongside to turn them. They ran because they followed their wild blood, they couldn't get away from it, the same thing my mother said.

Iris and John let the oxen go, the wagon dragging behind them, the canvas with the painted slogan Oregon or Bust unraveling like a white kite tail seesawing behind the frame, landing in the dirt like their lives. The jolting and popping made wheel rims unspring from their felloes, and the wagon became a bullwhip yoked to their necks, and it was over as soon as it began. The yoke mates ran themselves to death and were dragged down with broken legs and spines. There was only one left alive, the strongest, who had stopped when he could no longer breathe and the weight of dragging the carcasses had become too heavy. The men came and butchered what they could salvage of the dead and cut the throat of the living and butchered him too because he was broken down and would never work again.

The lightning traveled toward me. I lay back on the cement of the reservoir, and thought about my mother. The anger fell away, washed off by the sage-tinted wind. The rage had fueled all of us—my father, my mother, my brother, and me—and I wondered how it could sustain me now that they were gone. There was no one left to rail against.

The hair on my arms began to stand up from electricity in the air. The storm was coming closer, like a lover. It pulled the strings of my nerves. The wind caught the nap of my hair and stroked it backward like the fur of an animal. The water under me felt alive and inviting. I turned over on my belly and propped my forehead on my fists. My lips dragged across the reservoir, kissing it just like the wind. There was another flash and I crawled forward and slid off the old wash bucket covering the opening of the cistern. I placed my head inside as if it were an oven, down into the giant box of a cavern. I took a deep breath of what had been carved out of the world.

The reservoir was precious, intoxicating. I never understood how our water could be so soft when everything else was so hard. My arm slapped down to the side, drunk and tingling, soft and damageable. I lifted my foot and dropped it, feeling limber and loose as a baby. I was turning into one, now that my mother was gone, and I loathed that feeling of vulnerability, of helplessness. The four of us hated babies, viewed malevolently their dependence, their mess. We saw in them what we couldn't stand in ourselves.

I thought about losing control of my body the way my mother did, and slipping inside the reservoir. My frame would become strong and heavy with the water. I would take on the weight of my father too, become both of them, stretch into his six-feet-four length. I could slide into his shoes, fill out his shirt that I now wore daily. He used to carry a notebook in his chest pocket, and I never knew what was in it. I wanted to know what it was like to be my father; all I had left of him was his glasses and how he saw the world.

Another thunderclap came; the shock jarred me as I listened to the reverberations of the water. The thunder always started someplace else and ended up inside you. It streaked into your torso and rearranged your heartbeat. The dusk had passed. It was very dark now. Bolts of lightning danced graceful and curving, sounding of war. They were artillery, then bombs. It sounded like cities imploding—first the crack and then the crash of collapse.

The land is forever, my mother had said, *a blessing and a curse.* Now she was gone, and all I had were her words. She was right, it was always the land. The Indians migrated later with their worship of the earth and exotic beauty. Horses made the warring of tribes as common as sibling rivalry. Afterward, Lewis and Clark called forth people like my family. Their diseases and guns eventually placed Native Americans on reservations, and the combustion engine relegated their horses to pets. But in the end, however battered and abused, there will forever be the land.

Another bolt of lightning stabbed the earth; a single cloud covered the moon in a shroud. Nothing by which to navigate or fold and unfold the covers of tide to hide the earth. It was utterly bare. Lying there on the reservoir, I looked into the blackness and thought of my father. *The moon is to hunt by,* he said. He stalked prey constantly, even at night, killed coyotes by the reflection from the moon. He never felt more comfortable than under that bittersweet light, which reminded him of the loss of day.

In the near distance, I heard an engine shift for the long pull up the hill. It came out fast on the last bit of paved road that ended at our driveway, after which gravel roads took over. The car rounded the corner where the signpost back to civilization stood. A totem with arrows of direction pointing to the four corners of the earth, like eagle feathers bound to a rawhide rope. I heard the car gain speed, the whine of tires coming down the hill.

I waited for the snarl, the guttural purr, the sound of the wheels as they passed our drive and went over that mean snare of a cattle guard. The noise of the crossing reverberated in the air, and I was struck by a quick wave of sadness. Eight years ago when the horses were turned out for the winter, my first pony, Fortune, was chased into it by deer hunters. She caught her legs down between the wide steel slats. We had to shoot her and saw off her legs in order to drag the body out with the D-6 Caterpillar.

I looked up at the granite sky, and I sat back on the reservoir. I stared at the gouged-out and robbed emptiness, there between the shining silver spurs of the downturned horns of the moon.

*   *   *

It was then I forced myself back out to save the yearling. I couldn't let her die, leaving me alone as my mother had. I drove there with a pump, a hose, and an eight-gallon bucket of water.

I noticed her calf first; she raised her head to look at me, still alive. But the yearling still lay there, had not gotten up since the birth eight hours ago. With her down, I knew her meager sustenance would be only the water I siphoned into her stomach. When I came upon her, I thought she was dead. The yearling opened her eyes when she heard me, and they had turned violet in the night. She panted for a moment with her tongue. It fell out of her mouth a deep blue, the color of leukemia.

I crouched down next to her with the end of the water hose. I threaded it through that cow's nose, making sure it went into her stomach instead of her trachea, watching carefully for the ripple of the end of the rubber tube to pass by her throat and into her esophagus and then on into her big belly. I held the bucket high and pumped water down inside her so she would live, and I thought of my mother and father.

My parents were almost the same person until I came, and then they parted forever. My father never saw my mother again in the same way after my birth. I realized everything about the separation repulsed him, seeing the bloody and blue rubbery grimness of me coming out of her vagina. It wasn't the blood; I think he liked our blood. In fact, after I was born, I imagined, his favorite time to make love with her was when she was bleeding, the red on his penis a clear sign of what he had done to her.

It was the contortion of her body, the stretching of it, the disfiguring that left her wide and gaping, open to the elements. I knew for someone who toils in the earth, the elements were something to be cursed and conquered, not something to lie down to. My brother, Jake, was cut out of my mother, and my father accepted this as the price for carrying on the name. But when I was born, she was ruined, a place he'd never want to put his penis because she had been taken over by me, still clinging to her breast.

I gazed at the calf curled into an impossibly small lump; she looked at me again as I set the water bucket down. I dropped my head back to stare at the sky, breathing out the liquor of my father. He used to tell me the Indian summer was so named because of the wars. Those were the years my great-grandfather, John Winter, had to fight late into the fall. It was the time when the beautiful Nez Perce and the cheating Cayuse didn't move to their winter places until November, and took their chances picking off the whites where they could. They would come with the wind, their magnificent horses with washboard shoulders dyed in the spectacular reds of the paintbrush plant. Blue-colored roman nose, jet-black mane, and the long magenta strands of tail were tied up into clubs.

My father said the Indians came in the harvest moons. They crossed and cleared the land with efficiency, killing everything off it, while my family continued to farm. Plodding along with their plows brutally embroidering the earth, they never discovered until it was too late that in those Indian summers there was nothing and no one around them but desolation. I looked back at the yearling and heard a faint gurgle. It was then I realized that in the dark I had pumped water into her lungs, not her stomach. She lay there drowned, just like my mother.

part two

6

THE HEAT WAVE BROKE ON THE DAY OF MY MOTHER'S
funeral. White clouds iced the sky and turned it cool enough to wear
the black dress. When I was fourteen, Mother bought me my first
Chanel for an evening wedding of a friend of theirs from the Cattle-
man's Association. Elise spoke of launching me at that event as if I were
some kind of ship. I remember the day we drove down to I. Magnin in
Portland, where she had a special charge account. The credit card came
with invitations to fashion shows and engraved sterling silver frames
every year. She spent so much money there, they knew her by name.

Whenever she went to events like weddings, fund-raisers, or the
dedication of a dam, she wore Chanel. Elise Steele had the beauty that
belonged to the realm of photographs, and she used her money the
same way she used her beauty, to keep herself away from us.

When my mother inherited her parents' estate, she set up her own
bank accounts, never merged it with what our family had grown
together. With that money she placed herself on the board of directors
of the Bank of the Columbia. That way, Ike couldn't walk in there with
the words *community property* on his breath. She trusted my father about
as much as she trusted the government. Ike, with his hot temperament, was too likely to buy things impulsively with her money. My
mother was the opposite of him—cold, shrewd, and able to bide her
time, hibernate if necessary.

I think she kept separate bank accounts with the hope of watching my father come to her and beg. He never did. He bought the cheapest, most dangerous equipment he could find, combines, trap wagons, tractors, and trucks. He frequented military surplus auctions and bankruptcy fire sales and bought like a bottom dweller. And then he made her children operate that machinery. Neither one of them said a word. A game of chicken right down to the end.

My mother and I rode down to Portland that day in her car, the Jaguar. Her father had told her he'd buy her a new automobile if she could pass the bar exam. She stuck it to him when she passed, requesting the beautiful curved sedan with red seats. It had long heavy doors and we never bothered using seat belts. Down the middle of the road she flew, begrudgingly touching the sideline gravel only for a wide-load semi or combine caravan. Everyone waved out where we lived except my mother. She perfected a two-finger salute from the top of the steering wheel, only to those few she deemed worthwhile.

That trip to Magnin's was special. I sat next to her in the front seat holding a photograph of her in her black suit to show the salesclerk so she could look for something similar. "What were you thinking there?" I asked my mother, pointing to the picture. She was standing in the middle of a group of people, with her head up, slightly tilted back. She didn't even crack a smile because that would ruin the perfect shape of her lips.

"I was concentrating on manipulating my internal organs," she told me, flooring the gas, passing a triple trailer.

I laughed.

She was serious. "You go crazy at a party if you depend on other people for conversation. If you depend on other people for anything."

Shopping at Magnin's first started as a reward for my having gone to an orthodontia appointment. My mouth was so sore after the orthodontist tightened the bands that I wasn't able to eat anything for a day afterward. So the shopping made up for the lost lunch. "It hurts to be beautiful," my mother said simply. It was what she always said about pain. Then she smiled one of her thousand-watters, her straight white teeth glamorizing the air surrounding her.

There was a routine to my mother's shopping. The first stop was the cosmetics counter. I sat on the high makeup chair out of the way and memorized the names and smells of perfume. Oscar de la Renta, Opium, Fracas, Chanel No. 5, and Chanel No. 19.

If any of the salesladies looked at me twice, I said, "I'm waiting for my mother," and pointed over at the Chanel counter with my pinky. Then I ignored them and went on minding my own business, crossing my Levi's-clad legs and bobbing my red cowboy boot daintily.

When I was twelve, a lady made up my face for the first time. I had inadvertently sat at her counter, and like a high priestess of beauty, she breathlessly told me, I had entered the Red Door of Elizabeth Arden. I made the decision right then that I would wow them back at the one-room schoolhouse by making my transition from kid to adult. Wearing makeup as opposed to working a twelve-hour day separated adults from children, I decided.

The day we bought the dress, my mother first purchased a big bag of face crap. By that time I was on my own "regime," which meant that I had to wash my face with black mud soap, rinse it in a soapy basin thirty-one times, then thirty times with fresh running water. I patted it dry and dabbed white-caked medicine all over so my skin dried up like a Japanese mask. This was all because my mother couldn't stand pimples on any child that came from her. Acne was a hideous deformity, suffered only by our relatives.

My mother wound up with a big bag of cosmetics, which was a tip-off to the second-floor ladies that she was in a buying mood. As we walked toward the elevator, Mother grabbed the photo from my hand. Elise Steele fixated on projects as if each were the last thing she would accomplish in her life.

"We're going to buy you a dress like that," she said, pointing to the picture of herself. "A woman with red lips and a black dress," she told me, hitting the elevator button, "is the kind of woman that men kill for."

I wanted to ask her how she knew that. Had Ike ever threatened to kill anyone over Elise, or had he just settled for taking things out on their children?

The dress we found was made out of fuzzy black Chanel wool that almost looked ratty except it couldn't be because it was designer. It closed with a smart collar at my neck and gold buttons that ran down the front. A pocket on the side held a fake handkerchief, which my mother replaced with a real one. During Elise's lifetime, I ended up wearing the dress three times, once for a wedding, once for my brother's funeral, and once for my father's. My mother's would be the fourth.

It was two in the afternoon, and the funeral started at four. I had fed the horses and the yearling's calf. I kept the calf in the tack room. It was cool in the day and warm at night. I knew this because I had slept down there with the calf the night my mother died. I figured for one evening I could turn my house completely over to the dead.

For as long as I could remember, 2 P.M. was the time when my mother went down for her daily nap. I roamed around Elise's room, as I had when she was alive, touching the Biedermeier furniture she'd bought when she married, a sleigh bed and matching dressers. My mother's things, her tastes, were different, lighter than the dark wood of the pioneer antiques. I found her jewelry case, an old leather-bound box that looked as if it contained Shakespeare's works, and took out her diamonds. My father had given her earrings when Jake was born. Sapphires surrounded two large diamonds, with platinum-capped pearls that dropped delicately down. When she wore them, I was convinced the pearls were full of her favorite perfume, Joy, which floated down drop by drop to her shoulders, making her smell of exotic places like the Alhambra, palaces I imagined my aunt frequented in Spain.

I slid on my mother's heavy strand of pearls, which draped down below my collar. Her wedding rings I wore on my right hand. They glinted and glittered when I brushed my hair, even in the dull light of the cloudy day. The black dress fit perfectly, the way it had when I first bought it as a fourteen-year-old. There was a time around the death of my brother and father that I had the thins, made my way by denying need. The dress hung on me then, and made me appear like a mannequin.

I looked at myself in her vanity mirror. My mother always told me I was like the land. But I didn't look country. You wouldn't see a round-nosed and freckled Pansy, or a Billy Lee, if you stared into my eyes. My features were sharper, my forehead higher. I think most people were reminded of my parents when they saw me. I had my mother's bones, but in truth, my appearance was most like the photos of my great-grandfather, John Winter, the immigrant from Norway, the horse trader who would do anything to make a sale. Bleeding horses to make them calm, smearing a brand, cutting a nerve so the buyers wouldn't know they were lame. He grew pure white hair, even lighter than mine. It made you think he'd seen something awful in his life.

One night, years ago, I had sat at the dinner table fiddling with my napkin, and my mother had traced the veins in my hands. "Look at the way they come down your fingers," she said. I stopped moving them momentarily, and they fell together looking just like the hills surrounding our house.

This fall I recognized what my mother was talking about. For the first time, I saw my family in the land. I was out riding over the range on the west bluffs of Rock Creek when I realized they were the shoulders of my father. His bony blades had become beaten down and rounded by the wind, tired of holding up the world, like Atlas after his daughters the Pléiades had committed suicide. My mother's hands, joined together waiting for a meal, formed Starvation Canyon to the north. My brother Jake's spine I saw outlined in the ridge opposite, my father forming the east side of Rock Creek.

I glanced in the mirror again. My tanned skin glowed from the Indian summer sun and the colored dust. It made the green of my eyes stand out. Covered in diamonds, the hardest substance in the world, I placed my hands over my face because I didn't have people, I had things.

Selva Wally, the undertaker, called to check on me. I preferred talking to Selva on the phone more than in person because she used the same makeup on herself that she used on the corpses. She had a wide, child-like expression that, combined with the thick makeup, made her look caught in a perpetual surprise. I couldn't help thinking her face had never gone back to normal after she embalmed her first corpse. But, despite my ungenerous thoughts, I knew Selva was a kind woman.

Over the years, she had done a good business with our family. So much so that I didn't bother going into the funeral home to discuss the service. Selva helped me pick the casket and headstone for my mother over the telephone.

"I think you should have the funeral in the church," Selva had said, clearing her nose by blowing air out like a porpoise. "The funeral home only holds two hundred."

"Do you think that many will come?" I had asked.

"They've been calling all morning." Selva cleared her nose again. "A fellow from Jasco County called an hour ago wanting to know what you looked like so he would be sure to spot you."

I laughed, alarmed.

"Sit upstairs in the choir," she said. "That way you won't get stared at too much."

"Regular grief convention," I said.

"When you and the other pallbearers carry out the casket, you can go on out to the cemetery at the ranch. That way you won't have to talk to anyone when they put your mother down. But afterward they'll be stopping by your house. Folks just can't stay away from this kind of thing."

At 4 P.M., the white church reflected the light from the clouds and sat like a beacon in the dried grass. It was pure and isolated like an Amish church. When I arrived, people were standing in the doorway and lined down the steps. Laura Stodemeier caught sight of me and waved me over. I avoided her, hurried in the basement doors, and climbed the back stairs to the choir loft. Red roses covered my mother's casket, and wreaths hung on easels spilled down the carpeted step to the congregation. The minister wore white; she looked different from when she had come out to the house to talk to my mother about dying.

The service was long. By now, I knew the prayers of death by heart.

My mother's favorite song was "Ode to Joy." I had asked the meager choir to end the funeral with that. They managed a decent rendition that she would have liked. She loved the indomitableness of that song. I could hear it, the toughness of it, even in the tiny church with the nineteen-person choir. I smiled when I caught the faint odor of flowers and thought of her Joy perfume.

I walked downstairs and joined the pallbearers: Gretel and Ed Davis, Judy and Dick Garnus, Martha and Charlie Mueller, Hugo Wagonchaff and myself. No one looked up but all of them placed their hands gently on me: on my back, on my arm, around my waist. These men and women had known Elise longer than I had—they had danced with her at the Grange before I was born. They'd cried at the funerals of her son and husband, worked the land until their arms grew strong, and now they would carry her home.

The organ rang out, and the eight of us walked down the aisle. The diamond rings cut into my fingers as we carried her out for her last ride.

Outside, the white light of the clouds blinded us. I heard the low background hum of a bagpipe. Scotty Jamison, best welder in the county, had learned both skills from his blacksmith father in Scotland before coming to the States. We took the things we couldn't fix to Scotty, and he always worked miracles.

Today, he wore the dark kilt he always donned when he came to the Fourth of July parade. The seven other pallbearers began singing under their breath. We moved in step. Everyone except me whispered the words, *Beat the drum slowly and play the fife lowly, and bitterly wept as we bore her along.*

We placed the casket on the platform of the hearse and moved it forward. They sang, *For we all loved our comrade so brave young and handsome.* The people in the church began slowly moving out. The driver came back and shut the doors, holding the handle open so that the closing sound wouldn't be so loud. He had a nice touch to him, sensitive. In the final verse I looked up and thought of the three dead members of my family. It gave me comfort to think they were all together. At least they would be at peace in the land.

The people spread over the steps and began to sing softly. Afterward there was silence. The eight of us squished into Selva's limousine, and the driver followed in tow of the hearse.

Our cemetery lay out at the Bar S, under the shelterbelt of pine trees. When Jake died, my father wanted to bury him on the ranch, not with the other relatives in Lona. Selva and my father argued, Selva saying it was against the law to bury someone just anywhere unless there was a family plot. So Ike bought a headstone, hauled it out to the ranch with the pickup, and dumped it onto the ground. He called Selva and told her that we now had a family plot, and Jake's funeral was the next day.

My father was buried next to his son, and now my mother would go down next to him. I noticed the gravediggers were waiting under the pine trees as we followed the hearse into the orchard. The car rolled and bumped over the natural ground until it came to a halt. Gretel Davis had been a friend of my mother's, and she helped me out of the car. She looked beautiful with her silver white hair cut short and swept up, light blue eyes, and a sky-colored shirt with a western yoke in the back and a black drape tied around her collar.

The wind started up and came through the pine trees like a flight of black crows. I used to love the sound of the wind but now it felt like a tornado, as if I was so slight, it could carry me away. I imagined I was at the top of a castle on the shore of a subjugated country. The wind was the sound of the range, empty and without shelter. It flapped our clothing like prayer flags on a forlorn mountain.

Beyond the pine trees, the barbed wire fence creaked and the winds leached out what little water the field had saved. Three hoops of coiled barbed wire hung on the fence, swinging in the gusts as if they were a series of family portraits, framing everything that had vanished.

We carried my mother to her grave and slid the casket onto the supports. Her curved white marble marker seemed to be the wings of a weeping angel. The nine of us stood with our heads down, our hands in front of us as the minister said the last words. A bouquet of yellow gladiolas lay at the head of her grave. Those were Elise's favorite flowers. She said the gold reminded her of wheat. During the summers of earlier harvests, she bought golden gladiolas from Smythe's store and placed them in vases on the dinner table for the crew.

Back then the harvest crew was made up of me, my father, my brother, and Henry. Henry was Jake's best friend. The two of them lived down in the bunkhouse during the summers because that way they could smoke cigarettes and drink on the weekends without my parents "knowing."

I turned to look behind me at my father's grave. There was a bottle of Early Times bourbon above the black granite block. Next to him was

Jake's grave, and on top of the rust-red stone was an opened package of Marlboro cigarettes and a packet of Western Family matches.

I grabbed my handkerchief from my pocket. A woman moved toward me from the pine trees. She had been standing back with the grave-diggers, and I hadn't noticed her. I thought I saw my mother alive again.

This woman walked closer, placed her hands around me, her cheek next to mine. I pulled back, and she reached up to take off her glasses. They were thick-lensed and black-rimmed. One would have imagined the person who wore these was almost blind. I noticed the faintest flutter in her hands. I realized I was facing Hanna.

She isn't stable, I noted, nervously. "I thought you'd have black hair," I blurted, holding my left elbow with my right hand. "Last time I saw you, you had black hair." She was white-haired now, like Lear, her body enveloped in a thick woolen navy coat. Her face had the look of someone who, while waiting at a train platform, had seen a stranger throw herself in front of an oncoming locomotive. Her kind eyes froze under delicate gray brows into a combination of sadness and surprise. I felt like apologizing for being so blunt; she was seventy years old after all.

"You and your brother always said whatever you wanted," she whispered. I nodded and scraped my shoe over some rocks in the cemetery. Hanna's face was much younger than her seventy years suggested. It was really unnerving how she hadn't aged. Schizophrenia did wonders for wrinkles.

Hanna tried to embrace me again, and I stepped back up on the wake of the grave. She released me as if separation were difficult and stepped unsteadily in her wide running shoes.

I picked up the matches and the cigarettes and, because everyone was watching, decided to leave the bottle of Early Times. I made myself stand still as Hanna caressed my hair. Her touch was uncomfortable and long, and I remembered how I had seen things when she touched me at Dammasch. I held my breath and wanted to back up again, but I was afraid to do anything.

"Walk with me to the house," Hanna said.

I nodded. "See you," I told Gretel. She and the others had gathered behind me watching Hanna with wonderment. I imagined they had met her before, when she was at the ranch the first time. I thought they probably wouldn't like her, would think she was a foreigner. I was wrong. The women, led by Gretel, surrounded Hanna and grasped her shoulders, and the men stood in line to touch her hand, their eyes cast to the ground. They were farmers looking to their hands and the land to relieve their sorrow.

Hanna and I turned and made our way toward the house in a surreal silence. I wondered how she had arrived—and, now she was here, how she would leave. If she stayed, I somehow imagined her coming into my room in the middle of the night with an ax and finishing off our family. Maybe that was what she meant by being done with us.

People from the funeral began driving in. They parked all over the ranch, wherever they pleased. Women carried cakes in Depression glass servers. Men hoisted the flowers from the church, building a little procession as they walked up to the grave site.

There was a side gate into our fenced yard, obscured by locust trees and lilac bushes. The latch had broken a couple years ago. Hanna walked directly to it. She didn't look around, even though she hadn't been at the ranch in thirty-one years, and instead reached over and unlatched the damaged gate from the inside.

The buzz hit me then, the unmistakable sound of a rattlesnake. I started and snapped my hand out to hold Hanna back. The two of us backed away from the gate as the snake sidewinded through. It moved fast, its head up in the air and twisted to face us, fangs bared all the while as it slithered out toward the field. Its tail rattled angrily, and I started to the house to get the shovel.

"I might still be able to kill it," I said. It was too bad my dogs, the border collies, were locked in the house; they were the best snake killers.

Hanna stopped me. "It won't be coming back," she said.

"Hell it won't," I answered. "It comes here for water. It was green."

Rattlers were colored differently depending on their surroundings. This one was clearly a yard rattler. I could tell because it grew brilliant verdant diamonds on its back. Wheatfield rattlers were the prettiest— intense yellow and black; those of the summer fallow were the ugliest, pale and brown.

"No," she said again, walking into the yard. "It's gone."

I squinted at her dress as she moved toward the rose garden. I couldn't tell if it was black or navy. Of course, she's wearing black, I found myself thinking. That's what people with second sight wear.

I followed her through the Pioneer roses planted by my grandmother. Hanna walked toward the crimson rosebush in the back, threading her way through the others. A rose thorn caught in my dress, as Hanna stopped and smelled that red rose. She knew it was the loveliest of all of them.

Behind her, I grabbed a large white rose, ripped it off from its stem. I picked one of the outside petals and dropped it. "How did you get here?" I asked, half not wanting to know. A person who lives in complete isolation as I did didn't like guests who arrive on broomstick.

She turned to stare intently at the house. I watched how her hands hung down; she didn't bother with crossing or holding them.

I nonchalantly placed the cigarettes in my pocket, while holding on to the matches and the rose. I picked another petal, fingered it, and then dropped it. A shower of rose petals fell to the ground.

"He loves you," Hanna said, still looking at the house.

I stared at the rose, but there on the hip remained one last stubborn petal.

7

I PLACED THE MATCHES TO MY LIPS. THEY WERE THE KIND that Henry and Jake used for cigarettes, holed up in the bunkhouse at the Bar S and Heart of the Beast. Henry first came to our house a month before Jake graduated from high school, and afterward, he rarely left. Henry fit into our family perfectly: he was Jake's ally, the second son Elise had always wanted, and he even managed to make Ike laugh once or twice. I had adored him from the beginning.

On the Tuesday night before Jake's graduation, I found Henry and Jake baking brownies. Because they were three and four years older than I was, I found everything they did fascinating. As they mixed in two packages of chocolate Ex-Lax, they recounted how several of the hard-ass teachers in Lona deserved a good comeuppance, specifically Mr. Sidow, the drill-happy football coach, and Mr. Klemp, the "Steele and Goodstand take ten laps" P.E. teacher. They calculated just when to place the plateful of goodies in the smoke-filled teachers' lounge (before the second shift lunch, when Sidow and Klemp would likely come in and chow down), and gave the little gift to Miss Humbolt, the leader of Future Homemakers of America. Henry asked me to write the attached note, in my most girly writing: *To our favorite teachers! Thanks for a great year! Love ya, the Rally squad.* I thought I added a nice touch by placing hearts above the final *i* in the Rally members' names: *Jodi, Susi, Lori, Molli, and Tami.*

Graduation night when Jake was waiting to receive his diploma, Klemp found Henry, picked him up by the shoulders, and pinned him to the hall wall outside the moist and body-odored gymnasium.

"Goodstand," he had screamed, "MY ASS IS BURNIN'."

Henry was a spark, a catalyst: once he yelled, "Don't give up the ship," and tackled Ike in the middle of the postharvest beer bust. The three of us then carried him down to the water trough and dumped him in. I watched how Henry stood over Ike as he lay in the water, smiling at him, ready to help him up afterward.

Jake and Henry traveled everywhere together. They were a handsome pair as they headed out to dances in Lona and Pendleton, or to hear bands in Portland. Henry stood tall and muscular, his tanned skin highlighting his blue eyes, white teeth, and sandy cropped hair. Jake was shorter, rounder, but still he was several inches over my five-foot eight-inch frame. His auburn hair grew curly and thick. Jake sported Levi's and logging shirts, Pendleton woolens in the winter and cotton in the summer. Henry wore T-shirts that allowed glimpses of the muscle in his arm when he reached for a beer.

Jake's eyes burned, though he didn't have mean eagle eyes like Ike. When a woman had a conversation with my brother, he could talk about boll weevils and she would listen for hours. He had a way of standing right—somehow a generous stander: never too close to invade space, not too far away either. Jake gave women the impression he was their long-lost twin. They would call at the ranch for my brother, and he carried on mysterious, sometimes long relationships. But he rarely brought them home, never wanted my father to have the opportunity to meet anyone that he might love.

Women could get in thick with Jake rapidly. Henry cracked jokes, was more likely to attract women because he was flippant and funny, but I never heard at school of Henry's having a girlfriend. I flattered myself and imagined he was waiting for me.

I dubbed Jake and Henry The Chick Magnets, as they showered to go out on their adventures. "Shut up," my brother would say to me. And then as they headed out the door, Henry would ask, "You ready?" and Jake would always reply, "Born ready."

I would stand there and watch them drive off, then walk down to the barn, saddle Jade, and ride the land in the moonlight. I wanted to go with them, I couldn't stand being left out of any of the exciting things they did. Before school started in the fall, Jake and Henry took off for the coast to fish and brought back the rare salmon. On summer Sundays, they hauled the boat to the river for waterskiing. And in the late spring, they were each other's support when we trekked east to Heart of the Beast.

Every June we traveled to my mother's land in the bright whiteness of melting snow. As soon as all three of us finished school, we packed up for a month of fence fixing, marking timber, and repairing roads. We loaded the dogs, the cattle horses, our Levi's, ten books apiece, and drove the one hundred miles to Joseph. Ike had lit out for the high country weeks earlier, seemed only to notice that he had a cook when Mother and I followed. Jake and Henry came last. My brother loved to linger where his father wasn't.

After dinner and on weekends while we were preparing the summer pasture at Heart of the Beast, Jake nursed those Marlboro cigarettes and the burnt-orange rage he felt toward our father. Vice versa bloomed in the big house. I never noticed it in myself, although the year I turned seventeen, it probably would have been clear to anyone watching.

The hundred-mile trip was a long drive. Our route threaded past Pendleton and La Grande, through small towns made up of a tavern or two and abandoned houses. Fired dead trees fell along the ravines like matchsticks. In the distance rose the sawtooth Wallowa Mountains. I stared at every rise and imagined myself living a hundred years earlier and seeing the same thing. Out here, the future looked the same as the past.

We proceeded along blue alfalfa fields colored of Mediterranean Sea to the town of Joseph, sprawled in the Wallowa Valley where the chief once summered his tribe. Shops of glass and paint, muffler repair, equipment rentals lined the streets. At the city limits, a sign announced the high school mascot: the Savages.

Mountain bowls surrounded the city, and a lake lapped at its edge. Halfway down the valley was my mother's place, Heart of the Beast—a 2,500-acre cattle ranch. The name came from a small mountain of earth, nipple shaped on the slope of a meadow. This was the formation the Nez Perce claimed had created them.

My mother took me up there when I was little to hunt for artifacts: arrowheads and unusual stones. The view looked over our entire ranch, spread out over several pine-covered mountains and valleys.

Over the years, I went up on that little peak less and less; too many things had happened there: flat tires, slammed fingers, lost hay hooks. I avoided it if I could. But the cattle flocked to the spot; they lay in the sun, pawed wallows, and chewed their cud. They loved the green grass; it was greener there than anywhere else on the ranch. I would drive the pickup to where the cattle congregated, and heave out salt licks and mineral blocks. They rolled out of the tailgate and sank in the earth strangely, as if the ground were particularly vulnerable.

I had always known there was something special about that ranch. It was the top of the world. Our hills held up the sky. Even in summer, jagged edges of snow ripped up the high precipices as if they were claws warning that something unusual gripped this place. When the sun came out, the mountainsides glowed green in the wind, catching the glint of grassbacks and alder leaves while above glimmered cherubskin clouds. As late as June, the new grass was just beginning to crack the ground asunder. Winter squelched spring, only giving up its stranglehold to summer.

Heart of the Beast brought out the worst in Elise and Ike, the worst in all of us, cooped up in my mother's small homestead and bunkhouse. But it was there I began work with Henry. Robert Frost said, "Something there is that doesn't love a wall," and it doesn't love barbed wire either. It was our chore to repair fence, miles of it.

The mending of fence at the upper place was done, in the four weeks we stayed there before returning to the Bar S to work the cattle, and then transport them to Heart of the Beast for summer pasture. Repairing the fence lines was when it all started, beginning with my observation of Henry's hands, stained dark and dirty with grease from changing oil, or tanned from building fence. Henry's muscular hands crowded out his veins until they bared themselves just under his skin. When we labored together, I stared at them. The sinew there was thick and brutelike. The hammer handle forced the pad of his hand into a fat curve, and stretched the tanned tension between his forefinger and thumb when he pounded posts.

His carved delicate wrists choked down the veins so when they flowed into his hand, they bloomed. I loved the way his body gave up secrets, those things as tender and personal as the way his blood fed his body. I knew the veins of Henry's hand like a map of home. I memorized how those blue ribbons came together. They flowed over one another, ran side by side, and crossed again like intertwined lovers.

Henry had such strong hands because he always hung on. His mother and father had separated when he turned ten. His father kept Henry and took up bourbon when the savings and loan he worked at went bankrupt. It was then Sonja Goodstand decided to leave permanently to become a diplomat. She took the Foreign Service exam, aced it, and enrolled in the Johns Hopkins Foreign Service graduate program.

"The Foreign Service is no place for a kid," Henry said. "That's why she didn't want me." A week into that year's stay at Heart of the Beast we were out repairing the north property line. While we mended fence, Ike negotiated the timber contracts, Mother cooked, and Jake fell prey to the odd and difficult jobs Ike thought up for him: moving old iron equipment from the junk pile, building roads with the dozer. Ike never allowed Jake to work with anyone, kind of the way repressive governments move their capitals away from the sea, away from insurgents.

Because neither of us was allowed to work with Jake, we ended up alone together, climbing the hills while we looked for downed wires where cattle could escape. I walked, the hammer looped through Ike's old military belt, staples and ties in the leather pouches. Henry rode the blood bay, Remley. A crop-out gelding, he didn't buck but he liked to run away. Across his thighs Henry carried the fence stretcher, and bundled behind his saddle, a butterfly of barbed wire.

It was a hot day. The air smelled and glistened of pine oil. Sweat dampened my shirtsleeves and I rolled them under my bra straps as I walked.

"Do you ever hear from your mother?" I asked, spotting a downed fence and pulling the fencing tool from my belt.

"She sends a card on my birthday."

"Big fucking deal," I said, though I thought it might have been too bold a thing to say to an abandoned son.

Henry laughed, and I was relieved.

"And she gives me advice," he said, standing up in his stirrups and sitting down again. The saddle creaked like the mooring rope of a ship. "Like what kind?" I went on, emboldened. "Go to school? Learn to read?"

"She says I shouldn't marry. Says men and women are incompatible."

I fell silent. That wasn't what I wanted to hear when I was working on a major thing with Henry. I looked at the blisters on my hands. The night before, Ike had given me Corn Huskers lotion. It went on thick and slimy like witch's brine and had created calluses over the welts. "What a bunch of crap," I said, pulling my gloves from my pocket and throwing them on the ground. "Excuse for her, more 'n anything," I said too loudly.

"Remember the time you tried to kill me?"

"What time was that?" I took a swig from my canteen and frowned at the two tangled wires where a cow had worked them loose. The barbed wires were old and rust colored. Lying down in the sparse forest grass and pine needles, they looked like snakes.

"Last week. When you taught me how to ride," he said, dismounting. He took the lead rope coiled around the saddle horn, and snapped it onto Remley's halter under the bridle. He tied a half hitch knot to the fence post, and then retied it again and yanked it for good measure. His Levi's caught on his lace-up boots when he dismounted.

I squinted at him in the bright thin mountain air. I thought I detected a smile, but I looked at him with concern, just to have the opportunity to stare at his face. "You were absolutely safe," I told him earnestly. I saw the sweat collecting on his forehead under the blue Nike baseball cap. I noticed the way his strong brow sheltered his bright blue eyes. Stubble did not cover his face like my brother's. He had been shaving, taking extra interest in his looks. I hoped it was because of me. "I would have caught you if you'd fallen," I said.

Henry looked at me, and walked over. My heart dropped. He was so close I could see the dirt creased in his neck and smell his sweet sweat. I considered that he used deodorant, another sign he was interested. Most ranch hands didn't care what they smelled like out in nature. He appraised the fence. "Learn by experience," he said softly. "Is that it?"

My face felt hot, an embarrassing red. "Yeah," I replied, averting my eyes, pretending to be interested in a dirt clod by my foot. The fence was tangled up right in front of me and Henry was to the side of me. It was like I suddenly forgot how to fix fence. It never occurred to me to pull on my gloves, grab the wire with the fencing pliers, and tear it apart.

"Well," he said, sighing as if he were going to discuss the finer points of barbed wire. "Even when you learn by experience, you still need a good teacher." He sort of leaned into me and whispered the last part.

I stood there, my stomach tightened. "I'm not a good teacher?" I asked, trying to keep my voice steady.

"I've seen better," he said, casually.

"Oh, I'm sure you've had a lot," I said. I pulled out my pliers finally. "Good teachers." I winked at him. "Going to college and all."

"Not so many," he replied. "Good ones," and he slapped my butt, low, and his fingers went so far, they hit the knot from the seams in the crotch of my Levi's. I jumped and I think I lost consciousness for the second his hand was on my butt, and then I stood there hoping I hadn't done anything completely stupid in that moment I couldn't remember. Like sneezing or worse, God, how embarrassing—once when I was little my brother pulled my leg and I had farted.

"What's the secret then?" I said, forcing myself to step forward and pick up my gloves.

Henry thought awhile, and moved over next to me again. "I think you have to be patient to be a good teacher." He cut the wire where it wouldn't untangle.

I slapped my gloves across my thigh, removing imaginary dust. Remley kicked at a fly with his back hoof. I considered Henry's tanned forearms where they came out of his rawhide gloves, watched the muscles tighten against one another and bulge as he snapped his fencing pliers. "Someday you'll have the opportunity to teach," I told him, grabbing on to the loose end of wire. I placed the two ends of the cut wire in the fence stretcher and began jacking that wire taut.

"When would that be?" asked Henry. He walked over to the saddle-bag, not waiting to hear my answer. He returned with a handful of staples and his hammer.

"When you run across a green hand," I said, glancing at him momentarily. His lips were smooth and generous, not even chapped from the dry mountain air.

"I'll look forward to that," said Henry, his eyes on the fence.

The wires sang tight. I held the two ends with the pliers, and then we twisted them back together whole.

A week earlier, to make the fence mending more efficient, Ike had given me the job of teaching Henry how to ride. The problem with that had been the Nez Perce horses. They were wonderful horses, but not for beginners. They loved to work, but every winter they were turned out to pasture and had to be rebroke again the following spring. They shied at anything—a snake, horsefly, tumbleweed, gust of wind.

"The reins are most important," I told Henry. "It's what gives you control."

I held Remley's bridle with one hand and the stirrup with the other. At first, Henry clung to the reins and the saddle horn when he mounted. His back was curved, and his heels were up.

The way to ride was to place as much weight as possible into the heels. That way the horse can't unseat the rider, and if you can stay on a horse long enough, eventually you'll learn to ride. But in teaching Henry, I wasn't thinking about his heels. The finesse of riding would come later.

"Tighten your reins," I said, setting them in his right hand. We walked around the salt lick at the corral for twenty minutes practicing how to stop Remley.

The corral at Heart of the Beast wasn't for working cattle like the seemingly infinite stockyards of the Bar S. Horse trading had gone on here, back during the Indian wars when my great-grandfather John Winter made his fortune selling horses to the cavalry. Built out of stripped pine poles, the corrals surrounded a Mother Hubbard–ish old white barn. The center of the building rose high for hay storage.

Around it was the animals' manger, which flanked the barn like a skirt. Windows placed at regular intervals allowed the breeze in during the summer and dried the mud in the winter. Out in the corral, a small corrugated-tin salt lick sweltered in the few days of heat.

I saw that once Henry gained confidence, he was a natural rider. Sitting Remley without fear, his back straightened up, and his heels came down almost immediately. Henry was good, except he became anxious when the horse trotted.

"Stop. Goddammit," he said, bouncing, bent over the saddle horn. "You know I think all women want the opportunity to teach men how to ride horses. Because then they have us where they want us. By the balls."

It was true. Every slight I'd ever received from Henry found its way back into my memory. "Grab the mane," I yelled. "And stand up in your stirrups." I looked back at him, placing my hand on Remley's shoulder, careful to avoid those big striped trotting hooves. That horse would try to pin a person who wasn't paying attention.

The striped hooves were the sign of a crop-out, or a solid-colored Appaloosa. I prided myself on how much I knew about horses. I read about them constantly when I was little—everything from how to care for them to what color and what type the kick-ass queens of history preferred. I researched Catherine the Great, Queen Elizabeth, Queen Isabella of Spain, and cast my lot with Isabella, who rode into battle on spotted or roan horses. She believed, like Shakespeare, that hair color represented the elements of nature and therefore a horse with all colors on its coat had the best temperament. White, black, brown, and red represented, respectively, sun, wind, earth, and fire. That was the kind of horse I picked. Jade was my roan Appaloosa.

Jade was not like the rest of the horses. She was more like a deer than a horse, soft and good-natured. She had only bucked once, and not when I broke her as a three-year-old. She had the personality of an angel and the fearlessness of a warhorse.

"Stop," Henry breathed jerkily.

I halted Remley and patted the folds of his skin between his forelegs. His coat felt like satin and shone like burnished metal. "Canter's better," I said. "Feels like a rocking chair."

"Even a dentist's chair's better than the trot," Henry said, looking at me sideways. "All right. Let's go." He kicked Remley forward. Henry didn't let anyone get the best of him.

"You sure?" I asked.

He nodded.

I led them out the corral gate, and slammed the locking stick forward. I grabbed Jade's mane and swung onto the saddle without using the stirrups. I showed off; riding was what I did best. No testicles got in my way.

We headed out. Ever since I was little, I've loved the thrill of starting on a ride, the way the riders and horses become used to each other. I straightened my saddle, which had been pulled off center with the mount. Jade's movement began to control my breath; she pushed air in and out of my lungs with her stride and my countering sway. The sound of the horses' hooves on the gravel of Heart of the Beast echoed life into the silent buildings.

Remley tried to turn back to the barn, but Henry caught him.

"Make him move out," I said, clicking and chucking my tongue at his horse. We passed through the gate of the barbed wire fence that surrounded the ranch site. A meadow unfolded up the side of the Wallowa Valley, and the hill for which the place was named arose there. Occasionally Henry and I had pitchforked hay to the cattle here when spring snow refused to relinquish the prize of the earth.

The sound of the hooves changed as we reached the meadow; little dirt clots, bits of grass scattered out from each hoof's landing. It sounded like rain. The smell of leather mixed with horse sweat. Remley snorted, his air muffled and forced through a wet, dense bag of nose.

I headed Jade around to avoid the peak, stayed on the lower pasture. The grass cushioned us as we walked, making it easier to negotiate than a cropped field. Horses didn't get so tired out in the turf; they could run forever. The only thing more glorious than galloping through the gold of wheat was galloping through green fields.

That was when I said something I shouldn't have. "Let's run."

"Okay," said Henry, gamely doing what I advised and grabbing the mane.

"Follow me," I trailed, "and hang on." I started Jade at a slow lope, and Henry's horse followed.

Remley began shouldering Jade over as we cantered along. I rode, instructing Henry all the while. The horses bobbed their heads in unison as they galloped through the thick soft earth. Watching Henry intently, I didn't notice that Remley had herded us up on top of the peak, and I certainly didn't see what spooked Remley. Whatever it was must have been somewhere in the tall grass at the top. Remley jerked his head down, and the reins came out of Henry's hands.

Henry grabbed for them, trying to pull them in. He hauled them into his stomach but Remley still had a free head.

"Shorten your reins again," I ordered.

His back was rounding and his butt began slapping down in the saddle. Remley raced with Jade. I set Jade down with a smart snap of rein. She crow-hopped, and it caught me by surprise. I lost my left stirrup. Ordinarily we would have had it out immediately; I would have turned her in a circle to keep her off balance so she couldn't buck. But this time I let her run on so I could talk to Henry, help him slow down.

"Grab on to the mane again, get your balance," I yelled from behind.

Henry clutched the mane with one hand, but his reins were useless and long. It only took an instant. Remley sensed the chance to run away. He tore off, bucking three times, his tail whistling in the wind as he snapped it back and forth.

I saw the back of his haunches pulling away from us, working hard, wrinkling that shiny hide and stretching it out again with his gallop. Remley veered to the cattle trail and headed toward the far corner of Heart of the Beast. He was still running at a full-out gallop. I envisioned the horse falling into a badger hole and breaking his leg, throwing Henry to a concussion. Worse, a barbed wire fence stood between Remley and a logging road that led back to the house. I knew what barbed wire could do to an animal, let alone a man. Ike would slap me as it was when he found out, even if Remley and Henry didn't kill themselves.

I turned Jade, and headed for the shale. The shale was what we called the only other road to the back side of our property. It went straight down the mountain rockfall, crossing the logging road halfway

down. Ike had ordered Jake to gouge it out of the rock slope with the
dozer so the loggers could pull timber off our property. The road
pitched at a hopeless angle. A person couldn't see the road when he
drove up, and driving down it, there was always the possibility the
driver would make the mistake of locking the wheels on the shale and
sliding right off the road into a roll. I didn't have a quarter of the nerve
to drive up the road, let alone down it. Only Ike, and rarely Jake, took
the pickup in four-wheel-drive Low on the shale.

I kicked Jade into a dead run, hoping to cut the blood bay off. Even
at that pace and over the top of the uneven meadow, she barely moved
her head. No one knows where the mysterious breed of Appaloosa
came from, what their heritage was before the Nez Perce perfected
them. Some say Spain, that Columbus brought the royal horses of
Isabella. But I knew all horses went back to one race. With her black-
tipped ears flat back, she ran like an Arabian, that lineage with millen-
nia of careful breeding that allowed them to negotiate the great ergs
and rock precipices with ease. Jade could do things at a run that would
break other horses' legs at a trot.

We reached the top of the hill, and I saw Remley and Henry halfway
down to the timber road. I reined Jade to where the shale started,
where the earth fell away. She leaped over the edge and disappeared
under me. I leaned so far back the cantle of the saddle bruised my back.
Luckily the saddle was cinched tight and didn't ride up on her neck.

She regained her footing and moved slowly, carefully picking her
way over the shard-edged stones. She hadn't been shod; working in the
mountains never required the iron of a blacksmith. Every few steps she
limped as an upturned rock dug into the soft frog of her foot. I leaned
backward to offset the weight on her forelegs as we tilted downward.

Jade kept limping, each step she took over the broken stones caus-
ing her as much pain as the last. I considered what to do. Hurry her
across as if she were one of those fakirs who traversed hot coals, the
faster the better? I thought about dismounting, leading her, wondering
if she'd fare better minus my 122 pounds. I pulled her to a halt, and
that was my mistake. She stood there blowing. I could feel her upper
back leg cocked, trembling.

Slowly her hindquarters shifted downhill. Panicked, she immediately pushed off with her resting foot. And that was what started it. Her whole back end began slipping. It wasn't a gravelly, pebbly sound. More a dull scraping, a deep reverberation with the weight of glaciers behind it. The shale hill gave way.

Jade didn't lose her head. I did. The red-hot heat of panic destroyed my composure the way it always did when I thought I was about to die. Jade wheeled around, dropping herself so her forelegs were in front of her. My horse fought to keep her balance. Every muscle held her body together, even though each of her legs could have slid in different directions. If she gave an inch she'd lose her balance on the running rockslide.

When she turned, I bailed off. I abandoned her. That was when I realized I had a serious character flaw. My slick-soled cowboy boots worked no better than Jade's hooves. I let the reins slip through my hands until the knot caught in my fist, which was still waving around as I balanced myself. I grabbed on to the stirrup, using Jade as ballast. I was terrified I'd slide down in front of her and be crushed if she fell.

The timber road was thirty feet below, and we were going to slide or roll down the entire way. At least I had enough guts not to let go of my horse. If I was a complete coward, I would have totally abandoned her and scrambled off to the side.

I spotted a solid rock outcropping that parted the shale as if it were a stream. I pulled Jade with me, and we high-stepped over to the boulderlike protrusion. The rocks continued to fall behind and to the sides of us even when we reached the solid ground. Here and there, a single rock broke free and twirled down the mountain.

Below us, Remley was about to come to the barbed wire fence. I could see he was headed toward the gate, where the wires were down. It was in bad shape; we hadn't mended fence down there yet. The top three wires were bent back on themselves.

From where we clung to the rock, there was no place for Jade and me to go but down. So I grabbed her reins under her bit, directing her head away from me, and I walked out on the shale. I thought she might balk. But of course she didn't. She stepped out carefully too, sat back on her haunches, and rode on down. I clambered right alongside of her.

We slid the whole way, sort of like surfing. When we were almost there, Jade stepped calmly off the slide and onto the road, snorting and shaking her head. By then I had seen her chipped and cracked hooves.

I looked up to see Remley jump the fence in one huge stride of his gallop. Henry landed with him, but landed hard. They ran on toward us as I knew they would. I glanced down again to Jade's feet. They were broken, fractured, and impossibly short. I wondered if she'd ever recover, if I'd ever be able to ride her again. Once a hoof is cracked up to the coronet, it's ruined. It never heals.

It was then I noticed Mother. She was driving the Ford out to meet Ike at some appointed time as he worked, marking our timber for the loggers. She stopped the pickup in the middle of the road and walked toward me. I thought she would lay into me.

But she didn't. She went past as if I weren't there. Mother was the one who had broke Remley. She never trained her horses completely; she and Jake had always liked something unknown that would challenge them.

That was until Remley's running away became routine. My mother rigged a trip rope up to Remley's front legs, and whenever he started to run away with her, she would yell, "Stop, you goddamn son of a bitch," and pull the trip rope that would send Remley and my mother crashing into the ground. It didn't take long for Remley to learn when my mother yelled he had better stop. And when Mother saw Remley coming over the fence with Henry, she hurled those words at her horse and he slid to a shuddering halt.

Elise walked up to Remley. His bloodred body was still shaking, terrified he was going to be thrown to the ground. She talked quietly to Henry, placed her hand on his calf. They walked in circles around her for a couple minutes. She turned them the other way, and they trotted around her in the opposite direction. Henry looked more at ease than ever. Then Elise motioned me toward them.

I was for sure in trouble, letting Remley run away with Henry like that, and then there was the jump over the barbed wire fence, which was the worst crime you could commit with a horse. It was my fault, and it was dangerous. I shouldn't have asked Henry to gallop the first time out on a horse, let alone risk Jade's breaking her legs on the shale fall.

"Iris," she said, pulling off her belt. As she approached us, I could see she was livid. She swung at me with the belt. It snapped wickedly on my T-shirt. Jade shied and I followed her. At ten feet, I brought my horse around to face my mother. The belt stung more than it hurt, and the worst of it was she had hit me in front of Henry. A completely humiliating thing, being whipped like an animal by your mother.

She stood there in her black lace-up boots, dark green Anne Klein pants, and pullover. Mother even wore clothes with lions on the tags.

She didn't have makeup on, never bothered with it unless she was going to town. Still, her countenance shone as if it were stainless steel. Even back then she looked as if she were a sculpture. Shadows made up her face; they gathered under her cheekbones, above her eyelids, below her sharp square jaw. Her ice-blue eyes flicked cruelly over me and my horse, and remained on Jade's broken feet. I wanted her to know that I had tried to stop Remley, that it wasn't my fault the mountain spooked him. She would scoff if I told her. I couldn't make her see things the way I did. I could never control my mother; that was why I liked to ride horses so much.

"Lucky you're off that horse," she said. "Because you won't be riding again until those hooves heal. If they heal."

"They're not that bad," I said.

"You wouldn't know," she said coldly. "You're no horsewoman."

She wasn't either, if you asked me, the way she broke her runaway. I stood there glaring at my mother. She always set her world up to control things and people. "I'll ride Remley out," I said. "He'll be fine." I didn't know how I'd fix fence or chase cattle without a horse for the rest of the summer.

"Shut up," she said. "Didn't you hear me? You are not to get on a horse again. Not until Jade heals."

"Mom," I said as I touched the welt under my shirtsleeve. "How do you expect me to work without a horse?"

"You can start with walking Henry home," she said, as she made her way to the pickup. My mother drove on by without another look at either her horse or her daughter.

We walked home, me between Remley and Jade. I caught my mother's horse by the bridle and punched him in the nose. "When there's nothing else, there's always work," I said. "And if you have children you have someone to take things out on. A whipping boy, and I can't wait to get the hell out."

"Quit complaining," Henry said. "At least you get something when they're gone." He pulled Remley away from me and kicked his tired horse into a run. Now that Henry had survived one little runaway he was all of a sudden an expert rider. He left me there, walking in the dirt.

8

WINTERS WERE HARD ON LAND, BUILDINGS, AND EQUIP-
ment, especially at Heart of the Beast. The housepaint peeled, the barn
broke apart, and the fences fell—everything returned to nature in the
long chill of the Wallowa.

While the rest of the family repaired, Ike prepared to pull down, to
destroy: that was Ike's job. He harvested grain, he selected the cattle
for slaughter, he marked the trees for clear-cut with red paint, and he
shot coyotes.

More than anything, my father loathed coyotes. He hated everything
about them—their independence, the way they preyed on calves, mostly
the fact that he couldn't kill them all off. He carried a rifle in the back of
the pickup, sometimes a .357 in his holster. He hunted deer, he stalked
elk, but mainly he killed coyotes. When he shot them, he threw them
in the back of the pickup. Afterward he gave the carcass to the dogs to
shred. He said it made a dog tough to tear up a coyote.

The spring I turned seventeen Ike and I began to fly together in his
plane, a high-winged red Super Cub. He strapped me into the copilot's
seat, turned on the gyro, and checked out the aircraft. I hated that
sound, sitting there waiting for him to look at flaps and fuel. It messed
with my inner ear. But I sat there just the same for ten minutes, while
he drained the nozzle under the wing, the jet A coming out a light blue
like the sky. Then he untied the wings from their tethers.

When he slid in, he placed his headphones on and that was the signal for me to do the same. Then he would revert to his military days in the South Pacific and say into the radio, "This is Papa 9 4 9 3 1, ready for takeoff." There was never any answer.

I thought it was odd that the military liked the word *Papa* enough to use it in their alphabet. No marine that I had ever heard about would be caught dead with his children calling him Papa. It was most often Sir. The last thing Ike did after strapping himself in was open his door and scream "Clear" when he started up the engine. It fascinated me that he did it every time, even though no one was around for miles.

We roared down the runway and took off into the blue sky of eastern Oregon. Besides using the plane to retrieve machinery parts, Ike looked for down fences and chased cattle with it. Flying terrified me, but that summer I never said a word because it saved me from walking miles of range.

My father and I shepherded the cattle together. In twenty minutes we flew back to the Bar S to check on them, spotting where the AWOLs hid, up canyons and cliffs, uncovering them in remote crevices feeding off the green markings that surrounded a hidden spring. Ike and I searched in the far corners of the range, sometimes finding them across the fence on neighbors' land; other times they hid in the underbrush at the bottom of the Creek Ranch.

I hated cattle almost as much as my father loathed coyotes. They tortured me because when they escaped, the job of herding them back in came to me, on top of any other chore I might have. I called them bovines and watched with disgust from the plane, packs of them lying in wallows chewing their cud. I detested how their fat backs upended themselves as we rooted them out of their hiding places. Stubborn sumbitches, they moved only if we were practically on top of them— only when we took a dive would they fan out at a run.

If it was a reconnaissance mission, Ike flew the fence lines searching for holes through which cattle escaped into the next county. When I walked out later to bring them in, I knew exactly where to look, and where I needed to go to fix fence. I never embarked without staples and wire twists tangled in my military belt and a fencing tool in my makeshift latigo.

My brother refused to fly in the plane with my father. It was as simple as that. Ike tried to make Jake steer the plane while he shot coyotes. Jake flew it all right. He grabbed his butterfly yoke and slowly pushed it in, the plane tipped its nose toward the bluffs on Rock Creek, and Jake held the course. Ike threw down his rifle and yanked his butterfly back. There was a struggle, until my father smashed his elbow into Jake's temple. Jake told me what happened afterward, and that was when I began doing my time beside my father.

When Jake refused to fly, Elise laid out the decree that she wouldn't either unless everyone in our family was crammed in the plane. Her philosophy was if the ship was going down we all were going with it. I thought it was simpler than that; if she had to die, so did we. That was the only way Elise agreed to take her share.

I was jealous of Jake, and was more than happy to take his place in the plane. I aimed to do better than my brother, who seemed to get all the attention, albeit good and bad, just because of his sex. When all of a sudden, Ike shouted, "Steer, goddammit," and motioned toward my butterfly wheel, I accepted my role with pleasure.

I grabbed my yoke, feeling the humming of the plane through the hard plastic that came up in my fingers with its molded grip. Ike's brows were furrowed; he had that enraged look in his eye that I never questioned. And there was the cigar, smoked down until it was just a long thumblike stub. He chewed it when it burned to that point, more than he inhaled it. My father had pushed his door out to the wing and retrieved his rifle from behind his seat. My headphones barely fit, but I could hear him all right.

"Hold'r in the canyon," he said.

I couldn't see over the instrument panel. Strapped in, I had no way to get up on my knees. But I had a damn good view of the turn coordinator; I kept those wings exactly on top of that white line, never pulled or pushed that butterfly in or out one millimeter. My heart pounded so hard it hurt.

Out of the corner of my eye, I saw Ike unstrapping himself. It was no easy task pulling off the gear that came down over his shoulders and hooked into the lap belt. But he unsnapped it in one click, then pulled out his .22 rifle and fired off four shots.

Afterward he set the gun down between us, laid it over the trim wheel. He seized his steering yoke again and turned it; my hands were still on mine. I held my yoke lightly, as Ike pulled out and we rose up. My stomach came into my mouth as we arced around and came back at the coyote one more time.

He discharged another four shots before he turned around for yet another pass. Ike was a good shot, even at speed. He usually made a kill and never went back afterward, left them there to rot.

After that day, he and I went flying often. Every time Jake failed at something, or refused, I did it. I flew the plane while my father shot coyotes. I hoed fields in 108 degrees, I drove combine, I skinned Cat, I herded cattle, I fixed fence, I cleaned the elevator, I hauled hay, I burned weeds. I did everything in Jake's place until I took over all my brother's purpose. I didn't complain. I did it younger, I did it harder, and I did it better, because I did it like a slave.

Without the luxury of riding Jade to fix fence at Heart of the Beast that summer, I lost weight. "Hiked it in." That's what Ike called it, just like the marines. He told me I could serve, I was tough, I didn't whine like my brother.

I wondered what my mother saw when she looked at her daughter. Not much probably. The extremities of my body hardened up. My hands tightened with muscle, and my arms hung away from my body from the brawn built up there. My yearly pair of new Levi's hung on me, ugly, hot, and dark blue.

Though our hair was the same color, I didn't have her curly tresses. Mine was long and soft, lighter now from the exposure, the color of palomino mane. I refused to guard my skin the way my mother did. She wore hats, a black Stetson with a silk stampede string. The darker I was the better; in fact, I was a photo negative of her. Everything white on her skin was dark on mine.

"My sister," Mother said once, idly touching her curls, "has hair the color of Spain." We were driving to Joseph for food and the mail. She told me that the king of Spain, Charles V, had so many lovers in the Scandinavian countries that a quarter of the population had black hair from him alone.

I laughed at her. "It's probably the color of Gypsies, Mom."

"What do you know about Gypsies? When have you ever seen one?" she snapped. She had been to Europe, to New York, San Francisco. Her parents sent her and her sister on cruises and trips because every farmer from the poorest to the richest hates being called "hick." They may not have had sons, but they had money.

"Not as much as you," I said. "Tell me about your friends, the Gypsies."

"Can't you be more helpful, like your brother?" she said, her thick Scandinavian lips tucked under bitterly. She placed both hands on the steering wheel and looked at my hand snapping the silver door handle nestled in the red leather. "Quit playing with that," she ordered.

"No," I said. "I'm not supposed to be a farmer, remember? The son always gets the place."

"Not if Ike has his way," she said.

"What about you. What if you have your way?" I asked.

She smiled and gave me a nonanswer, which was the Scandinavian way.

I thought about my parents as I sat there with her. It hadn't taken me seventeen years to know they didn't love each other or their children. Ike married Elise to get back at his father and she married him because Ike was a challenge. Unlike my brother and me, he was someone she simply couldn't rig a trip string up to.

That summer while I had been fixing fence, my brother spent his days on the dozer planning what he'd do when he ran the ranches. Since he'd turned twenty-one that year, he spouted off anytime at all. The program of planting seedlings after the clear-cuts. The erosion ditches to prevent runoff. Days off for the hired help. "Morale," he said, sarcastically, "is the most important thing for the crew."

"Morale," snorted Ike. "Don't talk to me about morale, unless you been in a war."

"I am in a war, living with you. You run this place like a boot camp," Jake told him.

"Christ," said Ike. "Get your lily-white ass out of here with your nose-picking complaining. You have no idea what real work is."

After that, Jake refused to eat dinner with us. He came in, dished up, and went down to the bunkhouse, wolfing down what he called his "grub." They went on and on like that; neither one would back down.

Even when I was little, I tried to escape my family at Heart of the Beast. The crystalled red cliffs, patterned like the wings of china pheasants, drew me in. In the spring, my favorite time of year, red rock precipices pulled water laced with ore from their quiver and shot it down the glacier-scrubbed face. The valley floor turned cold from the spray of it, the hurry of tea-colored streams riding down a toboggan course of logs, shrubs, and boulders. The rhythmic sounds of its rushing and charging beckoned the water off the cliffs to join the trip to the Snake, to the Columbia, and on down to the ocean.

Heart of the Beast lived between walls of rock that admitted to the cut of glacier. Some had recovered badly, propped up by buttresses of shale blotched and dappled as an ugly war pony; some were rounded and eroded away by wind and rain; others hid their weepy stains with pink dogwood trees.

I moved over the padded ground that sounded hollow when I walked, inhaling the smell of turpentine-painted trees that lay like a haze over the canopy of branches. I stopped here and there to move my hands over the worm paths I found in the black walnut tree trunks, tracing the designs like lizards, and the Nazca lines I had heard about, visible only from the sky. There was the Christmas of red bark and the green of juniper leaves that I fingered, harvesting their oil for perfume behind my earlobes.

It was an occasion, the yearly viewing of winter's damage. The spill-ways of trees and broken branches that tumbled through gullies, like a herd of animals run over cliffs by hunters with spears.

My own harvest came in spring, in the middle of the demolition. I collected what the hills fleeced, tiny particles of pyrite, fool's gold, pulled out from the mountains and left glittering the earth. I gathered the ore in alluvial fans simply because it was beautiful, and I hoped it would make me strong. Walking among the sage and yarrowed hills, I called it out from its sandy beds, placing it in the tobacco boxes I'd stolen from my father. I always ended my gathering at the argent doorstep of the hill named after Sacagawea.

At home the tips and heels of my cowboy boots shone with flecks of silver against their black leather. I showed the ore to my mother. I knew she'd love it; wealth was the only thing she ever settled on being faithful to. She cultivated my interest in mining; it was better than cutting up my dresses and shooting at my brother with my BB gun.

I placed the open boxes of the silver and pyrite on my oak floor and lit the old kerosene lamps, which filled my room with tallow light. I painted my mother with the gilt powder. I made her into a living sculpture, and I never forgot the image. Even at that early age, I kept trying to reforge my mother, to make her mine. But she remained an entity of gold that moved away, leaving behind glittering tears that mourned the vacuum left by her absence.

I took turns painting gold and silver, coloring her hands first. Then I placed it to her eyes, the lids silvered against the black of her lashes. In the creases lay dark metal, and the socket bone became a mirror. I brushed it along the veins in her wrists, her throat, and her backbone. "I'm going to make your cheekbones bronzed like the Incans and Indians," I told her.

"Don't be foolish," she said, and abruptly left the room.

I tried painting myself, but I fell down where my proud fingertips walked. I attempted to compose my bones into her beauty, but hers were wide and strong. When I finished, I walked around my room and watched the dried metal fall from my body, leaving skin soft, without wrinkle. I blew out the lanterns, and the light of the moon sparkled on the ore like a snowfall of riches inside my bedroom. Across the map of my palms, where the gold had fallen away first, my fortune was revealed to anyone who could decipher it.

All of us struggled to make our way that year at Heart of the Beast, but mercifully, it finally ended. Henry and I finished the fences, Ike cut his trees, Jake built his road. Too close, pent up, we were ready to kill by the time we returned to the Bar S for the roundup and the working of the cattle. That was the beginning, as near as I can tell, of the end.

It only took us a day to round up the cattle at the Bar S. All that night we heard their noise down in the stock corrals, cows calling constantly for their calves, for their herd. Once they were fenced in, they thundered, the dogs barked, the coyotes howled. Coyotes always followed the herds of cattle wherever they went, picking off the sick and newborn.

The second day was for working the cattle, readying them for the move to Heart of the Beast. Calves thrown in the early spring then needed vaccinations and branding; if they were male, castration. Before we turned the cattle out for the summer in the high country, we scarred them so we'd know they were ours. We made sure the lineage of the young males died and then we fattened them up for slaughter.

My father was a bull killer, a matador. If Ike were a country, he would have been Spain—a place of institutionalized violence from the Inquisition to the bullfights. When it came time for working the cattle, he rose in the morning extra early from the excitement of it all. Maybe he didn't even go to sleep.

On those mornings, he made an elaborate breakfast. Eggs scrambled. Flapjacks. Sausages. Coffee was the first thing we all drank in the morning, a jolt to get us going. Ike called us out of bed those days. Ordinarily, he would leave Jake, Henry, and me until our alarms went off, but when we worked the cattle, he started us out even earlier.

The day began with the sorting. Everything started with a judgment being passed. How old, how ill, what sex. The old, the sick, and the castrated were separated permanently, sold for their weight on the hoof. Then the various minor problems were diagnosed and dealt with, and finally, the calves were treated—vaccinated, branded, and cut.

After the sick cows and all the calves were separated from the rest of the herd, I ran them into a series of corrals that led into a chute and on down to the steel branding cages. There were two cages, red and yellow, lined up one after the other. The first was an operating table that tipped over sideways with a yank of a lever; that was for the castrations or other surgeries. The second was for the simple stuff: dehornings, branding, or vaccinating.

Cattle infections were gory. Cows contracted pinkeye and needed a dark purple stinging medicine sprayed into their eyes. I splashed diseased udders with the dirt-colored iodine. Boils were lanced and evil-smelling pus poured out. Horns grew into an eye or skull and had to be sawed off.

Jake had the job of herding the cattle down the chutes into the cages. He straddled the sides of the chute, sometimes pushing the cattle forward with his boots. Jake never wore the spiky hard cowboy boots like the rest of us. He wore round-toed lace-up boots, with soft, tender soles.

The cattle came down blowing challenges through their noses, looking for a way out of the enclosure. The instant they shoved their heads through the final viselike doors, I slammed down on the lever, shutting the clamp around their necks. That was my job. I stood on one side, Ike on the other. I watched him all day long through the dust and the prison bars of the cattle chute.

Once a cow was caught, a person had to stand back a minute while she fought the vise. She bellowed, kicked, and swung at us with her head, trying to gouge us if she had horns. If she didn't, she tried to take us out with her skull.

For the dehorning, a tonglike contraption went into the cow's nose, pinching down between the nostrils. It took Henry and me both to swing the cow's head around to the side, pulling on the rope with all of our weight. Ike used the saw and began sawing down at the base of the horn until he cracked it off. There was always blood down that far, close to the head. Ike saw my face.

"It's the only way to make sure the horns won't come back," he said.

I nodded at him and looked down, trying to hide the pity I felt toward the animals.

The calves were worked last. By that time, I had ground out all my fury in the torture of the mature cattle. When the babies came along, I was sick and sorry for them. Their shoulders were barely big enough for the whole brand to fit on their hide. A particularly small one would limp for a week or more from the size of the burn. I couldn't stand it after I saw the first few. The calves were so beautiful. Clean. Their white faces and legs were spotless. The brown and black shone from their mothers' licking. They weren't covered with shit like the adults.

I let the dogs take over for me. I just ran the chute gates and injected the vaccinations. I heard the bawling, but I wasn't there. I watched my father through the other side of the bars, working the electric branding iron that rested in a bucket of coal at his feet. It gave off the acrid, sweet smell of burning hair and skin. The iron was plugged into the outlet with a thick orange extension cord connected to the floodlight pole. That way if the branding wasn't done by sundown it could go on into the night. All his other tools lay within his reach—the knife, his antiseptic treatments, and his dogs.

The craziness of those two collies overcame everything. It happened when they tasted the first testicle. It turned them half wild like wolves. It amazed me, how they sucked in their stomachs and went everywhere at a trot. They hung their heads low and watched. Never did they look at anyone, except Ike. Those eyes followed the hooves and feet of the moving cattle. It was like pulling down prey, how they charged in on them—even if the calves were already caught and lying still between the breakaway iron bars of the chute. I noticed how they would reserve their utmost viciousness for the weakest calf. Both of them would attack it. Sometimes they actually downed it before I came over and kicked them off. The barking became an annoyance but I couldn't stop them. They ran on top of the benches alongside the chutes where my supplies were kept: cauterizing irons, iodine, KRS, vaccination guns, the saw and vise for dehorning. The dogs knocked everything over in their hope to get a mouthful of flesh.

It was sad enough for the female calves, but the baby bulls received the fold-down vise table. Once the chute was horizontal, Ike pulled away two of the bars by sliding a slip latch. That way he had enough room to cut. There was a rope with one end tied to the top of the chute. He looped the other end around one back hoof and yanked the hind legs apart, securing the foot up and back. He grabbed the still furry soft sack and took out his pocketknife. He sliced along the bottom of the sack. The baby bulls wailed. Usually the tongues came out and lolled on the dirt of the chute table, partly because the weight of the bars didn't allow them to breathe much. They had to open their mouths just to get enough air.

Ike squeezed the blue mass out of its encasement until he saw the two cords that connected the testicles and cut them. It was simple. He doused the opening with the ink-colored KRS. Next he branded them, and I gave them their vaccinations. The male calves usually didn't walk out of the chute. They couldn't. The castrated ones felt Ike's boot kicking them out with the rest of the cattle.

Afterward Ike tossed the testicles behind him into the dust and the dogs dove at them. Ace was bigger and always ate the prime pieces before his daughter, Dusty, could bolt down the leftover scraps.

Finally, we worked our way to the last group of calves. But Jake couldn't manage them. Four went into the chute but then stopped, reared up on their hind legs, and twisted their necks around trying to escape. It happened twice; Jake wasn't strong enough to muscle them into the cages. Before I knew it, Ike grabbed his stock whip and strode toward the V-shaped corral. The calves ran single file around the cell. Jake stood in the middle.

Ike entered the ring. For a moment, I stared at them as if they were strangers. Jake was much shorter and rounder, and he looked to the ground, while Ike's eyes searched for prey. The two men appeared as if they came from different countries; no one could have guessed they were father and son. It was like the architecture in Fez, the difference between the indoor courtyards in the houses of Muslims and the outdoor balconies on the houses of Jews.

Ike stood six feet four, and his frame never made the mistake of following anything but his lethal blue eyes. Wide shoulders cut a swath in the air, blue denim covered the blades with a yoke across the back, and his yoked heart mirrored it in front. In his pocket rested the bulging tablet with the figures from running his ranches. His boots had covered every inch of his lands. Their pointed toes and high-slant heels howled with distress and stories.

Jake didn't wear cowboy boots, didn't cut his hair, didn't shave, didn't tuck in his shirt, didn't carry whips or electric prods. Jake didn't force things, unless he was desperate. He cajoled, he coerced, and sometimes he didn't bother to do things at all.

"Get over there, goddammit," Ike yelled, throwing an arm in the opposite direction.

Together they cut the calves off, blocked them from running the perimeter. Finally two calves ran into the chute, and then Jake and Ike crowded the others quickly inside. The calves at the front of the line began balking again, rising up to turn around. Jake climbed forward on the chute sides straddling the calf backs. He quickly moved to the leaders, pushing their heads forward with his soft boots.

Behind him, Ike worked to force the rest of them in. He lashed his whip over the haunches of the closest calf, trying to force that calf to move all four ahead of him. It bawled as Ike whipped him and jumped on top of the calf ahead, cloven hooves digging into black hide.

The whip lashed down, hard and fast. Ike no longer beat the last calf but moved in, booting him forward with his knee and foot. The whip continued thrashing, black and searing, licking the sky as it came down on Jake straddling the chute. Jake released his hold on the sides of the chute to wave his hands. He started to turn and tell Ike to stop. The whip kept coming, and so did Ike, picking the calves up and moving them forward with his will, until two were in the branding cages and the remaining three smashed up against each other at the end of the wall.

"Get down here and hold them," he ordered Jake.

Jake crawled out over the calves, the tops of his hands bloody and full of welts. He walked down toward the bunkhouse.

"Where you going?" shouted Ike.

"Triage," Jake said. "Man down. Friendly fire. You cut my fucking hands, you crazy bastard."

Ike watched Jake walk away, then turned on me. "Goddammit. Get over here."

I did what he said and stood on the back of the last calf until he was in the cutting cage. When Ike finished the final castration, he turned to Dusty to give her the testicle. He wanted her to have at least one. He kicked Ace out of the way and handed it down to her, a puddle of pink inside his brown palm. I watched him from where I stood up on top of the chute, watched Dusty take the sweet meat from him. But I had taught her a few tricks, taught her to catch her food when I threw it at her. She snapped at Ike's hand, making a sucking sound through her jowls. She bit the tip of his middle finger hard. It caught Ike by surprise, and I wondered if he thought she wouldn't bite him just because she was female.

It was only in the evening, after the herd had been reunited, that the dust settled just enough to smell cattle and shit instead of ovened flesh. The world lay back down on itself again. There came a peace while the calves nursed their burned and cut hides, and the mothers rubbed the places where blood ran out of their heads instead of horns. In that calm I began breaking open the bales of alfalfa and spreading them over the corral, and I asked myself then whether we were any better than those pitiful animals that shat where they ate.

9

"Hard to believe what went on," Hanna said. She shook her head and took a sharp breath. The crickets began sawing in the far corner of the rose garden. A starling lit in the locust tree, and then disappeared again.

I thought of how my father had kicked her out thirty years ago. Mother had told me Hanna had run away upon learning that Ike was going to take her to the mental institution. But I imagined it had gone more like this: In one of his rages, Ike had tracked her down like a coyote. She probably hid from him, maybe in the bathtub with the curtain closed. Whenever I took a bath I wondered about the unexplainable crack in the tile; I always thought it was from some blow or fall.

"Nobody comes out here much anymore," I said. "They're afraid maybe the old house will swallow them up too."

She looked at me for a moment, then returned to studying the house. A soft breeze fluttered her white hair. "I think those people want something," she said, waving a hand in the direction of the shop. She seemed to sense things, like the broken lock, the rattlesnake, and now these visitors, without looking.

I glanced over and saw a group of men driving out to the field behind the machine shed. They didn't bother stopping at the house like the women and the rest of the funeral party, nor did they carry casseroles, cakes, or pies, food for comfort. The men entered my fallow field. One of them, Wade Runcid, caught his Levi's on the tight top strand of barbed wire. Wade was used to sloppy fences that gave way. Ours didn't. He reached down and dug in the earth. I knew exactly what he was doing, looking to see what kind of a crop it would grow next year. What kind of profit he might reap if he farmed it.

I thought about confronting him, the son of a bitch, but I just watched. He took soil samples from several layers of the earth, and then turned to talk to the other men. They walked out farther into my unseeded field. Tending to my mother and waiting for rain, I had fallen behind with the farming.

The others bent down and dug in the dirt, measuring the moisture, measuring the worth of the upcoming crop. They talked amongst themselves, and one turned to motion the outline of the field and then gestured to all the fields I owned. Then they walked back to their pick-ups. Wade threw the samples in the cab and climbed in after. His pickup rolled back and parked without his turning on the engine.

"Vultures sizing up the place," I said. A gust of wind suddenly blew through the twisted and parched wooden fence posts that kept back the savagery and thistles from our place.

Wade was our neighbor and a distant relative. My father always said we were lucky we didn't have relatives any closer than him. He was the first one to call with a joyful sorrow to express his condolences on Jake's death. Wade hired drunks off Burnside Street in Portland and used the excuse of their first bender to fire them without pay. He hosed down his wheat trucks to add weight before he took them to the river to weigh and sell. He always brought them into town with water spilling out the tailgate.

I looked back at Hanna still strangely studying the house. I wondered if she even remotely saw what I did, or whether she perceived something completely different.

"The sculptures are in the same room," I said. I crossed my arms and then deciding against it, placed my fists on my hips. "No one has touched them. Mother wouldn't let Ike."

Hanna finally looked away. "I need you to pose," she said.

"Why don't you finish it from memory?" I asked.

"I can cook," she added.

As she stood there wearing her black dress in the rose garden, I wondered if my posing and her cooking went together, or if she just left out the connection. She probably could sculpt, but I doubted she was capable of even making toast. I picked at a nonexistent hangnail until it bled. I watched the people coming down from the grave and entering my house. The wind blew my dress against my legs. I looked at Hanna, who remained silent and had gone back to studying the house again. I began to feel annoyed with her, the way she came in here with her eccentricities, her odd clothes and funny way of standing with her arms hanging down. "Well, what was it like?" I said, finally. "Being in the clink thirty-one years?"

Hanna pursed her lips.

Hanna wasn't a clairvoyant any more than I was. She was a psychiatric patient. "So, are you cured?" I asked impatiently. I doubted she had been healed of anything. I imagined her, walking the halls of the institution always dressed in black, the psychiatrist asking, "Still having the omnipotent witch fantasies, Miss Winter?" I stared at the ground, noticing the rose roots showing through the bark dust.

"It's not like there was one simple cure," Hanna replied softly, lucidly.

I looked back at her, surprised. I wondered if she went in and out of reality, or whether she just didn't feel the need to make other people understand how her mind worked. Maybe she'd lost the knack of making sense, being drugged all these years. Locked up, she probably didn't even remember how to relate to people. When I'd been out on the ranch for weeks on end, I felt I didn't make sense. "So you didn't just take a pill?" I wanted to take some pills to get rid of the constant ache. I wanted to take a lot of pills.

"It's working it over again. Over and over."

"What over?" I asked, narrowing my eyes. If she'd stopped taking her medication, I suddenly thought, she might be dangerous.

"Working it over until you understand."

I scoffed, shaking my head. "Too much has happened to do over," I whispered, and dropped the rosehip on the ground.

The heartbeat of the house floated outside into the evening air. It was the pump jack again, which had borne us water since the turn of the last century. Constantly moving up and down like a wooden man churning butter, it looked like one of the old oil rigs in the movie *Giant*. The sound of it was a low thud of pump paddles swinging around, and then the springlike rebound of the check valve closing and forcing water up the pipe.

I listened to it, a deep and long drag that echoed and rattled on back down the well to the center of the earth. After Mother died, I lay on the attic floor and imagined how it could have been for a baby resting there, with her head on the chest of her mother, hearing the heartbeat again.

Hanna looked at the pump house, a small red building with white trim on its paned peeling windows. All of the outbuildings of the ranch were the same red color—the barn, the two shops, and the oil shed. On top of the pump house stood an old windmill that used to power the water supply with the constant wind. Attached to it, a rusted triangular metal tail read Aermotor. It creaked slightly in an errant breeze and glittered in the light of the afternoon sun.

"How did you get out?" I knotted my hair into something that wouldn't fly away with the wind.

"How come you're still here?" Hanna asked.

I wondered how I was going to get her back to the institution. Maybe the way you put bait out for a wild tomcat before you shot it. "I like your dress," I said, finally.

"You think it's weird," she replied.

The edge in the evening air sent the horses racing in the corral. The setting sun gilded their flying manes and flaglike tails. I turned to watch them; they were beautiful, ethereal, like Pegasus.

"The horses of the muse," Hanna said.

A chill ran up my spine.

"Hullo, Iris," Bud Lerbert called, as he waved and entered my house.

I didn't know what to do with Hanna. I thought about calling the police, but I didn't want the neighbors knowing any more of my business. They'd jump on the Hanna incident, spreading it all over the county before dinner was over. As it was, I wondered how I was going to keep her from the guests.

"Come on," I said. "I'll show you to your room." If she stayed the night, I was certainly locking the knives, matches, and scissors in with the guns—and then locking my own door. I shook my head at the thought of the two of us in that old house, the survivors, the lucky ones.

On the front porch, next to the door, Hanna had placed an old alligator suitcase that reflected the sun in its hide. Several bales of clay sat next to it, wet inside plastic bags. I took the suitcase to her room at the far end of the ranch house, next to the windmill that reminded her of Spain. It was the room where my mother died.

I left Hanna in the bedroom, fingering the rounded wood of the headboard with one hand and burying her other hand in the snow of the chenille bedspread. I hoped she'd stay there, away from everyone else. I brought in the blocks of clay one by one through the front door, which closed poorly and never kept out the winter. I set the last block inside her room, on the dark wooden floor that glared under the old crystal chandelier of my father's house.

I took a deep breath and walked into the kitchen, which was where Wade Runcid cornered me. Viciousness in the kitchen. I was good at that. He had on one of those brown polyester western suits, a plaid shirt, tan knit tie, and go-to-meeting boots.

"Iris," Wade said. "I'd like you to meet my son Roy."

I knew Roy. He was between Jake and me in school. I gave Roy a grimace and shook his hand.

Roy was good-looking. He had thick white teeth except for one slightly darkened front tooth. I wondered if he had ever had a head injury. Farmers were notorious for hitting their children. Roy wore a cowboy hat. Even in the house. "You went to Oregon State, isn't that right?" he said.

"Good guess," I allowed, smiling along. Everyone out here went to Oregon State unless they went to Blue Mountain Community College.

"You major in agribusiness?"

I shook my head. "English."

"Boy," he said straightaway. "I sure liked that *Roots* show. That *Roots* was awful powerful." When he said *"Roots,"* he pronounced it Ruts. Roy thought television was literature, and thus that we had something in common.

"I don't remember it very well," I said. "I was about three when it came on."

Wade laughed so hard, he held his sides. I looked at his hands expecting to find a finger or two missing. They were all there. I noticed Roy watching me. He had a way of looking at women as if he was wondering whether they smelled rank without their clothes on.

"You got some good-looking fallow out there," Wade said, throwing a thumb in the direction of the field behind him. He was still laughing.

"Sixteen hundred acres of hope," I said coldly.

"That your property?" he asked casually. I felt my eyes turning to reptile. "I just didn't know whether that was your property or your aunt's maybe?" He craned his head around the room looking for Hanna.

Word had already spread that she was here. I moved to block his sight lines, and said nothing. I couldn't believe this conversation on the day I buried my mother. I picked up a knife and began slicing Betty Padfield's sour cream chocolate cake.

"Because me and my son here have been growing our place. We have the biggest operation in four counties now. Ranches are mergin'. In fact the only other place that's near as big as ours"—he paused, developing a stage whisper—"is the Griswolds'." He nodded at me and winked.

I tried to wink back, to be cocky, but my eye wouldn't cooperate. It behaved as if it had a tic instead. I balanced the cake on the knife and placed it on Mother's white-and-gold Ainsley plates. I didn't cut them any.

Roy breathed in with a hiss. "There's trouble there. You can count on that," he said.

"Marital," Wade added, nodding at me again and cleaning his ear with his little finger. "That marital trouble will bring down everything," he sighed, examining what he found. "I guess you already know that."

I grimaced at Roy again. Greed ran rampant at funerals. I wanted to laugh at their pathological machinations, but I took a big bite of cake instead.

"I wouldn't trust the Griswolds with any of my property. You'd never be sure the work would get done," Roy whispered.

"We noticed you were behind on your farming," said Wade with concern in his voice.

"You don't say," I replied, my mouth full of black cake.

Scotty Jamison, still wearing his kilt from the funeral, walked quietly around the corner and into the kitchen. The western wood paneling that glowed on the cupboards highlighted his red cheeks. Scotty looked not so much like a Scotsman, reedy, ruddy, and red, but rounded and solid. He was European, a walker. He loved traveling the land and rolling bits of Scottish cairns in his pockets as he strolled.

"I don't recall who you said owned that land?" Wade said under his breath, turning away from Scotty. He thumbed his finger again.

"I didn't say who owned it."

People moved into the kitchen from the green parlor where most of them had congregated to look at the heads. I remembered how, growing up, I was embarrassed to invite kids over. Having people see those statues was kind of like letting friends in on a dirty family secret, like admitting that my family slept with the dead. The heads had always been bizarre, and now they were more so—like the dead arising.

The bust of Hanna's grandfather, John Winter, had a corner of his own. He wore a crazed look the same as Sherman, maybe because he, too, was a veteran of the Indian wars. I knew he wasn't honest, no horse trader is, and that he taught his son Willy the art of the deal. With the recent letter, I learned of his seizure in 1873 of the land the Nez Perce called their own Heart of the Beast. Hanna left him in white plaster, his huge shock of white hair glowing.

The faces of Hanna's parents lined up next to her own simple sculpture, all with high Norwegian foreheads. After them came the first of the Steeles: the politician, Ingram, and his wife; then my father's father, the colonel, and Emma. Nearest the door and pedestaled together stood my family—Ike, Elise, and my brother, Jake.

I noticed Hanna had escaped into the green room as everyone else began ebbing into the kitchen to deliver their condolences. I started when I saw Henry standing with the pallbearers. He had come without my noticing and had probably been the one who adorned the graves.

He stood with his father, chatting with all of them, I imagined, talking about Elise. I wanted to be in that group. The nine of them huddled together, laughing, holding hard drinks and handkerchiefs. Henry was telling a story. My mother's compatriot, Gretel Davis, smiled and laughed. Her leathered skin rose delicately over her cheekbones. She was the only woman who owned diamond rings like my mother, the bigger the better. Gretel and Elise wore them everywhere: at parties, on cattle drives, running the water gun to fight fire in the fall.

I hadn't seen Henry since our falling-out a little over four years ago; I was twenty-four and he was twenty-seven. Since that time he had finished his internal medicine residency, and spent two years on an Indian reservation in Arizona and New Mexico repaying his debt to the government for his med school tuition.

"You got to get that seeded," Wade interrupted, loudly. I could tell he was becoming angry. He was bald, old, and used to getting his way. "Yesterday," he shouted.

"Maybe you could help me out, Scotty," I said, cutting another piece of cake.

"Pick a number," Roy growled. "Get in line. In back."

"Love to get in line," Scotty said, looking at me. He reached for the plate. "But I wouldn't stand behind you, Roy."

I saw Henry look up. He excused himself from the group and made his way toward us.

I felt tired, jumpy, as if I'd taken too many No-Doz. I moved aside to let Henry in.

"Shame it takes a death to get you back to town, college boy," said Roy.

"I've always picked my company carefully," Henry allowed, placing his arm around my shoulders and kissing me on the cheek. I felt a flush of heat around my collar and under my arms.

"Elise would have loved this," Henry said. "Everyone in three counties here."

"Loved to see it, I'm sure," I replied. "Especially you and Roy coming," I said to Wade. "Going to church. That's a first. And then coming out here, after she kicked you off poaching once before. Not too long ago."

My mother had loathed the Runcids. She couldn't stand the fact that once she married Ike, she was actually related to them. It embarrassed her.

"Henry, you remember Scotty Jamison, don't you?" I said, placing my hand lightly on Scotty's arm.

Henry and Scotty nodded to each other.

"Say, I heard a Scotsman joke," interrupted Roy, with a bad Scottish accent. "There once was a man named MacGregor. And he was getting drunk at a pub, complaining all the while. He said, 'I built this town. And I built these roads so they were smooth and hard. But do the people here call me MacGregor the road builder?'"

Roy waited for an answer. "'No,'" he lamented.

"'I planed the pier for the fishermen so it was sturdy and flush with the sea. And do they call me MacGregor the pier builder?'"

"'No,'" Roy lamented again.

"'I built the fences. Rock by rock so they were solid and indestructible. With me own hands I did this. But do the people call me MacGregor the fence builder?'"

"'No,'" he said disgustedly. Roy paused for a minute, setting up his punch line. "'But, you fuck one goat . . . !'"

Wade and Roy laughed out loud, the ladder laughs, those that rolled downward as if they were descending stairs. "They remember you for that!" Roy explained. "MacGregor the goat fucker!"

Wade wiped tears from his eyes with a white hanky and then blew his nose in it. Roy and Wade were the only ones laughing.

"What's that old saying, Roy?" Henry asked. "About humor coming from the truth?" Wade and Roy stopped guffawing.

"Nothin's as funny as Wade burning 'is house down," said Scotty. "Had a clog in 'is toilet," Scotty went on, glancing slyly at old Wade. "Too cheap to call a plumber," he said, with a high two-toned chuckle that punctuated most everything. "So he called me, the *welder*! I told him to unplug it 'imself. I said, Pour some gasoline in it and flush it. That'll clear yur clog."

I laughed. Wade's face turned an angry shade of red.

"Damned if 'e din't do just what I said. Lit the damn thing and the whole house exploded," Scotty practically yelled.

"Lucky you didn't get hurt," said Henry. "Didn't your mother teach you not to play with fire?"

"I heard you were working out at the reservation," said Roy, turning abruptly to face Henry.

"I guess the company you like to keep these days is a bunch of drunk Indians," added Wade.

"I guess I'd rather spend my time with Indians. And you'd rather spend your time with indigents. We're different that way," said Henry.

Wade glared. "Just don't bring any back here with you. Don't want you to marry no squaw."

Henry and I both looked at Roy. "You got a problem with marrying an American Indian?" I asked.

"I'm sorry, Iris," he said. "I forgot."

"You and your dad are forgetting a lot of things these days," I said, turning to look at a group of people coming my way. The neighbors, probably tired of the conversations of farming, the government, and the upcoming hunting season, closed in around us, saying their good-byes. Most of them liked to get home before dark.

"We're sorry about Elise," said Louis and Jimmy Cunningham. They were Nazarene, lived in Sherman County. "Heard you were letting some of the ranches go."

"Heard wrong, Louis," I said, shaking his hand. "I'm sorry about Elise, too."

"You selling any of that equipment?" asked Bud Lerbert.

The equipment, the land, it was what they wanted. I had the best equipment in the county. After my father died, Elise and I sold off all of Ike's rotting and ill-kept machinery, and then we bought new. An axial-flow International combine, a Challenger tractor, a Kenworth truck, deep furrow drills. It was my father's gift to me, his life insurance check, $1.5 million, most of it gone in estate taxes and equipment.

"No, Bud. Need the damn things too much."

"How's the seeding coming?" he asked, knitting his brows.

"Waiting for rain like everyone else."

"Not everyone. I seeded this September," he said, modestly.

I shook my head. "I guess you get all the rain then. You live in a regular banana belt."

Bud laughed. He placed his arms across his chest, hands under his armpits.

I knew it was coming. Bud couldn't resist asking. As rude as it was at my mother's wake.

"But I'd be real interested in that Cat if you ever want to, you know, sell."

"I'll put you on the list," I told him, smiling.

Bud smiled again, but in an uncertain way. He was trying to think who'd be on the list ahead of him. The fool.

Gretel and Ed Davis waved me over. As I moved toward them I noticed pockets of people congregated in groups according to their desires.

One crowd stood over by the entryway fingering the Civil War breakfront and the painting of Chief Joseph. We had had the painting forever, it seemed. The Oregon State Bar Association gave it to the colonel as a thank-you for his service to the profession. Janet Steptoe, Crystal Bettsort, and Sil Cotton chatted there quietly.

The Runcids and the Cunninghams remained standing where they were, legs spread apart as if they were trying to claim as much space as possible.

"You and Elise have a real nice place here. Never been out this way before. Real nice things," remarked Leona Walters.

"That's right, Leona," said Gretel. "She has the nicest place in the county. I've always thought that. It's why she came home to farm. And Ed and I are going to do what we can to make sure it stays that way."

I looked at Gretel. I just enjoyed watching how she said her mind. "It's neighbors like them," I said in a stage whisper to Leona, "that make living out here worth it."

I had had it with everyone else. I thanked them for coming, opened up the big door, and walked them all outside.

Henry came out of the house as the cars were filing down the road. I coiled up the hose with the sprinkler attached to the end. The grass wouldn't need any more water with the winter coming.

"You're staying then?" he said matter-of-factly.

"Of course," I told him.

"If you need any help, give me a call. I don't have much free time.

But what I have is yours." He said it simply, and walked out to his plane. I hadn't noticed it, parked up where Ike used to park his. Henry started it with a low buzz, and vanished down Ike's airstrip.

When I went inside, I found Hanna and Scotty across the room from each other in the green room. Scotty excused himself as I entered, shaking my hand with a welder's grip. Hanna still stood in the room of the heads, near my mother and father. They rested on black walnut pedestals, their armatures bolted into thick blocks of wood spattered by plaster and color wash. My mother's face was covered by a deep green shade, competing with her husband next to her, splashed with a blood-colored tint. In the summer, their warring heads attracted bees into the house, buzzing around their foreheads looking for some sweetness in the shiny finish of their faces.

Near the windows to the front yard was the sculpture of my brother, in plain brown clay. He was done when he was still a child, as if Hanna knew that was all he would ever be. As I walked in there, I felt short of breath. The heels of my shoes curved under my arches like the hooves of a foundered horse and sent echoes into the basement stairs where sometimes I fancied I still heard my father's footsteps.

Hanna had covered the heads with transparent shrouds of black silk so that their eyes peered out from behind their veiled shelters. She was standing motionless in front of her sister, looking silently into her eyes, and from where I stood, I thought I saw my mother crying.

10

THE BLACK DRESS CAME OFF, AND I LAY DOWN ON MY BED thinking of my mother. She had been the beginning and the ending. The parameters of my life lay somewhere inside her, as if all I would ever be was an unrealized portion of her capacity. I thought of her constantly, and wondered if I was going to go down like her.

My mother would have expected this at the wake, the vultures. She knew already from Ike's funeral about the gawking, the stupid things people say. How is an English major going to run a ranch? At least I *have* a degree, I told them. But she was wrong about one thing: she thought *no one came to the funerals of women.* The men had the biggest funerals because when they died, there was land at stake. When the women died, always much later, they were an afterthought, more like a period at the end of a sentence.

The softer sex. Soft hearted. Soft white wheat. The women in my family had always talked of agriculture. We grew soft white winter wheat. Hard red wheat made bread and loaves for eating gravy. Our wheat was for pastry and pasta. Hard red trafficked on futures, was what men traded in, and what people grew who lived on the plains with buffers of mountains surrounding them. In the Northwest, ordinary shields didn't exist where we lived tucked in winter's shadow. Our insulation was scraped from our bones by the winds that came from the Pacific and swirled around our heads. The chinooks and the arctic gales penetrated my body like a blacksmith cutting through iron.

Women came and went in winter. Dagmar, my mother's mother, arrived during the months when skin grew shiny white as the cushioning on open caskets. It was after her husband, Willy, died, and when my father took over all the ranches. Dagmar went to Willy's funeral and asked my mother strange personal questions about him. She asked why Willy wasn't buried on his hands and knees.

"What for?" Mother asked, surprised.

"Forgiveness," Dagmar said.

"He doesn't need forgiveness for anything," Mother had almost shouted.

It was when my grandmother came to live with us that my mother really began to devil me. I couldn't explain why, other than Dagmar just set Elise off. The women in my family followed in each other's footsteps as if there were some mental imprint in us. It was then I began to think Elise too had always been a little crazy, just like Dagmar, just like Hanna, maybe just like me.

Dagmar hid things—savings bonds and tobacco cans full of Indian head nickels. Once I caught her suffocating, with vicious mashing jerks and pressure, the childhood doll that I kept on my bed. She knew what it meant to rub out life and enjoy it.

My grandmother owned a snoose-colored box labeled "Factory Seconds" in which she kept her cards. They were not for playing solitaire. Yellowed, and with the gold halos of martyrs, they were cards of the female saints. She studied their biographies written on the back sides, and practiced sortilege, placing the cards in formations that sifted out a single card each time she played. After the third revolution of this, she would collect the winnowed cards. To me came St. Anne of fertility. To Elise, she gave St. Elizabeth, patron saint of widows. For herself she saved St. Joan, burned at the stake.

My twelfth birthday, the year I learned to drive combine and to reap seed, I told my mother that I would no longer participate in the world as it was. A constant ache, my period, had begun for the first time below my stomach. "I'm going to give myself a hysterectomy," I shouted to my mother as I ran to the bathroom. That morning, my hereditary insanity came for meals and sustenance, and lived at my house for good. I fled my room, smashing a summer pear sitting in the Depression glass bowl. I couldn't stand their leaking milk, their sweetness, their shiny mottled hides that sweated and waxed unnaturally into the air. I wanted to kill it, kill anything. I just wanted to get away from the cramps, the furious grief in my belly. I stalked through my mother's kitchen full of the smell of ripe red apples that made redolent rural grocery stores, and of bleeding tangerines harboring the stings of cold sores. Standing there, I discovered the hiding place that Dagmar never forgot. It was where she concealed her favorite things: bottles of ammonia, plastic nipples, and the *TV Guide*. She hid them in the oven.

I found myself in the bathroom heaving but would not open my mouth for the wicked bile. I stared at my expressionless face in the mirror, swallowed, sat on the toilet, and crushed toilet paper into the soft spot of my body. I knew of tampons and pads. The idea of having to grow up and use them enraged me. "There is nothing different," I said out loud.

Dagmar waited for me outside. She knew my body was in menarche, and that I was beginning to loathe what I was becoming. She squatted down behind a kitchen cabinet, made furious sucking and smacking sounds, and jumped out at me from behind it when I walked past. She aimed her milking lips toward my breasts, and said with swollen eyes, "I feed from you now."

This woman used to tell stories. She knew Sahaptian, the language of the Nez Perce. Dagmar talked about the nontreaty Indians of Lolo Trail, thick-necked savages who were ugly and obstinate. She said she was not afraid because she knew the language. She tried to teach me the tongue the first day I sat on her knees. The only words of Nez Perce I learned from her were *Kapsiis token*. It meant bad Indian.

Dagmar had a Severe Brothers saddle that she called Suffrage, and I wanted it more than anything. She saddled Suffrage on whatever horse she turned her eye to, and we rode over scabland full of scoke and pokeweed, riding together because she had given me my pony, Fortune, an Appaloosa gelding that came from the Snake River. She bought him from Ipsewahk, because she knew how to bargain too.

Sometimes Ike and my grandmother would work together. Her favorite thing to do was to spray the perimeter of the house with DDT. My father kept a stash of the pesticide in barrels after the government had banned it because of birth defects. Everyone in the area agreed it was the best for keeping snakes away. My family never believed anything unseen could poison them, even though we lived near the Hanford Nuclear facility, the Umatilla nerve gas repository, and a garbage and toxic waste dump. This was normal for farm country.

I tried to be kind to my grandmother before she died because I wanted that saddle. But as time went on, Dagmar became worse and worse. She began producing articles and advertisements and leaving them in my bathroom and in my bedroom. There was the December issue of the *Wet Set Gazette*. She had highlighted articles entitled "The Breast-Feeding Sag," "Bladder Problems and Pregnancy," "How to Overcome Stretch Marks, Leg Cramps, and Varicose Veins," "How to Be Pregnant and Still Be Attractive to a Man." She began substituting snap-open bras, placing them in my drawers and stealing my others. I found pads for seepage and leakage of the breast and back support braces stuffed in my underwear drawers. There was a bundle of antiabortion literature tied with a red bow on my pillow.

It might have been Dagmar who crystallized my hatred of children and the idea of not carrying on the family. She had a way of ferreting out what a person couldn't stand and using it against them. My mother learned the tricks of my grandmother well. But Hanna was a mystery to all of us, her strange appearance and her artistic mind. I couldn't decide if she was really connected to us or not. But she fascinated me just the same, and now that she was here, I wondered what to do with her.

As I lay in my bed, I remembered how Thursday night when my mother died, I had stayed up late, drinking, and collecting Hanna's things up in our attic. I saw the drawings that my aunt had done as a child. A grade school teacher had placed them in a book for her. On the back cover, I noticed Hanna's handwriting, as if she had gone back to look at them as an adult. *Reality is never beautiful*, it said.

My mother told me that Hanna left Heart of the Beast for art school on an Easter Sunday at age eighteen, fifty-three years ago. Willy had been proud that there was an artist in the family, someone who moved his name off the hillbilly list. He supported her, gave her anything. Besides, he couldn't have helped noticing her art. From kindergarten on, her teachers saved her paintings and drawings. They were that good.

By the time Hanna was born, Willy was an old man. Semiretired from horse trading, he spent his time telling stories about the extravagant bank robbers that his brother Cole had encountered. In the attic, I found a *Tribune* article about Jesse James that Willy had saved. It described how James and his gang, along with fine European furnishings, had come around the horn and worked their way through the Northwest.

The James boys' downfall, Willy used to say, was that they called attention to themselves. It was in the way they rode, two by two: Jesse and Frank James, then Cal Younger and Horse Thief Campbell, and pulling up the rear were the two Ford boys. More than anything, he envied them. Willy was a horse thief through and through, and the James boys rode on the most outstanding stolen horses in the world.

It was when Cole encountered James galloping down a lane shooting bullets into every fence post that he sold him an unbroken horse of my grandfather's. He traded for a .45 Smith & Wesson six-shooter. Willy Winter never forgave Cole for selling his horse and shortly thereafter committed the worst crime possible among the Winter brothers. He married.

He wed the youngest, most beautiful woman he could find. Dagmar was twenty-one years his junior. His sibling, the Norwegian bachelor, argued with him against the urge to tie the knot. A wife would just drain the money, Cole had said.

The word *poverty* never meant much to them living off the richness of Heart of the Beast, but if you asked them why they loved money more than people and had a fondness for unequal love relations, they'd lie and tell you it was because they grew up poor. They wouldn't say it was because they were afraid of being abandoned.

Cole was so undone by Willy's desertion through marriage that he began an affair with a younger sister of Dagmar's, whose name was Hanna. As in most cases the youngest are the wildest and have the most need. Cole impregnated Hanna and, faced with the loss of his newfound love to a baby, started the gunshot suicides. Only Dagmar knew what had happened, and she sent money for Hanna to get an abortion. In the end, the operation made her sterile. Dagmar and Willy named their last child Hanna, as if to replace the offspring of their dead brother and sterile sister.

As I looked at Hanna's early drawings up in the attic, I felt she must have known instinctively the circumstances in which she had come about. The first picture I looked at was of a slave sale. The slave seller stood on his own platform wearing black boots with patches of red at the knees, purple pants, a black coat with a white collar, and a red bull-whip raised in the air. He was a Napoleon with sunken coal-colored eyes, a curling mouth, and a mustache. His ears were hooks with great yellow bands in them. Hanna stood below him holding a drooping yellow flower, wearing an orange dress with waves across it. The sky was midnight and the clouds were colorless. A mother and daughter were the slaves; they bore earrings, and their mouths were open and screaming. They stood on a separate platform with the word *slave* written on it. Other people gathered in profile, all hanging on to one another's hands. These women were bidding on the slaves, while above them water rained down from uncurling ferns. In the air floated christhearts that read *"Sob, Sob"* and *"Ha, Ha."*

Below her drawings, still resting in the black trunk with the gleaming bronze locks, I found copies of her favorite artwork. Some of them lay bound in books with Spanish writing, *Las Pinturas Negras*. They were the black paintings of Goya. As I uncovered them, they glared at me as if angry they had been exposed. For a long time, I studied the one of Saturn eating his son. And below that, I found the letter. I picked it up and read it.

Circuit Court of the State of Oregon
In the county of Horrow
In the matter of Hanna Winter,
Notice and citation alleged
To be a mentally ill person.

To Hanna Winter:
You will please take notice that a notification in writing has been made by Ike Steele in which it is alleged that you are

mentally ill, and because of this mental illness you are in need of treatment, care and custody. You are cited to appear before honorable Judge John Johannson, Judge of the Circuit Court, in this court or at such other place specifically designated by the judge thereof 4:00 P.M. on the 29 day of October 1969 for a hearing on notification of mental illness. This examination will be held in the examining room, Courthouse, Thursday afternoon, October 12, 1969, 4:00 P.M.

I gripped the letter as I heard Hanna moving things around in the green room where, in the morning, the light would come in from the north-facing windows.

"The best light comes from the north," she had stated as she invaded my house.

I walked out to see what she was doing, looking at the lights, suspecting she had placed some kind of filter on them. The house smelled of furnace oil; winter had finally touched down. Warm yellow-colored air filled the rooms.

Hanna laid a tarp down over the dark wooden floor. On top of that, she found four pummy blocks, which she used as supports for an old unhinged, unknobbed door. A draping sheet partially covered it as if it were a table.

"I want to be done with all this now. It's time," Hanna said.

"I have to finish the seeding. You can mold your sculpture or whatever you want to do, but I have to work in the fields." The sunset streaked the sky with red. I placed the letter in my back pocket, poured myself some wine, and walked out on the back porch to look at the colors. In the two days since my mother died, it seemed, winter had clamped down in earnest; the air had turned cold and no longer smelled of fall smoke. The dew on the porch seeped into my gray wool socks.

Hanna joined me.

"Do you want to know how it happened?" I asked. "How it was with Elise when she went?"

My aunt turned to look at me. Her brows closed together in alarm.

"She spent her last month at the dinner table, sleeping pills in one hand, a fork in the other." I looked down at my hands. The glass was smudged with my dirty fingers. "Elise told me, 'You haven't lived. Unless you've contemplated taking fifty-one sleeping pills and a fifth of Wild Turkey, and at the same time stared at a plate of food worrying whether there might be some bacteria on it that could kill you.'"

Hanna's brows trembled where they came together.

"Wild Turkey's good," I added. "You ought to try it." I didn't tell her what I had said to my mother. *How much pain can you take?* I had asked her. I wanted to know.

As much as you give me, Elise had replied. *Do you think I don't notice? Notice what, Mom?*

The mess you are.

I had laughed aloud. I found it hilarious that she was complaining about having to watch my deterioration. *I guess you and I are the same. A couple of wasted and bitter old women.* I watched her for a reaction. *How did we end up here, Mom?*

You'll always be just like me.

No, I had told her. *I won't.*

I couldn't stop thinking of Elise now that Hanna was here. She had the same lovely skin, high cheekbones, the thick lips and aquiline nose. I stared at my aunt, thinking of my mother. I half hoped Hanna was actually Elise come back to life, but quiet now, pensive. I wondered if Hanna's coming might signal the end of this genetic female bad luck. My mother and I had resolved nothing in the resentment and blame game, and now she haunted me constantly. I knew I could never repair anything between us now that she was dead.

I remembered that the closer my mother came to death, the more she urged me to cast the heads.

It'll cost thousands, I argued with her. *Not to mention time. And who'll want them? Just a bunch of junk to take care of.*

They're in you, my mother said. *Bring them out. You can't bury what you won't look at.*

Yes, I can, I had told her. *It's called denial, Mom. I'm sure you've heard of that word.*

Maybe Hanna thought if she finished those sculptures, she'd be healed. I kicked the dog's water dish on the porch. I wanted to smash something, and I suddenly felt hysterical again. I turned to face Hanna, thinking of my parents.

She returned my stare silently.

I took a deep breath. "I've had those heads here," I said, knocking on my chest. "I've looked at them for fucking twenty-eight years," I told her. It began to annoy me that Hanna looked so much like Elise. "I'm sick of them. I don't want to look at them anymore. They're ugly and they're mean." The sun had set, there was no more brilliant cloud show. The sky was dead, everything was dead.

Hanna placed her hands to her eyes and breathed in.

I didn't see how finishing the sculptures could accomplish anything. I wiped the tears from my eyes disgustedly.

"Take off your clothes," she instructed. "You're exactly like your mother. So do something about yourself."

"Just go to hell," I said, laughing. This was ridiculous. She meant to sculpt me, I understood her to mean, full body and nude.

I contemplated the things a person could do for the only other living family member. I could pose naked for my aunt, sit down for hours while she remolded me. I would open my hips and breasts for the interpretation of an artist, a scientist, and tell this crazy woman my stories. After all, I thought maybe only a crazy person could understand the way I felt.

I reached for the letter in my back pocket, and glanced over at my aunt. Nakedness meant certifiable, I remembered suddenly. I had watched the programs about how the craziest murderers committed their crimes: it always involved nudity somehow.

She turned to look at me.

Slowly I removed the letter and unfolded it. I handed it to her.

Hanna took it, her hand blue under the rolled-up sleeve of her white mannish shirt.

I watched while she read it.

She started sobbing.

"Tell me everything," I whispered. "Everything," I said, as I reached up to the top button of my father's shirt, "and I will pose for you." I suppressed a laugh, thinking if I took off my clothes, that meant I was certifiable too.

Hanna turned away from me. She nervously clasped her hands together, and walked back into the house.

I wouldn't tell but listen, I decided as the sunset made my hand glow. I followed her inside. "What was it like to go over?" I whispered again. "And then come back. Or have you really come back?"

"All right," she said, wiping her eyes once more. "Deal."

So, she could be lucid if she chose to be. If I tried hard enough, I wondered if I could understand Hanna. Besides, living with a crazy person had to be better than being alone.

I undressed and Hanna watched me. I dropped my clothes into a dark pile. My skin began to feel like wax, and I crawled onto the horizontal door with the crumpled sheet covering it. I caressed the sheet, folded like waves, and I felt myself let go.

part three

11

July began the month of harvest and of lies. Farmers fibbed about their crop, the land lied about its bounty, and everything went to hell the summer of Henry's runaway horse. After we returned from Heart of the Beast, we busily began preparing for harvest: tracking down parts, readying the trucks, and the worst—cleaning the elevator. Ike gave that job to Jake. He stuck him down in the hole with rotting wheat, white worms, and malignantly thick dust.

The menial preharvest jobs of running to the co-op for small parts and cleaning out the trucks fell to me. Rodents found truck cabs perfect for making homes. The day before harvest, I drove the trucks to the water spigot, smelling the nests full of rat piss before I uncovered them. Rounding up the dogs, I made sure they were near; then I flushed out the seats with the hose, running water through the floorboards. That didn't work, so I pulled the bottom cushions off the seats and flung them outside to the ground. The dogs attacked the mother before she ran under the oil shed. Then they ate the babies, the tangle of clean-looking pink that screamed and squealed when the dogs wolfed them whole. I couldn't stand to watch it, always wondered if they were still alive down in that trench gut.

After I finished the trucks, I drove speeding into the co-op. We called it Grain Grabbers because they masqueraded as a sharing cooperative but gave the agribusiness operations huge discounts on their fertilizers and chemicals. Then they passed the bill on to family farms in the form of higher rates. I needed to purchase a new sickle bar for the combine. Starting harvest the next day, we didn't have time to re-rivet the teeth.

"You harvestin' yet?" I heard a voice from behind categorized parts: wing nuts, gaskets, bearings, and pulleys. Almost everything needed to fix anything on a ranch resided there.

"Starting tomorrow," I said, tapping my fingers on the dirty counter where farmers slapped down buttery ball bearings, broken belts, sheared sockets. The co-op smelled of rubber and gleaned steel.

Clem from the parts department hailed me down. He was the worst gossip in town next to Noel. "Old Mandrake's already going," he said. "I seen 'im smorning east of Nine Mile." There was a subtle slander that you weren't a good farmer unless you were harvesting by the Fourth of July.

"I wonder what he's getting," I said.

"Said seveny-five."

"Hah," I said at him. "That's crap." Workers at the Grain Grabbers didn't think too much of me. First, I was female, and second, I didn't dress up for men. That was a problem. I knew what they saw: my clothes and hair were always dirty; I wore a head rag because I was afraid of catching it in machinery or a running belt. Anyway, I didn't have loads of hair. Huge hair was in back then, and the men in the county judged women on whether their hair was blond, curly, and plentiful. Mine was simple, straight; the right color, but wrong style.

"What you think you'll be getting then?" Clem asked, eager for details.

"A hundred if Mandrake's getting seventy-five," I told him, running the sickle bar into the pickup bed. There was competitiveness in wheat farming that came down to lies.

That night, my father, Jake, and I drove the fire truck and the trap wagon down to the Creek Ranch. Ordinarily the fire truck led on the day of the caravan, because it was the most crucial vehicle in harvest, and Elise would drive it. She had devised her own air-conditioning system, carrying Cold Water All detergent bottles refilled with water and frozen in the walk-in. Everywhere she went in summer, she took her coldness with her.

But the year I turned seventeen, my mother refused to operate the ranch equipment in the heat. If she was going to be out at all, she drove her air-conditioned Jaguar. After Dagmar died, the more delicate and yet the harder Mother became. It was as if the longer she lived, the more her survival mechanisms were stripped away, and the real Elise Steele glared.

The next morning Ike wired the Jaguar with the yellow-and-black Wide Load sign. It hung down from the radiator grate as if it were the bucket of a dozer. The Bar S brand was burned into the wood on either side of the words. Mother sat at the beginning of our drive, her car idling, prepared to flag down passing pickups, grain trucks, and sunbirds' campers to a halt so we could inch by. As it was, the combine headers barely cleared the sides of the narrow roads.

I had started operating combine five years before, when I turned twelve. Ike instructed me to drive in the middle of the convoy; that way the police couldn't stop us for my not having a license. At least that was my father's theory; it never happened that we ran into a cop, because they occupied themselves giving fines to the outfits hauling too heavy loads of wheat into town, or harassing any Mexicans they could find.

Working the cattle had kicked off Ike's favorite time of year, but the harvest was his highlight. The reaping season lit the entire countryside with activity, beginning with the caravaning of equipment out to the fields. Our wheat land spread over two ranches: the Bar S and the Creek Ranch. And wherever the wheat was ripe, chewed hard, and spit white, we cut.

We advanced our machinery past neighboring ranches, waving at the sorry children too young to do anything but hang around the house. They scrambled toward us in diapers and shorts to sit on the fence and watch us go by. People knew who you were by the numbers. The more combines and trucks you owned, the bigger the outfit you ran, the more notorious you were.

The convoys from ranch to ranch reverted to the time when my great-grandfather first started farming in the state. He labored over wagons and equipment drawn by horses in great Sahara-like caravans that crossed over the hills of our land. When they delivered wheat to town, they drove the longest horse team in the state until 1912, when the Morgan horses died of a mysterious disease called the bleeding. After that he bought mules and carried on with the farming until he contracted with Caterpillar to purchase the twelfth diesel Cat ever constructed, the 1C-12, old Tusko. My father named it after the elephant at the Portland Zoo.

Only a few of the first Cats shipped to the American mainland. Two went to plantations in Hawaii, but most of them went to Europe to build the Albert Canal. They had more money in 1931. My grandfather farmed for 7½ cents an acre, and the price of wheat is the same now as then. He then loaned the Cat out free of charge to all his neighbors. He was a good friend, but hell on his son.

It was inevitable that the first day of harvest was the hottest in the year. It boiled tempers and flared grudges. Elise started us; Jake followed in his combine. It was the first time he led the combines; maybe his turning twenty-one that year compelled him to take charge. I followed him, then Carl came, then finally Henry and Ike in the wheat trucks. That was how it went; there was an order to things.

Henry drove the truck we called the Monster, an army surplus Auto Car my father bought at auction for cheap because it needed a new engine. Ike loved purchasing from army surplus sales, loved feeling as if he were in the middle of a war.

I believed a ghost possessed the Monster. It sounded as if it would rattle the elevator down when it came in to dump the grainloads. It had a mean roar and a long-lived rat that neither the dogs nor I could kill.

All the equipment, not just the Monster, had personalities—the buildings too. They were haunted, had life other than from this world. The elevator was a silent old man with stooped shoulders. The Caterpillars snarled like dragons, blowing off black smoke when the clutch engaged.

Most of all I loved newer model combines. The way the cab sat over the hunched body of the machine made it look like the one-eyed Cyclops. I spent the hours driving, thinking about the race of giants that ate men and tended sheep. The machine screamed when kicked into gear and sounded like a jet engine. It ate the wheat as easily as if it were greased glistening fat. The bats of the header were like Venetian silver teeth, grinding the fields into gold.

In the afternoon heat of harvest, the Cyclops hailed the storms. Chagall-like clouds rolled in first, as if they were flying, screaming people. Then came the vast purple sea led by thin waves of white meeting the blue-sky shore. And at the end of the day, the Cyclops called thunder and lightning down from the clouds in pairs. The earth boiled with the clean smell of ozone, nitrogen, and smoke, ready to shoot the bolts up to the sky all over again.

That morning, the caravan flowed smoothly, and by the time we traveled the eight miles to the Creek Ranch, it was noon. We ate our lunches under the shaded side of Jake's lead combine. The rest of the equipment we parked on the side of the road in the order we came.

It was one o'clock when the reaping finally started. There was no rule of when to start except that you didn't on a Friday. Bad luck. It was more Mother who feared Fridays; Ike didn't give a shit about much, including superstition. He wanted his crop harvested, the sooner the better.

"I want you to cut the first land in a long rectangle," Ike said to Jake. He sounded his *t*'s harshly with his razorlike tongue. My father pointed down the fence line toward the canyon. "Head out," he said. "Follow the fence to the first canyon. Then cut up to the fallow, and come straight back to the road." Ike's eyes ate up the sky as he spoke. Below, a wad of snoose bulged his black-and-silver whiskers.

There were many things to consider when cutting a land. The lay of the furrows, the direction of the wind in case of fires, the access for trucks.

"How about we cut it lengthwise," Jake returned.

I felt my body tense up. Even though they sounded like reasonable words—a question, a discussion, something normal people did all the time—in the world of my father, his child questioning him was anathema.

"Go up to the elevator and back down," Jake went on. "It's still a rectangle but north-south instead of east-west."

"Cut it like I told you," Ike said curtly.

"There's going to be a sumbitch of a tailwind," said Jake. He walked over and threw his lunch pail in the Jag.

The east wind had blown in, that was why it was so hot. Once Jake, Carl, and I made the first round, the entire trip down the fence line would have the wind burning up my father's old and cabless combines, carrying chaff and dust right into us.

"That's right," said Ike. "You got a tailwind, and I'm not ruinin' these trucks going a half mile into the fields to pick you up."

My father might say it was to save the trucks, but he didn't care about equipment.

"Is there tarweed out there?" I asked. Tarweed was the worst thing that could happen to a combine driver with a tailwind. It should have been sprayed out, but Ike never bothered. Now, when the combine thrashed the wheat and tar, the weed sent out razor-sharp nettles into the chaff. It collected around your neck, eyes, hands, clothes, and caused welts and the swollen eyes of a pugilist.

"There's a shitload," said Jake, his voice shrill as a saw. "It's all over this field."

Henry handed Jake his frayed coat, which he had brought for the cool morning. It was useful to keep the tars off his neck. Jake threw it to me, hard. It shocked me. I almost fell down trying to catch it. He gave up his shield.

"Quit pickin' your noses and get your asses in gear," said Ike, spitting a fat streak of snoose onto the gravel road. I wondered how my father could have such white teeth the way he chewed tobacco.

Jake walked toward his combine, his shoulders hunched. I moved to mine. I saw Jake swing a leg at the ground like a left hook. Jake was first. I followed him, and then tried to do better than he did.

"East wind will burn up the field if it gets lit down in the corner," Jake said.

Ike didn't hear him at first. Jake throttled up his combine. "What?" Ike screamed over the engine.

"Goddamned labor camp," yelled Jake, and he pushed the hydrostatic drive forward. The man-sized wheels of the combine moved slowly, grinding the earth to powder.

Jake maneuvered the lumbering machine into the field. I could see him over the grain bin, standing at the wheel while his hands worked the control levers of the header. He throttled down, and yanked back the gear, starting the machine cutting. Small parts shook and rattled. Dust clouded out of the back of the combine. It roiled down the straw walkers into the canvas box, which collected the chaff into haylike mounds. The cattle survived off this when we turned them out on stubble ground in fall. Jake opened the chaff gate and what was left from last year—ants, dust, corrupted wheat, and straw—dumped onto the ground. He lowered the shaking, cutting header and crawled into the field. The harvest began.

Elise collected the lunch pails. She walked over to Henry's truck, picked up his pail, threw it in the Jag with the others, and floored it as she took off down the gravel road. Dust bloomed as she drove the way pain comes when a scab is ripped off.

"After I set these machines, I'm going to Walla Walla," Ike told Henry. "You'll have to keep up yourself. Leave an empty truck in the field for the combines to dump into while you're gone."

The trip for parts was not a surprise. My father always let his equipment run down. He was too busy with the cattle and keeping up with all his ranches to bother with maintenance. The machines constantly broke down in the fields in the middle of harvest. They slowed the progress and meant waiting for hours while Ike flew up to Pendleton, or across the Columbia River to Richland and Walla Walla, to retrieve the repairing part that would suffice until the next problem.

I watched Ike walk into the field behind Jake's combine. He stuck his hand out to collect chaff from the buzzing blades of the straw walkers. He dug through it on the ground, looking for grain—things he figured he owned that slipped through the threshing.

Ike shook his head and jogged up to the side of the combine. While it was still rolling, he adjusted the concaves and straw walkers. It made me nervous to watch him walk next to the threshing machine. His hands fiddled with the settings on the crushing concaves and knifelike straw walkers. His feet marched in the mashed tracks of the enormous front wheels and barely kept ahead of the never-ending roll of the back ones.

Ike, covered with chaff, never bothered to shield his head with his hand as he walked behind the combine. The white husks blasted his face. The pearlescent powder glistened on him as if he were a mine worker. Oblivious, he dug again in the furrows behind the machine to find his lost treasure, the tiny kernels of wheat.

I saw him jump on the ladder, climb to the top behind the grain bin. He stared critically at the gold augering into the tank. He grabbed a handful of it and placed it to his nose. We all loved the smell of just-harvested wheat. It came into the combine hot from the sun, giving off the smell of earth, water, wind, and time. Freshly harvested grain was the smell of longing, of infatuation.

All of us chewed wheat during the harvest. No one smoked in the fields because of the fire hazard; we ate wheat instead. It tasted of rain. The grains boiled up white in the mouth the way anise turns milky on the tongue and teeth. I ground it down, worked it until finally I was chewing a tiny white ball full of the taste of baking bread.

Jake turned around to see Ike disappear down the ladder. My father stayed on the last rung this time, watching the belts and listening for machine trouble. Ike could detect a ball bearing that was going out, or a slipping belt, just by hearing it. Jake must have pushed his speed up a notch because then the combine lurched forward. Ike's cowboy boots slipped on the rounded last rung of the ladder. He clung to the sides of the stairs as his boot was knocked down toward the ground by the oncoming back wheel. Then I saw my father buck himself free. He landed in the stubble, clear of the passing wheel, but he had ripped open his hand on the rough steel ladder step.

Jake didn't notice. He kept looking down at the header, working the levers on either side of the steering wheel, keeping the scythes on the reaper from running into the ground.

Ike and I were the only ones who knew what had happened. I was just outside the fence waiting to be called into the field by my father. He motioned me to come on, and I kicked the machine into gear and drove into the field, cutting my path just beside my brother's swath. Ike repeated his examination of the settings on my machine, and climbed on top, ducking his hand under the auger. He came up with a fistful of blood orange; the wound mixed into the gold of the grain. Then he bit into the wheat and spat red over the side of the combine.

Ike's face was toward the sun, and it glowed back the way a mirror turns sunshine into fire. He stood up to his full height on top of the creeping reaper, and he whistled. He placed his tongue into his teeth and pierced the air like an eagle. It was his hunting call. He was blissful watching his grain harvest, the reward from twelve months of the land's work and his. Smiling there on top of the machine, he let out a victory cry. He saluted me as he took off to set Carl's combine, and I settled into the work. I think even more than the excitement of the harvest, my father was beaming because he'd cheated death once more.

The nature of fieldwork—harvesting, plowing, seeding—was slow, rhythmic. It was long days full of journeys into thought and memory. It became fun when Ike wasn't there. We were doing the best job in the world, bringing in the harvest. I wore Jake's coat, even though it was hot, to keep the tarweed off my skin. I pulled down my head rag so that it covered my forehead and I found a handkerchief in one of the pockets and placed that over my nose like a bandit. I sat with my leg propped up on the railing, leaning to the side, my hand on the header lever, watching for rocks and the edges of the sickle to drag. I fancied myself a gunslinger shooting beer cans off a fence post. I knew I looked ridiculous and was slightly embarrassed every time I got into a position where Henry might see me.

Henry jockeyed the full trucks into the elevator one after another. I saw him sprinting between rides. We filled them faster than he could keep up with, and he looked exhausted. The heat of the afternoon made the field appear melted. To the south, the rangeland looked blue and cool. Everywhere looked cooler than where I was. The clouds haunted as the late afternoon arrived. Thunderhead apparitions, massive curled ropes knotted around each other, appeared as if they were planet formations in the birthplace of galaxies.

Around three o'clock, the time when I started getting sleepy, I was still pretty close to Jake, though I tried to stay far enough behind to keep out of his chaff. Operating in another combine's debris or a tailwind was miserable, like being blasted by ground-up yellow jackets. Jake stood covered by it, frozen at the wheel like Ahab.

Suddenly I heard the sound of a gunshot, and I looked up, slamming the clutch. Ahead of me Jake's combine had veered off its course and mowed aimlessly into the field, like a riderless horse. It crazily chopped along into the center of the land. Black smoke billowed from the engine and then I saw the flames shooting up into the sky from the exhaust pipe. The air curled with the heat; I barely made out Jake with his fire extinguisher on the other side of the inferno. He hadn't even bothered to stop his combine; it still cut along into the field.

It was then I saw the wind carry the smoke and fire toward the dark gold wheat. Everything melted into the same color as a dying sun.

I threw my combine out of gear and set down the header, leaving it throttled up. I knew I was going to have to make a run for it if the wheat caught fire.

The extinguisher was on the grain tank. I grabbed it, jumped off the catwalk, and hurried to Jake's combine. It took forever, it seemed, reduced to human-size steps after riding on the giant tires of the moving houses.

I kept my distance from the still cutting combine, motioning to Jake to stop it. The machine wasn't halting so I skirted around to the other side and jumped on the ladder while the wheels continued to roll along, just as Ike had. I pulled the pin on the extinguisher and shot it at the engine.

Black soot painted Jake's face. He stood rigid, bracing himself against the railing, spraying the fire extinguisher at the flames. White foamed around the silver exhaust, and the muffler sizzled, as the fire kept burning on engine oil.

"Get the hell away from there," Jake yelled. "You're on top of the fucking diesel tank!"

I looked down and realized there was no place to stand because of the heat except for the tank. "Kill it!" I screamed, spraying my extinguisher at the fire.

"Can't," he screamed. "Get off there!"

I turned then to see that sparks had floated down into the wheat field and begun burning, licking and swallowing the grain as fast as the wind bore it along. And then I saw Ike's plane overhead.

He had just returned from getting his parts with the bird, which was what Ike called his Super Cub. Whenever he flew, he buzzed the harvest crew before he left and again when he landed. He let us know he was watching by cutting the fuel from one of the tanks, revving the propeller, and then shooting gas back to the motor as if the plane were taking off over our heads. The noise became fat, expanding like a balloon, and let out a scream the way a fighter plane sounds when it pulls from a dive. We could hear that sound even over the roar of our own machines.

Ike made a low pass practically at our height. He always flew anywhere he wanted, regardless of telephone poles, fences, or fire. Half the time he wasn't even steering because he was shooting coyotes. I saw his red face in the square window he had opened. Before his eyes, his crop was being destroyed, and he was pointing at my combine.

I knew right away I needed to get my machine out of the fire's path. "Just turn it off, kill it," I yelled at Jake. And then the motor went silent with one last backfire. Like a cannon shot it stopped. I thought I had exploded with the diesel tank. My legs were trembling and I lost my balance.

I saw Jake throw his shovel and his water sack to the ground, and then he disappeared down too. I stayed with my fire extinguisher still discharging on the engine. The heat made the metal crack and sing. I stood there hosing down the exhaust pipe, flogging a dead soldier until my extinguisher finally quit. Then I jumped down just like my brother.

Jake ran to the fire truck, a pickup with a water pump on it. I saw Henry moving the wheat trucks to the fallow ground. I turned toward my combine. Jake yelled something to me I couldn't hear. There was no sound but the singing of the wheat fire.

The last I had seen of Ike, he was circling the plane to land. He could bring the bird down anywhere. That Super Cub was tough enough to touch down on the range, a gravel road, or wheat field, and Ike circled us once more, looking to bring her in right beside us.

"Oh Jesus, no," I said. He had probably thought about using the field as a runway, then he considered the road, until he realized there were telephone poles alongside of it. He pulled up and circled once more, I imagined, heading up to where the road separated from the fence and those dangerous poles.

I panicked, and ran to my combine. Watching Ike's plane disappear over the hill and the rising curl of white that followed, I wondered if it were dust or smoke, whether he had landed safely or had had another one of his many incidents with the plane—the propeller breaking, the wheel falling off, a wingtip hitting sagebrush.

Carl hadn't been paying attention and had just then pulled out of the row. He raised his header and hurtled his combine toward the fallow ground. The only thing that stops fires in eastern Oregon is fallow. Roads will only slow them down momentarily before they jump over and are off again. It was bad that Jake's combine had cut into the middle of the wheat. There was nothing we could do now.

The smell of the smoke knifed into my nose. It was not the same as the sweet smell of smoke in the fall, the smell of log fires. Wheat fires have the smell of death, and it was huge after only ten minutes. Stubble burns slowly with white smoke. Sagebrush burns blue. Wheat burns the fastest and angriest of all. There was something about burning all that money, I thought, that made a wheat fire black as a devil.

An ominous cloud of soot exploded into the air. It was a call for help. An unwritten rule during harvest held—every harvest crew that could see wheat fire smoke was to stop harvesting and come immediately. It meant an accident had happened. It meant someone was losing their crop, their income, and more. But the real reason the neighbors came was that their field could be next.

I climbed up on my combine, yanking it into fourth gear, and followed Carl to the fallow field. Both combines were racing along, their headers in the air, in a massive movement of equipment to save machine from fire. Henry had started up the Monster and began speeding along with us. All of the engines lugged down in the thick stubble. We didn't care. The fire could take us all in a second. It moved that fast.

The Kregs were the first to come. Their outfit had four men with shovels and a pickup with a water hose. Old Adameye and his crew arrived next. Three men with shovels. I shut my combine off immediately, didn't bother with cooling it. I grabbed my shovel and crawled down to meet Henry and Carl, who were waiting for me with their firefighting tools.

The three of us jogged on the fallow until we were behind the fire line. Then we worked our way over to where Jake had parked the fire truck and was operating the hose. Two more harvest crews came, and we were all spread out, four people to a pickup. One drove, one ran the water, and two shoveled and sacked the fire.

I operated the hose, working the pistol-like nozzle. Jake steered, made the decisions where we fought the fire. Henry and Carl spread out beside us and sacked. Two of the crews wetted down the wheat around Jake's combine. The fire had burned slightly south from there. When I looked up, I saw that the smoke was starting to head west fast. Those east winds were problematic. They blew the strongest, could go on for hours. Or they could change in an instant.

Someone had called the rural fire department, which owned two big red tanker trucks that could never get to the place they needed to be and were notorious for quitting. And as it came down the dirt road, the second tanker died. They were young college kids running the fire truck, probably killed the engine because they popped the clutch shifting. It was just a job to them, something to pay for next year's tuition at Blue Mountain Community College.

"Those two are going to be in trouble," I hollered, pointing to the water tanker.

The driver rolled his window down, and I could see him leaning forward trying the ignition, his body bouncing from working the gas pedal. They both saw the fire shift direction and come their way. The smoke blew toward them, thick and choking. Where the flames were behind the soot, a person never knew.

The partner climbed out and on top of the cab and waved at us. We saw him intermittently as the smoke whipped around.

"Shit," said Jake.

I stood there holding the hose on the fire in front of me.

"Henry," Jake yelled, jumping out of the pickup. He climbed in the back, dragged a chain across the metal bed, and dropped it at the tailgate with a coiling thud. Henry ran over, threw his shovel in, and sprang into the pickup. I slid in the driver's side to the middle. I had one of those lifty feelings in my stomach. I usually had them when Jake or my father drove the pickups. I knew I could be dead from their driving.

Jake stepped in, shoving it into gear before he had his door shut. He floored it. Henry and I locked our hands onto the ceiling, and I slid down in the seat, my feet braced against the floorboards. Things began to happen in slow motion, like when you're in a car wreck. The feeling of losing control and of just surviving took over. I saw Jake's hands up high on the steering wheel, gripping so hard they were white. We hit a ditch and almost bottomed out in the thick soft sides of the crevice. Jake gunned it, and we came over the top, fishtailing. He pulled out of the field so he could back up to where the tanker was. We were going to tow it out of there.

The road was smoother here, and I had a chance to look at the fire. It was about a hundred feet away. The black smoke was coming fast. It reminded me of pictures of Vietnam. It was the color of an ugly, unhealed bruise, orange and brown, like what I imagined napalm released as it burned.

Jake craned his head out the window, concentrating on backing up. I turned around too and saw the partner of the tanker driver jump down from the roof. He stood in front of the truck's winch, trying to pull the cable out so he could hook it onto our hitch. It wasn't releasing.

"Fire's coming, Jake," I hollered.

"Shut up," he yelled from outside the window. "You do not leave somebody," he shouted. "Never, ever, is it excusable to leave someone stranded out here like this." He screamed this time.

We were flying backward. I glanced at the speedometer. It surprised me that it could register above forty miles per hour in reverse. I wasn't afraid of crashing; that would be better than the fire. Henry opened his door, positioned to jump out as soon as we stopped. Jake slammed on the brakes, and we slid twenty feet on the gravel. I turned in the seat to watch Henry and the young guy trying to get the winch to unroll. The fire was just about to reach the fence posts along the side of the road. The heat scorched the pickup.

Jake held the clutch in and pumped the gas pedal, the engine cranking and raising up and down from the pressure of the motor.

The kid abandoned ship, leaving Henry alone, and tried to outrun the fire on the other side of the road. "Henry," I screamed, and slid across the seat. Jake snapped his hand out and caught my wrist, yanking me so hard that I fell back on the seat.

"Do not get out of this cab, little sister," he growled. His voice had changed. It was colored blue and smooth, coming out of his throat like the violet flames at the base of the fire. The smoke reached us, covered us. I couldn't see Henry anymore through the back windshield. I heard him pull the chain out of the back, heard the rolling sound of the links as they clanked over the tailgate. There was silence for a minute, and I began inhaling my breath and holding it. I couldn't see anything but blackness. And then I heard Henry.

"Go. Go!" he shouted.

Jake let off the clutch and the engine just revved up. It went nowhere. I heard Jake retry it; he shoved it into first gear again. I couldn't hear the engine engage. There were sizzling, snapping sounds all around us. "Fuck me, you bastard," Jake spat.

"It's out of gear. Shit," I said, groping around the baseboard until I found the four-wheel-drive lever. I gave it a long hard yank down into Low, and we felt the pickup jump.

"Hold on," Jake said, and he let the clutch out again. This time the engine roared in a spasm and caught. The chain chattered, strained, and then tightened into a tow. We moved forward slowly as if we were pulling an entire ocean.

Jake couldn't see where he was driving. There was nothing but smoke. Then the wind whipped around, and we saw clearly for an instant. My brother rolled up his window because he saw the flames coming at him. They were jumping across the road. It was then that both of us saw Ike.

He had fired up the D-8, the trenching Cat. It was a big mother-fucker of a beast, with tracks as wide as a snow Cat's. Behind him, the disk clawed into the ground. It gouged up the earth and turned life so completely under that the flames had nothing to feed on. Ike roared toward us. He was carving a firebreak and was driving right through the fire.

"Crazy son of a bitch," said Jake in a high voice, staring at his father. "It's going to seize if you go through there."

That the engine would seize was the danger for all of us—the smoke would starve the motor out of oxygen. There would be no getting out and running. That would be the end of us all. It had happened the year before to Ralph Plath. He and his new Case were caught draw-

ing a firebreak to protect his ranch up on the bluffs of Rock Creek. The
fire never reached his property in the end. It was satisfied with just eating Ralph and the Case.

"Drive straight," I shouted, and then I screamed, "Henry. Hold on
good enough."

The fire came completely over us. I expected to die there crouched
down lying sideways on the seat. A feeling like autism took over. I
remembered being kicked by a horse when I was a child, I remembered
Ike taking me to my first day of school. I distinguished the smell of
burning engine oil from burning wheat. I tasted the fire, and I thought,
At least I will die knowing what fire tastes like.

The smoke cleared as quickly as it overcame us. I noticed Jake had
driven true, and that we were in the grooves of the gravel road. I looked
through the back window at Henry. He was balled up under the side of
the pickup bed. His hair wasn't even singed. The driver of the tanker
was white-faced; he had an inferno-fired look in his eyes.

No one said anything. I crawled out to sit on the windowsill of the
pickup to try to get sight of my father. I saw the D-8. It was still moving. He rode that tractor through the fire, cutting off its source of food.
The flames had halted there on the other side of the disked earth and
the road. The dust from the great plow mixed with the smoke like an
extinguisher, covering the ground with a blanket of new dirt and ash.
The fire stopped there at that line as if it were an angry mob.

Jake drove well ahead of the smoke, pulled off the road where there
was room, and stopped. I climbed out slowly and hung on to the
pickup for a moment. As I walked back to unwinch the tanker, Jake
stood by his door looking at the singed paint. Henry jumped down
from the pickup bed and walked aimlessly in the road. Ike drove by us
in the Cat, making sharp cutting signals across his neck.

"Quitting time all right," said Jake.

12

Shock still ruled. I unhitched the tanker and walked dazedly out to the fallow to join Carl in retrieving the combines. When I finished emptying my grain into Henry's truck, I turned the header into the wind. That was the way we parked during harvest, letting the blasts clean the machine. Ike must have called Elise on the CB radio, because she arrived with beer and pop for the harvest crews who helped fight fire. We weren't invited down because Ike didn't want us talking to the other ranchers. The old farmers loved gossip, though they never talked themselves. Tight-lipped true loners, they listened and drank their beer quietly, hoping to catch some hint of calamity about somebody else.

On any other day, I loved quitting time—when the setting sun turned the wheat into red-gold, and the air cooled down enough to allow itself to be breathed again. My body would be numb and open from the vibration of the sickle. At the day's end a person was always a little raw from all that reaping. Those nights my Levi's felt good, tight against my skin. But tonight they were simply something to hold me together after the inferno.

The throttling down of the engine was a release. I lowered my header to the ground and sat there cooling down with the motor. Shaking out my scarf, I poured water over it, the spilled water bubbling up on the catwalk in the chaff that clung there.

My face itched, especially my eyes, and I touched the cold rag to my

lashes and wet my forearms. I reached up to the bars that held up the
canvas canopy. It took a good stretch to unrack my bones. I hung down
from the bar, rolled my neck around, and caught Henry watching me.
He was sitting in his cab waiting for Carl's last load. The door was ajar
and his lace-up work boots were resting on the hinges. I saw his book
on the dash, *East of Eden*. I had seen him take it out that morning. I
watched everything Henry did.

Jake walked in front of my combine and Henry joined him. I gathered my things—coat, water jug, and coffee thermos. I glanced at Elise
passing out beer to the crews and the tanker drivers. My mother in her
element, best-looking woman in five counties smack in the middle of a
bunch of appreciative men, handing out beer on a hot day. It might as
well have been manna from heaven. She might as well have been wearing a solid gold dress.

"Let's get the fuck out of here," I overheard Jake say.

I hurried up to get my grease gun from the toolbox behind the ladder so I wouldn't keep my brother waiting.

I felt Jake's weight jump on the back of my combine, dieseling me up.

I climbed down on the header, walking the thin iron, balancing
between the steel twirls of the header's auger and the ground spiked
with stubble.

"Hurry up," Jake said.

"You in a rush?" I asked, knowing good and well he was.

He nodded. "I want to get this over with," he said sharply, as if he
didn't want to tell me his business.

I ignored him. "Going someplace?"

"Pendleton."

"What for?" I asked.

"What do you think?" he said. He pulled the diesel cap out of the
nozzle and held it by hand so the diesel would flow faster. "Bars," he
said. "Booze."

"I'm coming with," I told him.

"The fuck you are," he said, as if I had asked if I could watch while
he urinated.

"I'm not stayin' with them tonight," I stated, doing a cartwheel off
the header as if it were a balance beam. My boots snapped the brittle

stubble as I landed. I occasionally practiced gymnastics on the machinery, backflips and whipbacks off the cab of the wheat truck into the grain, hip circles on the chain that steadied the racks, round-off dismounts from the combine. It was a holdover from when I was twelve. The fire made me feel a little out of touch with reality.

"I got ID," I said, walking over to the back wheel and looking up at Jake as he dieseled. Verna Merle had given me her license when she turned twenty-one. She was overweight and had brown hair but no one ever bothered to look that close. "I don't want to stay home tonight," I told him.

"Ask Henry," he said tersely, pulling the nozzle slightly out of the tank and monitoring the gushing thick bronze liquid. "We're leaving as soon as we shower. You can't take forever or you're not coming with."

I grabbed the grease gun by the black hose and pulled it out of the toolbox, letting the lid slam behind me. Henry's door was open, and I placed my boot on the running board. I smiled at him because my teeth would look like sunshine against the blackness of my face. I wore a light green shirt that day so my big emerald eyes would bleed green for Henry. The shirt advertised Foster's beer. "It's What's Down Under That Counts" was written across my breasts.

"I'm going to Pendleton with you," I stated quickly. "I already talked to Jake." I balanced the grease gun across my knee, jerking and playing with the hose. My boots were black from charcoal.

Henry shrugged and took a drink from his water jug. "Fine with me," he said, tossing the jug onto the seat beside him. The water dripped out of the spigot and trickled back into the crack of the seat. He ran a hand down to his knee. The three of us were totally black, covered in soot, earth, and the remains of crop. Only our teeth, eyes, and tongues rolled with wetness and glared. "It'll be a rough night," he said. "I've seen that look on Jake's face before."

"Yeah, I've seen it too," I said, again too fast. "And I think it looks like fun."

"Trouble," he said.

"Trouble is fun," I told him. The nerves in my pelvis were rolling up inside and around me. The day had left me manic. I felt as if I had electricity between my thighs. I smiled at Henry again.

"You may have to drive home," he said. "Better not get carried away."

"You got a date," I said, and quickly turned to finish greasing. I noticed Henry's hands again. The white of the moons on his fingernails glowed the same color as the water-softened sheets that I had helped Elise place on Henry's bed before he came down the road to our house.

As I moved away from him, I turned around to see if he was looking at my body. I wanted to know if Henry was imagining me undressed, if he would uncover the soft places on me, taste them with his eyes, his tongue, and his beautiful rough hands.

He wasn't. He was staring straight ahead through the tiny windshield of the Monster at the blackened Cat Ike had driven through the fire. I turned abruptly back to my machinery, sure Henry had no interest in me other than my being the little sister of his best friend. My stomach turned cold. I wanted beer now, like my brother.

"You'd better get busy and service your combine," said Ike, walking past us in the stubble.

"I'm not servicing my fucking combine. My engine's burnt up," Jake said.

I snapped to attention.

"Help her then. Grease, change the oil, change the filters," Ike said, pointing. "It's Saturday, and we service on Saturday."

Life with my father was this way, completely arbitrary. I knew Ike well enough to know servicing the combines was not a maintenance issue—we had only run them a half day. It was punishment for my brother and me, as if we were responsible for the fire.

"You don't give a shit about maintenance," said Jake. He now stood on top of the trap wagon. It was an old black 1942 flatbed wheat truck. He slammed the diesel pump lever off and hung the nozzle violently. It was silent, not even wind anymore. Jake stayed there, glaring at his father. I stood staring at my brother. I envied and pitied him for letting his rage take over. I had the rage, but I never let it destroy where I lived.

"I'm not asking you," Ike said, walking toward the trap wagon. He threw an oil spout with the knifelike opener at a box on the flatbed. It missed the box and landed at Jake's feet. "Goddammit. Get a move on."

The crease between Ike's eyes seemed to split him in two. "That's the way you get yourself killed," Ike muttered. "Doing things your way."

"You were the one who almost killed us," Jake said. "If you had any decent equipment that ran." He kicked the spout back over Ike's head. "My engine exploded," he shouted, bending over toward his father as he kicked. "Goddamned flames coming out the exhaust. That's your idea of maintenance." His voice was hoarse, no longer high-pitched. I saw ropes and cords in my brother's neck.

"This equipment," Ike stated, throwing an arm at the combines, "runs fine. Did you check your oil before you started this morning? No," Ike answered, sarcastically. "If you had, you'd known something was wrong with that goddamn engine. Christ almighty, lazy-ass kid," he said.

"They always break down at harvest," Jake said softly, as if he'd discovered the riddle of the sphinx. "You don't take care of shit, old man."

This was different. Jake wasn't screaming anymore, calling my father "old man." I studied everything my brother did, how he had given up pretense. Jake didn't bother shaving during harvest, and earth-colored stubble covered his face. A black streak of charcoal ripped across his forehead where he wiped sweat. He wore a bandanna over the top of his head, which blew with the wind into something like curved horse withers.

Elise wouldn't have liked this; she didn't want her children to be too pretty, but she hated having ugly ones. It was perfect that Elise wasn't here. My mother always disappeared when Ike started in on his children. As long as I could remember, my mother had been a sieve through which my father's rage poured onto us.

Jake looked down to where Mother was parked and giving out refreshments. She could barely be made out, wearing a pink sundress with a matching scarf rolled up as a headband over her white bangs. I knew she wore her short cowboy boots, black with sewn silver eagles in front. They showed off her beautiful white legs, highlighted the way the curves of her calves narrowed to her knees. She hung around the Jag, sat on the hood talking to the men, never too far from the cool black car.

"She never once lifted a goddamned finger against him," Jake sneered under his breath. His long brown hair, dulled by the soot, clung to his neck. The wind blew errant pieces across his grained face. His Levi's were streaked and ripped from where he had used them as an oil rag for the last five days. The plaid collar of his shirt stood up from warding off chaff. The tails drifted in the breeze.

I heard footsteps coming, the snapping sounds in the stubble. I knew it wasn't Carl; he never interfered with my father and his children. It was Henry coming around the other side of my combine to join us. He had a perfect view of Jake up on the trap wagon, me by my combine header, and Ike, standing in the stubble in front of us both.

"If you don't like it," Ike said, in a low voice, "come down here and tell me."

"I don't. I hate it," my brother announced, leaning forward in a bow. "I hate the whole fucking lot."

"Iris," Ike said, turning. I thought I detected some relief in my father when he yelled at me. He knew I took it, I thrived, but only because my brother didn't. "You stupid idiot," he spat. "Getting up on a burning combine. Your mother and I raised two morons," he said, shaking his head.

"You can try to kill me," Jake said flatly. "I'm not going to let you take her, too. She doesn't know any better. Trying to put out your fire. I'm sick of putting out your fucking fires, old man."

What Jake said surprised me. I always thought he was completely indifferent to my safety. Of course, this wasn't the first time either one of us almost died. There was the carbon monoxide poisoning two winters ago. Ike told me to check his cows with the motorcycle, said to run out the engine fuel when I returned home. Another completely arbitrary exercise, just to make sure his children followed his orders.

I didn't want to ride the gas out, in –10 plus windchill. So I sat freezing in the garage with the motor running and the door closed. Ike just happened to come in there looking for paint. I didn't understand why he got so mad, why he dragged me roughly off the motorcycle, shook me, and then snapped his finger into my skull. I guessed it was because I hadn't gotten the gas lever of the motorcycle all the way to Off. That engine would have kept on running, long after I stopped.

"Don't you know any better than that?" Ike asked me.

"No," I answered.

"Of course she doesn't know any better," said Jake. "She's only seventeen years old."

"She's been doing this since she was twelve," Ike said. "Five years, didn't learn a damn thing."

"Fucking slave labor," shouted Jake. "I'm not servicing, I'm not fighting a fucking war for you, I'm not dying for you. I don't give a shit about this equipment. I don't give a shit about you."

Henry came farther around the header and stopped, again watching Jake above on the trap wagon and Ike below him.

"Let me tell you," Ike said. His voice was the hitting voice. "Come over here." He yanked me over with a movement of his hand. "You don't know a goddamned thing about work. Either of you." He shook my arm hard. He looked from me to my brother. "You think driving these things is work?" He raised my shoulder to my ear, and pointed to my combine with his free hand. "Your precious little asses have no idea," he yelled, casting my arm away as if it were a rotted fence post. "Try sowin' and buckin' sacks by hand. Drivin' a team over ten thousand acres. I risked my life for you, you whining little shits."

"You risked your life for your ranch. For your land. Not us," Jake said. "I quit."

"Get out then," Ike ordered, nodding down the fury in his voice. "And don't ever come back here," he said, dismissing us both as he stalked off. We stood there watching him disappear over the hill toward the plane. The low drone sounded as he took off. I thought it reverberated like a laden zeppelin, the kind I imagined bombing over London.

13

JAKE DROVE, I SAT IN THE MIDDLE OF THE TURK, THE
turquoise International pickup. We hadn't eaten anything. That was
the first mistake. The second was buying the twelve-pack of Oly at
Bristol's on the way.

My brother hunched over the steering wheel, burning a hole in the
road with his auburn eyes. The broken windows down, the summer
wind swirled around our heads with the dusk smell of wheat fields and
car crashes.

"I say we're lucky," I told Jake, and took a noisy sip of beer. We all
drank loudly. "That's why we're not dead now."

Jake put his arm out the pickup window and undulated it over the
wind with the movements of a roller coaster.

"Lucky my ass," he said. "Nobody is lucky who gets Ike. Ike. Ike."
Jake spoke Teutonic, like a Nazi.

Henry popped another Oly. He took a loud suck and gave me the
ring. I placed it on my ring finger with the three others, intending to
make a bracelet out of the beer tabs. I liked the feel of the cool edge of
aluminum around my wrist.

Jake rounded the corner, dipping into the opposing lane of traffic.
None of us reacted. The yellow lines of traffic were routinely ignored
in eastern Oregon. I leaned into Henry and let my body stay on him

when we came up, righted again, and hurtled down the road, our hair flying, the smell of beer and immortality in the air.

"Fate," said Jake. "That's why the fire didn't explode that engine. That's why I didn't die. That place is going to be mine someday."

I sucked my beer, said nothing. Selfish bastard, I thought.

"You'll have to kill 'im to get it," said Henry.

"I'm destined to take that place away from Ike," said Jake, mock dramatic. He brushed his hand through his postshower shining brown hair. "All right," he said, hitting the outside of the door in a smart beat with his hand.

"Going to be a lot tougher to get it now you quit," said Henry. "Hard to knock Ike off boxing groceries at Safeway."

"Better than sucking up to the despot," Jake replied, whacking his green-and-yellow tassel from the University of Oregon, which hung on the rearview mirror.

It was just another problem between Ike and Jake, when my brother went to U of O instead of Oregon State. Everyone in my family had gone to OSU for its agricultural program. My family had enrolled there from its beginning, ever since my great-grandfather donated money to build Steele Hall. Eugene was a hippie town, and Jake had majored in journalism because of Watergate. My father never even went to his graduation. I think deep down it was because he knew his son was smarter than he was.

"I wouldn't call working with Ike sucking up," Henry said after another loud sip.

"Henry's gonna save the whole goddamned universe," Jake announced. "He's going to help those poor Indians out th' reservation. Goverment'll put him through U of O med school as long as he goes out there an' takes care of a few gunshot wounds."

"Shit," Henry said, irritated. "Beats payin' the hunred thousand I don't have. What about you, Jake?" Henry talked with his beer can. "What're you going to do with your life?" he asked. "Oh, I forgot. You quit."

"I'd like to take that motherfucker out and shoot his ass is who I am," said Jake.

I didn't say anything. I didn't have to have a voice as long as Jake was around to carry on the fight with Ike.

We all sat in silence for a minute, sorry we had even brought Ike up. I fiddled with the dial of the radio. "Purple Rain" played on the one noncountry music station. The reflection from the headlights blazed through the windshield, casting a glow on Henry's face, bronzing his skin. His sandy hair fell to the side and glinted in the night.

We all started singing. When we discovered something other than country-western music on the radio, it thrilled us. Jake turned it up. He pounded on the thin steering wheel.

"Everthin' is random," I said. "Life is hard and then you die. People are either assholes. Or they're decent."

"Shit," replied Jake. "We're fucked, little sister."

"Yep," I said quickly. "What's it you have to do again after med school?" I asked Henry.

"Three years workin' outta a four-by-four army truck converted to an emergency room on a reservation."

"Which one?"

"Hell if I know," he replied. "Bumfuck, Nevada."

"Four years medical school, two years at a reservation. Then you're done?" I asked.

"Nope," he said. "Three years of residency comes first."

"Is it worth all that?" I said, alarmed.

"We *are* put here for a purpose," interrupted Jake, earnestly. "We just have to figure out what it is. Then we have nothing to do but follow our fate."

"Do I think it's worth it?" Henry asked. "I don't know. I don't know about a lot of things."

I turned to watch Henry in the light of the cab.

When the song ended, the announcer came on and started talking about Miss Budweiser's troubled trip to the Columbia Cup speedboat race. Jake turned off the radio. "Let's go to the Let 'er Rip Room," he said.

"I don't want to go there," I told him. "It's a sexist shithole."

"Nothing to fear," he said. "Those people are harmless. It's either the Let 'er Rip Room or you have to duck down so me 'n Henry can cruise the gut."

I finished my beer and threw it at Jake's foot. "That what you have in mind?" I asked Henry. "Play a little hide-the-salami in the back of a pickup?"

"Anywhere but a pickup," Henry replied.

"At least you're discriminating," I said.

What was wrong with him, anyway, I thought, some kind of stupid chivalric code? Maybe he just plain didn't do green-eyed blondes. Henry should have made his intentions known by now. Despite the fact women could make the first move these days, when a woman has a Columbia River–sized crush on a man, it is way better to have him make the play first.

Plus my brother. I never had the last word with him. He had an annoying way of making me feel like I was twelve. "I don't like that place because of the drink policy," I replied finally.

"You need to go to the Let 'er Rip," said Jake. "Every revolutionary needs to find out what the enemy is doing."

"Sometimes I think you are the enemy," I told him.

"You know who the enemy is," he said, whistling as he exhaled. "Besides, you were the one who wanted to come on this trip. Didn't want to stay home tonight with Mummy and Daddy." He looked for a parking spot. "Tonight you grow up," he announced harshly.

He parked the pickup on Dorian Street and we walked to the bar.

"You should become a civil rights lawyer," said Jake. "Then you and Henry could save people. Wouldn't that be wonderful if you could save people from themselves?" Jake laughed at the absurdity of salvation.

There was a line out the front. I stood behind Jake and Henry while they were ID'd; Henry had fake identification too, since he was still twenty. I held my breath as Verna Merle's worked. Forged ID works best in dark bars with a shortage of women.

The Let 'er Rip Room was small and it seemed even tinier packed with people. A picture of that famous bucking outlaw named Warpaint shimmered on the wall, a rangy-looking, splay-footed rascal with a matted mane and tail and a wide-open mouth. I found myself wondering why horse mouths slapped open when they bucked.

The champion cowboys of the rodeo hung on the walls: the first black cowboy, George Fletcher; the Nez Perce, Jackson Sundown;

Bertha Blancett, only woman to compete in the all-around. She grimaced like a pilgrim with her rounded hat and shawl. Above the bar dangled a sign that read, Old Oregon Trail: The Longest Road in Human History. Mule riggings hung up alongside the sign and miners' lanterns glowed cheaply over the whiskey bottles.

I walked off to buy a drink without looking back at Jake and Henry. I also noticed there weren't many women here under three hundred pounds. Henry and Jake deserved whatever came their way. A sign behind the bar directed, Please Keep Your Clothes On.

I squished through the red Naugahyde stools and tried to get the attention of the barkeep. Behind me, a guy with old-man eyebrows that jutted upward placed his hand on my back. I jumped, and he took it off.

I wore jeans and a pink-and-gray striped V-neck shirt that showed off my tan and my breasts. I usually thought myself lucky that I had big breasts, but not tonight. I crossed my arms over my chest and anchored my hands under my armpits, which was the way most of the men stood when they weren't holding beers. I wanted to go home.

"Can I buy ya an Oly?" the cowboy asked.

"Bud," I said. "Thanks," I added as a period to our conversation. I kept my arms crossed tightly, hoping the cowboy would get the hint I wasn't in the mood for any action.

He leaned over me to reach the bar, and I ducked and backed up, looking around. Henry and Jake stood on the other end of the bar getting drinks. Henry looked right at me, and I smiled what I considered a copy of my mother's best smile.

"Jack Purchase," the cowboy said, handing me the cold bottle.

"Cheers," I replied. "Nothing better than a red, white, and blue cocktail." I took a rough swig of my beer and set it down hard on the bar. I didn't want to send any subliminal signals about blow jobs.

"Nothing better," he said, kneading me with his elbow as if we were having a great private joke. He licked the tips of his teeth with his tongue. They shone a bright white and crooked, seemed to be converging at the center of his mouth.

The truth was, the cowboy would rather I had ordered Oly because of the dot covenant. It held that after a man bought a woman an Olympia beer, and she drank it, he could rip off the label and look underneath. There he'd find one to four dots printed on the back. One dot signified a peck on the lips, and four dots was a damn fine fuck. The only remaining problem with the covenant was that the man had to convince the woman in question to sign her full name to the thing for it to be legal and binding.

I took another drink of my Bud and looked around again. I spotted a woman with thick long hair that hung down below her ample butt. The weight of her hair stretched her part wide, like the Amish down in the valley with the two-inch crack running through the middle of their head. She stood against the wall with those western jeans that I hated, the ones that make women's asses look big as houses. Every two seconds she would reach her hand up to her neck, scoop up her hair, and run her hand down the length of it, letting it flop on her back pockets. I decided she was under the mistaken impression that butt-length, mouse-brown hair was sexy.

The room looked to be full of lowlifes. One group, the secessionists, the Ruby Ridge and Posse Comitatus types, huddled very privately. They appeared to be holding their buttholes as tight as humanly possible, all the while plotting their next assault on the government. Then there were the rodeo circuit cowboys, habitually scamming for all they were worth as if women were just another ten-second bronc ride. And finally the squatters, who preferred the nomenclature of miner, and they would tell you so.

We saw these people all the time up at Heart of the Beast. They bought mining rights for a couple of dollars and then squatted on the land for free afterward. It was a big damn fraud, and they all knew it. If anyone raised a fuss about their being there, or if they just plain liked the property, they could buy the claim for fourteen dollars an acre. All because the water and mining laws hadn't been changed since they were drafted for the first time back in 1845.

"I didn't get your name," said Purchase.

"Iris," I replied. "Iris Steele."

"Oh." He nodded. "You live over in Horrow County."

"How do you know?" I asked.

"I know the name." He paused for a moment. "Your father's the asshole."

"You're an asshole," I told him.

"No," he said, laughing and kneading me with his elbow. "I'm just kidding you."

"Do you know him?"

"It was a joke," he said.

"It's not a very funny one," I yelled over the barroom din.

"You sure light up easy," he cajoled, placing his hand on my shoulder.

"What do you do?" I asked him. "How do you know my father?"

"Why don't we get some music on in here," Jack Purchase yelled to one of his friends. He leaned his head back so his neck crowded his jowls.

I recognized the buddy as Lance Dicky. He'd played football and basketball against Jake and Henry in high school. He was from Krump, a real dump of a town.

"I'm sorry," he said. "What did you say?"

"I asked what you were doing these days."

"Hauling potatoes from the circles," he announced proudly.

"Oh wow," I told him, smiling. "Orelda. Those are the best French fries. Better than A&W."

Jack Purchase grinned, pleased. This guy was stupider than I thought possible.

"I don't haul for Orelda," he admitted. "I haul down to Krump, feed for the stockyards."

"Oh," I said, smiling. "The slaughterhouse." I finished my beer and sat on one of the Naugahyde stools.

"You want another?" he asked hopefully.

"No, thanks," I said. I wondered how drunk I was. I looked back at Lance Dicky. I hated him, I decided. Before Jake changed to contacts, Lance once pulled Jake's glasses out of his football helmet and smashed them with his cleat while the referee wasn't looking. Cheap white trash.

The jukebox began with that song "I Got Friends in Low Places." Everybody in the bar seemed to like it. Even the bartender flipped bottles on the part where the chorus says "O-asis."

"You harvestin' yet?" Lance asked.

"Started today."

"What you gettin'?"

"Seventy bushel."

"No," he exclaimed. His brow turned conspiratorial. "I heard there was a big fire out there," he whispered.

"It was on our place."

"No," he said again, this time whistling that whistle that says You don't say. "I heard somebody died out there," he went on. "I heard they had to be taken to the hospital in a plane. I heard it got so out of control it took eight harvest crews and burned up three ranches."

"No," I corrected him. "It was just on our place. My father stopped it with the Cat and the disk."

"Well," he said, feigning relief. "You don't look like your pretty little lashes got singed none."

"Not this time," I told him.

I took a deep breath, and sat up straight on my stool because I thought it might help me get some air. I had that out-of-body feeling when there are too many people in a room, too-loud music, and too much smoke. I moved my hand through the thick fumes, and watched them curl and swirl around my fingers.

A song ended that I didn't know, and people moved out of the center of the room. It wasn't really a dance floor, but people swayed around there anyway.

"You mind getting me a Coke?" I asked, reaching into my back pocket for money. "Here," I said, shoving him a crumpled ten.

"Ain't no way, darlin'," he replied. "I never pass up the opportunity to buy a dollar drink."

I looked around for Jake and Henry. I caught sight of a couple standing in the middle of the floor. She was another one of those long-haired women. I couldn't tell the color of it in the dimness, other than it was dark and she looked to be Indian. Her eyes fluttered closed, and her tongue searched for her partner's mouth. They stood about the same height and missed each other's mouths entirely in their groping search. The woman's arms, tanned and long, reached around his head in a clumsy embrace.

Gypsy hands full of silver rings on all of her fingers gripped a hank of hair, knocking the man's cowboy hat off. The couple remained oblivious. I noticed one finger bore a ring with a slave chain attached to a bracelet. I decided they were the kind of hands shown in pornographic pictures. The kind that caressed naked, spread legs. A photo where there was no head to the woman, it was just her open sex organs that had been bought.

Jack Purchase returned with my Coke. He followed my eyes to the couple and said, "Oops. You didn't see that."

"I see that all right."

The man pulled her shirt out of her Levi's. She redoubled her efforts on his face while he tried to unhook her bra.

I found myself strangely interested in the kind of bra she wore. Women take a huge interest in their bras, how they hold their breasts, how certain bras look under clothes, whether the nipples show through when they turn hard or are obscured by thick padding.

I was wearing my best bra, one with an underwire so I could cinch it high to hold my flesh full up and together. It was silk and made of one piece that went over the whole breast so that there were no creases under tight shirts. Tightness and thinness were the key to good bra wearing; that way everything showed through. I wore it hoping tonight Henry would notice me. He'd watch me move around him wearing something other than a diesel-covered T-shirt. I used everything I had to make him want to hold me, kiss me down my neck, my chest, take off that baby blue bra and everything else along with it.

I looked back at the couple. The man, frustrated in the process of undoing the hooks with his clumsy hands, shoved her dark T-shirt up around her armpits the way a toddler might push at its mother in a tantrum. He stood there planted on the dance floor weaving and staring at her chest.

I began to get nervous. I stood up. She wore a ratty-looking thing, not the kind of undergarment one would choose thinking it was going to be romantically taken off by a lover. Too small for her, it held her breasts like a shelf. The straps in the back flapped sloppily. It was a frayed old shitty bra with holes in the wide elastic that went around her sides.

She swayed forward and tried to grab hold of his head to steady herself in order to kiss him some more. The frustrated man grabbed between her breasts and gave the garment a wrenching twist. It broke free and the Jell-O-like mass of flesh came out shuddering and shaking from the trauma. Tan marks from her bikini bathing suit glared in the shoddy light.

Two men encroached on the couple.

"Do something," I told Jack Purchase.

"Ain't no way, darlin'. I can't do nothin'," he said with a nervous laugh.

I hated him, too, that fucking chickenshit. I set my drink on the bar.

I made myself look back at the couple. He was still squeezing her, but his tanned hands on her breasts kept falling off. He couldn't stand and feel her tits at the same time. She kept trying to pull his face closer to hers. He slowly bent forward, and then inched toward her nipple with his mouth.

She jerked him to her and looked up at the ceiling as if she were experiencing some great sexual excitement. He placed his mouth on her nipple for an instant before he lost his balance and quickly grabbed her waist to right himself. He stood there with his head at her naked waist, holding her and laughing. He started to unbutton her Levi's, his nose on her belly button. The flesh of her waist slightly fell over the waistband as she swayed. The saliva on her breast shone in the night light and highlighted the red of her nipple and areola, sloppily and loosely spread over her breast without boundaries, like she was.

There were five men around them now, close enough to touch the couple. They hooted mostly and whistled. One of them angrily hissed, "You can do it. Give her a fuck." Then I saw Lance Dicky take out his knife. I started to sweat, and I could feel my heart.

"That's your buddy," I said. "Go tell him to stop it."

Lance was a short, stout man with feathered hair and a shirt that read, If You Sit On My Face, I'll Guess Your Weight. He walked up behind her. The couple was oblivious and slow, barely keeping their balance. She hadn't closed her mouth, was still looking at the ceiling. His hands kept falling off her hips but returned to hold himself steady. They both swayed.

Lance pulled up her bra straps hard.

"Fucking two-year-old," I said.

He cut the straps with one slice of his knife, held the bra over his head, and walked back to the bar. The men standing around the couple behaved as if they'd just observed a Super Bowl touchdown. It was the drink policy at the Let 'er Rip to offer the whole barroom a round of free drinks if some cowboy got second base lucky and removed the bra in the process. The bartender took it, rang a cowbell, and began passing out liquid refreshment.

Then the couple slipped and fell on the floor. I saw my chance and walked right in.

"Get off her," I said, hitting the man in the eyes to make him move. He landed on top of her, and she spread out, her long hair sticking to the beer-stained floor.

"Did you hit your head?" I asked her as I bent down.

She numbly looked at me, then her gaze slipped away. I knew she couldn't focus. I pulled down her T-shirt and saw stains that looked like vomit. I heard the men behind me yelling, "Ah, no. No! What is she doing in there?"

"Can you hear me?" I asked her. I was crouched down next to her shoulder like a wolf.

The woman nodded and then turned her head to the side and started coughing and then spit. Then I felt a coldness pour over me, and looked up to see Lance holding an upside-down Budweiser bottle over my head.

"You fucking bastard," I screamed at him.

"You got a problem with that?" he said innocently. That was when Jake jumped him. He overshot and missed his head, but managed to get his arm around Lance's neck and hit him three times in the temple, his fist sliding off the eye socket bone the last time. Lance fell down on top of the woman's legs, Jake on top of him.

"I got a problem with you, motherfucker," Jake yelled in his ear. "You fucking fuck."

Two of the five friends made moves to grab Jake, and I clutched one of their pant legs as he went by me, tripping him. He landed on the woman's legs, too. She didn't even move.

Jake scrambled to his feet and kicked Lance, his foot glancing off his thigh. Then Jake fell down, Lance's friends on top of him. I knew that he was a fighter, had moods like the one he was in tonight. He wanted the violence. But Henry was another story. He was a healer; the most violence he'd ever contemplated was instructing me what to do if a rapist ever attacked me: hit him in the Adam's apple, rip it out if I could. I saw Henry pull someone off Jake; I watched his screwed-up face, expecting him to reach for the throat. He didn't. I heard him say, "You little fucker," as he kicked the guy in the balls as hard as he could. Afterward the man fell to the floor, inert.

The bartender pulled down a metal cage that protected the bottles of cheap whiskey and himself. He stood there with his hands crossed over his chest, watching intently.

"Let's go," I told the woman, placing her arm around my neck and pulling her up. She stumbled out of the bar with me, and I sat her down outside on the concrete next to the building, then ran back into the bar. Henry was helping Jake up off the floor, and I hurried over to them.

Everyone was silent as we walked out. I thought I heard a voice, and I turned around to see Lance Dicky stand up. He spoke like he was reciting a *poem*. "We'll be around," he said to us. "If you come back," and then he breathed, "into town."

"Fuck you," said Jake.

"You'd like that, wouldn't you," said Lance. "To go around back and get butt-fucked. You'd like that."

"Not as much as you, little Dicky," said Henry.

Outside, I watched Jake help the woman. He held her as much as picked her up. His hands caressed her stained shirt as she twisted to stand. The four of us left the Let 'er Rip Room, walked to the pickup on Dorian Street.

"What's your name?" I asked the woman.

"Kappy," she said hoarsely. "*Kapsiis token.*"

I remembered a little of Dagmar's teachings. "You're not so bad," I said.

Jake listened intently. He glanced sideways at her as she brushed the hair out of her face.

"*Kapsiis Sooyaapoo,*" Jake said.

"Not as bad as them," she said, and spat.

When we reached the pickup, Jake opened the passenger door for her. He jimmied the broken window down and helped her into the ripped, sunken seat. Then he closed it carefully and crawled into the back.

"Where we headed?" Henry asked me as he climbed into the truck.

"The reservation," I said, as I slid behind the milk-colored steering wheel.

14

I STARTED THE PICKUP AND WE ROLLED THROUGH SILENT downtown Pendleton. As he sat next to me, I noticed Henry smelled of summer, soap, and sweat. The scent of his clothes strangely reminded me of my mother, I guess because she cleaned them. A slight perfume arose from the oil in his body. It was like myrrh. It made me think of the tropics, the red-flowered island of Rhodes. I wanted to travel with Henry, to see a world other than the one I lived in.

As we reached the interstate, Kappy opened her eyes and the door. Hanging half in and half out, she said, "I'll walk to the reservation." I imagined her walking off a drinking binge on the freeway. I squinted at her bent back. I wondered how many times she had been picked up. Raped? Had she felt a knife at her throat? Her toughness fascinated me.

"We'll take you home," said Henry. He grabbed her gently around her waist and pulled her back beside him. The door slammed loosely shut.

We drove on toward the reservation. Five miles east of town it spread out like a puddle below Cabbage Hill. Kappy pulled herself away from Henry and leaned again on the rattling door. She laid her head on her arm; she looked as tired as she was drunk. I glanced at Jake through the back window. He huddled in the pickup bed staring at Kappy. He looked cold even in the warm night.

I slowed down, coasting off the exit. Here, reservation dogs lay in the street in front of us. Some were thin, small, Third World dogs, others monstrous and huge. We drove slowly by groups of men standing and talking around their cars. They stopped what they were doing and turned to look at us as we glided by, a beat-up pickup with a bunch of white kids driving around lost.

White people didn't go onto the reservations. All the way up and down the Columbia River, the Indians that lived, fished, and worked along the river refused to have much to do with whites. And vice versa.

A few days off from being full, the moon's white light cast a gunmetal shadow on the land, underworld and rude. It seemed no real buildings stood on the reservation, only tract and mobile homes. Between them was vast and gray space where the air smelled boiled and reused.

"All right, Kappy," I said. "Where do we go from here?"

"The end of the road," she said, throwing her hand forward.

I drove on down until we reached an old mobile home. A porchlike corrugated plastic addition hung over the entrance. I turned off the pickup, and Jake climbed out of the back and opened the door for Kappy. He slid his arm around her waist and walked her down the road for a minute. They turned in unison and headed to the house. Henry and I followed.

It was about 12:15, I noticed as I knocked on the front door lightly. No answer. We walked in and sat Kappy down on the brown-and-gold tweed couch. Jake seated himself next to her. On the prefabricated canvas-covered walls, I noticed an unframed poster of the Happy Creek Diorama. It was the spectacle about the West, staged each night of the Pendleton Rodeo. The name Happy Creek came from the stream that ran through the reservation. The founding fathers of Pendleton had placed the Indian reservation next to a creek so their excrement would be carried away.

Next to the poster hung a starkly framed picture dated eight years earlier of Kappy, a princess in the pageant. I didn't recognize her at first; she was slightly thinner then. In her white, beaded buckskin-fringed shawl, she stared gravely at the camera with sharp brown eyes under intense brows, regal and startlingly somber. In one hand she gripped an eagle feather fan and in her other flowed a block-lettered banner that read Happy Creek Princess. Her thick black hair, parted and plaited with fur and beads, glowed like moonlit water. Abalone shell earrings glittered from her ears as if they were lures.

I looked back at Kappy and Jake sitting together on the couch and wondered what she conjured with her dangerous dangling beauty. Despite the events of the evening, Kappy was a compelling presence. She still had the look of the young princess in the photo, but now she was older and harder. I noticed next to the couch a small table cluttered with beer bottles, and an overfilled ashtray threatened to collapse.

Kappy slumped down against Jake. She placed her head on her half-opened fist and sobbed.

I shifted uncomfortably. Henry picked up a miniature toy horse that stood on the table. He galloped it away from him down his arm, onto his hand, and then out into thin air.

"Kappy," I asked, "do you want to get ready for bed?"

She stood up, staggering back into a short hall leading to a bathroom and then a bedroom.

Kappy sat on the end of the bed. A crumpled crocheted afghan bedspread slid onto the floor as the cheap mattress sank with her. I reached under her pillow to look for her nightgown and found a frayed white cotton shift. It smelled of sweat and cooking oil.

I grabbed a tortoiseshell hair clamp and a brush off the floor. Throwing them onto the bed, I climbed on all fours behind Kappy and started smoothing her hair. I brushed it softly and slowly, pulling it back from her scalp where the beer and dirt had ratted it. I straightened and coaxed the waves and mats of her thick hair into a shining pool as if I were calming the sea.

Kappy sat upright and threw back her head. I twisted her hair around my finger and clipped it up out of the way.

"Ready?" I asked.

She nodded and stood up, her hands over her head. I touched her shirt, rolled it up as I took it off. Kappy unbuttoned her pants the rest of the way; she hadn't closed them after the bar. She leaned over to pull her jeans off, her breasts falling forward into a point, contrasted with the perfectly outlined curving bones of her back. She wasn't wearing underwear; I wondered where she had lost them. Kappy shocked me;

she didn't give a shit who saw her naked or drunk. I stood there tensely gripping her nightgown, waiting to place it over her, wanting to cover the mess.

I hadn't noticed before that she was barefoot, her feet marked with rainlike rivulets of dirt. She wouldn't care, I thought, but I hated going to bed with dirty feet. I reached for her hands. They were bigger than mine, and lay limp in my stronger, cut-up, callused fingers. We started into the bathroom. Jake stood at the door of her room watching us. I didn't know how long he had been there. He moved off into the darkness of the hall as we went to the bath.

I gave her three aspirins from a bottle I found in the medicine chest, and had her sit on the side of the bathtub as I washed her feet. Kappy held her nightgown in folds at her thigh with one hand and hung on to my belt loop with the other. She had pretty toes, high arches, and beautiful, smooth, tanned long legs. I soaped her feet, rinsed them, and dried them with a towel thinned down by age. Then she looked at me and said, "I haven't heard Nez Perce since my mother died."

I led her back into her bedroom, pulled down her covers, and she placed those long beautiful legs down into the whiteness of the sheets. I removed her comb, and her hair spread out above her like a halo.

"How did you end up here?" I asked.

She remained unmoved. "We got kicked off, told never to come back. We're bad. Always have been." She pushed her head back on the pillow.

The light at the built-in cabinet glowed dimly. I noticed she used decent makeup—Almay skin care products and Clinique mascara. A picture of two Indians in a turquoise frame hid behind the makeup. A woman carried a baby in a beaded bundle, and a man stood behind her with a tall, raven-colored hat. His face held the saddest expression I'd seen since the Curtis photo of Chief Joseph.

Picking up her T-shirt and pants, I turned off the light. I threw the shirt in the trash and soaked her jeans in the bathroom sink with some strong-smelling hand soap.

When I walked back to the living room, Jake was lying down on the couch as if it were a bed. I looked at him. "What's going on?" I asked.

"I'm staying here," he answered.

I stood in the middle of the room, staring at him. I wanted to run and beat the hell out of him. "You really think you're something, don't you?"

"No," he said, covering himself with another afghan. "I'm nothing."

"You've always done whatever you wanted, like it was owed to you or something. Like you're the center of the goddamned universe. Just because you're the son, you're the name. You think you have everyone wrapped around your finger." I stopped suddenly and looked at Henry. I didn't want him to see Jake and me fighting.

"Shut up," Jake ordered. "God, I hate little sisters."

"Kappy doesn't want you here," I muttered, moving toward the door.

"Does this mean you're leaving me for someone else?" asked Henry, feigning insult.

Jake flipped him off. "You'll find someone else," he said.

"You think he can just stay here?" I asked Henry as I opened the door.

"Well, he can't go home," Henry replied.

"You know, Ike and Elise may care what you do," I observed, turning back to Jake. "But out here, it's another world. Nobody gives a good goddamn about a white boy like you."

"Go on home," Jake answered tiredly. "I don't have a home anymore."

"Don't be stupid," I said, holding the door open. "Let's go."

He shook his head. "I just want to talk to her," he stated. "I'm leaving in the morning."

"It's really arrogant of you to assume you can just stay here. Talk to her," I said, rolling my eyes. "It'll scare the shit out of her when she wakes up and finds you."

Henry walked outside. "Come on, Iris. Let's go."

"You tell Ike," said Jake, "I'm going to rot out here on the damn Indian reservation. And make sure Mother is there when you do it."

"He'll disinherit you," I scoffed. I imagined telling my father. Ike would never mention Jake's name again. And I wouldn't either. It would be Elise who wouldn't forget. Her weapon when she fought with Ike would now be Jake. They always fought, especially around the stress of harvest. My father drank whiskey; she drank aquavit and picked fights until he smacked her. I saw it perfectly; that would be the time she would bring up the name of their lost son.

I leaned into the cheap door. Even though I had wanted it, I suddenly dreaded seeing myself working the ranch for the rest of my life. Stuck, the farmer's little daughter hung out on a fishing pole to catch a son-in-law who could really do the work, because everyone knew a daughter couldn't ranch. "You're a quitter," I said. "You son of a bitch."

"Fuck you," Jake said. "Wait till it happens to you. Bring it on. Let it rain," he said, laughing ruefully.

Henry looked at Jake and smiled futilely. "People make choices, Iris," he said.

We didn't lose our way leaving the reservation. We drove past the same men standing by the same cars. They were in the middle of the road this time. The moon cast their long shadows across the gravel road and out into the sagebrush. As we approached them, we slowed down. They all stared at us. They knew where we had been. They moved out of our way one by one. They were laughing, cracking jokes.

A car with one headlight came down the middle of the road like an erratic bat. Henry stopped the pickup to let it negotiate its way by us. An old woman was driving it. She leaned her head out her window and pointed a crooked finger up at the sky. "There's rain coming," she said. "When the moon is upside-down like that. You can be sure the storm's brewing."

Henry and I rode home on the interstate, staring down the road as if it were an enemy. I kept thinking of Kappy on the dance floor, wondering what would make someone let herself fall that way. I thought about how her feet were blackened from the places she had walked that night with her excuse for a date. Creosote had colored her soles with thick tar, and had turned the bottoms of her feet to pounded pavement. I imagined down at the railroad tracks was where she drank her mind away, inhaling the Popov vodka from the distillery of Hood River while the smell of creosote blackened her lungs.

Pendleton was a true town of the Old West with a famous rodeo, a lumber mill, a prison, an insane asylum, and an old tar plant. That was the worst, a rusted metal tepeelike burner with a rounded cage over the top that belched out that nasty smell of road building. The water towns along the rivers of the Northwest bore pockets of heavy industry like scabs where the river met the earth. From miles away they glared, clotted with aluminum plants, lumber mills, weapons-grade metal factories. It was the industry that built the town in the first place. Everything depended on that river, I thought, as we drove home. I watched it spread out to the right of us, glinting like a smooth ocean of bourbon flowing down the gorge and sailing on out to the sea. I wanted something that could wash me clean.

I remembered the picture of the Happy Creek Diorama on Kappy's wall. I went once when I was eleven with Elise, to the parade and the Happy Creek festival. An entire reenactment of American history unfolded right there in the roundup grounds against a painted sunset backdrop. It was one of those hot September days, and we stopped on the street for the Westward Bound Parade. There were teams of oxen so long they couldn't negotiate the corner between Dorian and Court Streets. We saw some mules, their long rabbit ears flopping back on their heads and buckskin-colored noses bobbing.

"These are the things that keep you young," said Elise, a scotch-and-7 in one hand, her black Stetson in the other. I noticed all the men looking at my mother. She was wearing a bright yellow dress, her white hair cut short and swinging like Marilyn's, and I wondered what she felt like pushing me around, an eleven-year-old in a wheelchair. I hated it; the doctors had given it to me for a month because of the accident.

I knew my mother felt guilty because of the knife she had left on the floor. That morning I had bounced on my parents' bed, practicing my gymnastics. I attacked it, completing a front summie with such force that I was propelled onto the floor. A pain started in my foot as if it were splitting. I started screaming, and I couldn't stop.

I was just about to pass out, when I looked at Ike, his face blue-red, the color of mine. He had this combination of rage that this little kid was interrupting his life and, I think, concern somewhere in the back of his mind that I might be the one who was exactly like him. As Ike bandaged my foot, I calmed down. No one said anything, but the knife was there because Elise had been cutting up her boxes. That's what she did when she was mad, took the butcher knife and destroyed cardboard boxes.

Afterward, my mother drove me to the emergency room, which was two hours away. It wasn't much of an emergency room, I thought, staring at the river beside us. If you were going to die, you'd be dead by the time you arrived.

I glanced back at Henry; he'd been silent so long. "Your dad ever take you to the rodeo?" I asked him.

"We went every year for a while after Mother left," he replied, running his hand through his thick hair. "After the savings and loan went bankrupt, we quit going. He never wanted to see his friends after that."

"You go to the parade?"

"Once," he said. "It was a hot day. Damn hot. Got a hell of a sunburn to remember it by."

I recalled how after Elise and I went to the parade, she let me wear her hat, and it came down over my nose, banging on the back edge of the wheelchair. I made Mother push me to the front so I wouldn't get those *Oh look at the poor crippled child in the wheelchair* looks.

"Your great-grandfather had the longest mule team in the state," she had said, getting really chatty the way she did after she'd had a drink. "Back before Tusko."

"How do you know?" I asked skeptically. I played with the brake on the wheels of the chair.

"I used to ride with the colonel," she said. "I'd drive him around the ranch in the Jag. I'd just gotten it. We'd drive for days out looking at the crops, and when he had enough he'd say, 'Bully,' and that's when I turned it for home. I loved looking over the land, talking about the settlement."

"Where was Ike?" I asked, accidentally pinching my finger between the metal brake wedge and the wheel.

"Your father wouldn't ride like that," she said. "He always wanted me to take care of the colonel."

"Something wrong with Grandfather?" I asked, holding my pinched finger.

"Oh, I don't know," she answered with a laugh. "Something's wrong with all of us."

I turned around to look at my mother.

"I didn't mind your grandfather," she said lowly, gesturing toward the parade. "He was history." My mother took a sip of her drink. "And that was our story."

As I watched the parade, I thought about the hulking old wagons, combines, and plows from the turn of the century that were deteriorating in the back canyon of the Bar S. Their carcasses covered in shadows only served for making forts and climbing on. The rabbits and mice overran them, turned them into hovels. I used to ride by them at dusk on my way home, and I felt I was passing something haunted, the souls of the hired hands still riding those old and broken-down ghost reapers.

I remembered then seeing the float for the Happy Creek Indian Princesses silently sliding by. Two Indian girls stood on it dressed in dun-colored fringe. The beadwork on their dresses traced their shoulders with vines and flowers the way I imagined Eden. They wore the colors I loved, greens and yellows. Wide puka-shell chokers lined their necks, and when they waved, turquoise rings flashed. They looked me in the eye and smiled at me.

I noticed a sign at the bottom of the float: Don't Throw Money at the Indians. Respect Our Dignity.

"Do they need money?" I whispered.

Elise nodded her head, bending down to me. "Indians are very poor. They need all the help they can get. So nice people give them money."

"But they are telling us they don't want money," I said, looking back at the float.

"That's right," she announced, raising her voice. "Some people just don't want to be helped." My mother was putting on a show. She talked loudly so that the people around us would see what a good-looking, smart woman she was.

"If they're poor why don't they want money?" I raised my foot up. It felt numb.

"I guess because it turns them into beggars. That's why they do this parade, that's why they compete for the Best-Dressed Indian award. Fifty silver dollars in a Hemlay steer-skin pouch," she said with a touch of awe in her voice. "Then there is the award for the oldest married Indian couple registered in the Indian village. See, we're trying to keep the families together," she instructed. "There is a beauty pageant, and a junior beauty pageant. It says right here." She pointed at the program. "The winners receive a blanket from the Pendleton Woolen Mills and six hundred dollars for their effort. Money," she said. "That's why they do this."

After the parade was over, she wheeled me in to the diorama. The pageant began with how the Indians existed before the white man came, and a long time was spent on how they prayed. Then the white people immigrated over the stage, in hokey outfits straight out of *Hee-Haw*. They pretended to move the Indians out, and the inevitable war happened.

A fake fight started between one of the Hee-Hawers and a tomahawk-wielding Indian riding around on a paint horse with orange hay-bale twine tied around its bottom lip. Then the life of the frontier town of Pendleton was set up, complete with the Chinese laundry, dance halls, saloons, and blacksmith shops. Two accidents occurred at this point. An Indian knocked over a Chinese man from the laundry, and a homesteader pulled an Indian off his horse and then exited victoriously stage left, which was the direction of the past, not the future. It ended with the announcer talking about how the white men and Indians lived in peace now, and how many of the participants were descended from ancestors who had starred in the original show that toured Europe with Buffalo Bill Cody and Sitting Bull at the start of the Indian pageant craze. Even Queen Victoria came out of her decades-long isolation after the death of her husband to see the Wild West show.

I looked around me; the stadium was full of people. There were a lot of kids, mostly younger than me, and none in a wheelchair. Their mouths were open and there might as well have been slobber coming out. They really believed that shit, I remember thinking.

Then it was over, and Elise wheeled me out of there and through the gambling arcade set up just as it had been since the rodeo started back at the turn of the century. Elise pulled the slot machine while I watched.

"I won! I won!" I heard her scream, and the fake Indian head nickels came running like a river out of that machine. "We got luck on our side, kid. Luck on our side." A crowd gathered around her, and everyone stopped playing for a minute to look at the beautiful woman with the crippled child who had won the jackpot. Then they all resumed what they were doing, I thought, kind of the same way they did when Jake, Henry, and I were on our way out of the Let 'er Rip Room. The bartender opened the cage that he had pulled down with one hand and held up the cut bra in the other. "One free round for everyone. One free round."

Butterflies started in my stomach as Henry navigated us slowly up our gravel drive, careful not to shake the pickup on the washboards. It was awkward driving home, Henry had been so quiet, and I wondered what he was thinking all that time. We parked along the line of vehicles in the front of the house. The dogs barked until they sniffed us as we stepped out.

"Shut up, Ace," I said. "Come here," and I pounded on his hollow-sounding side. Their fur in the night felt cold. "Damn you dogs, anyway."

"You want to come down?" asked Henry.

I nodded, walking with him toward the bunkhouse. I had beer in my hair and on my shirt. I wasn't drunk anymore, and I had the image of Kappy on the dance floor playing over and over in my mind. But just the same, a thrill rippled through me when he asked.

When we reached the bunkhouse, Henry opened the old door with a shove. Built in the teens, the bunkhouse sagged at its edges. Unlike the rest of the ranch buildings, the bunkhouse was neglected after the huge harvest crews vanished. Scuffed wooden floors held a great stove in its middle. Dormitory rooms lined up around the main room. Jake filled all but one with his guitars, books, records, and clothes. Henry's room lay on the opposite side from Jake's. A weeping willow tree scratched against his window at night.

"Leave the light off," I said, partly because I was shy, and partly from fear of Ike and Elise.

Henry struck a match and lit candles in Budweiser bottles with colored wax drippings decorating them. He placed one on the old stove. "Do you want to go in my room and just lay down for a while?"

"Okay," I said, shrugging my shoulders as if it were something Henry and I had done thousands of times, but my stomach jumped. I walked into Jake's bedroom to get his pillow. Lighting another candle,

I went to the bathroom and looked at myself in the mirror. My pink lipstick sparkled against my tanned face, and my hair shone bright white against my dark skin where it hung down, dried in strings. I brushed my teeth with my brother's toothbrush, pulled up my hair and tied it in a knot. I couldn't believe this was happening tonight of all nights.

Henry was already in bed when I returned to his room. He had taken off his clothes except his boxers. He leaned forward on his elbow and opened up the covers for me.

"Don't make me nervous," I said. "I've never done this before."

"You don't have to do anything," he replied.

"You know women can't just undress like men can down to their boxers. They have to reveal stuff," I said, thinking maybe this wasn't the right time after all.

"You don't have to take your clothes off," he answered.

I nodded and walked out to the stove, blew out the candles, and then came back in. I stood in front of him. I pulled my shirt off over my head, unbuttoned my Levi's, pushed them down, and stood there. "Shit," I said, as I stepped out of them and climbed in with Henry.

I never realized what an organ the skin was until then. The first thing Henry did when he wrapped his arms around me was to take off my bra. His hands caressed my back, sending my body into his, as he pressed his chest into mine. He let out a sound when we touched together, and his body felt smooth and warm. It was a living blanket. I pushed my legs into and around his. I rubbed the tops of my feet under his arches.

His skin was like a bath. I reached my fingers into my mouth to see if they had heated up to the temperature of Henry's body. I sucked on his earlobe. It tasted like wheat, like bread.

I smelled and touched him. His sweat wasn't sharp; it was clean, as if he'd just showered. His body was like oil, everything was like oil. I decided it must be sex sweat. I touched his cold, thick hair, my palm sliding down the back of his head and onto his warm neck. I breathed him in, closed my eyes, tired of enjoying the sight of him so long without his taste, touch, and smell.

The bed had one of those old wire spring supports that collapsed in the middle. Gravity pulled us together. My skin caught fire with his.

His silhouette moved darkly against the moonlight that cast a slanted shadow through the window. It was a bright night. The wind rubbed the weeping willow branches over the glass.

His penis scared me; I didn't know what to do with that thing, so I was just as glad he kept his boxers on. He ran his index fingers down the sides of my neck where the pain was from working all day; he knew how to relax me. His hands flowed over my shoulders down my arms and cupped the sides of my breasts. He traced the centerline of my stomach with his thumbs to my underwear and gathered the fold with him as his hands continued down my body.

I started to say, "Na-uh," and stiffened, pushing my butt into the bed so he couldn't get them off.

I was lying there thinking, If these come off, there will be no part of me hidden from Henry. My underwear was completely wet. How unbelievably embarrassing. If I let him take them off, he'd know. I was still at the age where my body was an enemy; the natural things it did and it wanted—the things I couldn't control—were the things I hated.

Henry kept kissing me slowly over the bones of my hips, down my thighs, pushing my legs up while he licked down to my toes. I had perfumed my entire body. It wasn't as if he had caught me by surprise; I had gotten ready that night, hoping we would end up exactly where we were. He came up again on all fours.

"I must have dreamed a thousand six hundred times of doing this," Henry said, looking directly into my eyes. "I never wanted to start something unless I was sure I could hang on."

The thrill of being with Henry rose completely then, I was sure he loved me as much as I did him. That was when I reached down and bucked my hips out of that underwear and threw them onto the floor. Henry pulled off his boxers, and he stayed there over me stroking me softly, closer and closer. He lightly dragged his hand across me down there, and I think it was a growl that came out of him, nothing discernible. He lay down beside me and pulled me up on top of him. I felt him pushing into my stomach. I got nervous then. He felt my jawbone go rigid, and he backed off.

"I hate being so nervous," I said. "You have to do everything."

Henry kissed my throat.

Until then, I had always associated penises with gross old men, horses, and bulls. I expected skin on a penis to be crusted and hard, and for it to smell bad, so I held my breath. I touched him with my index finger, tracing down it and on between his legs. Henry's skin was alive, moving against my hands like the inside of a cheek escapes and enfolds over food. I started breathing again and touched my tongue to his tip.

He lay his head back on the pillow, and closed his eyes. It was because Henry had released me from his eyes that I could look at him and really see him. He squeezed the tops of my crouched knees with his veined hands, and I realized I controlled him. He had given himself over to me. I had the power to contract his heart, to move his blood; I was a warrior as much as a lover. That was when I decided I wanted to give it all back to him. I wanted to shake like him.

I crawled up his body to his blue-red lips that shone with the smoothness of kissing. Thick sandy hair spilled on the cream sheets and shone against the distressed paint of the batten-and-board bunkhouse walls. His rounded shoulders pushed up by the two pillows let his arms splay to the sides, opening the tufts of black hair under his arms. I memorized the way the hair grew on his body, his chest, his belly, arms, and legs. I took in every detail. I knew I would go over and over them when I worked the long hours of the harvest, and the days into the rest of my life. I memorized him in case he should leave me. That was the first time I knew I loved the landscape of Henry as much as I loved the land.

There was no way I wanted to get pregnant. But the danger was part of the excitement. It was just so good to lie there and feel him gently starting to move up inside me. The pushes were tentative at first. I felt him squeezing in and then falling out when he released. That was when the fire in me started, and I began to believe.

No one at school ever talked about it, but I think everybody who didn't share a room with a sibling at their house masturbated so they would know whether orgasms were possible. That was how you'd find out if you were going to be any good at sex, or if you were going to be one of those poor frigid women you read about in the trashy magazines at the checkout line. Out where we lived, it was that way for everyone except for the poor Stone sisters. There was a rumor that their mother made them sleep four in a room so they couldn't masturbate. Other than them, I think everyone pretty much knew whether they were able to have orgasms or not by the time they were twelve.

That feeling started, and I opened my eyes and I started to push a little myself when Henry did. And then he penetrated me, opened me up. His lips drifted and nipped at my body, I pushed my weight down on him, I caressed his face with my breasts.

It came in waves—a desperation part at first, an uncontrolled drowning; and then there was a red-seeing part, a fainting part. It was the lose-four-of-your-five-senses part, everything except touch.

I lay on top of him afterward, him still inside me. We fell asleep there, the way you do after a meal. It was like I had taken food of him, nourishment, and sustenance. I never wanted to eat real food again. I was a cannibal; I had the strongest and weakest parts of Henry inside me forever.

I woke at dawn. I kissed him again, rolled off, and covered him with the sheet.

I dressed and walked quietly out, not shutting the door completely. The sky had swirls of clouds that looked the way hair does underwater, and the sun was just touching them with its red paint. The birds hadn't started, and I walked shivering in the damp dawn air. Nothing mattered to me then but the world of Henry and the world of our bodies was what I was thinking when I walked in front of my parents' bedroom window. I didn't care.

I started when I saw a little round glow of light. It was Ike standing there watching me through the window. The glowing red tip of his cigar flamed up as he took a drag off life.

part four

15

MILES EMMERETT'S LAW OFFICE BLED RED. MAROON walls supported a moose head and a five-point deer. Clubroom leather covered the furniture—riveted chairs and bolstery couches. Whenever I went there, I felt a twinge of guilt because I hadn't carried on the family law legacy. The smell of law books permeated his office like time ticking away, hours on end; it made me feel slightly ill. They depressed me somehow, reminded me of wasted and lost youth.

Miles sat slowly back in the big lawyer chair, his arms behind his gray head of hair. He was a long drink of water who wore a bow tie and white Stetson out of doors. His eyes shone like blue blown Chihuly glass.

His family was pioneer, came out from Salem, Massachusetts. Miles's ancestor had been tried for practicing witchcraft, and had died under a stone press. Instead of giving up his land, which would have saved his life, he suffocated with the words *more weight* on his lips.

"Iris," Miles said, leaning slowly forward in his lawyer chair. "Damn it," he added.

I smiled at him and gripped my mother's legal briefcase. She had inherited it from the colonel, a leather clutch tooled with the likeness of an eagle on both sides. Mother had chosen Miles as our attorney after she quit practicing. She'd picked him because the colonel had liked him, said he was the best lawyer in the state.

"I knew your father all my life, and there was no finer woman than your mother." He stared at a neat stack of papers on his desk blotter. "Good people. Hardworking sons a guns," he said, knitting his eyebrows. He touched the corners of the paper with gnarled fingers. "They're finally going ahead with it. They want the land back. The whole twenty-five hundred acres of Heart of the Beast."

"Who exactly is suing?"

Miles looked up suddenly. "It seems to be a band of Nez Perce that's behind it."

"I've never heard of a sovereign nation suing a U.S. citizen," I said.

"Happens all the time," he replied, wrinkling his nose as if he smelled something foul. "The tribes get into disputes, and they sue. They've been doing this for the fifty-two years I've been practicing law."

"It's just that Indians usually don't win," I said.

"Well, that used to be the case," Miles countered. "We're up against some pretty tough precedents." He looked at me intensely; two deep creases formed between his eyes. "I want you to know, there are a few things in this world that people will fight for. And land is one of them." He was starting to raise his voice. "I will do everything in my power to fight this suit."

"Thank you," I said, meeting his eyes. I shifted in my chair. Until they wanted my land, I had sided on everything with the Indians, and most of all with the Nez Perce. They were the ones who two hundred years ago had saved Lewis and Clark when they stumbled out of the Bitterroot Mountains starving and delirious. The Nez Perce gave them food, and horses, and gave Lewis a load of shit because he was ugly enough to have developed a taste for puppy meat. They knew one never ate beings as loyal and devoted as dogs. The Nez Perce were known amongst the whites as the most honorable of the Indians.

That was before the problems began with the homesteaders and the government. The resistance then started, which bled into the Trail of Tears. It was Sherman and Sheridan's idea to try to end the tribe and the trouble by sticking them on a swamp in Missouri. They wanted to kill Chief Joseph and the Oregon Nez Perce once and for all. What was left of the tribe dwindled from 400 to 150. This enraged me as a ten-year-old. My father and I had arguments at the dinner table. He gave me crap about how Indians are better off now.

There was no arguing with me because I had read *Bury My Heart at Wounded Knee*, in fourth grade. My brother gave it to me; it pleased Jake that we found something in common to hate Ike for. Reading it, a curtain lifted to the adult world. It made me realize that the planet is full of enemies, and I could be killed just as easily as the Indians were, say, because I was a girl born in China, Pakistan, or India. It was the way maybe a Jewish child in Hebrew class learns about the Holocaust. But a Jew living in Hitler's Poland had a better chance of survival than an Indian in America in the 1800s. The world is never the same after you learn certain things.

"The tribe is claiming your land was acquired illegally," Miles went on.

"What about statute of limitations?" I asked, remembering a few things from my mother. I needed her now, her sharp mind that never shut off.

"Well," Miles said, smiling at me. "There is one, 28 USC 2415. But this statute is for monetary damages and would not include land." I watched Miles's face, thin and long. He spoke drolly until he came to the punch line. Then he would whip out a document, or hold up the missing evidence and show a toothy Cheshire smile. At first he gave the impression he was inept, sort of like a southern senator; but like those southern senators, he'd come at you with a cannon instead of a slap on the wrist.

I liked that Miles appreciated my knowing something about the law. He probably imagined my mother and I had spent hours talking about her favorite cases. But we had talked about her career only once. She told me how she had successfully defended a man accused of committing rape. I never asked her about the law again because from what she told me, I knew that man had committed the crime. She did too, but she had gotten him off and was proud of it.

"This suit, Iris, is part of a larger movement. The restitution movement. Seems that's all Indians do anymore, legally. Seek restitution. I don't know if these tribes would exist if they didn't come together as victims. In this case, the tribe is trying to assert control of a vast amount of land and river systems. Among other things, they want to get rid of the dams. They say they're killing salmon."

I remembered reading how two hundred years ago the Nez Perce introduced Lewis and Clark to salmon. They didn't care for fish; they preferred red meat of any kind. "A lot of things are killing the fish," I said. "The drift nets off the coast, the Indians themselves. Gillnetting all the time, hauling salmon in just like the old canneries in The Dalles." When Jake, Henry, and I had boated on the river, sometimes we'd see the floating fish the Indians had neglected to retrieve from their nets. Of course, we surmised they'd been too drunk to tend their nets properly. The hell with them, I thought. They weren't meeting tribal needs; they sold it by the pound. Lewiston would be a dry dock if they breached those dams. I read in a wheat grower newsletter that over fifteen billion dollars of cargo barged through the Snake-Columbia system, and they just expected that to halt?

"They'll never get rid of those dams," I said. "Unless they get somebody to bomb them."

"That might happen," Miles said. "They got some crazy goddamned Luddites out in the world today. Twenty-four-hour armed patrols guard the dams of the Colorado. The Snake could be next."

I hugged my briefcase to my chest. The truth was, of course, they'd breach the dams. The farmers who used the river to barge their wheat didn't have much political clout. And that's what everything came down to. If the dams stayed it wouldn't be because of farmers, it would be because of the consumer complaints about the increase in power rates caused by the loss of the electricity.

"The tribe would pursue different tactics," Miles mused. "They're influential and have a lot of highly educated members. They're among the state's top ten political donors, have legislative liaisons in Washington, publicists. They've placed a petition to build a casino there, and they claim the casino profits will go to charitable organizations, schools, and museums all over the state. They appoint federal attorneys and state senators to be on their boards. Some of them are only a small part Nez Perce and are coming back to help with the return of the tribe." He ran his crooked hand over his wavy thick gray hair. "Of course you know the fastest growing minority group in the U.S. is Indian." He winked at me.

I smiled. "I guess I'll have to post No Trespassing signs. Once word gets out this is a sacred site, I'll have New Agers and groups of men coming on the place looking for sweat lodges." I wondered about giving the Nez Perce Heart of the Beast and whether I could receive a cut of the profits when the artisans showed up and started selling off bits of their culture and religion in the form of knickknacks.

Miles tightened his face and smiled back at me. "The thing is, this is about money and wealth and it's always been that way. It has nothing to do with preservation of nature." He leaned back in his chair. "The ecological Indian is a myth. When they killed buffalo, they ran them over cliffs by the thousands. Took only the tongues and fetuses. Fired the grass behind them as if that helped Mother Earth." He eyed his bookshelf. "Practically wiped the deer out of the South. Thought the blood of a dead deer begot live deer. Same for the beaver."

I squinted at Miles, thinking this information was a little farfetched, thinking he was one of those snoose-spitting revisionists. I wasn't surprised. There has never been multiculturalism in the West, there was only the big fat melting pot. The Indians were murdered. The Chinese came in, worked at the land and the barren mines that the whites threw away. The immigrants of Jewish heritage left their menorahs and yarmulkes back East if they were coming. The black cowboys stayed down in Texas except for a rodeo rider here and there. In our household, as in most of the ranching families, racism was commonplace. When my parents brought me home from the hospital, Jake took one look at the bruised newborn me and told my parents that I was dark. My father whipped him with a belt.

The Indians drove Ike a little crazy. It was as if all those dead siblings had come back to life and were getting all the things Ike never received. All of a sudden they had fish, casino money, land, and the right to do whatever they wanted on it.

It grated on me, too, them coming at me. "Why hasn't this been brought up earlier? Why now?" I asked, shaking my head.

"Their movement is simply gaining momentum. The crux of the issue in our case is how your great-grandfather obtained Heart of the Beast. Do you have the title?"

"No," I said, taking out a pen and yellow legal pad from the briefcase. "Once your letter came, I looked everywhere. I have wills, insurance policies, vehicle titles. But I don't have the title to Heart of the Beast."

"Because the Nez Perce must have a pretty good idea what that title says, or they wouldn't have brought this suit. This law allows for only the United States to extinguish Indian title to land. If the state or county or individual negotiated with the tribe for property and obtained it as a result, it would be a violation. Any land proven to have been taken in breach of this document will result in compensation to the tribe—sometimes to the tune of millions of dollars. There's been several cases where tribes back East have been successful with this tactic."

"If John Winter did buy it from the Nez Perce directly, what will happen to me?" I asked hesitantly.

"You'll probably be one ranch shy," Miles said grimly.

I wanted to laugh and cry at the same time. Letting go of my mother and her things was, on the one hand, what I wanted to do. But when it came down to it, I absolutely hated having things seized from me.

"So our job is to prove John Winter bought that land legally. I shall make a trip to the Union County Courthouse in La Grande. Wallowa County wasn't separated until 1887. The index book should have the deed records of Heart of the Beast. Handwritten and recorded. We shall see," he mumbled as he wrote a note.

I found myself leaning over the table to see what he was writing. His breath smelled bad: old and calcified.

"They'll probably also say that the laws in effect when the transfers took place were archaic. And they'll use the cultural heritage argument that the land is sacred to bolster their case, something like the Indians who sold property were taken advantage of, intimidated, coerced by the dominant culture." Miles turned to his filing cabinet. "Do you know of anyone at all who could support our case? That your great-grandfather acquired the land legally?" He spoke slowly, methodically shaking out a file.

"Who?" I asked incredulously. "Who is still around?"

"Well, it's difficult," he agreed.

"Maybe we could hold a séance and have a few ghosts show up for depositions," I said.

Miles looked up at me nervously and smiled. "Is that what you've been doing out there all alone?"

"Naw," I replied. "I don't need to hold a séance to see ghosts." I thought of Hanna walking around in her white shirt.

Miles paused, and then laughed again uncomfortably. "There aren't many who could remember back that far to establish that this was a reasonable transaction," he went on. "But we need something that will prove our case." He licked his finger and paged slowly through the file. "Can you think of anyone? Someone who had firsthand knowledge of the transaction. The historical society." He stopped paging and wrote his idea down. "Or an old city clerk," Miles said, writing again.

"No," I replied, thinking of every person I had done business with since my father had died. "Hanna mentioned something about John Winter buying things from the Indians."

A look of concern crossed Miles's face. "Hanna's with you?" he asked.

I nodded.

He started to say something and then stopped himself; he was careful about what he asked. "I shall speak to her by telephone, but I would advise you not to discuss Heart of the Beast." He furrowed his brow and thought a moment. "Besides," he added, "Hanna's memory can be discounted in court. They have to find something more substantial than a person who has been in a mental institution for thirty or so years. She's not credible for either side. I shall mention this when I speak with the attorney for the Nez Perce."

"I don't want to drag Hanna through anything," I said, dropping the briefcase on the gray carpet. I imagined lawyers grilling her on her electroshock therapy and her madness. "The Indians knew what they were doing," I said angrily. "They wanted the money. To buy booze. Buy horses. They're just like everyone else; they wanted fancy things and when a little money was waved under their noses, they gave in to it. It happens all the time. Still goes on. It's no revelation what happened here." I slapped my hand down on the yellow pad futilely.

"It's nothing personal, Iris," Miles said quietly.

"When someone wants to take your land away from you, it is extremely personal," I said.

"If it helps, I understand completely how you feel. It's infuriating. And it's a bad precedent. They want to do anything they please on their land. They want to become a true sovereign nation." His hands shook, from the exhaustion of having concentrated for so long.

I had a sinking feeling I was on the losing side of the battle. Miles could barely make it through a day's work, let alone see a trial through completion. "Sovereign nation," I scoffed. "What's that mean? They can put a nuclear waste dump on their land without consideration of anyone else? They can build an amphitheater for rock concerts and blast thousands of decibels without regard to any other community?" It was in the news everywhere how tribes in the Northwest and Midwest were trying to make money off their property however they wanted.

"Yes," said Miles. "That's what they think sovereignty means."

"They have another think coming."

"That's right," Miles chuckled. "Another think." He stood slowly up, walked to his liquor cabinet behind me, limping once. He poured himself a glass of whiskey. He held the bottle toward me.

Miles was worse off than I thought. I shook my head.

"What about documents?" he went on, slightly bent over and limping again as he returned to his desk. "Are there old letters from John Winter or any other written records about how he purchased the property?"

"I don't think so. I've been through most every building on the ranch. They kept all the old tractors, but not much paper." There was silence.

"Well, hell." He drew the words out into four syllables. "At least we have one thing on our side," Miles said slyly. "The federal court judge was appointed by Reagan."

"Conservative?" I said dully.

"Conservative," he replied, nodding with pride. "Reagan was the one who changed the national mood toward Indians. With Nixon, Ford, and Carter it was pretty sympathetic to the tribes. You know, living up to the rights and promises in the U.S. treaties. But back then they didn't want so much."

I nodded, hating that I was agreeing.

"But Reagan said— You know what Reagan said about the treaties, don't you?"

"No, I don't," I confessed. Aw hell, I thought. "What did my long-armed hero say?"

Miles's eyes bored into mine. "We've done too much already. We stole it from them fair and square."

I looked away from Miles to the animals on his walls and thought of the dream I'd had the night my mother died. The Nez Perce cut up and bloody, their children screaming and running to my house.

16

WINTER CAME EARLY THAT YEAR; THE TIME BETWEEN
the birth and death of days grew shorter rapidly with my mother's
absence. I prepared the cropland, as much as I was going to. I had fertilized the ground last spring, but it hadn't been weeded. There wasn't
much use for the rods when the drought killed even the thistles.

Every morning Carl met me in the machine shop at seven. We discussed what needed to be done with inertia grown from a hatred of
nature, and drank the bitter seeds of coffee. He shoveled wood into the
stove that barreled heat into the freezing cement-floored building.
Inside paraded a never-ending rotation of undone machines: the D-6
crawler blocked up and trackless while the bull gears were being
replaced; the Kenworth truck, its cab pulled and facedown toward the
oil-stained floor; the combine backed in and engineless, the motor still
dangling from the cast-iron hoist. Carl loved mechanicking and, like
my mother, he loved the winter.

Scotty Jamison arrived for coffee one morning. The three of us sat
staring at the furnace while we talked equipment. Scotty was solidly in
his late forties. He wore the same one-piece coveralls every day—and
the ad nauseam discussions about machinery made me think he was
much closer to old Carl's age than mine. I found myself looking at his
hands, gripping his thermos-top cup. His palms, stretched out and
elongated, looked disproportionate when he held delicate things like

cups of hot coffee. I couldn't get the idea out of my head that his hands looked like a chimp's. But those hands piped fabulously, and Scotty had brought his bagpipe with him.

He came again and again to our place. Arriving before dawn, he walked out on the land the way he did in Scotland. It was strange: my aunt working all day and night in the house, wearing her broken glasses with the black electrical tape, and a bagpiper skirling at dawn like a crazy rooster call. I told Hanna that she ought to go out and greet him, so I could get some peace as I ate breakfast.

One day he left the instrument sitting in a chair by the stove without asking me, as if he were marking territory. Every time I saw it, I wanted to take it out back of the shop with the rest of the junk that wasn't mine.

I didn't like it when the land froze up, but at least it gave me a break from the rigors of farming. Winter was time for vacations. It used to be, anyway. My mother and I took four of them after Ike died. She wanted to see the Taj Mahal, the Pyramids, Jerusalem, St. Peter's.

I also had the down-season jobs, painting the buildings, fixing the torn tin on the elevator, and rotating the wheat. This was work I loved because of the immediate gratification. I could start and finish something in one day. But mostly winter was a waiting game until spring, my favorite time. It was then I felt the sun in my feet, and I could get back in the fields again, plowing the harvested ground, preparing it for the following year's crop. Since Ike had died, we began rotating our fields for conservation, planting them every other year instead of annually. This was called summer fallowing, and I decided to do it because of the drought.

Carl and I talked about the weather, and why it wouldn't be a good time to start seeding the fallow. Too cold. Frozen. Too windy for the spray.

"Might have to think about spring seeding," he said, sipping out of his thermos cup.

"Ike didn't like to spring seed," I told him. "Never got much of a crop with spring wheat. Not as hardy as winter wheat." I was a young farmer, inexperienced, it was true. Like most of them, these last three years I generally followed what my father had done before he'd died. Of course that was dangerous, blindly following.

"It's getting late," Carl said, staring at the welding table. "Got to get the seeding done," he repeated.

I hated the waiting, the feeling I was losing things as the winter rolled along. "I guess we have no choice," I replied.

And then at eight o'clock exactly Carl stood up to spend the rest of his day with equipment: more transmission overhauls, housing replacements, welding rods on the weeders. I ventured out in the cold to the barn, looking at the land, barren and dry.

I fed the horses, threw them their hay on one side of the barn. Then I mixed the powder, a spoiled-egg-smelling concoction called calf manna, and fed it to the yearling's calf. I heated water in the tinned bucket until it was lukewarm and then shook in the milky mash that I mixed with my hands. It occurred to me, looking at the orphaned calf, she was the only child I would ever have.

I named her Midnight, and she came running for me when she smelled me but did not know what to do with herself. She stepped her hooves on my boots, the way kittens tread on the milk-ringed teats of a mama cat. She placed her head between my legs and butted up at my body. A creature like myself who had no natural instinct for doing something in the correct manner, she learned survival by force.

Midnight sucked on my middle finger, which I palmed to her. She would have starved, never realizing she wasn't getting food, but I squirted milk from the nipple at the bottom of the bucket into her nose. She pulled on the breast of the tin bucket too hard because she didn't know it was a gentle thing. To her it was a vicious business, and she tipped me off balance to get her neck in the best position for the manna to swish down her gullet.

Every day when I came in from the morning work, I sat down for Hanna, a Bloody Mary at my side.

"I'm almost ready to let you go," said Hanna. She continued to wear the same thing, a white shirt covered with reddish smudges of clay. Any variation of clothes must have been too threatening to her.

"Why aren't you doing my head like the rest of them?" I asked again.

"You needed to be whole," she said, touching her clay-covered fingers to her forehead. The tips of her white hair curled around a rolled blue paisley bandanna.

"How much longer?" I asked, hot and embarrassed. I realized, sitting there, I was envious of her—as crazy as she was, at least she was connected to something, not floating and severed like me.

"Until it takes over," she said, intensely smoothing the clay. The form appeared sloppy, spread out on the armature, an uncontained misshapen mass.

"What?" I asked.

"The pregnancy." She began whistling. I thought I detected a Chinese opera.

I realized Hanna thought she was pregnant with art instead of a baby, viewed the art as her baby. I tightened my stomach, which gravity was pulling toward the sheets and the door I was sitting on. "Pregnancy," I said, "is the most disgusting thing on this earth." I thought of the yearling giving birth to the calf. I looked at Hanna and shook my head, pregnant with something that wasn't a real baby. I realized then, I had felt nauseous since we started working on the sculpture of me. Maybe I was having sympathy pains for Hanna's creation; maybe it was something else. Really, I had been feeling sick talking to her about what happened in my family.

Hanna's blue eyes stared intensely at me. "The body moves in a forward direction, if you let it. If you are not too filled with envy, anger, jealousy." She listed each emotion as if she knew them as friends, as if she could recount both their faults and high points. I watched her perusing her art tools. "The body works to create," she said, picking out a fork and returning to the sculpture. "The trouble comes," she added, carving the clay delicately with the prongs, "when you can't stand what you're carrying." My house had been taken over by her production; clay dust covered everything. And her tools spread out, scrapers, clay pointers, carvers, bent wires, files, saws, pliers, paintbrushes, armatures, chipping tools, and triangular makeup applicators.

"Is that what happened to you?" I asked, thinking how odd she still was—believing she was pregnant, yet wearing her mannish outfit, the same thing every day.

"I was doing my parents," she said, waving her hand back to their heads and the rest of the sculptures in the green room. She sighed as she balled up clay and added it to my form.

The way she breathed soothed me, deep and long, like an endless and clear spring. Most springs I had seen were contaminated from the animals that had died in them.

"You are unhappy, the same way I was," she said, bending down to my sculpture, to me, and attaching clay, substance onto my being. She smoothed it with her thumb and turned the sculpture around on the lazy Susan to see the other side.

I shook my head. "There is no rhyme or reason to unhappiness," I said. "It's just life. It's human nature." I was getting more and more uncomfortable, frozen there while she sculpted.

"Human nature," she repeated, frowning. "Desire, impulses, unhappiness."

"I have to do some work this afternoon," I said suddenly as I broke out of my pose for a moment to take another drink.

Hanna looked up and watched me. "A life wasted is a life wasted," she stated. "It doesn't take thirty-one years in an institution to waste a life." She stepped back to her table and picked up a bamboo stick. Momentarily placing it next to the sculpture, she measured it with her thumb, and sawed it off at an angle.

"They found you going through garbage cans?" I said, feeling slightly defensive.

"The nothingness took over, the white light," she replied. "It's made of all the colors, but all you can see is pale, death-colored white. When I tried to make my family whole, make them fit together, everything fell apart, and I thought I was dying, too."

I remembered how I'd wanted to float in the cool water of the reservoir the night my mother died. I wondered why re-creating her family, instead of losing it, had sent Hanna over the edge. I took a drink and thought about the things humans do to survive—foraging in garbage, numbing the brain with alcohol. I recalled the insane things people had done that Henry had told me about from his rotation in the emergency room. But the alternative to crazy coping skills was certainly bleaker.

Hanna placed the bamboo in a base of clay and then made a bridge to the sculpture. I watched how she worked on my entire body; I wondered if Hanna thought she'd be complete if she made me whole this way. But still, I couldn't see anything recognizable as me in her project.

"We can stop now," she said, walking toward the kitchen and pulling off her bandanna. I sat up and began to put my clothes on. Though she didn't frighten me anymore, everything about Hanna was just plain odd. Like her skin. Of course it was of a seventy-year-old woman, but it looked like the skin of a woman in her forties. Maybe the lack of normal concerns somehow unburdened her countenance. Hanna didn't seem to need to talk either. Yet I found myself understanding her, and felt a small thrill, because the line between sanity and insanity was finer than I thought. At times, I could bridge it, at least with her.

Hanna returned with a piece of white cloth from the rag drawer. I recognized it as an old shirt of Elise's. She watered it down in the sink and carefully wrapped my clay in swaddling. Then she retrieved a clear plastic bag from her toolbox. Hanna dipped it in water and placed that around the sculpture too. "I'll work on it later," she said.

"It looks like it's incubating," I mused, pulling my socks up under my Levi's and shoving my feet into my boots.

"Takes time." Hanna walked back to the kitchen and placed a cup of water in the microwave for tea. While she waited, she picked up something and studied it, interested. It was my grandmother's watch, the only thing my father had left of his mother.

I looked out the window as I pulled on my coat. "I don't have much time." The wind had finally stopped. I realized for the first time I felt hopeful. It was spraying weather, with no wind; I could ready the land for the spring seeding. I heard the whine of a crop duster.

"Everyone has time," she replied. She pulled out her tea and looked momentarily into the cup and blew. "After all, what is it?" Hanna dangled the watch from its delicate thin gold band. She stared at it swinging back and forth.

I headed toward the door and looked back at her. "I don't know," I said. "What do you think time is?"

"It's only a measure of separation."

17

I couldn't stand sitting for Hanna. I felt I was doing something good and couldn't tolerate being good anymore. So I tore out of there to diesel up my machine. Four in the afternoon rolled over in the cab clock, a late start, and a vintage Ike maneuver. My father always began projects at the oddest hours and expected me to finish, even if it went on until midnight.

The D-6 was down at the Creek Ranch so I picked the Challenger. I grabbed the key and turned the engine over. I loved the smell and sound of a diesel engine. The motor roared the way a dragon might, snorting fire out of its nostrils.

Irritated, I stood there and finished dieseling the Cat. I was angriest at missing the opportunity to plant winter wheat. Carl was right, the only option left was to buy spring seed and hope for the best.

I hitched up the rod weeders and started out. As I was lowering the implement, I noticed the leak in the hydraulics. The oil sprayed like a gusher. For a woman, mechanicking is hard. That old saying about Ginger Rogers having to do everything that Fred Astaire did but backward applies here. Women have to be twice as smart as a man to figure out how to move the sheer weight and stubbornness of everything on the ranch. I owned all kinds of leverage implements and placed them in the cabs of each vehicle I drove: hollow steel tubes for wrenches to torque down on nuts that refused to release; WD-40, sledgehammers, widowmaker jacks, I used anything for an edge.

The one thing my father had supplied me by dying was new machinery, and it never broke down. But there were still the flat tires, the hydraulic hoses that leaked, the spray boom that wouldn't lower.

And it was a hydraulic hose that cold winter day that made me stop in the middle of the field with the 85 C Challenger. "You motherfucking sumbitch anyhow," I said, and crawled out of the cab.

That's when I saw the clouds coming over the Cascades like an army of blackened soldiers. Down on our southern border a blow had started. I scrambled back into the cab and throttled down, grabbing the binoculars. A great plume of dust rose from my field like a benevolent fire. I couldn't find any landmarks, not even the fence on the south side of the place. Nothing, until I realized I was looking at seeded ground, and then I saw Wade Runcid's great green Steiger charging up over my hill.

The worst part of it was that I was stuck out in the middle of the field, with the pickup back at the house, miles away. I looked again, spotting the canyon that I used for a marker as I swathed across the fields. He had seeded over everything. Seeded up the canyons over the conservation ditches that I had made to keep the rainwater from running off. I was on an indistinguishable piece of land now. I couldn't tell where my property started or ended, and Wade was still going, seeding slowly back and forth up toward the house.

I shut off the Challenger, stepped out of the cab, and walked toward the blow. I felt the kind of anger I imagined people did when they disappeared—the spontaneous combustions that happen in India, the subcontinent of overwhelming rage. The wind started up again. It snapped my clothes. I crushed the top of each furrow, sinking into the ground like my feet were branding irons melting flesh.

It took about thirty minutes to get across the field, and I became angrier with each stride. I heard the Steiger louder and louder as I walked up to where he'd come back for the next pass. I stayed there seething, in his path. The top of the tractor came slowly up over the hill. I heard that old engine lugging down as it pulled the drills. I stood there in his way with my arms crossed, and he came on like a locomotive. I waited for him to slow up and ease out of the pull, but he kept coming right at me. Suddenly, he shut the throttle down and hit the clutch at the same time. Then he turned it off.

"Shit," I hollered at him. "You don't even know how to run a fucking tractor." I could see it was Wade. He looked more wizened than ever, covered with the dust of seeding. I remembered when I was little he used to give me silver dollars and tell me he would pray for me. My father always told me to bite on them to make sure they weren't one of those fake chocolate candies. Really, the worst of the worst were the pious crooks.

We stayed there looking at each other. I knew he wanted me to acquiesce. He was trying to pull age rank on me so I would walk up to his cab, and he wouldn't have to get out. I remained planted where I was and said, "You get down here, you fucking old man."

He took his own sweet time, but he knew he had to come to me. I was surprised, actually, that it was old Wade himself. He usually sent one of his sons, Roy or Marvin, to do his henchwork. The children in that family ran amok; last year Marvin's son attacked the Hatzapple kid at school. Pulled out a sawed-off shotgun he stole from his father and told Hatzapple, "I'll give you five seconds to tell me one good reason not to kill you." The poor kid couldn't think of one good reason, so Marvin's son became a convicted murderer and lived at the boys' correctional facility in Portland.

Wade climbed down out of his Steiger, after taking a large drink from his Coleman. He walked toward me limping, exaggerating the pain from sitting in the tractor for so long.

"I just got to thinking," he said, shuffling up to me. "You not getting your seeding done on time and all. I thought maybe something might work out for the both of us. If I helped you out. I figured I could farm this piece for a bit. You wouldn't have to pay me anything. I'd just take the grain off the land and call it fair."

"Sure you did, Runcid," I hissed at him. "What in the hell gave you the idea that you could trespass on my property? Bring your tractor, a goddamned piece of shit, wheel tractor," I cracked, slapping the back of my hand on my palm. "Powder up my land, trying to seed it." I glared at him. "When it's bone dry, and winter. And then say you want to take the crop?" I was incredulous.

"I thought I was helping you out," he replied sweetly.

"The hell you were. Tearing out my fence. Trying to steal my land." He didn't think he would be caught until it was too late and the field had been seeded.

"Tell me what you really think?" he said slyly.

My father had warned me well about the Runcids. He warned me about slander. Ike had caught Wade in a water meeting secretly taping him, hoping my father's temper would boil, and he could trap him in defamation. Wade Runcid was a conniving little fucker.

"Get off my property," I ordered. I walked over to his seeders and pulled a length of barbed wire off them where they caught on my fence.

"What about remuneration?" he asked innocently as he followed behind me. "You couldn't get it done. It had to be done. So, I did it for you. The going rate for seeding is a hundred an acre."

"It is my land," I screamed. "If I want to pave it and have a fucking chess tournament on it, it's my own damned business."

He paused a minute, looking at the earth. "You know," he said slowly, as if starting on a long oration, "your grandfather is the one who gave me the idea I ought to help you. He used to work his neighbors' land when they needed it. Your father would have done the same thing for my sons. You're too young to remember."

"I remember it," I said. "My grandfather worked his neighbors' land for free. He never expected anything back for having done it. Not land, not money, nothing." I came close to that old man so I could smell the snoose on his breath. "He did it for free because he didn't like to see his neighbors suffer. That was the way things used to be before you agribusiness assholes fell off the turnip truck in our neighborhood." I turned on my heel and walked, branding the furrows again as I strode. "By the way," I said, spinning around, raising the barbed wire to him. "You will replace the fence. Right, neighbor?"

He didn't look at me when I spoke to him, but his shoulders hunched up a little higher than they already were.

That night the dogs started barking. Coyotes, I surmised. I walked back toward my room and noticed my sculpture was turned from lying on its side to standing up. Hanna had placed the barbed wire I had taken from Wade's seeders around it. The sculpture was stretched and bound, like Michelangelo's slave that Napoleon stole from Italy. Hanna was working late into the night now, as if in a hurry to finish and leave here for good.

"Looks like hell," I told her. I stared at the sculpture of me, small, weak, and violent-looking. I studied it closely. Despite myself, I began smiling. Hanna had captured exactly how I'd been feeling since the trouble had begun with Heart of the Beast.

My appearance depressed me, and I carefully pulled the barbs from the carving. I stared at what remained. A pattern of welts and pocks stamped the earth-colored clay. I felt like crying.

I couldn't go to sleep after that; I wondered how I was ever going to liberate my life. I listened to my brother's CDs, went through my mother's files searching for the title to Heart of the Beast, and avoided the liquor cabinet. I found taxes and savings accounts, but nothing else. Springsteen was singing "The River." To my brother and me, music was the closest thing to love and nirvana.

It was around eleven that night when the knock on the door came. The Border collies barked crazily once more. "Shut up," I told them, moving them to their den with my hard stare. The cattle dogs, the eye watchers, their light blue eyes locked on mine now because everyone else was gone.

Ace growled again. "Goddammit, Ace," I said. He looked at me, and I pointed at their den under the TV table. My father's ashtray, made of the bottom of a World War II missile shell, still rested there. I couldn't bring myself to clean the cigar ashes out.

I opened up the thick green door. It was Roy, Wade's younger son, dressed up in a white plaid western yoked shirt with pearly snaps. I wanted to chew him up and spew him out.

"Sorry about my dad," Roy said. He had his cowboy hat in one hand and carried a casserole dish in the other. It was green with white daisies and had a matching white lid. "He gets it in his head something needs to be done and he takes it upon himself to do it." He paused, studying my face. "I brought you some dinner."

I noticed he cradled the casserole the way he might a baby. I didn't throw him out immediately. "Thank you," I said, taking the casserole and opening it up. Meat loaf.

"I cooked it myself. Our own beef," he added hopefully.

I stood there regarding Roy. I thought about the loaded pistol in my bedroom, and my brother's rifle in my closet. I started to tell him to get lost, and then I laughed. I flung the door wide with my shoulder. "Want some?" I said.

"I thought you'd never ask," he replied, smiling. He teeth glowed there where he had a slight overbite. He followed me to the kitchen and slumped down into the chair at the counter. He slapped out a snappy eight-beat tune as he waited for the grub. I doubted he was hungry for food.

"Want a beer?" I said.

He gave me a big smile. Apparently I was speaking his language. "You got Oly?" he asked hopefully.

I shook my head. "Bud."

"Thas all right." He stood up and looked like he was getting ready to say something. He reached down and pulled up his Levi's by the thick leather belt, one hand in front and one hand in back.

I walked around and gave him the beer.

"I can open this with my teeth," he said.

"No," I replied. "You cannot," and I hit him on the shoulder. I hit him hard. It caught him off guard, and he looked alarmed for a minute. Suddenly he smiled, and I thought he was going to hit me back, but he shrugged instead. "See for yourself."

He placed the bottle to the side of his mouth and looked at the floor, concentrating. I heard the hiss of air escaping the bottle. Roy raised his head to look at me, the beer cap in his mouth. He smiled, and his teeth sparkled, except for the dark one in the middle. I watched his oil-stained fingers take the beer cap away. He said, "I've wanted to make love to you since the moment I saw you."

He lunged at me with his tongue, and he placed his hand on my breast. I just stood there, curious to see what would happen. He jerked, and he sweated as he touched me. I imagined making love with Roy would be something like a bull running at a cow in breeding season, knocking her to her knees. His thin lips felt like an empty glass placed over my mouth, and I knew Roy was as vacant as his father. The sight of Roy somehow made me miss Henry so much I started tearing up a little.

It took Roy a while to realize I wasn't responding to his lovemaking, and he pulled back and looked at me, probably mistaking the tears for frigidity. Some men in eastern Oregon thought frigidity was a disease as common in women as pinkeye was in cattle. Word was Roy had raped Jeanette Lightner in high school. She called the police when she returned home, and they went round Roy's house to investigate. She was having her period at the time, blood all over the damn place. Enough evidence to convict, but Jeanette's father made her drop the charges.

"Aw," Roy said. "Ain't no way things so bad."

He had no idea.

"You know what I think," he went on, reaching for his beer. He tried to keep watching me as he grasped, and he knocked the bottle over.

"Better not think too much, Roy," I said, wiping the beer off the floor, throwing the rag into the stainless sink.

"It could be a good life," he allowed, finally giving up his coquetry. He looked into my eyes and grabbed my shoulders as I came up. "It won't feel like you've just settled for long. We'd have more money 'n Roosevelt. And then that empty feeling will be filled up with something else. Something everyone in the county will be pantin' over."

"Tell me about it, Roy. The just settling part. Because I think that idea's about as interesting as a blunt, dry turd."

"I've learned to make compromises," he responded in a serious tone. "We could help you out," he went on, moving his body in toward mine. "A great deal."

"I could live a lifetime without the help I got today."

"My father an' me, we're set up pretty good," he said, blue eyes sparkling. "But we need more equipment." He paused bashfully. "And land. You could come up with that. See. This's the era of agribusiness. We're taking over. And then the only thing left to do would be to get the government off our backs."

To some farmers, especially the likes of the Runcids, women and the government were whores you occasionally had to fuck when you were desperate.

"You sign up for the program this year?" I asked casually. The farm program was a lifeline to family farmers when the wheat price was down around two dollars a bushel. I went to the kitchen, sliced the meat loaf, and slapped it on a paper plate.

"Shit, yeah," Roy said. "Last year, we even made more money than the Indians."

I handed him a fork.

He sighed wistfully, picking it up.

I shoved the ground beef in his direction.

"My daddy an' me got ourselves three different corporations, one in my name, one in my dad's name, and one in the ranch's name. We signed up three times."

"Sounds like a good deal then, agribusiness," I told him, opening the refrigerator. "You get the discounts from the co-op on fuel, fertilizer, chemical. You sign up for the government programs three times. You take over the family farms."

When I turned around, Roy stood there with his Levi's down. He pulled his penis out from his tight whites. It was pointing straight at me, and was big. Catherine the Great big. "It's a good deal," he said. His head was to the side, and he wore a relaxed smile on his face as if he was already imagining me sucking on his dick. "You interested?"

"Maybe," I replied, pulling the ketchup out and banging it loudly on the counter.

I saw Roy jump out of the corner of my eye. "Think about it, would you?" he said.

"I will," I told him enthusiastically. I felt a little masochistic, like the sculpture showed.

"I mean really think about it," he stated again.

"Okay," I replied, smiling.

"Well." He said it *way ell*. "I better be going after all. Fish aren't biting." And then he made like a grouper with his mouth as he pulled himself in. "Don't look like I'm gonna get you to smoke my pole. Not tonight anyway." He smiled at me and winked.

I started toward the door to show him out.

He couldn't help himself. "What year is that axial flow and that Challenger?" he asked, following me.

"Bought them two years ago," I said, opening the door for him.

"Mind if I kiss you?" he whispered.

"Mind if I kill you?" I replied.

Roy did a double take. And then he pretended to pull a stray hair from my chin. I knew Roy would always find his way. "Oh, by the way," he added. "What are you going to do with that land out there? That yours, or your aunt's? You going to leave it fallow this year?"

"Half of it's mine," I said. "The other half might belong to some Indians."

"Eeuw," mouthed Roy. He wrinkled up his face.

"Still interested," I asked sweetly, "in working for Indians?" I shut the door in his face.

Afterward, I finished looking through my mother's taxes. It was another hour or so when the dogs started barking again. I went to the door and opened it; there was no one. The dogs wouldn't quiet down, so I walked to my closet for my brother's rifle. I stood out there on the back porch, aimed at the stars, and pulled the trigger. The noise echoed down to the river and back, and then there was silence.

18

Jake RETURNED HOME THE OPENING DAY OF THE FALL HUNT-
ing season, a full four years after he left us. Smoke cluttered the air and
the deer heads returned. The nearing of the hunting season always
meant carnage around the ranch. I never knew where I was going to
find it—poking around behind the shop or shed for extra hydraulic
hose or chain. I hated that aspect of fall, couldn't stand being surprised
by a bloody piece of animal.

The dogs' dragging game remains back to the ranch was the cause
of the problem. With their noses that smelled for miles, they were
always searching for things like deer skulls discarded by poachers.
Those were the worst—I knew the head was cut off because it was a
female not a buck. The fur still clung to the bone, matted into clumps
of black drips around the empty eye holes and severed neck, where the
dogs had mauled it trying to get licks of gristle.

Sometimes I encountered whole body parts when I searched the
side of the combine shed for equipment. It was usually some length of
a leg or a whole hindquarter hidden in a tuft of grass where Ace had
tried to bury it. I began to approach things cautiously, expecting to find
something bloody and broken.

After Jake left, Mother began to disappear, and her rituals of cleaning everything with pure ammonia began, as if the chemical would kill
the mess that thrived at our house. More and more she lay in her bed

dead tired but with the shades drawn up in full daylight. Her arm was slung over her eyes as if she were warding off the sun with her dagger-like elbow.

Dinners at our place were grim. Mother cooked food for Ike, Henry, and me as if it were killing her to do it. She watched us with disgust, especially when Henry and I ate together. The ranch kitchen was set up so that Mother stayed in it during dinner, theoretically so she could hash for the crews. But the room was more like a life vest that surrounded her. Everything she needed was barely an arm's reach away. Most of all I think she liked it because from that vantage point she could observe us. The way she sat there, eyes squinted, it was as if she were watching us have sex.

We sat along the long, low counter, eating elbow to elbow, never looking at one another. We used to sit Ike, Jake, and then me. Now, in the summers and early fall before school, it was Ike, me, and then Henry. All I could think about was how I felt we were like greedy pigs, sucking her dry. I read in a magazine somewhere that adolescents who have started with sexual relations have trouble eating. I don't know if that was it, or whether I just felt my mother was poisoning me. But whenever I ate her food, I saw the deer heads.

Ike replaced any talk of Jake with a new preoccupation. In the middle of the Columbia River, there at the great bend that leads it home to our house, he purchased an island. It was Ike's idea of a perfect cattle pasture, with the impenetrable fences of the Columbia. He began looking for something to float those cattle over and started stalking army surplus auctions searching for the exact right vehicle. He flew to Bremerton, Portland, and San Francisco looking for an LVT. It was an amphibious landing craft, the kind he had used in the marines to capture Okinawa.

That summer when Ike was off with his island, Henry and I essentially lived together. We had grown inseparable in the three years Jake had been gone. In the summers we worked together—Ike needed Henry even more since my brother left. During school, we saw each other every weekend.

We had brought in the harvest ourselves. I filled Henry's wheat trucks until the springs creaked and watched his dust as he carried the bounty home. Harvest had stretched into September, and Henry and I worked from five in the morning until dark. In only three days we would be leaving again for school—I, for junior year abroad, and Henry for med school in Portland. I was excited and sad at the same time about our departure. We would pack up our things in his mismatched bags and drive the Gorge down to the valley away from the security of home.

That weekend, the opening of hunting season, Ike and Elise were leaving the ranch to go to a bar association function. Hunting season didn't impress Ike. He didn't need a season to kill. I told them that Henry and I would stay home and kick the poachers off. Frustration at poachers always made me want to shoot things, a perfect feeling for the first day of hunting season. People from hundreds of miles away trespassed on our property; they flocked there with hunting fever, and somebody needed to patrol it.

"The hell you will," said Ike. "Henry can get his ass back to his father's while I'm gone. I'm not leaving you two alone together." His jaw muscle bulged as he set it into a hard line, and his eyes narrowed. I imagine he envisioned us doing exactly what we were doing. With Henry living at our bunkhouse, Ike gone most of the time, and Elise disappearing after sundown, no one noticed my absence.

"Fine," I said like a doormat, knowing full well Henry would leave and come back. That night I called Jake at the reservation. I stood out in the shop where the second telephone was, hoping Ike and Elise wouldn't happen to pick up the main phone in the house.

"I thought you might like to come back," I said. "Come back to hunt."

"Maybe," replied Jake. "Is the asshole going to be gone?" He sounded near enough to be in the next room. Though Jake hadn't been home in four years, I'd seen him once or twice a year. The three of us would go out to dinner in Portland. Jake was always alone, never brought Kappy, said she was going to school.

"They'll be gone," I told him.

"How are they treating you?"

"Usual."

"Still harvesting?"

"Just finished."

"Is Henry there?" he asked.

"Yeah," I replied.

"Get him," he said.

Henry was shooting baskets at the far end of the shop where years earlier he and Jake had bolted a hoop. The smashes of the bounces echoed through the cement floor up into the three-story rafters.

Jake asked Henry about his med school at OHSU. Then they talked basketball. It always amazed me how much men could talk about sports. Instead of the proper question, "Are you still fucking my sister?" I imagined Jake asked, "How're the Beavers looking this year?"

"Good enough to kick the Ducks' butt in the civil war," said Henry. He laughed at Jake's response, and then I heard him say, "See you Saturday."

The opening day of hunting season was the start of an obsession. All manner of campers, beat-up pickups, and Winnebagos descended upon us. People came from the big cities driving vehicles used only once a year for this purpose, and breakdowns littered the interstate.

Everyone in the county, including us, sped around from dawn until dusk. We slung bota bags of Jack Daniel's around our necks, tossed rifles over our shoulders, and emerged like warriors and thieves. Many times Jake, Henry, and I had hunted the Creek Ranch, where brush flourished for the deer to hide and feed.

Usually I dropped Henry and Jake off in the canyons to walk the hills. Jake was most likely to get the kill. Henry was the cleaner; he carved up their carcasses, studying the blood and bone of the wild. I patrolled down the creek road, moving people along who stopped to take a free potshot. It was the neighbors, especially, who weren't above poaching.

That fall afternoon, Jake drove into the ranch in a silver Dodge with a ram's head hood ornament. It annoyed me that he was late. I had asked him to arrive at seven in the morning, otherwise the deer would already be hiding out. I observed his gun racks mounted behind the seat, and saw that he had another person with him, a little girl. She looked to be about three or four years old.

"She likes animals" was all Jake said, walking quickly around to the passenger side of the pickup. He fished her out with one arm and held her there, looking at me. Curly black hair framed her round, cherublike face, and she wore a zookeeper's outfit with a badge that read San Diego Zoo. I noticed a miniature horse in her round fingers.

Children bothered me. In fact, I loathed them. This kid wasn't as bad as most, I decided. In fact, she wasn't bad at all, because she was older. It was more babies that made me sick. The way their mouths always slobbered, sucked, and revolved around something. The bald heads, the staring at people, having to have attention, crying for no apparent reason. It made me want to throw them against a wall. No wonder Elise had kept me in a pen until I was two.

"This is Tansy," Jake said.

Tansy dropped the horse, and despite myself I picked it up for her. She reached for it but missed, and it dropped again. Women and children never worked out.

Jake whistled. He sounded just like Ike, turning his tongue to reeds while an enormous black dog lunged out of the truckbed. Knots of flesh swung on its legs like flabby testicles. Its muzzle grew deformed and angular just like its geometric ears. It ducked its head down as if embarrassed by the sight of itself. Jake whistled again, and the dog turned its massive skull up to him. Its eyes smoldered like yellow fires, and its tail snaked around, slapping the sky.

"Whoa," said Henry. "Where'd you get the horse?"

"Reservation," Jake replied over his shoulder as he started down to the corral with Tansy. Suddenly my brother broke into a run. Tansy's hair blew back and I heard her laugh. I could tell she liked adventure, just like her father. He carried Tansy straight to the corral, leaving Henry and me standing at the pickup. "When are Elise and Ike coming back?" he yelled again over his shoulder.

"Tomorrow," I hollered back as he reached the corral. The dog barked at the horses outside the fence. It pawed the ground and placed its head under the lower railing, because it was too big to crawl under the big gate that let the hay trucks in. It barked again, with the look of a chaser. I didn't like it.

I walked down there quickly, with the irritation that came with my proprietary interest. I was the one who fed the horses, took care of them, and rode them. I didn't want my brother, his dog, or a kid down there messing with my stuff. I really loathed the way kids took over things. They never had any boundaries. They acted like they needed help when they were really invaders.

Jade lay down, curled and dozing. Her massive black tail covered the dust of the corral in drapes and swings, her black forelegs rounded together under her upright head. She had dreamy cat-iron eyes. Her obsidian hooves twisted around her were arrowheads pointing at her heart.

Jake walked in the gate, letting the dog in.

"Goddammit, Jake," I said. "Tie that thing up, for Jesus' sake."

It ran straight at my horse, rasping that mammoth echoing bark. Jade scrambled up, stretching her black forelegs in front of her, heaving herself to her feet. The dog orbited the four horses, moving them into a corner.

"Get that fucking dog out of there," I repeated. The sound of Ace and Dusty barking up in the house followed us down to the corral. Jake whistled and tried to call the dog back. I picked up some rocks, big enough to hurt, and hurled them hard straight at him. Rock throwing was a skill I had honed from chasing cattle. I hit him in the rib, then he was gone. He took off through a hole in the fence where Revolution the bull had once smashed through. The dog disappeared, loping around the ranch sniffing at the corners of buildings, tarps, and traces of jackrabbits.

Henry climbed the fence and sat on the wide plank top built for the observation of horse breaking and cattle cutting. Jake worked his way up to Jade. She was always pushed out by the other horses to face the humans because she was the tamest. She stood facing him. The blowing of her nostrils sounded like an intense and violent snore.

The minute Tansy saw Jade, she raised her hand. It was obvious she would not be satisfied with anything less than being seriously involved with this horse. The other horses milled around behind Jade the way wild horses do. "This is Jade," I heard Jake say. Tansy stroked her on the broad slope of her nose. I noticed she did not pat. Horses hated being patted on their faces.

I crossed my arms and hung back, kicking at a puncture weed. The sun was drawing the cold out of the air as it passed the prime of afternoon. It wouldn't be much of a hunting day, since we hadn't gotten up at dawn. The deer would be hiding out. It didn't take them long to know that the hunting season was on, about as long as it took to shoot one bullet at them. They fled over the hills in herds bounding with the smoothness of running horses. Then the bucks tore out, hiding with one another, usually an old one paired up with a young one as if to impart knowledge like a father to a son.

Jake and Tansy moved to the side of my horse, and Tansy petted the barrel of her belly. Jake talked low and soft to Jade. I thought I heard him call her Jadey. It surprised me that he talked so sweetly. All his life the horses had persecuted him, especially when he hauled hay for them. He usually called them the shitters because he said that's all they did, eat and shit.

"Careful," I warned.

It happened so quickly. Before I knew it, Jake hoisted Tansy atop Jade. She sat there, petting the fur on Jade's withers, smiling and breathless. I imagined the way her heart was pumping with the joy of living, just the way it had been for me when I sat on a horse for the first time. I started down to the tack room for a halter and grain so Jake could lead Jade and Tansy around the corral. I heard the faint sound of a car out on Baseline Road.

"What are you going to give me for letting the kid ride my horse?" I asked, turning around.

"A swift kick in the ass," he said.

"Yeah?" I replied. "That's what I ought to give you for leavin'."

In the tack room I placed a can full of grain in the thick plastic green bucket and grabbed Jade's halter. When I returned, I saw Henry jump down and walk quickly toward Jake. Jade had gotten away from my brother and was amongst the other horses now, milling in the agitated dance of the wild horse. Tansy still sat on top of her with both hands in Jade's neck, fists full of black mane. Remley was the only other horse that was tame. The other two I culled from the Nez Perce herd just as I had Jade six years before. I had naively hoped to have the time to break them this summer.

The herd instinct took over. The horses milled about and looked suspiciously at us. Every time we inched near them to try to get Tansy off, they wheeled as if they were circus horses and headed the other direction. They ducked their heads amongst one another and took turns moving into the middle of the pack. Tansy, with her black curls and round face, had fear full up in those startled eyes. She was concentrating on Jade, watching out for the snaking heads and rubbing shoulders of the other horses. I noticed she never cried, she never even once whined.

"Get her off," I said.

"She'll be all right," said Jake.

The horses continued to mill around one another.

"No, Jake. Get her off the horse," I said, anxiously.

The wild ones attempted to break out of the herd and run to the other end of the corral.

"What will you give me if I get her off?" he asked, mocking.

"I'll give you a ticket off of this goddamned place."

The black dog appeared in the corral again, his tongue hanging down and those yellow eyes glowing with intensity. He began stalking the horses, trotting with his head down.

"Beat it," I yelled. I ran at him, swinging the bucket to divide him from the horses. He dove at the black points of their hocks, and they bolted, running the perimeter of the fence. The wild horses, the leopard Appaloosas, Aerie and Banner, ran first with the instinct of survival guiding them. Jade and Remley followed.

"Tansy," Jake said.

She nodded.

"Oh, so finally," I yelled.

"Grab on to the fence, honey, if you get close enough," Jake went on calmly.

What an idiot, I thought, acting like she's on a goddamned swing. "Come here, Jadey," I cajoled. I shook the bucket of grain at her a little too nervously, while I held out a handful.

Tansy crouched down, still hanging on to Jade. She brought her legs up as if she were in a fetal position. She started singing. I could hear it faintly at first. The dog was still barking unceasingly. It had beaten us to the far corner of the corral where the horses had stopped their charge.

When I heard the corral gate close, I felt as if iodine had been injected in my veins. I turned to see Ike walk into the corral. As the hunting season started, Ike always carried a pistol strapped to his thigh. He was wearing new Levi's; the dark blue glared pure against the dusted things that belonged to the ranch. The pistol was in his hand.

Ike looked at Tansy, taking in her dark skin and intense expression. The dog remained barking crazily at the violently milling horses. Jake held his hands out to his sides in that crucified stance, trying to stop the horses from making another break for it. But of course they did anyway. It was Remley that bolted straight at Jake, between him and the fence. The rest of them followed, and Tansy was obscured by the powdered dust that rose from the favorite rolling spot of the horses. The grit of the land turned everything to dullness and darkness except the dog, which followed the horses excitedly, slobbering as it barked.

The gunshot shattered everything. I heard a scream. Dust mushroomed from the running horses. I ran forward, but I couldn't see anything. I felt I was drowning. The yelp of the dog broke the silence, and I saw it tear out of the dust and go down. It didn't die like a cat. Cats jump when they die; they roll and writhe, trying to claw the hell out of what it was that killed them even if it was the rubber of a tire. The dog just fell, and where cats are silent, the dog howled.

We all froze. Even the horses, blowing now and snorting, turned to face the gun. Ike walked over to the dog and put his foot on its neck. It kept howling through the tread on its windpipe. Without looking up, Ike said to Jake, "Who is that on the horse?"

Jake turned around slowly. "My daughter," he said. There was silence.

I had the feeling Jake had longed to say this. He had waited his entire life to do this to his father, just as Ike had done to the colonel.

Ike scowled at the girl, again taking in her dark skin, eyes, and hair. Then he looked back at the dog. He aimed the pistol at its head. "Get off my property," he said. "You are no longer family. You are a trespasser." Ike pulled the trigger, and the dog was silent.

The little girl screamed when the dog died. The horses jumped and started to run again. Her concentration momentarily distracted, she fell in the middle of the herd. Jade froze, and I yelled, "Stop, you goddamn son of a bitch" at Remley. He threw up his head, planted his feet, and nastiness poured out from his nostrils and eyes.

Jake ran in there and pulled Tansy up to him. She still wasn't crying. When I fell off horses as a child, I bawled my eyes out, and I wanted revenge. Dust streaked Jake's cheeks where tears were running down his face. I had never seen my brother cry. He stopped in front of me, setting his daughter down by his legs. She looked bewildered, baffled. I knew she must be hurting from the fall, but she never let on.

"You take her," he told me.

"What?" I asked.

"You take her with you," he said. He spat the words out one at a time, overenunciating, practically beating me with them.

I looked at him and then at his daughter.

"Tell Mother to meet me down at the Creek," he said. "Tell her it's the spot where we used to go fishing." He walked past his father still standing with his boot on the dog. When he reached the gate, he opened it and turned around. He looked at Ike, and my father returned his stare. Jake saluted Ike, but at the same time he smiled a one-sided smile and narrowed his eyes through his tears. As his hand finished the salute, it loosened into something like a dismissal. Then Jake walked to his pickup; he pulled his rifle out of the racks and set it beside him. He drove off, leaving dust and wind in his wake.

19

Tansy's head swayed below me. She turned to observe her father walk away, studied him until he was out of sight. I watched her look to the horses and then down at the ground, avoiding the dead dog.

I became nervous, wondering if she might start to cry. I thought I might. Tansy reached up with the back of her hand and brushed the hair out of her eyes. I did the same thing, looking up to the sun to burn my eyes so I could feel some physical pain. I looked down at Tansy, and when that soft purple spot that appears after you've burned your eyes good and hard disappeared, what I saw shocked me. She reached up to me. She didn't grab at me, she held her hand up and open as if she were searching for a rope to climb out of there with. And she waited. She waited for me to grab hold, too.

So I did. I gave her my whole hand, but it was too big, and she settled on gripping my middle and index fingers. I held on with my thumb, and that was how we worked it. I know something black in me died a little when I grabbed hold of her.

"You might want to go with Mother," I said to Henry. "In case you need to help calm him down."

"All right," Henry answered, walking up to us. He entered our circle, not liking to be cast out and alone with the ugliness of it all. I could tell he wanted to touch us as he stood there. He looked back and forth to me and then Tansy. But he kept his arms to his sides, as if he knew the sole purpose of Ike's violence was to isolate everyone.

Ike turned and strode out of the corral. He looked straight ahead as he left, slamming the lock bar of the gate so hard, splinters must have jabbed into his hand.

"Then I'll drag that thing down to the canyon," Henry said. "God, it stinks."

I didn't smell anything but dust.

"At least I've finished anatomy," cracked Henry, his blue eyes blinking rapidly. "No more dead dog dissection." His T-shirt hung untucked over his Levi's. One of Jake's Pendleton plaids was tied at his waist for the cool evening hours of hunting season.

I looked at Henry and smiled faintly. I wondered if somehow he thought his job was to drag away the dead, to cover them up and set the world right again. I thought deep down that was why he wanted to become a physician, to drag away death with a cure.

"I'll get Elise," he said, ordering himself around. "Then the dog." Henry walked past us toward the house.

I heard the thunder of the plane as Ike took off.

I expected Tansy to start that whiny cry, as little kids do when their mothers leave the room. But she didn't. Tansy wanted to walk; she didn't want to be carried. Her small tennis shoes negotiated the piles of cattle and horse manure and the weeds the horses wouldn't eat. It was clear to me that I was leading her somewhere else. Anywhere. She stopped before we reached the corral gate, and pointed back at the horses. They were still standing in the corner. She looked at me, and then back to the animals.

I called my horse. I pulled some wheat grass through the fence and held it out. Jade started forward, her head down, a slow and lumbering walk up the slight hill to the gate where we stood. I gave the stems to Tansy; she held them in her free hand since she still had not let go of me. Jade stopped short, stretching her head and neck as far as she could without coming a step closer.

"Come on, Jade," I said. "Get up here." She moved one of those ebony hooves closer, grabbed the grass, and nodded her head as she chewed. Jade took another step closer, sniffing at the tininess of Tansy, looking for more grass. "She didn't mean to hurt you," I said. "You'll have to get back up on her someday." Since I was Tansy's age, that was what I loved most about the horses. They never held a grudge if you fell, or were bucked off; you just jumped back on and tried it again. They didn't operate on revenge, the way we did.

Tansy let go of my hand, stood unsteadily for a moment, and then walked slowly toward Jade. She didn't even come up to Jade's wide chest. I thought about warning her to stand to the side, to be careful of Jade's teeth and her hooves, but I just stood there mute. She began to pet Jade on the forearms, at the place where the blue roan color disappeared into her shiny black stockings. She moved up to her chest, stroking the place where her heart pumped red into her blue body. Jade reached her nose down to the ground and snorted, blowing the corral dust. Tansy stood next to her, now stroking her neck where she could reach it.

"That's what a good horsewoman does," I said. "She gets back on the horse. And you are a good horsewoman. I could see it in the way you sat her."

Tansy's hand was now on Jade's leg again. She squinted and brushed her hair out of her face with the back of her fingers. Tansy wasn't a talker. She fit perfectly with our family, I decided. I didn't know how much she understood of adult language, but I gave her the benefit of the doubt.

"You must have inherited it," I told her. "Someone in your family must have loved horses."

Tansy continued petting Jade's legs.

"I got it from your great-grandfather," I went on. "I used to ride my first pony for him, Fortune. He would sit up on this fence right here, with his cowboy hat on, and watch me ride for hours."

Tansy looked at me and opened both hands up to the sky that was full of Jade's back. I grabbed a piece of black baling twine wrapped on the gate and looped it around Jade's neck. I lifted Tansy onto her once more; her body was still and frozen. She clutched at the mane, and I held on to the softness of her thigh where it came out of her zookeeper's outfit.

"It's okay," I told her. "You did it."

216 × JOYCE WEATHERFORD

"Off," she said, and then looked at me quickly with eyes full of discovered worlds.

"You don't have to stay there long."

She let go of Jade's mane and twisted down to me and that was how it happened that I held her in my arms and didn't let go. She sat over one hip, and I hoisted her with a "hup" so that her shorts were smooth and not bunched up. Tansy placed her arm around my neck and stroked Jade on the face as she said good-bye to her. "Jade," she said with a little convulsion, and then looked at me again.

"That's right," I said, noticing to my chagrin that Tansy was delightful.

She covered Jade's eye with her little hand.

"That is where Jade sees," I told her.

Then she put her palm over her nose.

"Where she smells. Now whenever you come back to see Jade, she will remember you."

This made an impression on Tansy. She waved to Jade as we walked out of the corral and she watched her over my shoulder as we continued to the house. Jade had followed us to the fence and stood there looking at us through the slats of the two-by-sixes of the corral.

The dogs escaped when I opened the front door. Henry had told Mother. She walked around the house holding her hands to her head.

"Didn't you tell him to tie that dog up?" she demanded, as she banged downstairs to the basement to get her jacket.

"Yes. I did." I held Tansy tight, and yelled down at my mother. "He doesn't listen to me. He doesn't listen to anybody."

Elise was not satisfied with this. She was trying to make what had happened sound better to her, and she was having trouble. "It must've had rabies," she said, returning with Ike's Levi's coat with sheepskin lining. "Was it foaming at the mouth?" she asked.

"No," I said. "You might want to wear the red coat," I told her. "It's hunting season."

"I know," she said, waving me off and walking into her bedroom. She returned with a red bandanna, let go of her head long enough to tie it around her blond curls. "I can't believe he did that. Shot the damn dog," she muttered. "Why did he come home?" she demanded.

"It was his birthday," I replied, looking at her.

"Birthday?" Elise repeated.

"And I wanted to see him before I left."

"Christ," she whispered. "And with a little Indian."

"This is Tansy," I said, turning to face her.

She stopped then. My mother walked slowly toward us, her hand on the knot in the back of the kerchief.

"Your granddaughter."

Elise stared at her daughter holding her granddaughter. "Oh my God," she said. She turned not red like Ike, but a cold blue-white. Then she shattered a little bit, shuddered. A grotesque smile appeared on her beautiful face and she started to sob.

I noticed Tansy's smell then, not one of those odious and suburban perfumes of baby powder, but a plain sweat, physical sweat.

Tansy watched Elise. Just as quickly as she started, Elise stopped crying. She yanked her coat on roughly, and walked out with Henry's name on her breath. "You drive," I heard her say as the door shut.

I think part of me went with my mother then. It wouldn't have gone with her a year prior, a day earlier, even an hour before. Tansy and I washed our hands in the stainless kitchen sink. I still held her on my hip. She did not make any attempt to get down in the strange house.

I poured some ice water and pushed our glasses across the counter. Walking around to the other side, we pulled up the old rocker. We sat together, and I gave Tansy her glass.

She drank it down. That amazed me; I could never stand the coldness of ice water on my teeth or in my body. Tansy pulled out the ice and began playing with it, placing it in her mouth, but it wouldn't fit. She sucked on it, rolling it around her tongue, and then pulled it out again with her cold fingers. It was too big for her mouth. She turned sideways on my lap and looked back at me. Her eyelashes were right up against the skin of her eye. They were long, black, and thick. I stared unmoved at her face. It was swollen, not like she had been hit, more like she had been crying or that she just hadn't shed the watery world of her infancy yet. I studied her as if she were in a petri dish, and I held her.

She looked at me with those brown eyes and made an offering of the ice cube.

I leaned my head down to touch the cold square to my lips.

Tansy watched me without expression. She watched my eyes, she watched my lips. Slowly she moved the ice cube into my mouth. A tiny rivulet of melted water ran down my chin and dripped onto her leg. She didn't notice.

I took the ice cube into my mouth. I sucked it down, rounding its edges. I pushed it back out of my mouth. I returned it to her, a much smaller, rounder ball of ice. She reached up shyly to take it from me, and placed it into her own mouth. I thought then about my brother, her father, how when we were little we used to paint flowers and scenes on the horses with Day-Glo tempera paint. Jake always wrote on one side of the big white belly of his horse, *Let me out.* Afterward we would ride bareback down to the canyon and wash them off by riding into the spring. Memories of my brother's and my childhood came flooding back to me.

Tansy gave me a fresh cube to melt. This time she leaned into me and held it in her mouth. I took it from her with my lips, water dripping now on us both from the melted ice. It shocked me that I was sitting with a child and wasn't repelled. But we did it, over and over and over again, until the last ice melted, until I heard a pickup driving in slow.

My mother entered the house alone. She walked into her room and returned with a black dress on a plastic hanger dangling from her hand. "Better clean up here," she said. "They'll be coming." She disappeared back into her room.

Tansy and I followed her.

"Henry found him," she said, rummaging in her closet.

I held Tansy a little tighter. A wave of bad adrenaline bloomed from the middle of my back outward, as if I had been stabbed with a knife.

"At the base of the black walnut tree. At least the bullet didn't tear his face off," she added harshly as if to punish me for making her say it.

I took ahold of Tansy's hand again. A snarling clawing cat landed on my back then, and I've never gotten it off. When the realization that Jake was dead hit me, I imploded, sank down and twisted, as if somehow I was trying to yank those claws out of my neck.

"He was just lying there staring at the birds on his chest," she said.

Tansy turned her face. She knew all right. That was what made her finally lovely to me. She looked away, and I buried my nose in the back of her neck. We left Elise staring into her closet, filling her eyes up with anything but her dead son.

I practiced routines, I filled the ice trays, gave Tansy more water. Now was the time to dig in, when death occurred. Once tragedy came, it fell down often. Accidents, cancers, bankruptcy; they came in threes. What a person couldn't do was panic, I told myself. If the panic took hold, then the second tragedy would strike you. It was like that old Bible story about not looking back at the burning city, or you'd turn to salt. I didn't look back.

But Tansy did. It shocked me, her emotion, when it came. She tried to hide in my chest. Imagine, I thought, a three-year-old covering her grief. I heard her sob and try to breathe through the flood. I pitied her for having to feel, when I should have pitied myself, because after that I never really felt anything. Because it was I who had invited Jake home to hunt, and placed the gun in his hand.

20

THE DUSK HAD PASSED, AND I HATED THE DARKNESS. ELISE walked out of her bedroom wearing the dress she'd had in her hands earlier. She paced with her head down, looking at her high-heeled Ferragamo shoes. A gold tee strap was anchored around her beautifully boned ankle. The metal glinted and cast out sparks that defended her balance. She sat in the leather chair in the green room. "The visitors," she said. "They will be coming. The news will spread like fire. Then the condolences." She crossed her legs into the position that she would retain all night. "Get dressed," she ordered.

There was silence in the house, except for the heartbeat of the well.

I felt eviscerated. "Where are they?" I asked. More than anything I wanted to see Henry, to look into his eyes, to hold on to the one good thing I had.

"He took your brother," she said softly. I could barely hear her.

"Where?" I demanded, alarmed. I remembered that Tansy probably understood everything we said, and I walked into the kitchen with her to distract her momentarily. I watched how she moved along with me as if she was used to being carried, and I wondered if her father had taken care of her while Kappy was in school.

"The hospital. For the pronouncement of death. They'll be coming then. The visitors. State trooper. We need to be ready for them," Elise went on. "Do we have coffee?" she asked.

"Yes," I called to my mother. I began to hear a faint buzzing, a hum. It became louder, with a low harmonic, the kind that comes in waves. It was a fat, thick sick engine sound. "What is that?" I asked, returning.

"That would be your father," Mother said, formal and detached. "Returning from his appointment with the loan officer at the bank in Pendleton." She stated it as though it pleased her.

"He wants to land in the dark?" I asked, walking to the window to look at the airstrip. I couldn't see anything. Then came the buzz of the engine screaming for air. He was dive-bombing the house, the way he did the combines. He circled the house repeatedly, buzzing louder and louder. It sounded like an air raid, sounded like he was yelling at me to do something. Without runway lights, landing a plane after sundown was exactly the same as crashing. Bad things happened in threes.

"We better get out there, so he doesn't take the fence down," I said, thinking even if Ike survives this landing, he'll wish he were dead when he finds out Jake killed himself. I was starting to panic. I sat down in front of Elise and held Tansy tightly with both arms. "Elise," I yelled. "He's calling us to get out there. We need to help him." Tansy sat tensely on my knees, on my faded Levi's with the ragged hole in the right thigh. She looked through the black windows to the garden, a pitch-black mirror, and fingered the fringe on my jeans, touching my skin with the palm of her hand as gently as she had my horse.

It sounded as if the plane was in a nosedive. It was a fast, high-pitched whine of engine, a sustained piercing note before a crash. And just when the noise became deafening, it dropped.

My mother was unmoved. She stared straight ahead. If you hooked her to a crane and pulled her up, she would be in the same position. Tansy looked at me. All of a sudden I became furious at my brother for including me in his tragedy, his daughter and me.

"He should go to the airport," said Elise. "He knows better than to land here at night," she went on icily.

"Ike *doesn't* know better, Mom," I practically yelled. "He's going to land here. We need to give him some light." Mother shook her head. "Just help me start up the rigs, shine their headlights on the fences so he knows where the goddamned landing strip is. There's no moon, nothing out tonight."

She didn't even react to my cussing.

"He's going to take down the fence if he can't see it," I said, picking Tansy up and walking toward the door.

My mother finally looked up, her face shined with satin makeup that appeared like infinite flecks of mirror. "Let him take one down," she said, low and cold, harder than the ice Tansy and I had sucked.

The heated air of the furnace lifted the blond hair on her forehead. It was the only movement. She sat stone still in the leather chair, in her Chanel suit, surrounded by the dusted furniture and sculptures in the green room.

We left my mother frozen and waiting for the callers, the neighbors who would come, hats in their hands, with food, condolences, and offers to take some land off my parents' hands, because everyone knew after tragedy struck, there was always opportunity.

Tansy and I entered the night; the cinders from the field-burning in the valley blew in the air. I could not get warm. The smell of smoke reminded me of smoldering leaves, and freezing people huddled too closely around that which would scar them. I thought of Thanksgiving, and Christmas, and the things that would never be the same now that Jake was gone.

The two of us climbed into the pickup. Mother had left the door ajar. We drove it past the elevator at the east end of the ranch where the runway started. I parked it at the far edge with the lights shining down on the barbed wires, the white tips on the metal posts reflecting like the spires on a medieval castle ready for the heads of the enemy to be impaled upon them. We abandoned the pickup the way we had left my mother.

I ran back, the fallow and Tansy's weight tiring me out. The blue night light of the ranch cast a pall on the buildings. Ike kept circling, the red and green lights on his wingtips blinking. We started the Jaguar and placed it at the opposite end from the pickup. Tansy helped me now; she crawled out of my lap when we reached the water tanker. We drove over the airstrip to place it along the far fence line so he wouldn't land safely but then crash into the stumps of the old fence.

I fired up the wheat trucks, placing wood blocks under their tires so they wouldn't roll, and parked them on the other side of the strip. The adrenaline shot through me from Jake's death, and what I thought could be my father's. I moved everything we had—the service pickups, the semi, the stock truck, and Henry's pickup. I was breathing hard, but still, I jogged down carrying Tansy to the beginning of the runway by the pickup's headlights. I stood panting as Ike circled around once more to land.

He came in low. I realized he could only see where the light illuminated the barbed wire fence. And then I knew he was trying to land close to the light. The plane was coming fast as it always did. The dogs barked incessantly. They loved going up to greet my father when he came back from a plane trip. They would never go to see him off, afraid they would be taken along. They hated flying, and I didn't blame them.

I heard a ping and then a scream as the wire tore away from the fence posts. I ducked to the ground, covering Tansy. There was a snap, and a whirling sound, like a giant bullwhip going around in circles. He had landed, but the landing gear caught in the fence and had buckled. The plane skidded, went dark, and came to a halt sideways. One of the shiny white wingtips was down on the ground, reflecting the light of the still running rigs.

I lifted Tansy over the shortened barbed wire fence and crawled over after her, scratching my palm on the stinging barbs. I picked her up again, and we ran up to see my father. He was slumped over the yoke of the steering butterfly, his glasses shattered.

I set Tansy down and climbed up under the wing, pulling open the shiny white latch. "Dad," I whispered. He pushed himself back with his hands still on the steering butterfly. "Are you okay?" I asked in a panicky voice.

"Lost my glasses."

"Can you move?"

"I think so. I don't know."

He lifted his long legs up, and I helped him place them out of the plane. He grabbed hold of my arm and the top of the door, slid himself onto the threshold, and then down to the ground. Ike stood up unsteadily, still holding on to my hand. He held it hard. There was nothing weak about his grip.

"Let's just walk slowly," I said, grabbing Tansy's hand with my free one.

I led him down the slight hill toward the house. It wasn't until we got under the blue night light that I looked back and saw the blood in his eye. He looked pitiful, old.

"Who's that?" he asked, listening to the sound of our feet on the gravel.

"Your granddaughter."

We walked down the steps to the front yard. His boots sounded hollow.

Elise was still sitting in the chair where I had left her. She looked at his bloody face, and I could see her practically say "Touché."

I led Ike to the rocking chair.

"Uncle Martin will be calling soon," she said as he sat down.

"What for?" Ike asked. Uncle Martin was another distant relative, a Nazarene minister and a thorn in my father's side. He had several times fenced across the public road, trying to cut off access to our Creek Ranch, claiming he, not the state, owned the road. My father always cussed him out and tore down the fencing. Martin sneered at the weeds spread by the cattle in my father's fields. Ike was too busy to worry about weeds, but Martin was obsessive. He hoed his entire fields by hand between rod weedings.

"The minister's always the first one to call," Elise said. "Wants to be the first one to break the news. He has the police inform him when there is an accident, a death, a dispute," Elise went on, unstoppable, eerily calm.

"Who died?" asked Ike, looking straight ahead. Of course he had to have guessed.

Elise stared at him. "Your son," she replied. "Suicide. Another one of your accomplishments."

Ike sat there, his eyes swollen and partially closed. Blood colored the white of his right eye. "Lay off, Mother," he said softly.

I thought about getting a towel to wash the blood off his face.

Elise turned to me. I noticed her face was puffy. She looked at Tansy. "Poor little critter," she said. "Orphaned."

"She's not orphaned," I told her, moving the ottoman away from her and sitting on it. I wanted my mother to tend to her husband. "She has us, not to mention Kappy."

"It is what Jake wanted, you know," stated Elise. "It's our punishment."

I thought I felt Tansy recoil. She held on to my neck a little tighter afterward.

"We're responsible for the girl now. What do you think of that?" she asked Ike.

"I don't want the little M.R.," Ike replied stonily.

"Shit, Dad," I said. Everything about us was stiff and breakable. The sculptures of the family surrounded us in the green room; they observed every detail.

"Those are her initials, aren't they?" asked Ike.

"No. *T.S.* Tansy Steele," I said loudly. I wanted to tell him there is no way a person could get *mentally retarded* out of that, but I kept my mouth shut because of Tansy on my lap.

"But she can't speak," he said.

I moved away from my parents permanently. They might as well have become clay statues then and there. Everything was changing. "What do you think is wrong with her?" I asked. "Same thing that was wrong with her father?"

Neither one answered me. They sat facing each other for the first time in their lives. There was silence for a long time. Finally, my father spoke. "I came home early," Ike said. "Because I wanted to catch you and Henry putting one over on me."

"What did you plan on proving? That you could run her off, too?" my mother snapped.

I gathered myself and Tansy to stand up.

"I just," he said, still staring ahead, "didn't want them making a fool out of me."

My mother placed her head on her fist. "Making a fool out of you," she uttered disgustedly. "But somehow it's me who's a man down, isn't it, Ike?"

"What the hell did he come out here for anyway?" Ike asked. He sat so motionless, there was no difference between him and his sculpture. His forehead red, the creases in his brows, his strong sharp nose and iron-colored stubble.

"I invited him," I said softly. "Today was his birthday."

My mother sobbed when I said that, like she'd forgotten it was her son's birthday until I reminded her again.

"Christ," Ike muttered. "Get me a drink, would you."

"Get it yourself," said my mother.

I looked at my parents—bleeding, half-blind. I took Tansy with me to get Ike his Early Times. Staring at my niece, watching her smooth, beautiful hair, I figured it was the least I could do for Jake: pick up his fight. That was when I began helping my father to anything that would place him down in the grave faster, and I had enough of my mother in me to be able to bide my time.

"Where's her mother?" Ike asked, when we returned. "I'm sure as hell not going to raise no Indian."

"I think she's at the reservation," I replied.

"Give her back to her mother then," Ike instructed. "Right now." It was as if the faster Tansy left the place, the better.

"Shut up, Ike, for Chrissakes. Just shut up," said Elise. She was still holding her head. "I'm tired of you shoving people around. You made my son, my baby, kill himself, goddammit. Did you have to push him and push him and push him?"

I thought Ike might be having a stroke from the accident. He couldn't speak clearly. "Don't you blame this on me," he finally mouthed. "You pulled that trigger. You pulled that trigger every day of Jake's life. You think I didn't see it. Undermining me through Jake, because you wouldn't fight your own goddamned battles yourself. Why don't you tell me what you've wanted to say all these years, because here I am."

Tansy held me, crying and shaking.

"You go to hell, Ike," Elise snarled. She pulled out a piece of paper from the side of the chair. She clutched it in her fist and waved it at her husband.

I took the paper from my mother gently. She stared at it as I unfolded it, and she started to cry again, looking at that paper.

"My baby," she cried. "On his birthday." She hit herself in the stomach like she was trying to beat out the pain that once her son had grown there, become beautiful, whole and alive inside her, and now he lay, top of his head shot off, in the black vacuum of a morgue.

It was a note, written on an old Oregon transportation certificate for cattle. On the front were pictures of cattle ears to describe what types of chunks had been cut out of their lobes to mark them. Below was a space to describe the brands as well. Probably the only thing Jake could find in the jockey box of the pickup to write on.

I thought about how Tansy would react to the note, no doubt as if she thought we were poison. The paper read: "All I have goes to my beloved daughter Tansy Steele."

"We found this too," said Mother, through her tears. She held up a dirty object. "Your mother's watch, Ike. It was in his left pocket when we found him," she went on shakily.

"Give me that," Ike snapped. I handed it to him, and he snatched it away. Ike dropped it in his shirt pocket, on the left side just as Jake had.

That night Henry and I drove Tansy back to the reservation. I wanted to talk to him about Jake, but we rode in silence because of Tansy. We arrived at Kappy's past one in the morning. She came to the door in jeans and a crocheted sweater.

"I'm sorry to tell you this," said Henry. He had to say it because I couldn't.

Kappy walked to her couch and sat down, her hands in her lap. She stiffened. Why else would we be here with Tansy and not Jake?

"Jake died today," Henry said softly.

"What happened?" she asked, almost as if she was checking to see if the reality matched what she'd seen in her imagination. Her voice was low, but not husky.

I could see Henry trying to say it so it wouldn't hurt. "He shot himself." He gave a few details so there wouldn't be questions. "We found him this evening around five-thirty."

Kappy shook her head, and was silent. I noticed there were no beer bottles on the tables as before. Instead, there were law books. Another lawyer in the family, I thought, just what we needed. I had a feeling this wouldn't be the last time I would see Kappy. I watched her sitting there alone. She had gained weight, maybe from the pregnancy. The small cost of a new life.

Tansy stood in the middle of the room. Her mother remained motionless on the couch. Henry grabbed Tansy's arm and led her over. Kappy looked at her daughter, and it was then she started crying.

I wanted to get out of there. I was useless amidst the pain of that house.

"He always talked about *ruling from the grave*," Kappy cried, stroking Tansy's hair. "How his family ruled from the grave. Now it's him down there. He was obsessed with getting revenge on Ike." She talked almost a cadence. "He goaded and goaded me to go to law school, and when I finally did something with my life," she stated angrily, "he started throwing his away."

"He got revenge," I whispered. "On all of us."

"He wanted Ike to have nothing. Nothing," she went on.

"Turns out they'll both have nothing," I said. "Except hate and guilt."

Henry laid his hand on my back. We started to leave.

"I know why he did it," Kappy announced, as we reached the door.

Suddenly I didn't want to listen to her. I didn't want to hear anything, or see anything anymore.

"He couldn't stand what he had become." Kappy stood up, holding Tansy to her. "Ordering me around. He was just like his father. That's why he shot himself."

I looked at Tansy. I doubted Jake had treated her the way Ike had treated him. I shook my head.

"If he was named correctly," Kappy said, laughing, "Indian style, he would have been called Snake."

"No," I replied. "It was my fault. I shouldn't have invited him back. I never should have," I said, and closed the door behind us.

Henry drove home. I sat next to him thinking about Jake's inert body, his bloody head. I remembered the clothes he was wearing, his favorite hunting shirt and the ever-present Levi's. I couldn't bear it; I fought back my tears. I considered canceling school, canceling everything, and just hanging on to Henry as he finished med school. I wondered about his friends in Portland and whether I could fit in. I was envious of them, and their fancy M.D. degrees. A Native American woman named Ingrid, adopted by a Swedish family, was one of Henry's best friends. She went to Stanford undergrad and had already gotten into residency at Harvard. So much for adopted Indians and fetal alcohol syndrome. I was afraid of losing Henry to her, losing him to a million things. I was an ugly, small, envious, shattered person. I felt that I was nothing, just like my dead brother.

"I'm thinking of dropping out of school," I said numbly, staring at the river as we sailed on down in the night.

"I would if I could," Henry said.

"What would you do?" I asked.

He was quiet for a moment. "If I had the money, travel. If I didn't, Peace Corps."

I thought about my upcoming fall and winter terms in England and France to study literature. Everything seemed pointless and stupid now, but at least I wouldn't have to listen to Ike and Elise.

We drove in silence. Henry exited the freeway and took the back road home.

"Did you ever want to be anything besides a doctor?" I asked after a few minutes.

"No," he replied. "The grind of the training is too hard, too long. You can't be distracted by anything else. You'll give up."

I listened to Henry. He was my lifeline. I wasn't going to be a quitter like my brother.

"Besides," Henry said jokingly, "after what I saw and heard tonight, you're going to need a doctor in the family."

I looked at him—we had never talked about marriage before. I decided to give up my life at the ranch. I'd cook, clean, be a perfect wife; whatever Henry wanted me to do, I'd do it. "Will you meet me in Europe?" I asked suddenly, thinking six months was too long to go without seeing Henry. Maybe in Paris or London, life would be different.

"You're not coming home for Christmas?" he returned.

"Ike says if I go, I'm not coming back till I'm finished." I made an attempt to laugh. "Ike likes things finished," I said.

"Of course," Henry replied. "Of course, I will come."

Henry drove me out to the point. The most beautiful location on the ranch, it was where you could see down Rock Creek to the Columbia, where Mounts Hood, Rainier, and Adams would be illuminated by the rising red sun. We sat outside in the cold for hours. I didn't care if my parents were worried about my safe return.

When Henry turned to hold me, I attacked him to get away from the pain. I stripped off our clothes, and we made love out on the ground, the wind cutting into our skin, and the rocks slicing our backs. I pulled him into me hard and rough like a punch because to really challenge death—to take a weapon out and fight it—the only thing to do is the act that makes life. The sun was just coming up as our tears finally came. The crying didn't stop until our bodies were covered with the fundamental elements of agriculture: rain, dirt, and morning sun.

part five

21

My land marked where the Columbia Gorge ended. There, the river's steep bluffs began to give way to younger rock, less violent, softened by earth, more flexible and forgiving. Downriver to the left, wedged between the cliffs, was my father's island, and to the right was Henry. Leaving Hanna disheveled and still carving at home, I drove the Blazer to the river, turned right, and headed up the green water, herding shadows against the tide as the midwinter wind blew the waves east with me.

I passed the minefield of one thousand and one nerve gas bunkers along the Columbia. It must have been someone's idea of a joke to put one thousand and one of them out there, something like One Thousand and One Nights. They hid just off the freeway, nestled down by the river behind a sign that read: Umatilla Army Depot, Accomplishment Through Action. The logo had a picture of an eagle and a globe.

The hidden bunkers held ton containers of mustard, nerve, and sarin gas left over from the world wars. The chemicals were absorbed into a body's cells, into the nerves that operate the vital activities. If exposed, you died by asphyxiation. Drowned in air. Stacked now in the little gravelike mounds, the containers leaked poison out there where the river widened. The West was full of problems no one knew how to solve.

Around eight in the morning, I dropped down into the swale that held Pendleton. The reservation stretched out and beyond, toward Cabbage Hill. The road turned treacherous and cattle guards grated my tires as I left the freeway, momentarily drowning out the radio. Since the liberal-leaning board heads and surfers arrived on the Columbia, our music had improved. Now, public radio came from Walla Walla and Spokane. I listened to NPR instead of KONA Kountry.

Kash Kash Road led past Cayuse Casino down to the reservation, submerged in the cavity of Happy Creek. Surrounded by Novas, tri-colored Datsun pickups, and Impalas, the United Tribes lived hidden from the rest of the world. Identical small brick houses lined the sides of the road. Tents stood pitched outside for sleeping, next to motorcy-cles and plastic lawn chairs. A silver fishing boat was parked on the street or in the drive of almost every house.

I traveled Immigrant Canyon Road, Paradise Road, and Mission. They were beat-up streets graveled at the edges where they disap-peared into nothing. In the middle of the day, men worked on their cars and children played in plastic jungle gyms.

An American flag flew at the Indian Center. I turned in, parked, and walked up the handicap ramp to the sprawling Yellowbird Tribal Health Center.

At the desk, a pretty young tribe member greeted me with a rich smile. She sported a T-shirt that read Dartmouth University.

"Hello," she said softly. I smiled back at her. She studied from a big red book called *Gray's Anatomy*. How irritating, another beautiful American Indian M.D. I wondered if Henry was involved with this woman.

"I'm here to see Henry Goodstand," I said, watching for her response.

"Do you have an appointment?" she asked, reaching to the tele-phone. I decided she was too young for Henry.

"No." I looked at the counter. It was full of pamphlets. "Tell him it's Iris Steele," I said in a voice that cracked.

"Dr. Goodstand," the young woman said. "Iris Steele is here to see you."

I noticed an old man sitting, staring at the floor in the great room. He looked as if he wasn't a stranger to waiting. Otherwise, the building appeared empty. Brand-new, track lighted, and freshly carpeted, the room practically shone. Exposed-brick walls bore old photographs of Indians, sharply framed and hung from the ceilings.

"Okay," the receptionist said. She hung up the telephone. "He's with a patient. He said five minutes."

"Great," I replied. I felt pinpricks inside my stomach. I tried to lower my expectations. It had been four years since Henry and I brought in our last harvest, Henry working on his three-week vacation. Later that same year, we had our fight. I was twenty-four, he twenty-seven, his first year of residency at Providence Hospital in Portland. I thought we had perfected the art of long-distance relationships. We had no trouble seeing each other during college. Only sixty miles apart, we talked on the phone, he came down to Corvallis for weekends, or I went up to see him. After I graduated, I talked Elise into sending me overseas again, claiming I didn't want to be the dread "hick." I think it was Elise's way of toughening me up, much different methods than my father's. I drifted through Europe, the Middle East, Africa, India, and Asia with her credit card and came home more certain than ever that I loved my place, my land, my work, and Henry.

Afterward I worked at the ranch as he completed his internship and residency. In the summers we labored together in harvest, and the rest of the year, I stayed with him whenever I could. But I hated the Willamette Valley. The rain, the smallness of things, the envy, the snap judgments, it all hung in the air down there like smoke from the fall field-burning.

It was then that Henry asked me to live with him in Portland. He wanted me to stay down there, cooped up and trapped. I said I wouldn't do it; I'd continue farming with Ike. I thought we could see each other on the weekends, but I couldn't live down there, becoming exactly like everyone else. A couple of days here and there wasn't enough for Henry. I said he was inflexible, and he told me I was obstinate. For someone who hung on as well as Henry, it devastated me when he set me loose after six years of a close relationship.

Since then I had lost track of him. I knew he had spent the last two years on reservation land in the Southwest, driving thousands of miles in a 4 x 4 army truck converted to a mobile examination room. It was his payback for medical school tuition. Two years ago, he sent me a letter when he learned Ike had died, though it was six months after the fact. It was postmarked Flagstaff, Arizona.

As I stood there waiting for him, a pamphlet on the desk caught my eye. On the cover an Indian woman knelt at a grave with a flower. What You Should Know About Smoking and Cancer was printed along the bottom. Inside it read, "In Indian country, tobacco is meant to honor life, not to harm life. Traditional people may use tobacco for spiritual ceremonies: to help our thoughts and prayers reach the creator, and to honor beings we have hunted." On the next page it said, "Indians have the highest growth rate of smokers in the United States, increasing among children, women, and men at a faster pace than any other population in the world. Cancer is knocking down our door. Stay smoke-free and healthy."

There were papers explaining the genetic reasons for Indians having the highest rate of diabetes and diabetes-related complications in the world. I saw kidney disease literature, stating the ugly percentage of end-stage renal failure found in the Indian community. Information on gang violence, auto accidents, domestic violence abounded. There was one entitled: "Alcohol and Illicit Drugs, Why the Highest in the Country?" I placed that one in my back pocket. I was looking at a light blue pamphlet, "A Call for Help: Suicide. Why the Youth Suicide/Homicide Rate in the Indian Community Continues to Rank the Highest in the United States." Then Henry appeared.

As disturbing as the state of Native American health was, my attention was on Henry the minute he rounded the corner, the minute he entered my air. I sort of turned and backed up, hitting the receptionist's desk with my boot. It echoed in the large waiting room; I imagined it disaligned the black-and-white photographs that decorated the halls. I felt foreign.

Henry wore creased khaki pants and a white button-down shirt. A stethoscope dangled around his neck. I suddenly remembered the last day of Henry's miserable internship in Portland, five years ago. He was on the ER rotation, scheduled to finish the final shift of the entire suffering year at 7 A.M.

Enid Hemple, my alias, checked into the emergency room at 6 A.M.

complaining of vague belly pain. I had planned it out carefully, previously asking Henry what was the worst thing an ER patient could come in with: vague abdominal pain was the answer. This required tests and complicated analysis, it could take hours, the last thing an exhausted intern wanted on his last day. I asked for a private room, undressed, and sat on the examining table holding a bottle of Veuve Clicquot, waiting for him to enter. Henry didn't knock on the door, more slapped it three times before shoving it open. His face was drained of color, his sandy hair stuck up with a rooster tail from the two hours of sleep he'd had in the last forty-eight hours. When he saw me it was as if he'd been liberated from prison. Drinking the champagne wasn't the first thing we did.

I wondered how much Henry had changed since those years, how learning to defeat death had transformed him.

"Iris," he said, his eyes sparkling. "Just drop by?"

"Picking up parts," I lied.

"Grain Grabbers at it again," he said, switching a pen from the right hand to the left.

"Yeah. And I wanted to see the place. See where you work." I sank down on one haunch and touched him briefly on the arm. I noticed his muscle was still there, obscured by the white of pinpoint cotton. He had lost some of the roundness to his face. Before, when he smiled, his cheeks rounded upward. Now they were replaced by delicate bone. I could see the sheen of baby hairs covering his cheekbone and the point where they stopped, where the shave had started. Henry looked clean; he looked sterile.

He removed his stethoscope from his neck and dropped it in a curl into his pocket. I noticed a pen callus on the knuckle of his middle finger. "Come on," he said. "Take a look."

"Love to," I answered, watching his back as I followed him. His sandy hair lay in a smart cut stopping just above the collar of his shirt. I felt as if I was in a museum, not a medical center. We reached a glassed-in room where a woman sat at a switchboard.

"The dispatch center," Henry said, looking at his watch. "Carolyn takes calls from the field. Our area covers five hundred square miles."

I raised my eyebrows and slowed to look at Carolyn. Headphones corralled her long black hair.

Henry knocked on the window and popped his head in the room. "Any train wrecks?" he asked.

"Lucky, so far," she said. Carolyn was efficient, businesslike. Her padded body crouched at the switchboard as if she were a Buddha. The lenses of her glasses were large half rounds, tinted amber. They gave her the look of an activist from the seventies.

"This is Iris," Henry said, motioning to me.

Carolyn twisted her chair around to look at me, keeping her head connected to the switchboard. She didn't shake my hand.

I felt out of place again.

Henry held the door open for me to leave, and I walked out past his arms. I hung back in the hall waiting for him to lead me. I hated not leading, not knowing where I was going.

"My office," he said, sliding a shoulder into a door. He took the stethoscope out of his pocket and placed it and his pen on the paper-covered desk.

I sat down in the patient's chair on the other side and looked at his framed diplomas on the walls. Oregon State University, University of Oregon Medical School. Providence Hospital internal medicine residency. They were colorful, orange and black, deep scarlet and gold. They looked like medals.

It was awkward sitting silently with him in his office full of medical gadgets, an otoscope, a reflex hammer, stethoscope, blood pressure cuff, and a tuning fork. I glanced around and then stared at his lip. I remembered his body, the way I had kissed his legs in the bunkhouse, worshiped his hands in the field, the way his hair trailed down his white belly and gathered into black fur. Those things that were once familiar territory now seemed alien.

I imagined it was the same for Henry as it was for me; otherwise, he would be married by now, probably to some nurse who followed his orders at home, the same as in the hospital. It annoyed me that doctors married nurses. His friends had all married nurses and then divorced before residency was over. Except for his friend Ingrid. She married her college basketball star sweetheart, and then he went to work as an investment banker on Wall Street.

Occasionally my college roommates had set me up on dates. But every time I went out with someone, I compared him to Henry. The two of us had a history together. I never fit as well around anyone else. As cynical as I was, I held out for what I thought was true love.

Driving up that morning, I had imagined all the possibilities. He could be engaged. I knew he wasn't married. I had kept up enough with his father, Earl, to know that much. Every several months, I took a load of garbage to the dump, and I would stop in and chat with Earl. The garbage dump was now the largest employer in the county, and after the bankruptcy of the savings and loan, Earl had gotten a job there. He showed me postcards Henry had sent him of the colored canyons of the Southwest, or of the red rocks of Sedona. It was bittersweet seeing Earl. I was sad that after the savings and loan failed, he couldn't find any job other than working at the dump. In addition, talking about Henry made me miss him even more.

I imagined at least Henry had a girlfriend. But suppose he didn't? I envisioned us going home to his apartment in Pendleton, buying a new bed together, one finally big enough for the both of us, shedding our clothes and never getting out again.

So I sat there looking at him nervously, and I cleared my throat. "Well, mister, I didn't come here to see the one-eye surprise." And I folded my hands over my backpack purse. I smiled and added, "If that's what you're thinkin'."

Henry laughed. He looked impish and younger, his wide crop-teeth smile cut dimples into his cheeks, and I briefly saw the boy who gave Coach Klemp diarrhea for days. "What *did* you come here for?" he said.

I scratched my back, felt as if that cat were clawing on me again. I didn't answer. And then I blurted out, because I didn't have anything better to say, "Fuckin' Runcid tore down the fence and seeded half the sixteen hundred."

"Does it ever end?" Henry said, alarmed.

"No," I replied. "The next thing I know, that excuse of a son of his came out to the house apologizing for his father, and he's got his dick out of his pants, inviting me to smoke his pole."

Henry stood up. Walked around to the corner of his desk and sat down in front of me. "Bastard," he said. "Like the sign in the Let 'er Rip Room," he cracked. " 'The Oregon Trail: Longest Road in Human History.' " By definition of the word *doctor,* Henry was the sympathetic type, but he had his limits. I remembered how he dreaded pain patients. He was one of those who tended to think the origin of chronic pain was the mind, and I wondered if he thought I was a chronic pain lifer.

"Yeah," I said. "Those poor people on the Oregon Trail didn't realize they had it so good."

Henry laughed and looked down at my boots. They were round-toed logging boots, the same as my brother used to wear. Now everyone wore them, and they were called Doc Martens.

"How come you came back?" I asked, crossing my feet at my ankles and pulling them under my chair.

"Medicine's not much better than farming," he said. "Four years' medical school. One miserable year of internship," he said.

I wondered if he remembered how we had celebrated that last morning. Lots of memories returned as I looked at him, how in winter after we made love my freezing fingers and toes would warm up and stay that way. We were so awkward now, reduced to remembrances.

Henry rubbed his mouth with his hand. I noticed his hands were even prettier than before. "Three years' residency, overlapped with two years on the reservation," he went on. "Find a career I love. Then the managed-care disaster hits. Didn't want to work for an HMO, so I quit and came back here."

"Does it suit you?"

He shrugged. "Doesn't much matter," he said, looking at me. "These people are sick. You know," he allowed softly, "nature will fuck you."

"No kidding," I said, thinking how many times nature had interfered with my farming plans—finding the easiest path for water, over a field instead of a dam; or the most unkillable, invasive weed; and now this global warming, dry-weather disaster.

"The change in the diet is a big problem," he said. "Eating lean meat and fish for thousands of years. Now oil, cholesterol, occasionally Mickey D's." Henry returned to his chair and sat down.

I remembered the way his lips looked blue the first time we made love.

"Then there are the infectious diseases," he went on. "It's really war. We discover a new antibiotic, and then the Hantavirus shows up, the plague comes back. Yesterday I saw something similar to mad cow disease. The patient got it from eating deer brain. She disintegrated neurologically."

I nodded. "Nature's response to interference. It's the same in farming, the erosion, the damming, and the cutting. The balance goes out of kilter. And once that happens, nature goes wild. It's like she gets mad, fights back like a beast. And she always wins," I said, smiling and shaking my head. "We think we're in control. But nature is."

Henry narrowed his eyes. "A patient came in the other day wanting to know about breast-feeding. I told her it was her personal decision, but the facts are that breast milk's the most contaminated thing on the planet."

The subject of breast-feeding appalled me. I was silent for a moment. Elise had never breast-fed. She didn't buy into that religion of being a good mother. In fact, the religion of motherhood went by her without so much as a revival. She was certainly not one of those females who claimed their latent goddess powers came through motherhood and breast-feeding. She told me once, "Good God, Iris. It's cannibalism." I think I was getting red in the face when Henry interrupted my thought.

"They released the final data on Hanford this year," he said. "There were twenty-three million curies of radioactive material released in all."

"I knew it was a lot," I stammered. My eyes watered. I felt poisoned from every angle, so I'd never even had the remotest chance to survive. I searched in my purse just to have something to do. This visit wasn't going the way I had hoped.

Henry leaned forward on his desk, resting his hands together amongst the medical gadgets. "Remember Three Mile Island? Fifteen to twenty-four curies. And they pulled the milk and the vegetables. Pulled everything because it was contaminated."

My mind drifted. I always thought the fact I wasn't breast-fed was the root of my trouble with Elise. The experts all chant "breast is best," like some kind of "om mani pad-me hum," and they threaten you with every manner of disease if you weren't breast-fed. The way I saw it now, if Elise had been a better mother, I would be dead by now, too.

Maybe contaminated breast milk was how nature was going to get back at humans for making a mess of things.

"Collects in the fat," Henry said. "Women live longer than cattle and it collects. The average mother's breast milk, if tested, wouldn't pass the USDA because of toxins. Anyway," he said, clearing his throat, "it's like I have inherited furniture. Furniture of the dead."

"I know what you mean," I replied, not finding anything in my purse but a half stick of gum.

"I learned all these skills, these tools," he went on, frowning. I loved the way his eyebrows framed his deep-set eyes perfectly. Henry looked at his fingers spread out on his right hand. "I learned the landscape of the body. The ecology. But you know," he said irritatedly, grabbing a pen from his desk, "the oath I took. You saw it. At graduation."

I nodded. I had gone with Earl to watch his son graduate from medical school. It was the happiest day of Earl's life. "Yeah," I nodded. "The Hippocratic."

"The one that says I will do no harm." He looked at his watch again.

"Do you have an appointment?" I interrupted, thinking I should leave.

"No," he went on, shaking his head. "That idea isn't always shared by my partners in healing. Some people embrace illness as a lifestyle." He paused. "And insurers make that inevitable."

I shifted in my chair. I felt slightly persecuted, as if he were talking to me. The moroseness, the drinking, the misery. I should just get on with it. "Jaded, are you?" I asked.

He looked at me quickly. "Yeah. Jaded," he whispered softly. "But there are fighters here. People who take responsibility for their health and their lives. One of them is worth all the rest."

I remembered Henry's ER rotation again. I was never so baffled, watching him have to work all night because someone had shoved an Idaho russet potato up their butt. When he told me the story that weekend, all I could think of was the pesticides that were on potatoes. The next night he had to pull out a condom filled with Cheez Whiz that had gotten shot up inside a rectum. "I guess that's what makes life interesting" was all he said.

"But the surgeries on tumors," Henry went on, picking up the tuning fork and dropping it so it hummed. "Looking at that black thing, sayin', You motherfucker, I'm going to kill you." He stared at me, his eyes hardening. "There is nothing better."

I didn't meet Henry's eyes. He could operate on tumors all day and night, and never need the likes of me. Never need anyone. I took a deep breath and decided to try once more to recover our friendship, if not our passion. "What about the science?" We used to talk for hours about everything from the capacity of the brain to the germination of seeds. "The pure science? The formation of the human body."

"That's really it," he said. "Why I love medicine. Why you love farming. The basic things of life. Growing it. Preserving it. There is only one word to describe it. . . ." He paused, searching my eyes.

At least he's trying, I thought, as I looked at him.

"Awe," he said finally.

I felt nervous again. The hope in me fell. I twisted in my chair and reached around to scratch my neck. "I don't think I feel awe," I replied. But the way my words came out, they sounded stupid. It was like the woman ahead of me in line at the gift shop in the Louvre. She pointed to a copy of the *Mona Lisa* and said to her girlfriend, "Ain't theyur sompin fayemos about that paintin'?" I finally decided I was ready to leave. The gulf between us was widening even more. We were as far apart as an atheist and an evangelical.

I hoisted my backpack on my shoulder to leave. "Have you seen Kappy or Tansy?" I asked. It wasn't just because of the lawsuit; I really wanted to know how they were doing, and I was tired of just driving by their house.

For six years, since Jake's estate had been settled, I had thought about Kappy and Tansy. All that time I had wondered when Kappy was going to come after us—what she said about Jake making her go to law school, his ruling from the grave. Jake had chosen a formidable mate, just as my father had. There had to be something my brother wanted from my parents, and I wondered when Kappy was going to ask for it. She had easily managed to negotiate Tansy's claim for Jake's meager estate, plus ten thousand dollars for herself.

When I went to Pendleton for parts, I always drove out to the reservation just to go by their house. I judged how they were doing by the shape it was in and the types of cars that were parked there. For many years, it was a blue Mazda pickup without a back bumper, and whenever I saw a blue rig, I looked hard to see if they were in it.

Henry's pager sounded; he reached down and punched the number up. His mouth pulled to one side in a frown, and he dialed an extension. "Dr. Goodstand," he said.

There was silence while Henry listened. He scribbled some notes on a clipboard with blue paper on it.

"Serious?" I asked.

"New patient." He looked at his notes. "Thirty-six-year-old Nez Perce woman with diabetes. Trouble balancing her medications. She fell from her horse. The second time this week."

"When's she coming in?"

"Coming in? She's seventy miles east."

"You have to get her?"

"Five hundred square miles is a big territory. Sometimes that means a long car trip. We have a plane for emergencies. But the problem with this job is we just don't have enough staff. Can't get nurses in cities, let alone out here." He reached for his Ghurka bag under his desk. "Just a minute," he said, typing into the computer.

I fingered the zipper on my backpack.

Henry furrowed his brows. "Kappy died."

I sat there stunned.

"Diabetes-related complications. Three months before I came."

"Oh God. Poor Tansy," I said.

Henry looked up at his diplomas and shook his head, futilely. "Disease is bad. Medicine is good. This is war."

22

IF YOU COME WITH ME TO EVACUATE THIS PATIENT," HENRY said, "I'll help you find Tansy. She'll probably be living with a guardian now. Someone of the tribe."

"I don't know anything about medicine," I replied hesitantly.

"No, but you can fly a plane."

"You'll be taking your life in your hands if that happens."

Henry gave me a one-sided smile.

Actually, I liked the idea of helping him. Henry had assisted us for so many years; it was the least I could do.

"Need to pick up some medications," he added. "And we'll be off."

Henry changed into another mode. His movements became smooth, efficient, fast. He wrote a list of things, contingency plans, necessary medications. Sweat dampened his white shirt.

I followed him into the pharmacy. Henry unlocked a white metal cabinet, took vials of clear liquid and small, dark bottles of tablets and placed them in the bag. Finally, he moved to a computer on the far side of the pharmacy and typed.

"What are you doing?" I asked impatiently.

"Flight plan," he responded. The monitor revealed a map of the Columbia Basin. The river, outlined in black, ran north up to the fork where the Snake split off into its loop around Lewiston. I saw where Heart of the Beast lay, hidden in the Wallowas. Beyond that was the beginning of the Blue Mountains; they flowed east, becoming the thick purple color of the Rocky Mountains. A vast, opaque area unfolded to the south toward southern Idaho, Utah, and Nevada. Henry glared critically at the screen.

"What are you looking for?" I asked, leaning down.

"To see if we'll be Scud-running or not." Henry tapped his fingers rapidly on the keys.

"Fighting Iraqis?"

"Flying in bad conditions. You look for these," he said, pointing quickly to a red section on the map over the Cascades. "Lenses," he replied. "Ripples of wind blowing over mountains. Updrafts, downdrafts, one after another. They'll take you down in a heartbeat."

"Where's the patient?" I asked.

"Smoke Lake."

Smoke Lake was toward the border of Oregon and Idaho. The air looked safe over there, I decided.

"And we worry about these," he went on, pointing to the text below the map. It read "Cumulo-nimbus forecasted southeastern Oregon. Storm advisory in effect."

"That's a hundred miles away," I stated.

"Except for the wind," he said. "Forty knots'll get it here in a hurry."

I stood up. "What are we waiting for?"

"I just need to check the temperature–dew point spread. When the temperature approaches the dew point, it means ground fog is forming."

"You can't just leave the patient," I said, walking toward the door.

He grabbed his bag. "Luckily the weather has never pushed its point. It's a decision I've never had to make."

"Henry," I whispered, following him outside and down the white gleaming halls. "Who paid for all of this? That equipment had to cost thousands."

"Casino money," he replied, rushing out to the parking lot. We jumped into his dirty blue Expedition and drove up to the summit. Opening the padlock on the Cyclone Fence, we entered the airport and sped across the pavement. Clumps of cheat grass broke through here and there. Miles of reservation spread around us, gray-colored flats. Henry turned between two opposing lines of tan airplane hangars, all of them with corrugated metal doors mirroring one another. We parked at number 12.

"Who owns all these?" I asked, throwing my hand back in the direction of the hangars.

"Tribe members," he said, giving the sliding door a yank.

Our plane gleamed, painted red and white like an ambulance. The sides of it read in bold black letters: THE UNITED TRIBES. Below, a silhouette of an Indian chief in full headdress stared nobly out, an aura-like circle emanating from him. The tail marking was R74727.

"The Romeo 747," I said softly. Perfect.

Henry removed blocks from the wheels. He flipped the cowling up over the engines, and strained fuel. It dripped out a light blue. Climbing up on the wings, he checked the gauge to determine if they were full, and tested the ailerons, the flaps located there. Henry was thorough; he walked around the plane making sure the cables were connected and the movement worked free and clear. Ike had never been so attentive. Then Henry dragged the plane out by its front wheel, watching that the wings weren't clipped by the doors.

He buttoned up the flaps, climbed into the cockpit, flipped the master switch on, and said, "Get in."

I heard the gyros winding up on the turn coordinator. I couldn't stand that sound, like a live wire in my head. It was not of this earth. It reminded me of Ike, the coyotes, and the last cattle drive when everything blew apart.

Henry turned the yoke, pulling it out and in. My copilot yoke mirrored Henry's movement as if a ghost sat in my seat.

"Open up your door," he ordered, "and yell, 'Clear.'"

I did as he said, screaming "clear" to the abandoned windswept hangars. I slammed my door shut just as Henry started up the propeller.

He handed me headphones that caused a nasty suction on my ears. At least it covered the noise of the gyro.

"Can you hear me?" he said, gesturing to my microphone.

I nodded. "Roger." My voice felt like thought instead of speech.

Communicating through the headphones inside the roaring plane made me feel as if we were twins, still inside a womb. I was disoriented, kept from oblivion by a thick black cord filled with spirals and kinks.

I picked up a pamphlet down by the trim wheel, flipped through it, stopping at the emergency approach and landing page. It outlined six steps of executing an emergency landing. "Determine wind direction and glide, find suitable crash landing sight, turn radio to 121.5 and declare intentions (Mayday, Mayday), fasten seat belts, unlatch doors prior to landing, touch down in full stall attitude holding yoke fully back to keep nose wheel off the ground as long as possible."

Henry rolled his eyes. "You don't trust me?" he asked, pulling down his seat belt. It came over both shoulders and attached at his lap.

"You'll be there to catch me, I suppose, if we fall?" I said, as I took my coat off and buckled my belt.

"Just like you were, when Remley ran away," he said, throttling up to full speed on both sides of the plane, testing the engines. The plane bounced around, almost lifting itself off the ground with the force of the propeller and the power. It moved slightly forward and side to side, as Henry checked the rudder pedals and brakes. He gripped a small televisionlike box, a global positioning system, and stowed it along with a radio and a telephone below his seat. I recognized the GPS because the agribusiness concerns had to use them to find their best land.

I was acutely aware that my seat belt was only a lap belt, but strangely the pit in my stomach disappeared.

Henry's siphoned voice went out into the world, "This is Romeo seven four seven two seven, ready for takeoff."

There was no response.

"Uncontrolled air space," he said. "It's like reporting in the blind." He popped the plane forward, grabbing a map. He studied it for a moment, steering with the rudder pedals. Finally he pointed to a place due east of us. "There she is," he said, and gave me the map to fold down. We taxied out to the only airstrip. He turned the plane into the wind, throttled up, released the brakes, and then we were hitting and snapping down that runway.

We reached sixty miles per hour, then seventy-five and the plane was ready to fly, fighting to get up in the air like a horse pulling at its reins. Then came the steady push-in of the throttle, the easing up of the nose, and we were caught by the net of air, which comes in to catch those brave enough to throw themselves into it.

At first, all I saw was the nose of the plane and the sky. The motor had that low, lugged, sloppy sound as it took off climbing up the ladders of the altimeter. The engines couldn't have had more power than two Volkswagens.

Henry spoke once into the microphone. "This is Romeo seven four seven two seven proceeding due west." After several minutes, he turned the trim knob and the plane shifted slightly. The nose came down, and I found myself looking at the Columbia Basin. Lewis and Clark couldn't have seen a more staggering sight.

"Oh my God, Henry," I said. "I never knew it would be this beautiful." I had always flown with Ike for a purpose, chasing cattle or shooting coyotes. I never bothered to take a look at what was around me until now.

I forced the window open. It was difficult even to hold my hand steady in the wind. It blew my skin into warped forms. I stretched up in the seat and looked over the metal door. Nothing lay between the ground and us. We were floating there over the river, and I could see everything.

Down to the west were the bumps, the dangerous clouds coming over the Cascades. They formed prisms through which the sun came, casting beams of light that ignited the Columbia into fire. Nearer to us, clouds reflected in the river, billowing white sheets like sails. Directly below I followed the eddies and currents that turned the great river into a gleaming slab of green-gray marble.

The railroad tracks followed the curves of the riverbanks. Sections of it cut straight through the water as if a child had sloppily outlined the edges of the river in black. I saw the dams that covered the Columbia and the Snake with lakelike water.

Around us, the mesa of the Columbia basin spread out. There where the river cut through strata, millions of years of history flashed. I saw the thick black old rock they called Vishnu, after the Hindu god, the supreme spirit, the preserver. Above that, the layers of basalt fell away in contoured lines as if they were giant constructions holding back the mesa from the river.

We completed our turn and headed east, the Blue Mountains rising from the Columbia basin like the curve of a claw-footed bath. From the air, farming was a Euclidean dream. Thickly planted circles were bisected by irrigation lines. The square sections made an undulating quilt that covered the earth. From the air I saw which land was bad, washed out with white alkali, and which land was rich and laid down like chocolate silk.

I wondered where Tansy was in all of this land, and how I was going to find her. I sat there imagining what she looked like today. She would be beautiful, her shoulders wide and strong like her father's. They could carry quivers of arrows, cattle tongues, stoles made from storied pelts, and her eyes, bruised darker than mine, would be covered with scaffolding to keep the grieving clouds from pouring rain over her irises.

Below us appeared a runway with giant white Xs across both ends. "What's that?" I asked.

"Private," he said. "The Xs mean 'keep out.' You land there, you'll likely be met with a shotgun. They're all over out here. Terrorists. Meth labs. Chemical plants."

I wondered what I would find when I tracked down my niece.

Henry spoke into the air once more. We heard the tower at Pendleton talking to a landing plane. I settled in for the ride.

From two thousand feet, the ranch sites sprawled like toys, and the roads spread out as if they were lines drawn on a sandy beach. I could see truck tracks where years ago people had driven over the range.

More and more the land looked alive. Harvested fields were like the scarred coats of deer. Wrinkles of geography appeared as weather-beaten faces of old farmers. The canyons and crevices were covered with brush as if there were something embarrassing about the orifices of the earth.

The one thing I couldn't see was Hanford, hidden behind Gable Mountain. It should have been called Coffin Mountain, for the radiation. A person couldn't see the poison that came out of that place. The bone seekers. Strontium-90, plutonium-239. They were the worst, long-term. They seeped into your skeleton and kept giving off radiation for the length of their half-life: thirty years for strontium and twenty-four thousand years for plutonium.

When I took Elise in for her brain cancer, the doctors gave me a test, too. Then they told me what else to worry about besides the iodine-131. It was the bone seekers. They told me I was lucky. At least I wasn't Native American.

The diet of the traditional Indians was fish. Their practice was to honor the spirit of the whole animal they killed. They ate the bones. They caught fish below Hanford's reactors that were cooled by river water, which was then returned to the Columbia. The radioactivity spread everywhere, seeped into the meat and milk, the fish, the leafy vegetables. Everything fed by the air and water of the Columbia basin was contaminated, and no one knew for forty years, except the vague and shadowy "people" in charge of Hanford.

I pulled the window back into place and latched it. Henry glanced around constantly, taking in everything about the land and the air. I could see he loved his work. It suited and challenged him.

"What are you looking for?" I asked. It still bothered me to talk; I felt like my body was becoming amphibious, my fingers fusing together. I moved them like a mitt. The only thing that jolted me out of that sea was the intermittent chop of the wind.

"You have to watch," he said. "In case something happens."

"Like what?"

"Anything. The plane. A radio from the hospital."

"Run through it for me," I said. "Tell me what we're going to do."

"First. You have to have decided where to land. Before you get there."

"There's no strip here," I said. "It's the middle of nowhere." We had traveled past farming now. The range spread out before us, a winter shade of brown.

"I do the same thing Ike did," Henry said, concentrating on maneuvering the plane. "It's worse when I fly over mountains. There's less space to land. Less time."

"You had trouble?" I asked, feeling a wave of nausea.

"An engine quit on me once. That's why I made them buy a twin-engine plane." He throttled down.

I felt my stomach turn at the thought of Henry in a plane crash. I looked away at the infinite rangeland that spread out like longing. Seeing Henry made me miss what we had together, but it also made me think of Jake. Henry reminded me of lost parts of my life. It seemed they were flying back to me now, landing in my solar plexus full of desires and impulses. And now I wanted desperately to find Tansy.

"I look for a paved road first," Henry went on, making a series of left turns. Henry glanced at the global positioning system as we neared our destination.

I noticed we were over a small ranch site, turning around and around it as we descended an Escher-like spiral staircase to land.

"Check to make sure there are no telephone poles," he added. "If there isn't pavement, I go gravel, then dirt. Range is better than cropland. The stubble wraps around the wheels. Pulls you down and can flip you. Fallow is bad, too. Too thick. Like landing in mud."

Henry wheeled the trim tab and throttled the engines lower. The plane felt to be pointing practically straight down. The throttle hummed uncomfortably close to zero.

We were landing on gravel, the road to the house. Luckily, the telephone poles stretched across the range, not the road. Otherwise, we would have had to touch down in sagebrush. As high as it was, it could rip off a wing.

Henry pulled the nose down even farther for the landing. From where I sat, we came into the ranch like one of those carny rides that whip you around as you barely miss the ground.

At the last minute, Henry lifted the nose up. I didn't feel the back wheels hit; they lay down on the earth as if they'd never left. We slowed as he placed the front wheel on the thick gravel that builds up in the middle. The plane steamed through it like a ship.

The road led into a homestead surrounding an old white two-story house. We drove in, the nose and propeller of the plane angled up into the air whipping like a bomber. It was a small place with a shed to the right of the house and a barn to the left.

A heavy-set woman came running out of the house waving at us.

Henry stopped the plane, and the dust cleared. He grabbed his bag and was out the door before I removed my headphones.

I heard her voice as I walked up the broken concrete sidewalk.

"We found her horse. It come running back to the barn. I went looking for her," she said, slowing to breathe. "Found her on the side of the road. She couldn't have been there very long. Not more 'n fifteen minutes."

"Then what happened?" asked Henry. His voice was loud, but calm.

"I brought her in here. Laid her down on the couch. I gave her some insulin. It happened already once this week. She fell off. She's been having trouble with her medication."

I pushed open the screen door. It had no weight at all. It stayed open as I entered the house. It was dark and smelled of incense. The floor sloped. It undulated with warp and was covered by boomerang-patterned linoleum.

I walked down the hall. There were pieces of fabric hanging on curtain rods, circular ornaments with beads and feathers. I followed the voices to the living room. Henry shone his penlight while holding the woman's eyes open with his thumb.

"What's your name?" he asked, his voice steady but hurried.

The woman mumbled something I couldn't make out. She was dressed in jeans and a T-shirt. Her hair was cut short. Henry examined the patient's skull, delicately touching it and checking to see if his fingers came up red.

"Where are we?" Henry asked.

"Lapwai," the woman said.

Henry gripped her hand and pricked her finger, testing her sugar. "What day is it?"

"August."

It was February 7.

Henry inserted a needle into the soft inside of her elbow for IV access. Then he bolted. He ran right by me, grabbing my shoulders and moving me out of the way. I went numb again. Nothing in the world struck me as a good idea except to sit down on the floor, and that was what I did. My mind shut off. I wanted to cry.

I heard Henry scream "Clear," and he started the plane. Then he ran

back in carrying a bright yellow plastic body board and a blue cushioned brace.

"If I knew where she hit, I could drill a hole."

That didn't make any sense, I thought. For a diabetic to have a hole
drilled in her skull.

"Iris," he said. "Give me a hand." He had the board at the patient's
side. "Just lift her up. Slightly roll her."

I inched my fingers under her hips.

"I need you, too," he said to the other woman. She came over
silently.

"Don't lift," Henry repeated. "Just roll her. Hang on to the brace
there. And her shoulder."

While we moved her, Henry deftly placed the board under halfway.
He cautiously slid her onto the platform. He strapped the patient
down. One thick band around her forehead, one around her shoulders,
waist, and legs.

"Grab that end," he said to me, motioning to her feet. "Hanford
Regional Health Center," he said to the woman. "That's where we're
going."

"No," she replied. "That's too far. I can't get all the way to Hanford.
I need to have her treated close to home."

"Look, Patty," Henry said in the same loud but calm voice. "The
patient has a severe closed-head injury. She needs a CAT scan and a
neurosurgeon. Hanford is the closest level-two trauma center. And
we're going there."

"I won't go to that place." She raised her hand to her forehead.

Henry and I started outside, and the woman came after us. He
pushed the board at me to go faster. I walked backward as rapidly as I
could, navigating the broken and ripped-up cement walkway.

The side doors to the plane had been flung open. I stepped up and
crouched inside, scooting back, setting the patient on a platform.
Henry secured her. He placed an oxygen mask over her nose and
mouth, and electrodes on her chest. He injected something into her IV
access and then hooked the bag to the plane's ceiling.

"I think she's unconscious," I said.

"I know," said Henry. "Strap yourself in." He motioned to a seat on

the side of the plane. "Ride back there," he ordered. "But you'll have to
fly if the patient crashes. Watch the monitor for me," he said, pointing
to a white box with a red continuous heartbeat.

I pulled down the shoulder harness, buckled it, and placed my
headphones over my ears.

"Are you coming with us?" he asked the woman.

She did not respond.

"Are you coming or not?" asked Henry, sliding into the cockpit.

"I have to stay here," the woman said finally. "I have to look after
the children."

"All right, then," said Henry. "We'll meet you at the hospital."

I knew what was happening now. It was the same thing that had
happened to Ike.

We didn't have the luxury of taking off into the wind. It blew from
the side, knocking us around malevolently. The front wheel was slowed
down by the gravel. It was a long run on the road before I felt us fly. I
sat there clutching my seat belt, my eyes riveted on the undulating
lights monitoring her heart.

I heard Henry announce our heading into the airwaves. He changed
channels and held his hand up signaling he was moving to channel 4.
"I need an ACLS with neurosurgeon on standby. I have an approximately thirty-six-year-old Native American female with a history of
diabetes. Appears to have fallen on horseback and suffered a subdural
hematoma. She's gone from conversant to unresponsive with mini-
mally reactive pupil on the left side. Flying to Richland. Will need to be
met by ACLS. Vital signs 190 over 100. Pulse 120. Afebrile. Respira-
tory rate, rapid."

Through the window, I saw the clouds that we had seen on the
radar moving in. They came with the wind. The plane was buffeted as it
rose in the air. At least we had beaten the worst of it, I hoped.

When we arrived in Richland the paramedics asked me to ride with
her. I wanted to decline. But we all rode together, anyway, to the Death
Mile Hospital. That's what everyone called Hanford Regional Health
Center. I was uncomfortable, and I definitely didn't have ambulance
manners.

"She's lucky," said the paramedic. "The head injuries from the rural areas are usually too far gone by the time they get up here." He was a tall, thin young man with freckles on the backs of his hands; he looked like the type who had climbed Mt. Hood and Mt. Rainier by the time he was eighteen. "It's pretty cool livin' in the great outdoors," he said. "Unless you get sick. Or you have an accident. Then you're screwed."

"Yeah, I know," I said. "It happened to somebody in my family."

The paramedic looked at me and started to say something, but I stared him down.

We pulled into the hospital, and the patient didn't look lucky anymore. Her hands and arms were rigid and straight out from her body. They called her breathing agonal. The pupils were dilated. They took her immediately into Emergency.

I felt as if I had fallen off a horse myself. I needed to go into the bathroom. I didn't know if I was going to throw up or shit. But I managed to walk to the admitting desk and fill out what I knew on her forms. I marked Indian Health Service for her insurance, listed her address as Oregon. I pushed the clipboard under the glass partition and sat down, waiting to be called.

A woman with a brown wig and glasses worked at the reception desk. She motioned me back immediately when she read the form.

"Do you have her Health Service information?" she asked. I thought I detected alarm in her voice.

"No," I responded. "It was an emergency. We came here in an ambulance."

The woman narrowed her eyes at me. "You don't even have her purse?"

"No," I told her. "But her physician is here. He's from the Indian Health Service, Pendleton."

"Where is he?" she demanded.

"They're getting a CAT scan. Her doctor can give you all the information."

I sat down again and tried to read a magazine. I was struck by the number of people in there. Six families. A lot of bored children. Old-timers.

After about forty minutes, Henry came out. "We got the CAT," he said, sitting down next to me. "She hit on the left side of her head. A pretty good bleed. They're getting her ready to go into surgery now."

"Will she live?" I asked, crossing my arms tightly.

"If she does, she'll have neurologic damage," he replied. "There is a better waiting room down here." He stood up and looked around briefly.

As I followed Henry through the emergency room, I wondered how he could be so calm, eerily calm. I expected Henry to be devastated, or at least shaken up from his patient's courtship with death. I doubted his pulse would even rise when he assisted the surgery.

People in green scrubs rushed to and from counters filled with medicines, cotton balls, tongue depressors, blood pressure equipment. On either side of us, blue-curtained cubicles overflowed with patients. Occasionally one of the drapes opened, revealing a middle-aged man with a bandaged hand, a woman fully clothed lying on her back, a terrified child crying.

I followed Henry through another set of plastic-wrapped doors and continued down the hallway. Signs pointing to either side of us were labeled: Radiology, Oncology, Surgery, Rehabilitation. We passed by the CAT scan room and the nurse's station there. One very attractive young, blond nurse looked at a chart. An older nurse retrieved something out of a cupboard.

"Drunk," the blonde said. "My guess is point two five."

"Damn Indians," said the other. "Drunks, fights, car wrecks, shootings, knifings. It's like the freaking Wild West in here."

When we walked by, the older one turned her back on us. The blonde smiled at Henry. She ignored me.

Henry stopped in front of the waiting room door and stood as I entered. The room reeked of anxious boredom. It was plain and uncomfortably chaired. Another family agitated in there, a mother and her son and daughter. The mother held her hand to her temple; the children sat next to her. Their legs splayed over the too large chairs, tiptoes turned in. Someone brought them crayons. They furtively colored.

After about two hours, the doctor entered to talk to the family. I could see the mother bracing herself.

He nodded to her. "We went cell by cell. We tested it all. I think we have clean borders."

The mother started to cry. The boy climbed on her, he grabbed her glasses. The girl anchored her hand in the V-neck of her blouse.

"He's in the intensive care now," the doctor said. "You can see him in about fifteen minutes."

I watched the three of them leave. Then I heard voices in the hallway. "You can't see her," I heard one of the nurses say. "She's still in the operating room."

A question shot out, followed by mumbling.

"The doctor will speak with you when they're finished."

More talking. Someone running. A young Indian man came in the room. He sat down for a minute and a half, all the while looking at the door. He stood up and ran out.

The hospital was cold. I walked to the nurse's station to ask them to turn up the heat.

"Can't," the young nurse said. "It's the temperature we like. For operating."

"You ought to work in a morgue," I told her. I looked down the hall as I started back to the waiting room. A group of people surrounded an old man dressed in traditional Indian garb. He raked the walls with his fingers and watched the ceiling, as if to keep an eye on it.

The nurse looked, too. "Jesus Christ," she said, and walked like a bulldog down there.

"You people come with me," she ordered. "I can't have you doin' a rain dance or whatever it is you're doin' in the middle of a hallway. This is a hospital. We need to keep this hall clear." She walked behind them, herding the group my way.

"You don't understand," said a woman. I recognized her as the patient's friend. "He has a method to what he does. It's ritual. There's work to be done at the Death Mile Hospital."

The nurse winced a little and continued herding them my way.

I quickly walked back into the waiting room and took a seat at the far end.

"This is a top-rate, level-two trauma center," said the nurse. "We do everything we can here. But we don't do hocus-pocus."

The group filed in one at a time, the young man I had seen earlier, followed by the friend, followed by the healer, followed by a little girl.

The medicine man walked into the room and spotted me immediately. He shuffled up and looked me in the eye. He was a slight person who appeared as if he bore great strength. His brown eyes carried white circles around the edges of the irises. I sat there looking at him, and he at me. He must have stood there for three minutes, staring silently. Then he closed his eyes. Finally, he moved to the center of the room and made elaborate and specific gestures to the four corners of the room. Then he began chanting.

But my eyes were riveted to the little girl. She was about ten, I guessed. She had thick black hair. It was below her shoulders and curled under at the ends.

The little girl did not look at me. The shaman carried on his mental surgery, chanting and singing. The beat of his instrument was transporting. I didn't know whether I was really there or not. I didn't know where I was. I wasn't acting like myself. When I reached out to touch the little girl's hair, everyone looked at me.

That was how Henry found me, the shaman chanting, the little girl staring at me as I caressed her hair and thought of my lost niece.

"Come on," said Henry. "Let's go find Tansy."

23

AFTER WE LANDED AT THE RESERVATION, HENRY DROVE me back to the Yellowbird Health Clinic. We entered the adjacent Tribal Administration Building. Passing through the heavy wood doors, we proceeded down a long hallway. Tribal Enrollment was the first door on the right.

Henry knocked; there was no answer. He pulled out his keys and tried several. The door remained closed. "I've only got one more," he said, turning the key gingerly. The door opened. "Anyone finds out I did this," he said, "my career is history."

The small room brimmed with plants: lilies, bromeliads, and spider ferns. It smelled like shrub perspiration, a greenhouse. Henry seated himself behind the desk and turned on the computer.

"Henry, you don't have to do this," I said, walking behind him to look at the computer screen.

"It would take you forever," he said. "No one would help. It's illegal to give out information—other than whether or not someone is a member."

"Just give me your keys," I said. "And if anyone finds out, I'll say I stole them."

He remained at the chair. He began typing. "Besides, Tansy is Nez Perce, so I have to access the Nez Perce Tribal Enrollment in Spaulding, Idaho. And even then, you might not see her. What they'd probably do is contact the custodial guardian first and ask if they wanted to accept contact from you. You think they'll want to hear from fourth-generation Narcissa Whitman?"

I bristled at his slander. "Okay," I said angrily. "Go right ahead. Lose your damn job."

Henry was silent for a minute. "I've never had a brother or a sister," he replied. "Do you know how many times I wished I had? Jake was the closest thing, and when he died, I lost even that. You have to find that little girl. She needs a family." Henry held his body rigid, the way people do when they're concentrating on not crying.

I fidgeted nervously behind him while the screen remained blank. "This place stinks," I said, changing the subject after several minutes.

"Yeah," he said, recovered. "Terry loves plants more than people."

"What the hell is a custodial guardian, anyway?" Anger was the best way to take away pain; I knew that much from experience. "I'm her aunt, for christsakes."

"After the death of both parents, a child becomes a ward of the tribal court," he said. "I've seen it happen a lot. Then they go to tribal social services, and after that, a foster home pending placement with a permanent guardian."

"I'm not even notified?"

"The Indian Child Welfare Act gives tribes first jurisdiction over a kid, even over state court. It ensures that they will be placed in a Native American home. But to be honest, Iris, why wouldn't they have done that? What contact have you had with Tansy over the last twelve years?"

"Nothing," I said, and took a deep breath. "Well, one time. The day her father killed himself." I gathered my hair together, and swung it to my back.

Henry sat with his hands in his lap, waiting. I imagined he didn't want to touch much for fear of fingerprints. When the screen materialized, he scrolled down the long list of names, addresses occasionally coming up from all over the world. Slowing when he came to the Ss, he found Kappy. It read *deceased*. Below that was Tansy's name, listed as living on 241 Prospector Avenue, Pendleton, Oregon. She wasn't more than five miles away.

"She's in a foster home. They haven't placed her in permanent custody yet."

"Oh god, a foster home," I said. Indian foster homes couldn't be any better than the ones you read about in the newspapers.

Henry shut off the computer. We left quickly and quietly. "Anyone wonders how you found her, just say you asked around," instructed Henry. "No one will believe that, but say it anyway."

I left Henry at the clinic and drove past Kappy and Tansy's old house, just as I had done for the past seven years. I wondered who owned it now that Kappy was dead. Two years ago, a solid wood awning replaced the corrugated plastic. Flowerpots on either side of the door bloomed. Since Cayuse Casino, the tribe prospered.

The knots in my stomach were tight, worse than they had been with Henry. I hunched over the wheel, my belly buckled under. I briefly thought about going home but banished my cowardice immediately. I couldn't stand the idea of a foster home. What if her foster brother was molesting her the way it happened to my high school classmate, Jan Lock, coming in at night while the parents ignored the noises, pushing her facedown on the bed and fucking her from behind. I started sweating. My palms itched, my neck and back hurt. I turned and headed toward Prospector.

It was a brick house, same as all the rest; a broken-down swing sagged in the front lawn. I knocked on Tansy's door, as I had her mother's twelve years ago. Tansy opened it slightly and peered out. I drew in my breath; her face was arrestingly beautiful. She squinted at me, auburn-eyed like her father. Despite her beauty, I noticed her jaws were clenched, and her sharp aquiline nose leaned ever so slightly to one side. It was as if half her face was tending, caring for the opposite half. She had a tiny scar at the edge of her mouth on the sheltered side. It pointed to her upper lip, which arrested into a pinkish nippled scoop at its center. She stared at me and caressed it with her tongue. She had not lost the nursing callus from her infancy.

Tansy walked back inside to watch television and kicked a leather bag out of the way. It careened across the room. In the corner of the living room a twin bed stood. The neatness of the house practically glared at me, defying any claim that she was ill kept. But the odor couldn't be hidden, stale, and old.

"I'm your aunt," I said gingerly. Indians said *auntie*, but I was just her aunt. I noticed the poster of Kappy as the Happy Creek Princess hung on the wall over the bed. I imagined it was one of the few things she had left of her mother. Like Henry, I tried to hold back my tears. I wondered how I could just appear in her life after eight years. I decided it was just what people did out here where there was nothing around to hem them in.

"I know who the hell you are," she said. "You look just like him."

I didn't think I looked at all like Jake, I thought, as I sat down on the couch with her. I was angry at myself that I had stayed away from them, furious at listening to Elise's warnings about how Kappy was dangerous, just out for herself. Who wasn't?

Tansy continued watching a movie, *The Wizard of Oz*, on the cable channel.

I looked over at her, wondering if she understood how much she had changed since I saw her last. She had matured early and looked like she was already a teenager. She wasn't that different from me; I was twelve when I took on the jobs of an adult. Tansy's body had rounded. She moved in handfuls of flesh now, rather than slices. She seemed unaware, as though she didn't notice the difference in her body. Her black thick hair was gathered in a ponytail. Delicate curls and waves of stray baby hairs decorated her forehead, just like her father's.

She kept her eyes on the television.

"You like livin' here?" I ventured.

She reached up with the back of her hand and pushed the curls from her forehead. Tansy's hair flowed strong and black. I was unfamiliar with such strong softness. What came out of our family's heads was marked by its inability to be depended on. Our hair was frail and thin. When you set it, it would not be styled when you were finished. One was afraid to look at it to see what it had become.

She ignored me.

"I didn't think you'd remember me," I tried again.

"Of course I do. I remember you. I remember the time I rode your horse."

I watched her speak, the way her rounded cheeks moved and the whiteness of her tiny teeth. "Jade," I said.

She nodded. "Jade, Remley, Banner, and Aerie," she replied. "My dad taught me all the horses' names."

"You here alone?" I asked.

"Been waitin' for you to come pick me up to go riding again," she said, straight-faced.

I stared at her. The eight years weighed on me. I shifted on the couch.

"I want to ride your horse again," she said, looking at me, expecting an answer.

I nodded. The last time she rode my horse, Jake had killed himself.

"My guardian lives here," she said, glaring at the TV. "Her name is Linda Blackwood. She gets paid a thousand a month for me to stay with her."

"How long you been here?"

"Six months," she said. And then she turned to look me in the eye. "Ever since my mother died."

I tried to offer a sympathetic smile. Tansy looked away in disgust. I should be going, I thought, but turned to watch the movie instead. We sat in silence for fifteen minutes.

"Look, there's the witch," she said, suddenly.

"Anyone else live here?" I asked.

"Her friend Charlie, sometimes. And two other kids." She tucked her legs around her and wiggled as she buried them in an afghan. "People don't understand. I'm a lot older than you think I am. Haven't you heard? Childhood's disappearing. Kids are growing up early. I don't need a guardian."

I wondered if those were Jake's or Kappy's words. "Until you're eighteen," I said. "It's the law. A judge will appoint you a permanent guardian, and, besides, the Nez Perce will want you back in their tribe."

"Like hell," she replied. "My mother told me they kicked us out of there. They said my family was bad medicine. It's how my mother got her name. They're not going to want me back now. That's how I got my name. *Tansy* means poison, you know."

"*Tansy* also means unvanquishable." I knew my weeds.

She mouthed the word silently.

"Of course someone'll want to adopt you."

"Oh, so I can carry on their cultural heritage for them?" She sat there sullen. "No, thank you. I already know as much as I want to know about being Indian. I know how to do the dances, speak the language. I know I can go to college free so I can get my MBA and come back here and run a casino. I know that I'm going to get diabetes just like my mother and die from it."

The room closed in around us. "Do the Nez Perce know your mother's passed away?" I stopped myself from saying "dead."

"Quit talking to me like I'm a kid," Tansy said, angrily picking at the afghan that covered her legs. "Of course they know," she scoffed. "Six years till I'm eighteen. That's nothing. I don't want to live with some family so they can get paid extra money. I've been taking care of myself since I was born."

Suddenly, I heard myself saying, "Why don't we get out of here for a while?" At the time, it seemed like the most natural thing in the world to do.

Tansy looked around at the house.

"There's nothing better than a drive to help a person clear their head. We can come back. Whenever you want."

To my surprise, she nodded. And I remember thinking, This is a bad sign—she just accepts offers from strangers to take off. I thought of how I first met her mother, and how Jake had stayed there that night, a family of coincidence and luck, or lack of it.

Tansy sat down on her bed for a minute, almost as if she had just woken up, and then grabbed the brown bag she had kicked. She stuffed it full of a handful of underwear, another pair of jeans, four shirts, and her boots. I didn't think she would want to come, let alone pack a bag and stay with me. When she was about to walk out the door, she turned and went back.

My heart pounded. I told myself this was good: maybe Tansy had more sense than I did. I knew it was wrong to kidnap a child, even if she was my niece.

Tansy walked back in the house, stood on the bed, and grabbed the photo of her mother. She threw her bag in the back of the Blazer and kept the picture up front, down by her right leg. Then we rolled out of there and started the sixty-mile drive to our house. The photo rattled against the side of the door. I imagined it was Kappy telling me how angry she was. I listened to the rattle all the way to Krump.

"You hungry?" It was nearing 6 P.M.

She looked at me. "Yeah," she said.

"What do you want?"

"There's a Burgerville by the freeway."

I pulled up to the drive-in window and ordered a cheeseburger, fries, and a milk. I glanced at Tansy.

"Same thing. But not milk. Chocolate shake," she instructed, again pushing the curls out of her face with the back of her hand. "Ask them for ten ketchups, will you?"

I nodded. We inched forward, picked up our food, and drove over to park alongside the Shiloh. "I probably should have ordered a salad," I said, as I took a bite of the burger. The Blazer smelled of greasy French fries.

Tansy sat ignoring me again. She ate her cheeseburger with both hands, didn't unwrap it any farther than she had to, and didn't speak while she ate. She was finished before I was halfway through mine. Then she started on her French fries, opening the ketchups and sucking the corner of the package after she took bites of fry. I watched her hands, noticing their delicate plumpness, the knuckles dimpling. When Tansy finished, she wadded the paper, stuffed it in the fry carton, along with the empty ketchups. She placed the whole thing in the white bag that sat inside the well between us, then leaned back in her seat and sucked on her shake. "My mother said people do nice things for other people so they can make themselves feel better."

I sat there and chewed my mouthful. I thought about turning back, but it was too late now. "Do you miss her?" I asked.

Tansy was silent. She looked to see if any wayward ketchup had lodged under her fingernails, and then she nodded.

"My mom died four months ago," I said abruptly.

"What from?" Tansy asked, looking up.

"Cancer," I replied. "Your mom?"

"Heart attack," she said. "Because of the diabetes."

I stopped chewing even though there was cheeseburger in my mouth.

"Do you miss her?" she asked.

I nodded. My eyes welled up sitting in the car, and suddenly I wasn't hungry anymore. I swallowed and laid the rest of my cheeseburger in the trash bag. "You ready?" I asked.

"Born ready," she said. She flipped through my CDs until she found Everclear. She looked at it for a minute, then threw it back and placed *Live Through This* in the tray and turned up the volume.

When Tansy and I arrived at the Bar S, I noticed Scotty Jamison's pickup at the shop. The two of us shivered as we ran inside. We found a mess there, the house covered with half-full coffee cups and chewed pencils. Hanna was in the green room working on the sculpture; she'd probably been there since I'd left at dawn. I saw dark commas of black under her eyes. She appeared every bit of her seventy years now.

The progress she had made amazed me. I was practically finished. My sculpture had grown flesh, it had grown muscle. I could see it was me, but stronger, tougher. There were scratches all over it as if it were a combination of sculpture and drawing.

I hardened, lightened, and evolved into the dried clay color of my parents. Strong fire grew out of my head; the left side of me was brutal as the rages of Ike. My sculpture now fit in with the rest of them. Hanna cut off the twisted slave body, sliced below my breasts. One nipple turned inward, grew convex; the other looked as if it had forces, green rays coming in and out of it.

My arms evolved into limbs like the Hermitage caryatids, strong enough to support the architecture of my family. The muscles, carved out, grew together, wrapped over one another, and disappeared into the traces of my yokelike shoulders.

When Hanna saw Tansy as we walked inside, she sat down, sighed, and placed a hand over her eyes.

Tansy looked at me uneasily.

"This is my niece," I said, introducing Tansy.

Tansy extended her hand, which shocked me.

"Jake's," Hanna said hoarsely as she grasped Tansy's hand. I thought she might cry. I immediately felt guilty, as if I had done something wrong, but I had told her about Tansy within the first couple of weeks of her arrival at the Bar S. She, of course, had said nothing.

Tansy rubbed her hand on the back of her jeans. I wondered if she was seeing the colors from Hanna's hands, just as I had at Dammasch. "You did all this?" Tansy asked, stopping in front of the statue of Jake.

Hanna nodded. She placed her hands to her eyes again and pressed hard.

"Your father," I told her. "When he was about ten." They looked eerily the same. Their lips, the way the upper one came to a point in the middle; their profiles, the line of the jaw, square and rigid.

"That's your grandmother," I said, pointing to Elise. Tansy turned. The curls at her forehead matched her father's and grandmother's.

Hanna had placed my clay next to Elise. On my other side was Jake. Finally, herding the family together, Ike glared on the other end.

I sat down, looked at all of us waiting to be cast and finally made permanent. But something was wrong. We all knew, as we stared at the sculptures, Tansy wasn't there. I wondered if Hanna was capable of another. It seemed it had practically killed her to finish mine. Up all night with insomnia, she talked even less than before, seemed to be thinking constantly about her work even when she wasn't sculpting. Her eyes were red all the time as if she had contracted sties.

We left Hanna sitting there, her fingers on her eyes; I imagined her trying to see the visions she had conjured in the past. I showed Tansy her new room. It had been Jake's when he was little. She immediately went to the closet and dug into the boxes of her father's things. Elise had kept them. Tansy pulled out a baby quilt with cowboys on it. She found plastic jets that Jake had hung from the ceiling. He treasured planes until riding with Ike ruined his love for them. Wooden combines and tractors filled one box. Tansy pulled each one out lovingly, probably with the thought that her father's fingerprints were still on them.

I went to retrieve the photo albums and when I returned, Tansy wasn't there. I walked through the house looking for her, but she wasn't anywhere. I found her, finally, down at the barn with Jade. She had swung up onto my horse without a coat, a bridle, or saddle, and was sitting there in the middle of the corral staring straight ahead.

Through the next two weeks, Tansy and I were constant companions. I drove her to register for school through the freezing fog. She wanted to get a hardship license, special dispensation to drive, which you could get in the rural areas because of the distances. Turned out she didn't need it because I drove her there and picked her up every day. I didn't mind; besides, the school had gone to a four-day week to save money.

She brought her homework back from class, and I helped her with it. We were a bit like mother and daughter but, given my frame of reference, more like friends. She told me she didn't fit in at school. The heroin and crystal meth users expected her to do drugs, just because she was Indian.

Every day we continued looking through Jake's things. He'd left practically everything when he moved in with Kappy. Tansy sang pieces of his favorite music as she went through old albums he'd discarded for CDs. Springsteen, Jimi Hendrix, Talking Heads, The Who, Woody Guthrie, Hüsker Dü, Beatles, Elton John, REM, U2. She sang the words of "One Tree Hill" by heart. I watched her in amazement.

She looked at me. "What? You think I only know war chants?"

I shook my head and smiled. "No," I said softly, "I think you know a lot more."

The house seemed warmer now that she was there. It was messier, of course, Hanna and Tansy being who they were, but that was a small price to pay for warmth. When Tansy and I found Jake's school pictures, she gathered them up and said she was going to make an album. Sitting there with Jake's music playing, I felt drunk without even taking a shot, and no longer was I jealous of my brother. Smiling, I realized Tansy idolized her father.

As she stared at the photos of Jake hunting with Ike, her hair swung down and hung beside her face. She looked at what she had left of her father. I looked too: Jake, pale and opaque-skinned, smaller and weaker than he had ever seemed to me at the time; his thin arms emerged from his short-sleeved shirt, bony and awkward. God, he looked so small.

He was no match for my father, who seemed to devour everything. No wonder my brother hanged the cat; he couldn't kill me, and it was the only thing left his size.

In almost all the photos, he wore the crew cut that I remember Ike giving him. Jake hated Ike's short shaves, said they made him look bad because they revealed all the scars on his head. But Ike went on giving them anyway. "Long hair is for hippies," he sneered.

Jake smiled for Mother in another photo, and the grin disappeared into nothing at the corners of his mouth. I studied the snapshot taken by Elise. Ike was walking behind Jake, wouldn't even stand with his son. He was half turned around, growling an order as if he wanted to take a bite out of them both for bothering to take the photo. I could imagine him saying, *If you have to take a picture of your life, you aren't living it.*

Tansy showed me one after another. I stared longest at the photo taken the Christmas Ike and Elise had given Jake his rifle. He held it above his head like a warrior running into battle. They had even given him the gun he killed himself with.

We retrieved Jake's clothes, and Tansy took his favorite Pendleton shirts. They fit her about as poorly as Ike's fit me, but she wore them to school anyway. She snatched up the worn-out Levi's coat I had used to keep the tar off my neck. She held it up in her fist and shouted, "An anarchy jacket! I've always wanted one."

Jake's first guitar, enclosed in a dusty black case, was wedged back in a closet corner. Tansy pulled it out and placed her small hands on it, trying a chord as she strummed. It was true and still is: the only song I remember Jake teaching me was "This Land Is Your Land." I showed her how to play it. She learned it immediately and started variations, thinking up new songs.

Every night we stayed up until almost midnight, later than we should have, especially since Tansy and I had to leave for school at seven-thirty. There were more and more boxes to go through, and we hadn't even started on the bunkhouse. Tansy was so preoccupied with her father, she didn't eat. I warmed lasagna in the oven, made salads, and cooked chicken. Though I tried to prepare things that were good for her health, she only picked at her food and then excused herself to thumb through more boxes. Hanna and I ate dinner alone together.

Hanna, on the other hand, seemed grateful to be there and always thanked me as I sat inside the kitchen just as my mother had done.

In the process of going through Jake's things, I realized everything of my dead family was still in the house: the clothes of my mother, father, and brother. I even had the colonel's uniforms hung up in the basement in the room off the walk-in refrigerator. Five months after Elise's death, I needed to sift through things, digest it, save what I could, and discard the rest.

I decided to ask Hanna if she wanted her sister's clothing. I noticed lately she had begun to vary what she wore. She replaced the white shirt with my mother's pullovers. Now Hanna took walks in the morning and needed the extra clothing for the chill winter air. She spent some time with Scotty out in the shop; I drove by after taking Tansy to school and saw them there welding.

Mostly, I stood by and watched everything Tansy did. She didn't seem to notice me, but that didn't bother me somehow. People who'd had trauma like she had weren't malicious, just preoccupied.

Whenever I looked at my niece, I started thinking of the things we could do together. I wanted to get away, travel through India, go to the Pushkar camel fair on the full moon of the celebration of Brahma. We could head out to the Thar Desert, return through Jaisalmer, then ride down to Agra and finish at the Ganges, where we would be enveloped in the magical river full of human souls.

Maybe, given our history, we could go on a world tour of cemeteries. Start at Westminster, then Père-Lachaise in Paris, get high at Jim Morrison's grave. We could take the train down to Santa Croce in Florence, afterward fly to see Novodivichy in Moscow, then the Ganges, and finish at the Ricoletta in Buenos Aires. There had to be some way to work things out.

Fourteen nights after Tansy had come, Hanna entered my room, waking me from sleep. She sat down on my bed. She looked so white—again wearing her old clothes—that she could have been an apparition. I jumped, afraid she was going to kill me after all.

"Jesus," I said. I turned on the light. She had the dry lips of Dagmar, as if the water had been sucked out of her body. "What?" I asked. I looked at the clock; it read two-thirty in the morning.

She started sobbing the way she did the day I showed her the letter that committed her to the asylum. She didn't cover her eyes, and she looked so tired, so worn down.

Thinking something might have happened to Tansy, I jumped up, pulled on my sweats, and followed Hanna out to the green room. One last armature was covered in a large formation of clay. I stood looking at it.

"Scotty built it today," she said. "But Tansy doesn't fit in with the rest. I can't even picture what kind of face she should have."

"Put your face on her," I said. "She's not that different from you. The family outcast. Maybe that's why you can't do her. Too close to home."

Hanna stood looking at me, her arms hanging down. She shook her head no, and I felt failure grip our house again in its familiar and ever-present embrace.

I sat down and stared at the sculpture for several minutes. As I stayed there, I began to wonder how long I could hide Tansy here. Someone would find out soon enough. And she would probably be taken from me. I also suspected the institution might be searching for Hanna.

Silently we looked at the unfinished mass there with the other heads. Somehow, it looked like a leak that would sink a boat. I wanted to turn away, to not look at the mess, but I stayed there with my aunt.

After several minutes, Hanna sighed. "I had a vision in my head for thirty-one years. She upset everything."

"I know," I said.

Hanna rubbed her white sleeve over her face, brushing off her tears.

"Just sit with it," I said, suddenly resolute. "You've waited a lifetime to come back home, what's a few more days, or years? Some things," I said, looking at the nascent sculpture of Tansy, "you just can't force."

24

THE DEAD OF WINTER CAME THE THIRD WEEK AFTER Tansy's arrival. Even in the house, the air remained cold and dry; I could hear Hanna's roughened breathing through two doors. I resolved to call Miles the next morning and tell him I had Tansy: it was the same resolution I had made every night of the past three weeks. But each day Tansy and I did something new, and I was so taken with her, so wrapped up, I delayed making the call until the following day.

I decided to teach her to ride, pulled out the mangers in the old barn and made an indoor arena. We saddled up Jade, and Tansy learned how to direct her, how to use legs and weight instead of reins.

When she became confident enough, we rode out together; Tansy on Jade, me on Remley. We went to the Creek Ranch, followed the trading trail and the route of the cattle drives. The edges of the winter-filled creek were frozen. We urged the horses forward, cracking the ice. They blew their nostrils at the frozen water, suspecting some treachery. We tied them to the black walnut where Jake had shot himself, and then climbed the precarious rocks up to the Indian cave on the cliffs above the waters. With the screen left over from the archaeology team at OSU, we sifted for arrowheads. Afterward we sat at the lip of the cavern crevice and surveyed the ranch.

To the west, the ranch and Rock Creek flowed down to the John Day, a bizarre title for a river, named after an eccentric man who even back then was considered insane, wandering about Oregon, raped several times by Indians. To the east our ranch reached up toward the Wallowa Mountains in the northeast corner of the state.

"I want to go up there," Tansy said, squinting as she looked into the distance. "Visit Heart of the Beast."

"Yes," I replied. "We'll go. I'm going to teach you to take care of the land you own."

"I own?" she said, looking at me in surprise. "I've never been able to keep ahold of nothin'."

I laughed. "Me either," I said.

"My mother kept a picture of an old man. She told me his name was Hush Hush Cute. Said he was the father of ten children. I remember it 'cause it was such an unusual name. And because she told me he was my great-grandfather. He sold some land, and it was after that my great-grandparents moved to the reservation. Since then we've been bad. Nothing but trouble comes from us."

I remembered the photo I had seen on Kappy's nightstand. She held on to it just as tightly as Tansy held on to the picture of her mother. A person had to grasp on to what mattered most.

"I'm going to see to it that you inherit your father's half of Heart of the Beast," I said. I realized afterward, I had told her this with pride. I couldn't figure out why Elise and Ike had never had that conversation with me. I imagine their constant work replaced any opportunity for reflection about life.

Tansy was silent for a moment. "Unless the tribe takes it," she said.

"Owning land isn't easy," I said. "You have to fight for it. You let it go, and you've turned against it."

Tansy looked away. "You're not telling me anything I don't know," she said coldly.

I took out my ChapStick from my coat pocket and found a piece of gum. I tore it and gave her half. Tansy definitely had moments like this when she was curt and sullen. I tried not to take it personally. I imagined she was this way with everyone, including her mother. "There are always people who will take your land from you," I said. "Neighbors, developers, relatives."

"And that's what's going to happen," she said, matter-of-factly.

"The Nez Perce tribe has to prove the land isn't ours. Only if they can do that will the land pass to them."

"What do they know? How do they know whether it was ours or theirs?" she said.

"Well, the tribe says it was theirs to begin with, and that we took it from them illegally. We say we bought the land fair and square."

"My mother studied law so she could take that land from you," Tansy said. "She said your family had more than enough land. But she died before she got it back. And now it turns out I own half of it." She shook her head, and inhaled hard as if that would stop her from crying.

"Your mother studied law because Jake wanted that land. He wanted to get back at my mother and father."

She looked at me suddenly, studying my eyes. "My mother spoke about you a couple of times," she said. "Didn't want to do you any damage, that you'd never done anything to her."

I remembered how we had taken her home that night at the bar, and I had helped her to bed. I pulled my coat tight and crossed my arms. "Tansy," I said softly. "How would you like it if I were your guardian?" I spread my fingers through the fine dirt at the edge of the cave.

Tansy brought her knees under her chin and held them there. She was silent.

"You could live here with me, go to school." I tried to think of things a twelve-year-old would want, things I would have liked back then. "You can ride Jade all the time. We could go on trips together. The Himalayas are beautiful. They glow. And the Amazon. We could catch piranhas and fry them for dinner." I searched for something else to give her, but nothing came and at the same time, too much came. Just let it go, I told myself.

"Hawaii," she said grimly, as if it were a painful burden that she'd never been there. "I want to go to Hawaii."

I laughed. "Sure," I replied, hoping this was just a phase of wanting things she'd been deprived of, like cheeseburgers and fries.

"I want to surf," she said.

I nodded. "And when you're old enough for college," I said lightly, "we can visit some campuses, see if you like any of them."

She frowned. "Stanford," she announced. "They got one of the biggest powwows on the West Coast."

"Oregon State's nice too," I responded. *"Merde,"* I said. "You could go to the Sorbonne if you wanted."

"What's *merde?*" she asked.

"Shit in French."

She nodded, as if she was going to remember that one. Tansy sat next to me staring out at the ranch that unfolded below us. But she hadn't answered the question I had asked first.

"Why don't you have any tattoos?" Tansy said suddenly, throwing a rock off onto the shale. "And you don't have anything pierced except your ears."

I thought a minute. "Reminds me too much of what we did to the cattle, I guess." I sifted the dirt and tiny rocks in my hand.

She remained silent.

"It's not something you need to tell me now," I whispered. "Why don't you take some time and think about it." I felt something hard, and there in my palm remained a perfect arrowhead, black, finely chipped obsidian. I turned it over in my hand, fingering the sharp transparent edge. I poked it into my fingertip, and through the dust and all the years, it still stung.

The Friday of our third week, I woke up to find Tansy going through my makeup. She was already dressed for school in jeans and a borrowed black turtleneck. Over it, she wore her father's aqua-and-black Pendleton. She rolled up the sleeves, and the tails followed her like a kimono. She was thinner now that she hadn't been eating.

"Looking for something?" I asked, climbing out of bed. I pulled on my gray sweats.

"No," she said, glancing at herself in my vanity mirror. She ran her hand through her thick hair and swung it around her shoulders.

"You want some makeup?" I said, going to the dresser for my socks.

"I dunno," she said, shrugging. But she still stood there picking up my compacts of eye shadow.

"I'll do your face. If you want," I said. I was good at makeup. Elise made sure I knew all the makeup tricks so I could do her face. She enrolled me in beauty classes when I was fourteen, and the makeup artists all wanted to pluck my eyebrows because they said if they did it early enough the hair wouldn't grow back.

I bought and studied books of Way Bandy and watched in demonstrations how to do his faces—the all-American face, the pouty face, the athletic face. I learned how to apply foundation, mix it so it wasn't too thick or too thin. I mastered the art of shadowing, contouring, and lip lines. I did Elise's face to perfection every time she had to go anywhere.

I stood next to Tansy in my soft sweats, my hair wrapped up in an elastic fastener, looking at both of us in the mirror. I sized up Tansy's face and realized this wasn't a countenance I knew how to do, because there were different tricks to doing different types of features.

Tansy sat down on the bench of the vanity that had been Elise's.

"My mother didn't like makeup. She didn't use much," Tansy said. "Just mascara."

"Just use the mascara, then," I said.

She looked at herself in the mirror nervously. "No. Do it," she instructed.

I stood behind her and pulled her hair back, looking at her eyes critically. Her eyebrows were wide and went sort of straight across her face with no lift to them. "I can pluck a few lower brow hairs and give you an arch," I said. "Just one or two."

She nodded.

I yanked one out and she jumped, slapping her hand to her eye. A small red blotch appeared.

"Don't you have a waxer?" she asked angrily. "My mother always had hers waxed."

"No," I replied. "I do it by hand."

Tansy felt the injury to see if it had swollen.

"Well, let's not worry about the brows." I went on, tapping out some foundation on my palm, adding a little water. "Close your eyes." I covered her skin, smooth without blemish. While her eyes were still closed, I added blush to the bone of her cheek, almost obscured by the roundness of her adolescence. Below that, I contoured her hollows with the big thick black brush. But her face was too round, and the contours ended up looking like bruises.

Tansy didn't have a lot of eyelid area, which was what I was used to. Her eyes were like Kappy's, small and the tiniest bit Asian. I added a little brown pencil at the corners of her eyes and touched some matte brown in the crease. "Look down, so I can get the mascara on."

She opened them, looking carefully down and forward.

I applied the mascara, and then drew some natural color on her lips. Hers were beautiful and thick like Elise's and Kappy's. "Okay," I said. "Open your eyes."

Tansy sat there motionless looking into the mirror. I saw her swallow.

Her face was striking, exotic, unnerving. She suddenly looked much older, not just like a twelve-year-old with makeup. I stared at her and thought of India again, how at dawn I had watched the red tongue of the sun slowly lick the Taj Mahal with life. It made it even more lovely than the cool blue light of moon. The exquisite beauty came from the mixture of cultures, I thought. I remembered arguing with my Indian friend about the caste system. He tried to defend it, saying that perfection came when people continued what they were suited and bred for. "Look at what's in front of you," I had said. "This building isn't Islamic, it isn't Indian, it's the combination of both. It's the collision that made this so incredible."

"My neck doesn't match my face," Tansy said, lifting her chin up to look. She grabbed a towel and began scrubbing her cheeks. Her skin turned red and tears began running out of her eyes. "It's not coming off," she cried.

"My neck doesn't match my face either," I said. "Nobody's face matches their neck unless they stay inside all their life. It's because of the elements."

"No," she replied, looking at me with streaked red eyes. "Your face is darker than your neck. Mine is lighter. You can never have lighter skin on your face." She spat out the words. "Your foundation is wrong."

I inspected her closely. A person could hardly tell, and her face was smooth, lovely, without wrinkle or blemish. "It's fine," I said. "It's beautiful. No one will notice."

"Yes, they will," she said through her tears. "Everyone will notice. They'll all stare at me."

"Just wash it off," I said, annoyed. She was making a federal crime out of my foundation. "You were the one who wanted me to do it."

Tansy threw the towel on the vanity and sat there looking at herself disgustedly. "But I like the eyes," she said.

"Suit yourself," I replied, walking out to the kitchen for some coffee and toast. Tansy didn't join me. She was still on her crash diet, living on the remnants of her father. But people did what they needed to survive.

When we walked out to the Blazer, Tansy shrugged her shoulder and asked, "How much does that mascara cost?"

"I don't know," I said, closing the gate after her.

"What do you mean, you don't know," she asked again, pulling the Blazer handle with a yank.

"I never looked at the price," I admitted.

"I know the price of everything," she said, slamming the door shut.

I dropped her off at school, and she walked in without looking back. As I drove away, I wondered if she'd be there waiting when I came to pick her up. Only if I happened to be the first one who came by, I thought.

Scotty Jamison's pickup was at the shop once more when I arrived home. Hanna wasn't in the house; it was silent again the way it had been after my mother died. I sat down at the kitchen counter and fidgeted with a Grain Grabbers pen, wondering what I would tell Miles.

I had several reasons for kidnapping Tansy, actually. I was going to give her a better life. I wanted to teach her to love the land, and how to be its steward.

I imagined a tribal court custody judge snorting and saying, "That's ironic." I would go on, despite him. I would tell him I was going to show her how to care for and ride horses. But most of all, I wanted to prove that her family didn't always abandon her. I started sweating, went to the sink, and poured myself a glass of water.

They'd take her away from me, I realized. I wondered how I couldn't have seen that. The tribal court would send her back to the small foster home crowded with four other people. And everything would be worse now, because, despite the rough spots, we were starting to know one another. Not in a fantasy, but really know about each other. I imagined seeing Tansy walk out that door, never looking back at me because it was too painful for her. It would be about as bad as looking at a gallon of my own blood on the floor.

It was then I received a call from Howard Milner, the principal of the school. He explained that for the last couple of days they had been doing research on Tansy's transcripts. It seemed when they had requested documents from Tansy's old school, they were informed she was a missing person.

Milner used a low and precise voice; probably how he imagined it should sound when one informed a fugitive from the law that the jig was up. I pictured how he had cleared his throat before he made the call. He would have cleared his desk, too. Milner couldn't think about and look at two things at the same time. This was probably the most upsetting episode to come to his attention since the Runcid kid had shot the Hatzapple boy.

"Thank you very much, sir," I said, hanging up. I immediately dialed Miles. It was surprisingly simple. I was to bring her to his office tomorrow, drop her off. She'd walk out of the door and out of my life, just the way I imagined.

As I sat there, I heard Hanna come in the front door. I walked into the green room and said, "Tansy's going back tomorrow. Maybe she's the lucky one."

Hanna knelt, her coat still on. Snow dusted her shoulders. As I moved to the window to look at the snow, Hanna opened a garbage sack full of items she'd collected from the ranch. She worked busily, as if she'd discovered a secret that had eluded her a lifetime. "Things never turn out the way you see them in your head," Hanna said, slapping her hands on her knees, cleaning the snow off there.

"No kidding," I said. "The crops never turn out like you hope." I pushed my face to the cold pane of the window, trying to freeze off the tears that were threatening to come.

I heard Hanna breathing as she sorted the treasures she'd found. I turned to look at her, musing that all ranchers had their private collection of valuables. Along with pyromania and a tendency to haul haphazardly, all ranchers and farmers share a proclivity to "gather treasures." Things they'd found by accident or on purpose: the arrowhead next to the broken rod, the twelve rattles of a rattlesnake, the errant bullet that almost killed them.

"I need you to help me gather her together," Hanna said.

"Gather who together?" I said, confused.

"Bring what suits her," she said, not explaining, but expecting me to guess, which I did. She meant bring my treasures for Tansy.

I went to my room, returning with the whole box full of agate, arrowheads, crystal, snake-eye, rattlesnake rattles, rope, literature and law books, horn, hoof, horsehair, Western Family matches, Early Times whiskey, Marlboro cigarettes, a silver spade bit, and grain.

As I carried them to Hanna, I noticed the snow began coming down hard. I told myself this was good, it would help the upcoming crop, unless the ground was frozen. If that happened it would be a heart-break, because the moisture comes down and runs off over the hard ground as if it's never been there at all, a figment of the imagination.

"I'm going to get Tansy, before we're snowed in," I said, watching Hanna at work on her sculpture. Tansy's head was beginning to emerge as a marbleization of the four elements—earth, water, fire, and air. Before I walked out the door, I decided she was the most alive of all of us, and the most essential.

Tansy and I returned as the evening darkened the sky. Tansy's sculpture had started to take form, but she didn't bother looking at it when she entered the house. When I told her she was to go back to the foster home in the morning, she began crying. She sobbed all the way home, didn't talk to me except to say, "How can you take me back there?"

"It's the law," I mumbled. "Fucked."

By five, about dark, the temperature was –2. A freezing wind blew in from the Arctic, which brought the temperature down to about –15. When I walked down to the corral to turn on the heater so the water trough wouldn't freeze, the snow seemed nothing more than millions of small downy feathers. I thought it was just a light dusting. But it was cold; the ground was so hard, it was like walking on lava rock. Even the horses had come into the barn. They huddled together in the back gathering warmth from one another where the wind didn't slice through the windows. A foot of snow covered the ground, and kept falling.

I realized then I needed the Caterpillar to break out of the snow in the morning. Tansy was to be in Miles's office in Pendleton the next day, or I was going to jail. The tractor remained where I had finished weeding after the Runcid incident, out by Baseline Road. I headed out into the blizzard, crossing the field instead of the road because it was shorter that way. On the verge of Tansy's departure, the idea of walking into the winter was appealing to me.

I wore two pairs of socks; my brother's round-toed boots so the socks would fit; two pairs of long johns; the bottom half of a ski outfit I had bought years ago with Elise; two wool ski hats, one with a mask; and ski mitts. Then over everything was the tan army coat—it might have been my grandfather's, it was so old. Over that I slung my bota bag full of aquavit, and in my coat pocket was a can of starting fluid and my grandmother Emma's old watch.

I knew the land by heart, knew every draw, every crevice, every crest. I wasn't afraid of getting lost. When I started out, the snow was still falling, and the wind had picked up. The ice hit me like a cat-'o-nine-tails. I couldn't feel it through all that insulation, but I could hear it cracking on my coat as it landed, almost as if it were crashing into a windshield. I heard only that and the sound of my breath.

Tansy had been packing and Hanna, of course, was occupied, so I left a note telling them where I had gone, and that I'd be back for dinner. I walked out past the old chicken coop, past the wagons from the turn of the century, past the back pasture, and up the first hill into the eleven hundred. The Cat was at the far end, and I knew even if I didn't find it right away, if I kept going I'd eventually reach it. Sooner or later, I'd come to the fence, and then all I had to do was turn right.

All the clothes I'd layered kept me warm, hot really. I took a couple of swigs of the aquavit, and I felt even better, slightly numb but with a burst of energy from the sugar. I plowed along through the snow as though it were nothing, as if I were simply threading my way through endless silk scarves.

I was tough, I knew I could do it. But lately, I caught myself getting soft. Instead of running Quicken for the bills every Sunday, I found myself roaming through the ranch with Tansy. Instead of rising before dawn for the down-season jobs, I slept in and drove her to school. And maybe that was why I went the way I did, to prove I could.

I missed the Cat completely, sitting up in the northwest corner. I wound up at the end of our property smack at the barbed-wire fence Runcid had replaced. I walked straight into it, fell into the drift that had already collected there at the obscured fence line.

"Sumbitch," I said, taking another swig. I turned north and hiked up the hill toward the corner. When I crested the rise, I saw the machine down at the gate. The snowstorm was letting up.

Usually diesels didn't start worth a shit in a freeze, all that business with the glow plugs trying to warm the engine up. But with the modern machinery, they had computers in them that did everything. I had brought starting fluid just in case. I grabbed the key and held it over for the computer to give the diesel a goose. Then I tried starting it. Nothing. I turned it all the way off and repeated my routine. I choked it hard to shove some fuel into the dragon's belly to get the damn thing to take off. This time it did. It rumbled furiously, and belched out black smoke I could see even in the night. I turned the lights on and sat there letting it warm up. My machine, the vast universe, and me. I told myself I was happy alone; I didn't need Tansy or Hanna. I took a swig and thought of my father. Above, the clouds cleared. I watched the Milky Way.

The hydraulics hummed as I raised them. I didn't bother unhitching the weeders, figured I'd do it in the morning. We inched into the snow. The Cat had to climb out of the drift to move forward. We moved ahead, then I backed up and moved forward again. Each time we cleared a little snow from the machine, and soon we were headed to the top of the hill to try to find our way back home.

When we crested the first hill, I saw their eyes in the darkness. Gold reflected back from the living. It was Tansy and Jade. When I hadn't come back, they'd made their way out to find me.

Jade saw that tractor coming at her and began running sideways, high-stepping over the foot and a half of snow. Tansy pulled her back and goaded her toward me until, trembling, she stopped and faced the oncoming machine. She was waiting for me to notice her in the freezing landscape. She demanded it.

I slammed in the clutch, the engine still at a full roar. The floodlights made the snow sparkle and glow. The lights surrounded the Caterpillar so when the critical time to seed came, a person could work day and night. Ike had done it many times, the floods ensuring the seeders weren't leaving skips in the land.

Jade and Tansy stood in the halo of light; the soft glow surrounded all of us. Tansy rode without a saddle. I imagined her running down to the barn, roughly bridling Jade, and jumping onto her back the way I had instructed her. I believe she had been afraid for my life.

Tansy looked at me long and hard, then leaned back and stared at the sky. Her hands were wrapped in Jade's frozen black mane, the reins icy stiff pieces of wood. Suddenly, Jade couldn't stand the fire-breathing monster anymore. She jumped sideways, leaping the snow with her bounding gait. As Jade bobbed her head, her breath exploded into the cold air like burned myrrh escaping from swinging chalices.

Tansy gripped her strong legs around Jade's barrel and slouched her back to take up the bounce in her horse's jumps, clinging like a burr in her mane. Jade's thick winter coat made a warm saddle for Tansy. Her legs were thrown forward and back with Jade's shoulders as she moved. She leaned forward, waved at me, and looked again up to the sky. That was how she had found me, I thought. She followed the brightest star in Orion the Hunter, up to the top of our place, the top of the world.

The sky was black granite and the earth was white marble. Well, certainly you could find one another in a black-and-white world. Tansy waved again, and I blinked my lights. I followed her in, our roles reversed from when she first grabbed on to my hand eight years ago in the corral.

Tansy worked Jade into a canter and circled me. I felt like a moving city. I was a little brightly lit community out in the middle of nowhere. Tansy and Jade made one trip around me, then another, herding me forward. Jade finally quit trying to run away, and the two of them settled on leading me home; Tansy and my horse loped and jumped the snow side to side in front of the raging Caterpillar. What I saw were Jade's flashing black stockings against the snow, and a small bundle with her hand up in the air in victory, waving at the world as she led the way home.

She was riding without hanging on, probably laughing, talking, and screaming because nothing could be heard over the roar of the engine. We were in another realm, the tractor deafening, like Armageddon.

25

WELL," SAID MILES, PLACING HIS BONY HAND ON MY shoulder, "now that's over with, we have to think about how you're going to win the judgment." At least he didn't scold me as if I were a child, and I thought I detected some sympathy. "Whatever it was that was holding the tribe back," he continued, "is gone. Definitely gone. I received another letter yesterday. The trial's scheduled for late March," he said, walking slowly back behind his desk. "We have approximately one month."

I sat down quietly in the nearest chair.

"I have not found the original deed to Heart of the Beast, and I'm assuming you haven't either."

I shook my head.

"However, I did locate a copy in the Union County courthouse in La Grande. It says clearly that John Winter bought the land from an Indian. We have a big fight ahead of us, and the odds aren't in our favor."

I had the urge to get up and walk out, just forget the whole thing.

"Now, I try to guess what they will present in their case," Miles said, passionately. The fight. It was what Miles loved, what he lived for. His blue eyes beamed. "They will allege the land was taken in violation of the Trade and Intercourse Act. Of course, you only have to testify to what you know personally." Miles looked up from his legal pad to see if I was listening.

"I'd like to go over the settlement of my mother's estate," I said.

Miles reached up to his forehead and pinched the creases there as if I'd given him a headache.

"I'd like Tansy to inherit her share."

Miles remained mute as the stuffed game on his walls. He laid the pen down, folded his knotted hands together, and stared at me.

"Is there any way to reinherit her?" I asked nervously. It seemed lately I never knew if I was doing the right or wrong thing. "Because my mother did not see to the sustenance of her only granddaughter."

"That's because she didn't want to," Miles interrupted. "You are going against her wishes. She left her entire estate to you. Elise Steele knew she had a granddaughter."

"Well, she appointed me executrix of her estate," I replied softly. "She left things to my judgment."

"Why, Iris? Why are you doing this?" Miles asked.

I looked at him. I wanted to tell him what I knew about loss. I stared at his light blue eyes, his gray hair, his bow tie from another era. He didn't have a wife, children. I had a feeling he knew about loss already. "Because she's what I have left."

Miles turned and looked toward the wall. He was silent for a long time, and I gripped my backpack. "There is a disclaimer right," he finally stated, picking up his pen again, "which allows assets to be passed on to progeny within nine months of the date of death. It would apply only to your mother's estate, since your father's has long been settled."

"That would work," I said. The smell of the legal books and his office was suffocating me again. "I would like you to pursue this on behalf of Tansy."

"It only works if Tansy is the only grandchild. This law would distribute the estate to all progeny equally."

"There is only one," I said. "She's it."

"All right," he muttered as he wrote. He looked up at me. "If you feel this strongly, Iris, you should consider trying to adopt her."

"Yes," I said softly.

"Actually," Miles erupted, "we have a problem there. Well, we have a problem and the tribe has one too. The Lost River Nez Perce will want to keep her in the tribe. They don't just give their children up. These groups have been disbanded for what—a hundred and twenty years or so. Now that they're recognized," he said, "they fight like hell to keep their members."

"But I'm her aunt," I said. "That ought to count for something."

"Caucasian blood doesn't count for much in the eyes of the Indians or the government. The Indian Child Welfare Act states that when a petition is made for adoption of a Native American child, if there is no Indian blood on the part of the adoptive parent, this fact need be alleged in the petition. If this is the case, then the registered tribe actually has the right to intervene and possibly veto an adoption outside the tribe."

"That's why I wasn't notified when Kappy died."

"I assume that's correct," said Miles.

I looked away from him. I stared again at the animal trophies mounted on his walls; I couldn't stop looking at them. They were so beautiful, as beautiful dead as they were alive.

"She has a temporary guardian now, assigned by tribal court order after Kappy's death. If, for instance, Kappy has a relative in Lapwai, or elsewhere, they would try to contact them first to place her in permanent legal custody. But the tribe will have a problem here, too. From what you've told me today about Tansy's new inheritance, they can't have someone appointed to be her permanent guardian," he said.

I looked back at him.

"Because they have a conflict of interest. They'll have to sue Tansy for Heart of the Beast if she inherits her share. And Tansy's permanent guardian can't be a member of the tribe that's suing her in a court of law. Conflict of interest."

"That's good," I said.

"So they either proceed with trying to get the land, the money, and the casino," he said. "Or they proceed with trying to keep their lost daughter."

"Why can't they do both?"

"It depends on the timing. They're moving damn fast in federal court now. Could be they're trying to get the federal trial over quickly," he said. "They know the history here. They'd like to get this finished before any loose ends unravel."

"Which will be the harder case to win?" I asked.

"Both," he replied. "But there is not much preparation we can do for the custody fight."

"I'm her aunt, for christsakes." I fingered a scab I'd received from the torn tin on the elevator.

"Doesn't matter. They take the survival of the tribe seriously. They're just like anyone else."

I was silent for a moment. "I'd like to get permission to take Tansy up to Heart of the Beast. Do you think I could get it before the trial?"

He shrugged his shoulders. "Probably only if you bring her back when you say you will."

"Of course," I said.

Miles squinted at me. "The trial is scheduled four weeks from now," he said. "It gives us a little time. We'll see what we can do."

I stood up, but Miles didn't see me out. As I left his office, I stared at the deserted grounds of the Happy Creek pageant. I didn't want to go home now that Tansy was gone.

I was beginning to think Willy was right; he believed he needed a lawyer in the family to farm. Willy had orchestrated everything. Mother served as his lawyer. Hanna was supposed to have been the farmer. He said every ranch operation needed a farmer and a lawyer. An accountant too, if you had enough children. He was probably right, but in the end, his organization didn't get him as far as being a good father would have.

I wondered what it would take for me to be able to raise Tansy, to have her in my life. I didn't need her to work for me the way my parents and their parents did. It was just that when I watched her, I became enormously proud to be in her presence, no matter where we went or what we did.

No one mistook us for mother and daughter, but I imagined I saw looks of envy when people saw us together, the blond Scandinavian and the raven-haired Native American. Did they wonder what kind of a connection we had? Did they think we were just friends? Did they think my ancestors had killed hers, or vice versa? Did they know we were the survivors?

I was tired of darkness following me. Death seemed to trail me like

some strange insane woman decked out with black clothes and a
porkpie hat. I wondered if I looked for it, somehow searched it out. I
remembered in college, after Jake had died, I tried to be like Henry and
turned away from live people and into dead science. It was a distribution requirement, biology. My favorite subject was cannibalism. I sent
worms through mazes. Some of them found their way through; others
were ignorant and could go nowhere. Then I cut up the smart worms
and fed them to the others. The stupid worms improved, were able to
get through the maze. I wrote my term paper on cannibalism and how
it augments the brain. Our family had been feeding on one another for
generations. I should have been a genius by then.

I wanted to move forward now. I thought of Tansy, her beautiful
strong black hair. And now she was gone.

I picked up my cell phone. I dialed Henry's number at the clinic. It
was busy. I waited and dialed again because I had all the time in the
world, and finally I had something lovely to say.

26

Henry lived near the wool mills, out past the mustard-colored rodeo stadium and the brick-laid correctional institute. The mills had inhabited Pendleton ever since the sheep and cattle wars last century. They were famous for their Indian blankets, originally an attempt to form a friendship with the tribes. Mostly it was an effort to sell to or trade with them. The mill sent designers to study blanket patterns from the Southwest and the Northwest and then re-created them in their wool looms. Long ago we had bought a Chief Joseph blanket from the Pendleton store.

On my way to Henry's apartment, I stopped to buy groceries at Safeway. I needed fresh things like lettuce, tomatoes, milk, and cheese. Our remaining food supplies came from the bulk warehouses of Costco: freezable items and canned goods. When it came to food, living on a ranch took planning; it was sort of like stockpiling for the apocalypse.

Henry's place overlooked the city on Immigrant Street. Darkness arrived by the time I reached his house. The trip in the plane had convinced me his career choice was perfect for him, but it hadn't convinced me he was entirely happy.

Turning Tansy back over to her foster family, I realized I wouldn't be able to spend that night alone. Linda, her foster mother, had rushed over and hugged Tansy, and Tansy had just stood there; she didn't even attempt to embrace her in return.

Maybe seeing Henry was a rebound maneuver, but the truth was I still wanted Henry. I had never stopped. After giving up Tansy, a hole in me opened up I thought I'd closed permanently. I craved a life with someone, with Henry and with Tansy. I wanted to grow old with them, work with them, travel with them, and argue with them.

This wasn't easy to admit, given my lack of success in familial relations. I wondered if I simply had immature and adolescent thoughts about relationships. In fact, I wondered if Henry had jumped ahead of me in maturity somehow in the last four years.

I knocked on his door. He wasn't in yet so I sat in the Blazer and waited for him. A little after seven, the Expedition turned in the drive. Wearing navy sweats and a gray shirt, he opened his front door and turned to wave at me. "Come in," he said. "I hope you weren't waiting long."

I followed him into the apartment. It was small but warm.

"I have some soup," he said. "Otherwise we can go out. Pizza place, or Chinese."

"Soup's great," I interrupted. "I just need to put my groceries in your fridge."

Henry looked alarmed. "You're not moving in, are you?" he quickly joked.

"No," I said, laughing. "I just don't want them to spoil." When I came back with the milk and butter, I heard the shower from behind the bedroom door. I opened the refrigerator and set in the whole brown bag. I noticed a partial six-pack of Chinook Ale, a half jar of salsa, margarine, and mustard. The cupboards were full of ramen noodles and Progresso soup. He liked minestrone.

I threw my father's sheepskin-lined coat on the chair. I perused everything in Henry's apartment. Generic hot pads and towels slung over the oven handle. I grabbed them, pleased that they weren't something cute, a gift from some flame who wanted to set up house with him. His furniture, solid but inexpensive, sparsely covered the room. A round wooden western table with knobs on the legs and chairs served in his kitchen. A dark blue–covered futon sat in the middle of the main room. The most substantial object he owned was a big TV; I imagined he kept up with sports.

Looking at every picture, I examined each one carefully. There was one of a pink-cheeked Henry dressed up as Pooh bear giving out candy on a children's ward. I found another of him, exhausted from climbing Mt. Adams, wearing shorts, a T-shirt, and hiking boots. Beside that, a group of people, Henry in the middle, celebrated New Year's Eve. I saw Earl, his father, standing at the side of their small house. And then I picked up the picture of the three of us, Henry, Jake, and me, taken the day harvest ended; the year before Jake left. A cowboy frame with boots, hats, and lariats surrounded the photo. My brother stood in the middle and smiled that quirky smile. I called it Jake's hot-ta-ha grin; it popped up when he tried to give me one. A hot-ta-ha was a pinch on a sore, but it really meant him chasing me around the house. It was a game we'd played since I was three: if he caught me, he tickled me until I wet my pants. It was the smile that said he was stronger, smarter, and ornerier than I was. I loved that smile, that attention, the best kind, the kind that a little sister provoked, knowing she was the most aggravating, the most important thing that could ever get into her big brother's craw.

In the picture, I gripped my Coke from the pop break because harvest had finished right around then, four in the afternoon. I held it in one hand, and grabbed Jake around his waist with the other. I was sixteen then, Jake twenty, and Henry hadn't yet turned nineteen.

Jake cradled his arms around Henry and me as if we were his prizes at the glorious moment of the end of harvest. The last of the long work of the summer and the unending grind of the entire year halted with the cease-fire of the reaping. The beer busts broke out with cold Oly beer. Afterward, when the machines were tucked in and buttoned down for the winter, only then did the time of depression come. But the day it finished was like the day school closed for summer.

I studied Jake and Henry. Henry was still awkward then. At the time, though, I thought he was the coolest person ever, next to my brother. Feathered thick hair parted in the middle. His tan made his skin look beautiful and smooth, had dried out any pimples from the nervousness of adolescence. His blue eyes shone even in the picture. Jake, as always, it seemed, was covered in dust. His dry, tanned skin, brown hair, and auburn eyes clashed with the red of his summer bandanna.

It occurred to me that Jake held the two of us up, grabbing us by our shoulders. He pulled us through the complete awfulness of adolescence, full of ugly family matters and self-loathing. But I couldn't figure out what I read on Henry's face—an expression I hadn't noticed before.

I was still sitting on the futon when Henry came out of the shower. His hair shone and stayed in the form the tines of the comb had left.

"Wonderful picture," I said, holding the photo up.

Henry came and sat next to me. "I love that one," he said.

"Henry," I asked, looking at it. "There is no easy way to say this."

He turned to face me, moving farther away in order to look at me fully.

"I think I've loved you . . ." I said, faltering with the math and the years, "ever since you came to live with us."

He was silent.

I looked at him long and hard. I wanted to know something Henry himself didn't have the answer to. "I just keep thinking of the reality of my life," I went on. "Like where I live. And where you live. And what went on in the past. And I can't stand going over it in my head anymore. I think this is as near as we've ever been. And I've started hoping," I said, matter-of-factly.

Henry rubbed his hand over his jaw. We both knew this was a conversation we should have had years ago.

"I look at this picture here. And what I wonder is. Whether maybe . . ."

"What?" he said softly.

"Whether all this time you were really in love with Jake."

We sat in silence. I was sweating, and I tried to hold my hands against my body so they wouldn't fly off like birds.

"The summer before Jake left," Henry stated bluntly, "I felt like a whole person. It was strange because it was the first time and the last time I ever felt that way. A couple years later, something happened to me. I don't know whether it was because of Jake's death or because I had fallen in love with you, or because I had started in medicine. Maybe all three."

I felt myself redden. My lips puffed out the way I hated.

"Once I began studying the body"—he searched around the room as he spoke—"there was a way things went together correctly. A pattern to the cadavers, and to the diseases. Everything was black and white. Cut and dried. I could find causes, treatments, cures. I could operate." He looked at me intensely. "In three, four, six hours, I could take out a tumor," he said. "I could just rid a body of a cancer, a growth. That was about the time I realized something was wrong with me."

I sat there, motionless. I didn't understand.

"Of course no one in medicine thinks this is strange. All of us try to be like little gods. And some of us are. We have the power to save a life. And the best doctors are that way precisely because they can't stand it."

"What do you mean, can't stand it?" I asked, narrowing my eyes. "What?"

"The fragility of everything. Of life," he replied. "They work compulsively. Immerse themselves in saving people so they aren't cut down by death."

"Like you said," I told him, waving him off. "People make choices."

"It was about this time," he went on with an insistence in his voice, "I was in residency; I began to be able to detect the smell of blood."

"Really?" I said, trying to seem nonplussed. Until that moment, whatever Henry's problem, I felt the need to take it from him. I stopped myself, then sat there watching him.

He ran his fingers through his hair. "Since you left, I wasn't interested in women. I just . . . my life was totally devoted to the medicine."

I gripped my hands together in my lap.

"But I realized somewhere along the way, that something had happened to me. It was then I noticed that I could smell blood. That I was becoming attracted to women who were bleeding."

I looked at Henry. This was something I didn't know. It wasn't overwhelming rage; it wasn't self-loathing; it wasn't hatred of his parents.

Henry smiled uneasily.

"Well," I said, laughing a little too hard. "So you're attracted to death. That makes perfect sense. Then you are attracted to me. We're meant for each other."

"It's not really a laughing matter," he replied.

"I'm dead serious," I whispered.

He started to speak and then stopped. Outside I heard the slam of a car door in the next drive. "I can't make love to a woman unless she's bleeding," he said.

I looked at his knees almost touching mine.

Henry took a breath.

"Saves money on birth control."

"Yeah," he replied. He attempted to laugh, but failed. Henry looked small, unsure of himself, completely different from the person I had known.

"Is it," I asked, sliding to the edge of the futon, "something you want to remedy?"

Henry ran his tongue over his lips, and looked down to the floor. His fingers opened, and he slid his palms along his thighs.

I waited there, staring at him, watching his shirt move in and out with his lungs. I fell in love with him all over again. But I noticed he hadn't answered me. Maybe that was what I found so attractive.

I stood up and pulled Henry toward me. I kissed him on the lower lip, walking him back into his bedroom. We moved slow and lumbering. His bedroom was small and square with a double bed backed up into a corner. It wasn't made; yellow sheets tangled in a mass at the foot of it. I pulled Henry's T-shirt over his head and untucked my turtleneck from my Levi's.

Henry's body had changed in four years. Where once it had been tanned and muscled, now it was white. I saw moles and stray hairs on his body. His stomach dove deeper, softer than I remembered. I buried my mouth in his belly. Kneeling there, I wondered what exactly Henry had meant. I wasn't on my period. Were the only options oral or anal? There wasn't blood, but at least there was no possibility of life coming from either option.

Henry was nervous, sweating. It occurred to me that I had been this anxious or worse when I lost my virginity to Henry eleven years ago. I pulled down his sweatpants, so he was standing there in his boxers, just like before. I sank down on the ground amidst his scattered shoes, taking the last bit of his clothes with me. There was no Ike anymore watching out his window, no Elise envious of love she didn't have.

Removing my shirt and the rest of my clothes, I stood in front of him naked. My body had changed, just like Henry's. We bore scars. We looked like the salmon returning from the sea, moving past the fish ladder windows at Bonneville dam, covered with gashes from sea lions, lures dangling from our lips. I'd grown wider; hollows appeared below my cheekbones and collarbones.

I searched for the burn scar located on Henry's thigh from the exhaust of the marble cutter we used to make patio stones. I found it with my tongue, licking it wet among the slick soft leg hair. I kissed his hands, wondering how many lives he'd saved on one hand and how many he'd lost in the other.

I pulled his arms around me, and we fell down between the shoes that had walked through his life, the loose change he had forgotten, and the discarded clothing that littered the floor like shorn hair.

He kept his eyes open, and we watched each other like twins delivered after a long and protracted separation.

"You can make love to me," I told him. "I'm not bleeding. But I'm dying as much as anyone."

Henry pushed his head sideways; tears ran down. "I could never live out there," he said.

"I know," I replied. Of course he could live out there. With a plane he could live anywhere. In his detached physician's way, he was afraid to submit to the vulnerability of love. If he fell in love with women who were dying, he never really had to fall in love. If he had sex when they menstruated, he never really had to face the possibility of life.

Henry breathed through my hair as he entered me. It hurt as he moved inside, I don't know why that was a surprise.

I could hear nothing but his heart and breath that filled his rib cage with air, shocked numb by the crack and sing of him. I felt his blood through the insides of my elbows as he lay over them, and I held him with my arms. My hands washed over his body as he moved. And I lost everything until afterward, when it came back, a dim pulse in my lower belly that was still clinging to him. After that, I was not sure the beat of it was mine.

part six

27

The morning of the trial, Hanna and I drove to the courthouse in Pendleton. A cross between a southern mansion and renaissance revival, it sat crooked in its own block. The edifice was the only lopsided thing in town, owing to a temporary lack of compass. All else was excruciatingly exact. At least the town fathers could say the streets were straight.

The trial started at ten. Nine-thirty inched by as Hanna and I walked up the stairs. Spring air blew in with a warmth that had seemed lost forever. As we entered the court, plush red carpet muffled sounds. The smell of the wood-lined walls lingered in the hall. Old pockets of air in the judges' chambers and the jury rooms seemed not to have been changed since the construction of the building a century ago. Pictures of old U.S. marshals with handlebar mustaches, former judges, and barristers lined the halls. I noticed a copy of the Bill of Rights on one of the walls.

Miles Emmerett and Tansy arrived. He had told me he was going to pick her up from the reservation before the trial. The documents for Elise's estate had been recorded, and Tansy was included in the distribution. She was also included in the lawsuit. I wondered if it had been the right thing to do.

I had also learned that after I signed an agreement to return her, the custody judge would allow Hanna and me to take Tansy to see Heart of the Beast after the trial. I received a warning, too, that if I didn't bring her back in two days, they would send the police after me.

Miles carried two huge briefcases with him, and looked winded from the walk upstairs. He ambled through the swinging doors of the courtroom; Tansy played nervously with her hair as she followed him. The judge's platform rose like a podium in front of the room. The deputy's desk and witness stand jutted out from that like a prow. Miles settled Hanna in the first row of observer benches. He motioned to the defendant's table for Tansy and me.

We perched ourselves at the huge oak desks, pushed together and surrounded by red leather-covered chairs. Miles was a buffer at the end closest to the plaintiffs. He handed me two yellow legal pads. "If you want to tell me something during the trial, write it down here and show it to me," he said. By the time Miles donned his glasses to read our writing, I thought, any opportunity for use would be long gone.

Apprehensively, I took off my mother's black coat. I wore her clothes as if they would invoke her strength. Tansy slumped down next to me. She slung her denim purse around the back of her seat. I looked at Miles's hand, hoping he had the same strength and stubbornness as his ancestor, the man who had motioned more weight onto the press rather than give up his land.

"The trial won't take that long," Miles said. "Two days. More or less. All of today will probably be spent with the tribe presenting witnesses that support their claim that John Winter illegally purchased Heart of the Beast. Of course after each witness, I cross-examine. Starting tomorrow, we present our witnesses. And they cross-examine. Then closing statements, and the judge takes the matter under advisement. We won't know the outcome for several weeks. Nonjury trials are always a waiting game."

"And what about the custody hearing?" I asked.

"I filed your claim in Tribal Court stating your desire to become her legal guardian. The tribe has delayed their response, probably until this trial is over. I imagine they will register theirs the moment the gavel comes down here. You can expect the custody hearing to occur shortly thereafter," he said, arranging his papers.

Tansy fiddled with her pen anxiously.

I didn't touch her, or look at her. I wondered if everything had been lost between us in the month we'd been apart. Our phone calls were limited to one per week, and I couldn't get a sense of how things were going for her. I suspected her foster parents were punishing her for leaving, maybe they were slighting her on food, or making her do more chores. In our conversations, Tansy had mostly wanted to talk about Jade: what she was eating, how fat she was getting, whether she had been missing Tansy, or whether she sunned herself in the afternoon, happy not to be ridden. She misses you, I told her. Jade stands at the gate for at least an hour a day waiting for you to come down and give her carrots. This wasn't even a lie.

Suddenly I heard the doors open behind us. A group of people walked in, led by a man in a double-breasted suit. Three of them made their way toward the plaintiff's table. The rest settled in the benches on the other side of Hanna. I recognized Linda Blackwood, Tansy's temporary guardian, whom I had seen when returning Tansy to Miles's office.

The man in the suit said hello to Miles. Miles nodded curtly. The two others sat next to him at the table. One of them, a young man, wasn't wearing a tie, even in court. He had a mean look and no lips; I imagined somehow they had been eaten off by his own invective. The woman next to him wore a floral beaded costume as beautiful as the one I had seen in the photo of Kappy.

Miles leaned over to me. "Cash Ogden," he said. "He's their attorney. He's part Nez Perce. Used to be a U.S. attorney."

Cash carried an easel to the front of the courtroom. He placed a poster on it showing a map of the Wallowa area. I saw the location of Heart of the Beast. It lay beside the lake in the southern half of the valley.

The deputy entered and rapped the gavel at her desk. An American flag with gold fringe around the edges waved as she walked by. My mother had told me that the fringe was a remnant from the time of the federal marshals, back when justice rode into town on a horse.

We followed Miles's example and stood up as the judge entered. He was in his late sixties and had an extraordinarily wide face. The black robe rustled as he sat down.

"Be seated." He grabbed a pen from his desk and rearranged his papers. "Are the parties ready?" asked the judge.

The deputy settled herself at the desk in front of the bench. I thought of my grandfather, buying off all the judges, never losing a case. I wondered how corrupt the law had been, how corrupt it still was.

"Plaintiff ready, Your Honor," said Cash.

"Defendant ready, Your Honor," repeated Miles.

I heard the door behind us open again and turned to see the medicine man I had seen at the hospital. He was wearing skin clothes, and the noise of his sliding feet filled the courtroom. He sat on their side, opposite Hanna. Side by side, I imagined, the two of them summoned what powers they could. Whatever the hex was, I didn't want it on me.

The deputy cleared her throat, announced the case, and described the property. Full of southwest quarters of sections, land lying west of the northerly and southerly fences on the west side of canyons, the property sounded nothing like the way it looked from the air, geometric and orderly. The description of the land was as chaotic as its history.

"Mr. Odgen," said the judge, when the deputy had finished, "proceed with your opening statement."

Cash stood up from behind the desk and began. He was smooth, and even Tansy, a twelve-year-old, was riveted by him. He talked about how the Oregon Nez Perce had almost become extinct in the long years since Lewis and Clark and the Corps of Discovery had crossed the country two hundred years ago. They were shot like deer, he said, laid out and counted, and the perpetrator of some of these crimes had been John Winter.

"How can he say that?" I whispered to Miles. He nodded but didn't reply. I squinted at Cash as he moved to the side of the courtroom. He had probably paid focus groups to tell him where he looked best when he talked. He didn't need to look good saying the things he did.

Cash talked about how the Indians weren't the only ones to suffer under the tyranny of the masses. He described how in 1857 a vote was put to the people on a measure declaring that free Negroes should not be permitted to reside in Oregon. The vote against free Negroes as residents was nine to one. "The measure reads," said Cash, walking back to his desk to pick up an ancient leather-bound book, "'Any free Negro or mulatto coming to the country should leave within two years; if he (or she) failed to leave the country after notice, he should be whipped on the bare back with not less than twenty nor more than thirty-nine stripes and flogged likewise every six months until he did leave.'" Cash held the book in both hands. "That measure, Your Honor, was not repealed until after the turn of the century."

I noticed that the judge shifted in his chair but kept the same stern-lipped expression.

"Abraham Lincoln," Cash stated, "in 1857 was offered the position of Governor of the Oregon Territory. He turned the job down because his wife objected to going to such an uncivilized part of the country. And the fact remains that Mr. Lincoln didn't come to Oregon," Cash said as he laid down the book. "Those who had come out on the Oregon Trail, the pioneers, were the ones to negotiate with my clients, the Nez Perce."

Cash took a drink of water. I looked at Miles; he wasn't taking notes, seemed barely to be listening. God, I wanted to just disappear. I was sweating, ruining my mother's dress. What did it matter? I thought. Didn't I know by now that a person couldn't become invested in anything, otherwise it would be snatched away by fate, God, or just plain stupid bad luck?

"Who were these pioneers?" Cash asked the judge as he raised both palms. "Your relatives, some of mine, relatives of everyone in this court-house. We Americans have defined ourselves by the West. It is what we have that differentiates us from our allies in Europe. Open spaces, Indians, cowboys, pioneers, the rugged individualist. As hard as it is to admit, the reality of these people was quite different from our fantasy.

"The ugly truth is that the pioneers were malcontents. Trouble-makers. People unable to scrape together a living in the big cities like Boston, New York, Philadelphia, Atlanta, Chicago. People not satisfied with the Great Plains states: Kansas, Missouri. Poor people unable or unwilling to make it anywhere else.

"They came, and they stayed here because there was nowhere else to move. This was the end of the line. They settled down and picked fights with their neighbors, then they stole their land. And they got away with it until now.

"The Nez Perce tribes have always been good neighbors and good stewards of their land. They gave Lewis and Clark food, shelter, and guides for the remainder of their trip. The Nez Perce count the son, the granddaughter, and great-granddaughter of Meriwether Lewis amongst their members. The Lost River tribe has a compelling desire for justice. It was fellow Nez Perce who lay siege to the Indians who killed Narcissa and Reverend Marcus Whitman and forced them to turn themselves over to the authorities.

"For countless years, we have had to depend on the kindness of strangers, who were rarely kind. The case we make today is that the particular property in question, the property that Iris and Tansy Steele now own, was special land, taken illegally. It contains the embodiment of the Lost River culture—the rock formations they call Heart of the Beast. And as Chief Joseph said, 'I would not sell the land that contains the bones of my father.' And so the Lost River tribe would not sell the skeleton of their creation. We will prove John Winter bought this land directly from the Nez Perce, extinguishing Indian title in violation of the federal Trade and Intercourse Act.

"Our adversaries in this matter probably seem baffled by the lawsuit," Cash admitted, motioning graciously in our direction. "They don't know anything about the transactions that took place. It was their parents, grandparents, and perhaps great-grandparents. But," he said slowly, "today we will have the pleasure of setting the record straight for everyone. Thank you, Your Honor."

Cash walked behind the table and sat down as Miles stood slowly up.

"Mr. Emmerett, your opening statement," said the judge.

Miles walked to the side of the courtroom, limping once. "We all know the tragic history of the Indians," he said. "But we are here today to prove that my clients legally acquired the land in question, Heart of the Beast. Thank you, Your Honor." He walked slowly back to sit down.

My heart sank. What a pitiful defense. I picked up my pen and rearranged myself in my chair.

"You may call your first witness," said Judge Barnes.

Cash stood up. "The Nez Perce tribe calls Miss Tansy Steele to the witness stand."

"Objection." Miles shouted loud and long from where he sat at the table. He pronounced the word *Ahhb-jection*. He scowled at the judge. "This witness is not on the witness list, Your Honor."

Cash remained standing. "Your Honor, she was added today at the last minute, because we were uncertain of her availability."

"Proceed," said the judge. "If you wish additional time for further testimony we'll take that up at the end of the day."

If Miles was under the illusion that the judge was taking any advice on order from him, he'd better think again.

The deputy stood up, holding a Bible. "The court calls Tansy Steele to the witness stand."

Tansy looked terrified as she walked to the chair. She held the railing for as long as she could the way a child who doesn't know how to swim does in the deep end of a pool. I recognized her dress as one we had bought at the Bon Marché in preparation for school. It could have been a garment of sacrifice for the Maid of Orléans; it clung to her as if it were melting. She stopped in front of the deputy, placed her small left hand on the Bible, raised her right hand, and took the oath.

"Miss Steele," said Cash, remaining at his desk, "have you ever heard the legend of Heart of the Beast?"

"Of course," she said. "Every Nez Perce knows it. Even you probably know it."

I winced. She wasn't careful with her words. No twelve-year-old was.

"Your mother was a full-blooded Nez Perce?" Cash asked.

She nodded.

The court reporter looked up. "I'm sorry, I didn't hear that," she said.

"Yes," said Tansy, a little more unsteady this time.

"That makes you one-half Nez Perce," he said.

She nodded again, and then she said, "Yes."

"Tell me, if you could, the story of Heart of the Beast."

"The coyote lived up there on the range. The coyote was the symbol of us. Of everyone. Of human nature I guess, how it could never be controlled or killed."

Cash stood up, walked to the front of his desk, and leaned back on it casually. "Could you tell us, if you know, what the remainder of the legend was?"

"In the beginning, there were two coyotes." she stated. "The second coyote was kind of crazy. It had grown into a beast, and was eating up everything in the world. First it took the grizzly, then the eagles, and then the fish." She spoke carefully, as if wanting to get it exact.

"The first coyote decided to stop the beast, and he fought smart. He made four flint knives, tied himself across three mountaintops, and teased the beast until it swallowed him with the whole of creation." She seemed to be growing comfortable in the spotlight of the witness stand.

"Once inside, the coyote saw that some of the animals were still barely alive. He then began carving on the heart of the beast. But the heart was strong, tough, and poisonous. So he gave the three other knives to the animals there with him. But that heart broke all four knives." Tansy exhaled. It annoyed me that she was dramatic, as if she relived the event. It was as if the force of her words invoked the myth into reality. "The beast lay down and roared, but it didn't die. The coyote thought he would never be able to kill it."

"And then what happened?" Cash asked. "After the heart broke the knives."

It made me uncomfortable to listen to him also speaking as if the events of the legend had actually taken place.

Tansy started again. "The coyote decided to start a fire in the belly of the beast. The animals fanned the flames until the beast burned from the inside out and all of them escaped. Once the coyote was free, he pulled the dying monster apart into five pieces, hoping it would never arise again. He flung those pieces to the corners of the earth, and they became all peoples of the world. And at last the coyote stood there holding the last fragment of the beast. It was the heart. And he wrung out that bloody, strong core, and the drops of blood that fell down became the Nez Perce people."

The courtroom was silent. Everyone watched Tansy. It was then I realized how the myth had become reality. It was what was actually happening to the Nez Perce now. Their lawyers who were former federal attorneys, their state senators, their lobbyists in Congress, their casinos—they had already been swallowed by American culture. Now that they were devoured, they carved on the heart just like the coyote.

Lawsuits, enforcement of old treaties, the tribe did what they could to vanquish their enemies. They had learned well: taking on the descendants of homesteaders and the state to get their land back; using the federal government for the environmental claims; making money by starting up casinos.

"Where do you think the coyote was standing when he wrung out that heart?" asked Cash.

"I don't know exactly," said Tansy.

"Do you think it could have been on your property, Heart of the Beast?"

"Ahbjection," said Miles. "Calls for speculation."

"Overruled."

"It could have been," replied Tansy.

"No further questions," said Cash.

Miles looked up from his desk. "Have you ever been to the Heart of the Beast?" he asked.

"No," she said. "But I'm going there after this trial is over to see what the fuss is all about."

The judge laughed.

"No further questions, Your Honor," said Miles.

"The Nez Perce tribe calls Ms. Hanna Winter to the witness stand," said Cash as he stood up.

I looked at Miles and then Hanna.

"Ahbjection, Your Honor," shouted Miles even louder than before. His wrinkled, usually white skin was red.

"Your Honor, she was also added today at the last minute because we were uncertain of her availability," Cash said, as calmly as before.

"Proceed," said the judge.

I watched Hanna take the oath. Her hands were sinewy and thin, her fingers stained from the clay.

I suddenly remembered reading the journals of Lewis and Clark. Lewis encountered an Indian chief when they camped on the banks of the Columbia near my father's island. The chief had fourteen finger bones taken from his slain enemies, and he kept them in his medicine bag. They were painted red like Hanna's and jingled together like chimes.

"Where was your place of birth?" Cash asked, again gliding over to the side of the courtroom.

"Oregon," Hanna replied, looking at me.

I smiled encouragement from the desk and leaned forward. I noticed Tansy did the same.

"Did you ever see Indians on your property?" Cash asked softly.

Hanna nodded. "Indians came. They talked to my father. He traded horses."

"You ever have occasion to talk with those folks?" he asked smoothly, as if we all were sitting round a damn campfire.

The judge watched intently.

"One Indian. Peo Peo Tholekt," she said rapidly. "He played with me." She looked up at the judge and smiled absently.

"Why did Peo Peo Tholekt camp on your family's land?" Cash proceeded.

"We let them stay. They wanted to go to McAlexander's place. Old Joseph was buried there until they moved the grave." Hanna's face was sincere, earnest, but I wished she'd just shut up. My mother always said you should never give out any more information than is necessary, especially in a trial.

"Why did they move the grave from Americus McAlexander's place?"

The judge leaned forward to hear her.

"Settlers were digging, taking things from the grave."

"Like what?" Cash asked expectantly.

"Krugerst, the dentist, took the skull."

Cash looked sincerely down at his hands, and clasped them together as if he were in prayer. "When Peo Peo Tholekt came to camp at your place did he call it Heart of the Beast?" said Cash.

"Objection," Miles stated. "This is hearsay. We can't cross-examine Peo Peo Tholekt today."

"Overruled. I'll accept it as farming background, not necessarily as a true statement," declared Judge Barnes.

"Miss Winter?" said Cash again.

"Yes," answered Hanna.

"Who was Peo Peo Tholekt?"

"Chief Joseph's nephew."

"How did your father know that Peo Peo Tholekt was Chief Joseph's nephew?"

"My father saw Joseph when he was an old man. He must have seen them together."

"Joseph came back to the Wallowa in 1891," Cash said, "with the representative from the Bureau of Indian Affairs to try and buy back land for his tribe. The settlers refused to sell to them. Could it have been then that your father saw Joseph? When he refused to sell the land back that John Winter stole in the first place?"

"Ahbjection," cried Miles. "He's asking her to describe events that took place forty-five years before she was born!"

"It could have been," Hanna said distractedly.

"Sustained," Judge Barnes offered belatedly.

"No further questions."

Miles walked up to Hanna.

I looked away. My heart was beating like mad, and I wondered if he was going to tear her down.

He smiled at her. "I have here a copy of the petition requesting permission to place a casino on the property in question. How do you think a casino would look on the land you grew up on, Ms. Winter? The place you were born."

"Objection, irrelevant."

"Overruled."

"Not pretty," she said.

"No further questions."

"Recross, Your Honor," said Cash, rifling through his immense lawyer bag.

"Proceed," Judge Barnes said.

"Do you remember who your grandfather bought the property from, or the details of the land purchase?"

I leaned forward once more and smiled at Hanna, encouraging her.

"Peo Peo Tholekt told me my grandfather bought the land from the Nez Perce themselves."

A wave of heat washed over me.

Hanna glanced at me and smiled faintly. "And he said he paid for it with sugar."

I remembered Kappy's diabetes and looked at Tansy, thinking of the delicate things she had inherited. Sugar. Of course.

28

Cash and Miles argued about bones and relics. A ponytailed, Birkenstocked anthropology professor from the University of Oregon testified about the age of artifacts found in the area. According to him, they were eight to ten thousand years old and proved the veracity of the Nez Perce claim on the land.

Miles cross-examined the witness about the Kennewick Man, and the theory that there had been other immigrants to North America who predated the "Native Americans" by thousands of years. It was impossible to prove with certainty, Miles conceded, because the Yakama and Umatilla tribes were unwilling to release the body for research. Miles ended his cross-examination, announcing, "The Scopes monkey trial showed us that oral history and creation myths don't mean much in the face of science." I thought Cash had rattled Miles a little; he wasn't near as smooth as he'd been in the beginning. He was angry when he stated his conclusion, more like William Jennings Bryan than Clarence Darrow.

The next witness had once been a clerk at the land title office of Nez Perce County, Idaho. Mildred McNabb wore her hair in a bun with a net and was as sure of herself on the stand as she was with her cable-knit patterns. She described how the government made one Indian sign away another's land. Cash asked her to identify some documents. The first was Grant's executive order of 1873 that gave the southern portion of the Wallowa Valley to the tribe. Then he asked her to identify one last document. It was the original deed of Heart of the Beast.

"Is John Winter's deed dated 1873?" asked Cash.

All I could think was that Jake had stolen it and given it to Kappy.

"That's right," Mrs. McNabb said, lifting her half glasses to look at the deed. "June 5, 1873. Same year as Grant's executive order that gave the land back to the Nez Perce."

"Who do you see sold the property to John Winter?"

"Appears to be an Indian named Hush Hush Cute."

I looked over to Miles and then to Tansy. Kappy was a great-grand-daughter of Hush Hush Cute. I wondered if my brother found her so attractive because of her or her family history. With no more than several thousand people living in eastern Oregon, the world was very small.

"From your best guess, what happened in this transaction?"

"Some of the Indians were notorious for signing away land if they had a little booze in them," she stated. "The homesteaders, shop owners, traders would get them drunk and bring them to the notary with a witness. Most of the Indian property went for one DC."

"What does that translate to, Mrs. McNabb?"

"One dollar and other consideration."

"Kind of like selling land for sugar?"

Miles interrupted with an objection.

"Overruled," the judge stated.

I stared at Mrs. McNabb and a feeling of nausea came. John Winter had gotten Tansy's great-grandfather drunk, bought Heart of the Beast, and paid for it with sugar. Why couldn't my relatives have been fighters against Prohibition instead of Nez Perce.

"No further questions," said Cash.

As far as I could tell, we lost the case right there. McNabb's testimony that John Winter bought the land from Hush Hush Cute was the violation of the Trade and Intercourse Act the tribe had alleged. I tried to decide what the judge had been thinking through all this. Because I knew what I was thinking. The Nez Perce deserved their land back. At the same time, I had an ugly feeling. If I gave this land up, I'd have to give up the Bar S too; as my mother said, it was all stolen. I had sunk to defining my worth by the land I owned, just like my relatives.

The tribe's last witness was an eighty-seven-year-old hunter named Louis Creech, who had worked the Wallowa all his life. When the judge saw this man, he laid down his pen and sat back in his chair. It was as if the trial had stopped at that moment. Cash did research on the judge, knew he loved to hunt. He drew the witness out, asking him whether or not he had ever hunted for bighorn sheep, extinct in Oregon now for fifty years.

"I hunted them in the Steens and the Wallowas. In the winter, they were as tame as you please, but come summer, they moved up t' the higher altitude. Impossible to shoot. Had t' track 'em for weeks. Usually got an elk and had to pack that out before I bagged a bighorn. Uh course, the easiest t' kill were the antelope. Dumbest critters on the face of the earth, 'side from porcupines. But you don't wanna ever kill a porcupine," Creech said, proffering a bent finger at the judge. "You never know when you might need a meal sometime."

The judge laughed and said, "I'll make a note of that."

I was furious, and wanted Miles to interrupt, but he was busy listening. As if he, too, had finally come upon something that captured his interest.

"And that was your livelihood, hunting and trapping? Could you explain a little about that?" Cash asked.

"Yes, sir. I trapped in the winter with the steel leg-hold trap. You needed 'em heavy to drown a beaver. I skinned 'em, took the castor gland for bait, and the tail for me to eat. Then I stretched 'em over frames of willow stick 'n' branded 'em with my mark. Sold 'em two dollars apiece.

"The grizzlies were around back then," Creech went on. "Now all you got is black bears. But the grizzlies, I never went out of my way to mess with 'em, but occasionally one would come at me. I froze and tried to wait it out, bucause once it come at you, you couldn't shoot enough times to kill 'im before he killed you. Then there was rattlesnakes. I musta used fifty, sixty bales of tobacco to spread around the cabins to keep 'em from getting under the foundation. And the wolves. Always taking your kill. They gone too." Creech would have gone on all day if Miles hadn't interrupted.

"Objection, irrelevant," said Miles finally.

I fidgeted, irritated that the judge was letting everything in.

"Overruled," stated the judge.

"Did you ever see any Nez Perce on or near Heart of the Beast in the time you lived out there?" asked Cash.

"No sir, I did not. I saw a lot of miners. Chinamen. Had to run 'em off the place otherwise they settle, and you never git rid of 'em. Convicts. The convicts come 'cross the Lolo Trail from Montana, headed to Portland. Them people never said a word. You couldn't shut a miner up. But convicts. If a man didn't answer when you called, better t' leave well enough alone. Let the man pass."

"You knew the Winters all your life?"

"I met John Winter only couple times when he was ridin' after cattle. But I found lotta his handwork. He used t' kill coyotes with strychnine. John Winter rode around all day with that strychnine in his pocket, eating raisins out of the same pouch. That was quite a man, John Winter. Strychnine eatin', horse swindlin', Injun killin'."

I looked at Miles, wondering why he wasn't objecting.

"His son Willy was just as bad," Creech went on. "Never felt good buyin' horses from either one," said Creech, laughing. Creech practically hee-hawed. He was hard of hearing, but it seemed to me the worse things he said about the Winters, the louder he became.

"Objection," said Miles finally.

"Overruled," replied the judge, leaning forward.

"What was your experience with Willy Winter as a horse trader? Was he an honest man?"

"He'd do jus' about anting to sell a horse. Filing teeth, smearin' brands. Kept 'em real thin so they'd make like they was tame. Bled some of 'em. Nerved a couple I seen."

"Nerved them?" asked Cash.

"Yeah, cut the nerve in the heel. Make a lame horse not feel nothin'."

"Where'd Willy Winter learn these things, trading with Gypsies?" Cash said, casually.

"Naw," replied Creech. "Nobody trusted Gypsies nuff t'do bidness with 'em. Learnt it from his dad."

"John Winter was known as a swindler?"

"Objection," Miles said.

"Overruled," the judge responded.

"No sir. Only the people that played cards and drank whiskey wid him thought he was crooked. An he only sold lame horses to folks going through. Down to parts west. So most people thought he was all right. John Winter made most of his money sellin' to the cavalry. Stole crop-out Appaloosas from the Indians, and turned 'round and sold 'em to the cavalry."

"Describe a crop-out Appaloosa, if you could," said Cash, smiling as if he had discovered gold.

"A crop-out's a solid color, didn't have spots," Creech yelled. "Solid color's the only kind the cavalry'd buy. Two Appaloosas bred together throw a spotted foal only 'bout thirty percent a the time. S'why Appaloosas so rare."

"He stole horses from the Nez Perce?" asked Cash.

"No!" Creech shrieked. "He wouldn't steal 'em. He'd buy 'em cheap from somebody else a stole 'em. They was a couple gangs that migrated around. They came from parts south and stole for a livin.' Then John Winter'd buy 'em cheap an sell 'em to the cavalry afore anyone knew any differnt."

"When the cavalry came, they needed fresh horses and provisions, isn't that right?"

"Yessir," Creech said.

"So what would a homesteader do to bring the cavalry in?" Cash inquired.

"Homesteaders cooked up troubles with the Nez Perce, claimed their cattle was stolen, 'n' blamed it on them Indians. An' then the cavalry come to move the Indians off, bucause the homesteaders had been wronged. An' when the cavalry was on their way out, Winter'd sell 'em provisions and horses at souped-up prices. A homesteader'd make good money selling supplies t' the army. Back then the govment reimbursed a man hunred fifty dollars a head for a good cavalry horse."

"Wouldn't a good way to keep doing business with the cavalry be to settle on some property that was sensitive to the Indians? Someplace that would be likely to upset them by whites just being there? Someplace like the sacred ground called Heart of the Beast?"

"Yessir. That'd be a good way to drum up bidness. If you dint get killed in the meantime." Creech started laughing. He leaned over on one haunch and placed his hand on his knee, palm turned out. "There's a rumor that General O. Howard tried to kill John Winter."

"General O. Howard, president of the Freedman Society, founder of Howard University, leader of the battles of Antietam and Gettysburg?" Cash asked incredulously. I decided, he'd probably done focus groups on Howard, too.

"Thas right. Only folks round here didn't think much a Howard. But the General come out anyway madder 'n hell bucause a what happen to them horses."

"Describe what you mean, sir," said Cash.

"John Winter captured them horses of the Nez Perce chief, Tih-po-ax. Musta been close to a thousan' head. General Howard wanted them horses to use in the quartermaster department 'n' to replace the broken-down animals of the cavalry," said Creech.

"What did John Winter do with these horses?" asked Cash.

"Slaughtered every damn one of 'em," Creech yelled. "Wanted to keep the supply down. Story was that it took 'im three days to do it. Did it on his own property, right there on Heart of the Beast. Everyone said it made that hill a little higher, all those bones of a thousan' horses."

"No further questions, Your Honor," said Cash.

After that, I didn't want to continue. When Miles called me up to the witness stand, the next day, I walked up slowly, wondering if my very existence somehow defended my family. I took the oath as if I were outside my body. The stand was cold and hard. I glanced at Miles with apprehension.

He asked the usual questions—where I was born, and when, about my parents and brother. I started crying right off the bat. I was embarrassed and mad at myself. I noticed the judge writing something down on his notepad. But the strangest thing was that Tansy started crying sitting there at the defendant's table. She didn't have a Kleenex and just used her palm to wipe the tears. The judge gave me a box of Kleenex as fast as a cat. I thought, How ironic, here he was worried about one woman's crying when he had the power to decide an entire tribe's fate.

The night before, Miles and I had discussed what I would say on the witness stand. Miles never mentioned he was going to bring up my family. He said he would ask what I knew about the property. I had to admit, Miles used me well. The judge took it all in.

"Did you ever hear the stories Mr. Ogden asked Miss Steele and Ms. Winter about?"

"No, never."

"How did your family acquire Heart of the Beast?"

"I don't know, I assume they homesteaded it."

"Have you ever heard any stories about the settlement?"

"A few," I said. "My mother told me that my great-grandmother lost seven of her children crossing the Oregon Trail. From cholera and meningitis, I believe. I know they walked all the way because they didn't want to burden the oxen, and that there were ten graves to every mile of trail. When they crossed the Platte River my great-grandfather carried a calf on his shoulders so the cattle would follow him, and my great-grandmother drove the wagon across and watched her brother drown." I sweated even more, positive that my face was blood red. "Then the Indians stole some of their stock, and they lost their team at the Applegate cutoff."

"No further questions."

I took a deep breath. I eyed Cash as he stood up. Judgment Day had arrived.

Cash slid up near the witness stand. He spoke softly. "Your grand-father Mark Steele wrote some books on Indians, did he not?"

"Yes," I said, looking at Miles. Miles nodded back at me. "He did."

"Are they rare? Hard to find?"

"Very." The truth was that we owned boxes of his books. The colonel had thousands printed, but only gave out a few, to his cronies, and to judges he wanted to curry favor with. Ike had told me he was going to take them out and burn them, just to get rid of the things, exactly what I wanted to do with the heads.

"Do you own copies of all his books?"

"Yes."

"From your statement to Mr. Emmerett about the Oregon Trail, sounds like you've read some of them. Is this true?"

"No, I haven't. My mother told me the story of the crossing."

"John Winter was someone your grandfather knew and admired. He wrote about him in at least two of his books. One about the Nez Perce war and the other about the Paiute wars. Isn't it true that John Winter fought in both of those?"

"As far as I know."

"Objection, Your Honor." Miles finally stepped in. "The witness has no firsthand knowledge of these books or what went on last century. It is unfair to ask her this information."

"Overruled."

"In fact, according to these books, John Winter had long been an Indian fighter before the Nez Perce war. He wrote several letters to President Abraham Lincoln, because he believed Lincoln was an old Indian fighter himself. Winter complained about the inability of the military to protect the citizens of the territory of Oregon. But your great-grandfather became frustrated by the president's inaction and lack of military support, because of his preoccupation with the slavery question. And so John Winter formed a militia with the stated policy of complete and total extermination of the Indians. His battle cry was 'take no prisoners.' Was it not?"

My stomach tightened. I felt pinpricks of heat under my arms. "I don't know, sir," I stammered. "I never heard that phrase before."

"Let me give you an account of how your family ended up with the land called Heart of the Beast. It is an excerpt from a book written by your grandfather Mark Steele. These books were purchased in the rare book department of Powell's Bookstore, Portland, Oregon. I submit this book, *The Sahaptian War*, by Mark Steele, as Exhibit Fifteen, Your Honor."

"Documented," said the deputy.

"Request permission to review Exhibit Fifteen," said Miles, smiling again.

"Granted," stated the judge.

"This is a letter written by Major General Timothy Cordon on behalf of General Howard to President Abraham Lincoln," said Cash, holding a copy of the letter in his hand. He waved it around lightly as if it were a perfume stick in the cosmetics department. "In it he describes how John Winter advanced into Nez Perce territory, capturing Heart of the

Beast. Once there, he was outraged at the lack of compensation for the 'just claims incurred in the prosecution of this war.' This was shortly before Winter captured and slaughtered those one thousand horses, and General Howard was forced to put a stop to John Winter."

This was just like Ibsen's *Ghosts*, I thought, taking another deep breath. I tried to remember what happened to the son in the play; I think he went insane because he contracted hereditary venereal disease. I thought again of the sins of the fathers revisited on the children, Scandinavians just couldn't get enough of it. You can never get away from your blood, like my mother said.

I noticed Cash glancing at Miles before he went on.

Miles did not look up from reading *The Sahaptian War*. His legs were crossed high like a lady's as he perused the book.

"'Dear Mr. President,'" Cash began. "'The entire number of hostile Indians who have surrendered themselves, as accurately as they could be counted, is twelve hundred twenty. It is a number that would have taken many years to exterminate, had that been my policy. Even had I been in favor of extermination, which I am proud to say I was not, it would have been an impossible task. At no period of time have I had in the field more than two hundred sixty men. Of this number, upwards of one hundred came up in the steamer with me as recruits from New York. They had never had a day's drilling, and the policy of extermination would have proven difficult to carry out with them on account of their want of skill.'"

I looked at Miles. He stared at Cash expectantly, as if he'd read this account before. I squinted at Miles, wondering if somehow I was missing in him some sign of the complete alarm that was raging in me.

"'The policy of extermination,'" Cash read on, "'is reserved for those quasi troops who were called into the field without law, retained without necessity, and were instructed to "take no prisoners!" The organizer of these servicemen is one John Winter, a trader who on occasion provides resources to the cavalry at inflated prices. His claims are dubious at best. I am sir, respectfully, your obedient servant. Timothy Cordon, Major General for General O. Howard. Department of the Columbia, Vancouver, Washington.'" Cash walked smoothly back to his table, looking first at Miles and then glancing at his notes.

It was difficult to concentrate. One minute I was furious at Miles for not calling this trial off. The next I was thinking *Well, they don't have any proof John Winter killed anyone,* and the next was *Of course he was a murderer.*

Cash looked back at me and paused for a moment. "Would extermination of twelve hundred twenty American Indians be the actions of a law-abiding citizen?"

"Of course not," I said loudly.

The judge looked at me.

"What do you do with Heart of the Beast currently?" Cash asked abruptly.

"We rent out the pasture to neighbors for their cattle in the summer and rent it out to hunters during the deer, elk, and bird season."

"Have you ever been told that running cattle on property harms the land? That the cattle grazing in the riparian zones exposes the land to extreme erosion?"

"We only have cattle there one month of the year," I said.

"According to the Department of Fish and Wildlife, grazing cattle for any amount of time on sensitive land causes destruction which takes years to rebuild. It's our sacred land, Your Honor, endangered land. It has been taken illegally from us years ago. We are the rightful stewards of Heart of the Beast. The details from *The Sahaptian War* show how John Winter deliberately took this property. He did so with an intent to exterminate this tribe with his take-no-prisoners attitude and by calling in the cavalry. He then profited by selling provisions to the very same forces that rid him of his enemies. And finally, he arranged to trap the Indian Hush Hush Cute into selling him this land, now proven to be in violation of the federal Trade and Intercourse Act. Mr. Creech, Ms. McNabb, even Ms. Winter corroborated this."

"Objection, Your Honor," said Miles, looking up from the book. "These statements are out of order and usurp the authority of this court."

"Mr. Ogden, please save your statements for closing," said the judge.

Cash remained standing with the letter in his hand. "It is time to right these wrongs. We must have justice. Thank you, Your Honor." Cash sat down abruptly. I noticed he continued to grip his paper as he watched Miles.

Miles stood up slowly. I pinched the fat between my thumb and fore-finger.

"Redirect, Your Honor," said Miles. "I know you haven't read these books, Ms. Steele. Perhaps I could read you some statements from them and then ask you a few questions. Before John Winter fought Nez Perce, there were apparently many skirmishes with the other Indians, the Coeur d'Alenes, the Paiutes, the Palous, and the Umatillas. He states on a number of occasions that there was one band of Indians that contin-ued to help the white forces exterminate or remove the other tribes."

"Objection," said Cash loudly.

I looked around nervously. The older Indians on his side of the room remained unmoved, but the younger ones looked at me with scorn. Feelings between whites and Indians hadn't changed, and I wondered if they ever would.

"Overruled."

"'The friendly Nez Perce,'" Miles read from the same book, "'were employed chiefly as spies and guides in our efforts against the Indians. Toward the close of the action, they attacked the enemy hiding in the brush and timber on the Spokane plain. On another occasion, they engaged the enemy advancing upon our flanks. The Nez Perce have given exemplary conduct and are worthy of special notice for their bravery, and valuable auxiliaries as instructors to our soldiers in the mode of Indian warfare.'" Miles laid down the book and crossed his arms. "What do you make of that, Ms. Steele?"

"That the Nez Perce helped place other Northwest Indians on reser-vations," I said.

"What do you suppose the benefit to them would be in that?"

"They wanted to keep their land and did whatever they thought would help accomplish that. Even if it meant turning on other Indian tribes."

"Sort of an end justifies the means."

"Yeah. Sort of."

"John Winter goes on to say in a letter to the governor: 'The enemy has endeavored by every means in their power to embarrass and crip-ple our county's manifest destiny. They have resorted to indiscriminate warfare; they have set a lake of fire before us. It would be worse than madness to plunge into this barren waste to attack. However, it would be more mortifying to fail in accomplishing the objectives of this great nation. Yours sincerely, John Winter.'"

More words on the founding of this great nation, I thought bitterly. The murderer John Winter speaks in his defense. I might as well cede the stand to him and all the rest of the ghosts come back to life.

"John Winter was a patriot," said Miles. "No more, no less occurred in all parts of the United States. He was a popular man amongst the people of the Northwest. Perhaps he was taking too much glory from the likes of General Howard."

I looked at Cash; he watched Miles intently with a pen in his hand.

Miles walked toward the judge, again limping once. He held the book up, a crooked finger marking a page. Everyone in the courtroom looked at him. His behavior was choppy, probably because he hadn't had time to study the book before the trial. But he had found those pages so smoothly; it was as if he'd read them before.

"Mark Steele writes a small epilogue on the last page of this book." He paused, searching with his finger for the paragraph. "He writes of the largest irony in the Sahaptian war." He gave me the book to read, a flimsy paperback, barely a quarter inch thick.

"'The humor of the story to all parties,'" I read, "'was a colossal mix-up the size only the government could make. When President Grant signed the executive order in 1873 to give the land back to Chief Joseph, he obtained the wrong geographic information. Originally, they intended to split the valley: the northern half, more settled by whites, was to stay in the homesteaders' hands; the southern half was to go to the Nez Perce. President Grant returned land in the Wallowas to the Nez Perce. But,'" I said, looking up at Miles, "'it was the wrong land. The deeds were incorrectly written, as so many were back in that time period. The tribe was given the northern half of the valley, where the settlers had already staked their claims. And the government took the southern half where the Nez Perce wintered in their return from the Imnaha. And thus ends this chapter of American history.'"

The courtroom was silent. I looked around. The judge was motionless, his pen still in the air. Cash stood up. Tansy wiped a tear from her cheeks with the back of her hand.

"What does this mean to you, Ms. Steele?" asked Miles, standing in front of me, reaching for the book.

I sat there stunned. I handed the book to him. "I guess the Nez Perce got some free sugar," I said, haltingly.

"What you mean to say is that John Winter legally bought the land since, as you can see on this map, Heart of the Beast is clearly located in the south."

"Yes," I said. "It appears he purchased it legally." How did Miles find this information so quickly, I wondered. Had the colonel given Miles a set of these books? If he knew this, why did he let this go to trial?

"Owning Heart of the Beast is not a crime," Miles said. "John Winter was merely doing what the founding fathers of this country set out to accomplish, the establishment of the United States of America from coast to coast. When Thomas Jefferson initiated the Lewis and Clark Expedition, the desire was to claim the Oregon Territory for the United States from everyone, including the Indians.

"Iris Winter had nine children, Your Honor, seven dead crossing the Oregon Trail. Of the two survivors, only one, William Winter, would live to have his own family. I submit that there were many sacrifices made during the creation of our country. Evidence of these still exists today. Losses occurred for all parts. No one was singled out or spared. Thank you, Your Honor."

The judge nodded, gathered up his papers, and left the courtroom for a break before closing arguments. There wasn't much more to say; the lawyers had said it all.

I suddenly felt a strange sensation; the hairs on my arm stood up and that prickly heat came down my neck like blood.

I looked around the courtroom. I saw the plaintiffs and, behind them, waiting for justice, what was left of the Lost River tribe. I hadn't noticed until then that Henry had been in the courtroom all along. He met my eyes and smiled. I nodded to Hanna behind me. I reached for Tansy's hand. Her face was drawn, and her cheeks pale. She didn't look Indian anymore. That was when I saw him. The medicine man. He stood there looking at us, the tiny blue rings in his irises burning, and I thought I heard him say something. "What?" I whispered, but he turned and headed out the door, shuffling in an almost musical gait.

I looked at Tansy again, and picked up my pen and paper. The lawyers had done enough talking; it was time for me to talk. Everything in life was a trade-off. Dams or salmon. Life or land. Children or childless. I was just like my relatives, the horse traders, after all. I was ready to bargain, a life for land.

part seven

29

THE NEXT MORNING TANSY, HANNA, AND I CHARGED OVER the roads headed toward Joseph. I almost collided with a passing cattle truck as I rounded a corner, but I jerked the Blazer over, and we hurtled on east to the foundry—the three of us, plus our ancestors in the form of fourteen heads of clay. Before we left the ranch, I had packed old Dutch Boy paint and International Harvester boxes with the life-size busts, carefully wrapping them in cotton towels and newsprint for support. After the trial, I wished I'd just thrown them in; maybe then they wouldn't survive the trip. At the same time, I wondered what good erasing us would do—as if nothing but blowing wind had ever occurred out here in eastern Oregon.

"I told the truth," Hanna said suddenly. "Sets you free." She stared out the window at the grass pasture full of Appaloosa horses and the windrowed fields of violet alfalfa.

"Free," I responded. What would set a person free, I wondered, as we passed Old Immigrant Hill and Poverty Flat Road, following the trail my great-grandparents walked into the state of Oregon. Truth. Restitution. Forgiveness. Love. Alcohol. Of course, suicide would do it, as it had for my brother. I looked at Tansy in the rearview mirror. She sat behind Hanna, watching the landscape slip by.

Hanna placed a CD in the player. It was music of bagpipes, like what Scotty Jamison had played at Elise's funeral. It echoed through the car, reminding me of Wales, abandoned fortresses in the useless defense of the motherland. I glanced at Hanna, seventy years old and only now accomplishing her lifelong goal. The failed versions of her parents and mine finally ready for casting. And right alongside them sat my own clay head encasing a steel armature, a circle inside another circle, the axis of the earth pointing east to Heart of the Beast like a compass.

For seven months I had lived with Hanna, and during that time I had talked about my family. She seemed to understand everything, nodding along as she sculpted. And at times, I had felt better discussing things with her. But the truth was, I hardly knew my aunt.

Tansy had spent only three weeks with me, but I could see what made her happy: she liked things that older people ordinarily did, thus her hardship license. And I knew, for instance, it pissed her off that the kids in school assumed she did drugs because she was Indian. She loved peanut butter and honey sandwiches, wore size 6 shoes, size 7 clothes, and had two fillings in her teeth.

But Hanna was unto herself. In her spare time, she didn't say how about going to a movie at The Dalles, or how about going fishing, or let's paint the bedroom. She doodled. Always heads full of curls and whirlpools, curly hair, curly eyes, circles, serpentines and more circles. When she wasn't drawing, she was carving. She'd make an observation here and there that was usually true, and then she'd close up again. Hanna mainly had a relationship with her art, and with me only by extension.

I inhaled sharply, thinking of Hanna's imminent departure. The Blazer smelled of old things, stale and forgotten, cigarette smoke, deteriorated newsprint. I realized the clothing Hanna was wearing had lain away in boxes for thirty-one years, ever since she went into the institution. It wouldn't be too long now before she'd be finished with her art, and then I imagined she'd leave. It's a pity, I thought, that we weren't able to have more of a relationship. In a way, she was just like her sister. After what I heard in the trial about the ruthlessness of their parents and grandparents I wondered why they weren't even worse off. I had to admit they came by their craziness honestly.

"I've always thought this land looks like Van Gogh's land," said

Hanna, continuing to stare out the window. "I could never look at his paintings without being reminded of home."

"Why'd you leave?" Tansy asked. "It's so beautiful here."

"Looking for something else," Hanna replied. She shook her head and then looked down at her lap. "It wasn't so much what I was looking for, but what I fled," she said finally. "I was forced to travel, to ward off the apparitions assembled in my brain."

It sounded like a quotation, like a poem, the way she said it. I thought it might be Rimbaud. An amorous English student had given me *A Season in Hell*. He was about fifteen years older than I. Gaunt, tall, and pale-skinned, he confided his secrets to me over coffee at Burtons, quietly and sincerely telling me that weekly he swallowed the same piece of string and timed its passing through his body. He said it pardoned him, absolved him, helped him transcend. He told me I should try it, and gave me a piece of twine. I had thrown it in the trash and placed Rimbaud on the shelf.

"It was a long time before I could work on people," Hanna continued. "But I was drawn to the flaws. Sometimes flaws make beauty."

I thought of how when she first came she had talked about completing her sculptures as if they would complete her. Then when she had started working, she sculpted my whole body, as if somehow she needed to go through all the steps to resolve her quest. When Tansy came, Hanna had begun all over, operating once more in an entirely different manner. I thought about the sculptures and about the trial and wondered if true resolution existed.

"Everything always came out looking different," sighed Hanna. "Your mother complained," Hanna said, looking at me. "She said it didn't look like her."

I laughed, thinking nothing could be perfect enough for my mother.

"But you have to take the good and the bad."

Tansy turned her head to listen. She pushed her hair off her forehead and chewed on a fingernail.

I shook my head, and we barreled down the road, a procession loaded with that which had never seen the light of day. Clay rubbed on cotton, rattled on newspaper and the printed word as we drove into the parking lot of the forge. I backed the Blazer up to the loading dock, the same way I unloaded cattle from a truck at auction. The morning blued the foggy spring air, illuminating trees covered in a white cloud batting. The forge fired heavily in the middle of a series of fifty-three Quonsets.

A middle-aged man with a Fu Manchu mustache opened a small door alongside the dock. He greeted us with a grimace and said his name was Gary.

"You got business here?" he asked warily.

"Fourteen sculptures in the back of that Blazer," I said, pointing, "and an appointment to have them cast."

He rolled up the loading door and helped us carry in the boxes. We set them in the middle of the room on an enormous wood-slab table. The fourteen sculptures covered the table in various stages of decay, like the broken heads of kings formerly surmounting the portal of Notre Dame.

Around us loomed fully finished sculptures waiting for departure to their final destinations. An enormous series of shelves spilled over with the bronze statues like an iron ossuary. Some of the bronzes sparkled in their packaging of bubble wrap, others sat ignored. Square marble bases in all colors lay strewn about on shelves, tables, and the floor. White walls darkened with scuff marks supported foundry workers' clothes hung on racks. Ironsmith chaps stood on their own from rigidity and overalls dangled in the chill air.

The room, with a cold cement flooring polished meatpacker gray, sucked heat out of my body. Swinging doors on two walls led into different parts of the foundry. I heard music coming from deep inside the forge, slightly louder than the drilling noises and compressors going off.

"Most of the stuff we do here is western art," said Gary. "That's a Jarad Spade," he added, pointing to an uncovered eagle alighting. "Those claws," he told me, "they're silver. We use cyanide for them."

I began carefully lifting the heads out of their boxes. Hanna helped me, moving more deliberately now. The few lines in her face disappeared. She looked very young again. The door swung open and the drift of an industrial fan lifted her clothes and swung them about her like the housedresses I remembered my mother wearing. I felt a pang in my throat. I couldn't stand how vulnerable she looked, how vulnerable my mother had been. Hanna looked closely, lovingly, at the crescent moon hair of my mother's and her own sculptures. The women all had moons sculpted in their hair that cast bittersweet shadows across their faces.

My aunt's fingers, still red-brown from the constant immersion in clay, rubbed and caressed the foreheads of my mother and father. I forced myself to look at them. "They don't look like my parents," I said, sad, disappointed, and empty.

"They don't have to," Hanna replied. "You see what's inside you."

I stared at Ike and Elise, cataloging every ugly feature I remembered. I found the grievances, the lack, the violence, the fault, and I just wanted to sit down and quit. The eyes of Elise had never looked at me when she was alive, nor did they now. Hanna captured the essence of people, and that was the essence of Elise and me.

Ike, on the other hand, looked directly at me, because I was always in his way. Seeing my father now, I realized the house had swallowed some of his rage. Ike's brows furrowed, and his eyes shone even in the hardened clay. His mouth still frightened me, lips dripping together as if screams still flowed from his mouth.

Hanna moved to look at her parents, Willy and Dagmar. Willy's shifty-eyed expression looked almost comical next to Dagmar's Norwegian grimace. Hanna stayed there with her parents, and I wondered if she had accepted them finally. How strange that she wore clothes she'd owned before her madness. She's still so fragile, I thought, but I had a feeling of her strength, too. A life wasted is a life wasted. But here she was, accomplishing a lifelong passion.

Placing the palm of her hand on the head of John Winter, Hanna moved on by. He remained with the same expression of hate, the crazed look in his eye of a Donner Party survivor. I imagined he would have eaten his family if he needed to.

She passed Ingram Steele, the lawmaker and the founder of universities. Beyond glowered the colonel, self-satisfied with the lascivious lip like Rodin's Balzac. Next to him, her face grazed by mourning and fear, his wife, Emma, looked on in condolence.

Finally she arrived at Jake and me. She touched the rounded corners of her clay, examining me as if she were a farmer searching land for moisture. She stayed longest resting her gaze on the head of her favorite, Tansy.

Tansy's sculpture glittered with what we had collected that evening. Her head sprang out like a fight from her neck, which was the trunk of a sage tree. The branches went through Tansy's jaws like strong fingers, and on the bark Hanna had hung the things we had gathered, obsidian arrowheads, agate, tiger's-eye, wheat, sugar, tobacco, and horns.

The branches came into Tansy's forehead and lifted her hair as if it were a barn raising, full of crossbars and beams of planed wood. Whiskey moons, the kind Ike loved, decorated her bangs. She was a growing tree, and her head was permanently blown back by the wind through her branches.

I noticed the final thing Hanna had done was to add, down by the base of Tansy's bust, a cloak. It swirled around her, undulating, but closed tightly at her neck. It pulled down her shoulders by the weight of it. There was a landscape reflected in the cape, two opposing rocks. Tansy's neck looked bruised and battered. A darkened stream ran down her face into a damaged patch behind her ear. It dripped below and pooled in a spot of blood on her cape, that of a bull killer.

I stood looking at the fourteen of us, a transient family about to be made permanent: all of us looked away from one another.

"What's this for?" asked Gary. "I never seen anything like it. Is it an installation?"

"Yes," I said.

"Where is it going?"

"Bar S Ranch," I told him. "It's a private project."

Hanna gripped her purse, her hands so red.

"What do you call this one?" Gary asked, fingering the sculpture of Elise.

"Mother," said Hanna, looking at me.

"That's good," replied Gary. "That's gonna sell. You have to name 'em names like that. Vague, even if they are about something personal."

Hanna stood transfixed, listening to the sounds of the forge. Sweat appeared on her upper lip: she nervously patted it with a handkerchief she'd brought in a beautiful embroidered handbag. I was sure both had been Dagmar's.

Hanna couldn't hide in her art anymore. What I saw made me pity her, for the butchered life she'd lived, for the years in the institution, for the electroshock therapy. The most she could make out of the waste were these fourteen sculptures. More than anything, I felt I was on her side. I wanted to help her. I wanted her to finally accomplish what she'd dreamed of.

"You just need to write me a check then. For the fourteen of them in bronze. You want bronze, not stainless?"

Hanna shook her head. "Not stainless," I said.

He scribbled some notes on his pad. He looked up suddenly. "Well, you can't cast this one the same way as the others," he instructed, pointing to Tansy's sculpture. "We only cast clay. There looks to be at least twenty other substances in that one," he said, narrowing his eyes.

"Everything we have in there is part of the sculpture," I said quickly. "It has to stay."

"Best we can do is put on a fixative and then a patina to preserve it."

"Fine," I replied.

"Five times thirteen. Let's see. Sixty-five thousand. That'll cover it."

"Good night," I gasped.

"It's a costly proposition," said Gary.

I noticed a burn scar under Gary's mustache. The hairs grew sideways there on his jawbone. The forge had left its mark.

Hanna opened her purse, pulled out a check. "I . . ." she stammered. "I don't have that much." She was crestfallen. "I have thirty-seven thousand dollars in savings." I thought she might cry.

Gary looked at her. He closed his book. "Metalwork costs as much as blood," he said.

"I have the rest," I blurted. "Or I know where I can get it."

Tansy looked at me. Tears spilled from Hanna's eyes.

"All right then," he said, opening his book again. "What can you pay me now?"

"Take the thirty-seven, and I'll pay the rest when they're done," I said.

Gary took Hanna's check and placed it in his chest pocket. He stepped back and rubbed his hand over his long hair. He walked the four corners of the table. "We'll start with two," he said. He hovered his hand over my parents' faces, obscuring them between his fingers. "You pick," he said, looking at me because I was the only one who talked in our strange group.

"Those," I said.

Then he lifted the sculptures of Ike and Elise, motioning us to each carry one. I collected mine, and Tansy and Hanna picked up theirs. It surprised me how Gary embraced the art—how personal and reverent he was with it. Yet at the same time, he bucked them up, as if they were bales of hay.

We followed him through the foundry. He moved the sculptures quickly, as if he wasn't sure he would find safe passage. We walked to the patina room first. I noticed the music then, piped inside the building.

Men stood at their projects covered with gray striped work overalls and leather aprons. They breathed into respirators or welding masks. Blowtorches blazed on differing ranges of inferno. These people swaggered with toughness. They looked like loggers that had run out of business when the trees disappeared; they were muffler welders, auto body workers, but earnest in their work.

Darkness filled the room, except for the glow of flamethrowers. Some shot honed dark blue cones; some shot yellow and orange licking tongues of fire. Baths of evil-smelling cupric acid, sodium sulfide, and liver of sulfate lined the path we followed. The walls were blackened here and there where the blowtorches had gotten away. The black stains flamed up the walls in nasty triangles. I recognized the song that was playing as "Breed" by Nirvana. It was everywhere in the fifty-three rooms of the forge. The drums knocked out a few of the blowtorches; the electric guitar was like a chain saw that whipped up the scalded and transformed air into a deafening balm.

I walked into the room where they chained the just cast bronze pieces back together to re-form the original sculpture. Strong women with rasps looked up and nodded at us as they filed off the edges of the seams. Their hair was pulled under caps and bandannas, and they wore thick white gloves and aprons. The smell of the soldering rods burned my nose. A woman welded a bronze piece of face. With my naked eye, I looked at the sparks that flowed down the forger's leg like a waterfall of light. It was the one thing Ike was always careful about, warning me to not look at the blue-white embers of the welding torch. "You'll go blind," he told me.

I don't know why I paid any attention to Ike. I would have just as soon gone blind, I decided, as I listened to Kurt Cobain's vacant voice. I stared at the sculpture, and despite my efforts, I saw the face of Ike. I grabbed ahold of Tansy with my free arm as she tried to make her way past me. I held her hard.

"Don't you want to stay with me?" I screamed at her over the music and the creation.

"What?" she yelled back.

"Stay with me!" I hated myself for begging, but I did it anyway.

She looked at me blankly, and then shook her head, pretending she couldn't hear me, I thought.

I stood there holding her arm down to my side. It was then, gripping her as my father had gripped me, that I realized I wanted Tansy to do my work for me. I thought having a child would make it right. She would somehow clean up and redo the mess that was all mine.

"Come on," she yelled, and pulled me through with her.

We entered the room where Gary and Hanna had stopped, the wax room. Red paraffin spilled and dripped everywhere on the floor and ceiling, as if a massacre had happened here. Women with scalpels and lamps hovered over the minutest details of the sculptures, now transformed into wax.

"This is where the lost wax process starts," Gary yelled. He placed the sculpture of Ike in a bath of wax. It came out with a thick coating of white. Then he cut the mask of the sculpture into two halves with a guitar string. He took each side and filled it with the red wax. When they hardened he attached the halves together.

"I have to make the trees," he said. "So when the bronze is poured into the mold the wax can escape. You can wait for me in the silicone room," he said, pointing through another set of swinging doors.

We moved toward a cloudlike white room. It wasn't painted, but covered with a silicone spray, used layer by layer to make the molds. It looked like heaven, like the clouds in the *Last Judgment* of the Sistine Chapel. Two workers, tall young men, were covered in train conductor clothes. Hanna examined one of the molds they had just finished. The pieces of the sculpture had been dismembered and hung on a tree so the wax could drip out when the molten bronze was poured inside.

"Ordinarily, we don't let people watch the casting process," said

Gary, returning with the molds. "Too dangerous. Something goes wrong, falls in the crucible, and the whole thing explodes. We make exceptions when the artist is here. Stand back," he ordered.

The two men came forward with fumigation wands as their weapons. They pulled down their masks and transformed themselves into buglike creatures. The air compressors started up, almost drowning out "Something in the Way," but I could still hear that beautiful requiem of song.

White material similar to insulation covered the sculpture of Ike. The air grew gray with particles of sand and glue. The grit caught on the blond hairs of my arms and covered my Levi's and T-shirt. I breathed in dust, remnants of Ike.

I remembered Hanna telling me that all she had thought about while she was doing the sculptures before her breakdown was the myth of Sisyphus. The doing over and over. The impossible task. Hopeless words of Kurt Cobain took over my mind, and I wondered if I was going to be cursed like him. I can't do this, I thought. Tansy's leaving, Hanna's leaving. I wanted to disappear, too.

It was then I noticed a vibration. It felt like a tank coming my way, growing louder and louder.

Gary came over to me, still wearing his terse expression. "The furnace," he screamed.

I nodded, but I wasn't listening.

He shook his head. "Do you hear it? The furnace?"

A roar slowly drowned out the compressors, the music, everything. The noise and the vibration took over my body and divorced me from feeling so completely that I wouldn't have known if I were urinating down my pant leg or having an orgasm.

Gary beckoned me forward just as the silicone completely covered Ike and Elise. I wondered why he was telling me to come forward. I walked by more shelves of white-colored molds. Hanna and Tansy followed me. He led us through heavy steel doors into the roar.

I walked into it, and the heat of the furnace struck me in the face. White silicone particles softened onto my skin. The smell of fire and smoke was overwhelming. An immense wind hit me from the fire of creation.

My feet felt fettered. I looked down to find I was standing in sand.

Hanna touched me on the arm. I noticed she was shaking. "You asked what it was like," she yelled. "To go over to the other side, and to come back." She nodded her head toward the furnace. "Torn apart and remade," she said.

Working in the corner of the room were three men covered with thick silver suits. Shiny masks pulled down over their faces, they looked like menacing iron men with their barrel-shaped bodies and trunklike legs. Shield gauntlets covered the thick black logging boots. The gold glow from the crucible of molten bronze glittered on their shoulders, the front of their coats, and the sharp black masks.

Gary leaned over to my ear. "We have to use sand because concrete will explode if there's an accident. If the molten bronze spills."

I wiped the sweat from my eyes on my shirtsleeve. Gary moved over and grabbed a steel rod to dip into the crucible on the other side of the furnace room. He looked as if he were stirring a pot full of meteorite.

"Twenty-one hundred degrees for bronze. Thirty-five hundred for stainless steel," he yelled when he walked back.

The other two men disappeared and then returned with the molds of Ike and Elise. They placed them in a coffin-shaped grate full of ash. Beneath the grate was a fire pit.

"We need to heat up the molds to at least a thousand degrees or they'll shatter when the bronze is poured," Gary said.

I heard Ike's mold start to crackle.

Gary returned to the crucible, continuing to monitor the temperature inside the three-foot blackened witch's pot. The molten bronze glowed and bubbled like the sun. Suddenly he closed his other fist, and the two iron-clad men swung a winch over the crucible. They fastened it to the radiant hot kettle. Slowly they worked their way over to the molds, careful not to tip the molten bronze.

The moving glow cast a light over the room. It hit the huge boxes of the fan above us and lit the ribbing of the insulated airways that traveled across the ceiling. The light cast a patina on Hanna's black glasses. It turned Tansy's skin to gold. It fluttered my hair with blasts of heat.

The glowing bronze poured in an arc from the crucible into the mold as if it were little bits of sun, otherworldly. There was no more cracking, just the roar of the furnace when they backed away. My parents' forms held the bright light, cast off their own power, their own source of energy, like a star. They warmed my face, my hands, and pressed a blanket over my chest.

"That's the first of them," announced Gary. The men slid the hoist back over, and it was finished. Carefully, they lowered the crucible onto the ground and unharnessed it. Gary turned off the furnace, and the roar slowly eased down. The men removed their shields, rolled up the door to the outside, and reality returned.

"It's beer thirty," one of them said. They walked out of the oven room and slid into their pickups. It was four-thirty, quitting time. We had spent almost all day there, and I hadn't even noticed.

Gary exited without a word. I walked closer to the molds. Hanna looked exhausted, drained. For the first time that day, there was silence. A snap caught me by surprise, and I jumped. I looked at the molds, and watched a spark fly out. An imperfection had burned off. Then another. The sculptures continued to draw me in with an embrace. I imagined my forehead was getting tanned from the sun of it, the warmth of my newly formed parents. I looked above us at the vent for the heat to escape. I watched the last remnants of smoke drift through the chimney. The fired air of the furnace flew out the roll-up door. I thought I felt water.

A dark purple bruise began to gather around the edges of the molds. They grew more earthly, the muddied color of heart or liver. The bronze began to shrink as it cooled. It became smaller and didn't threaten.

I reached into my pocket and pulled out my grandmother's watch. It belonged with Ike now. I held it by one end and carefully dropped it into his molten metal. It didn't explode. It disappeared slowly down into the gold, until there was nothing left. It was hers, and now his, without the colonel to always snatch it away.

The bronze cooled down, went from glowing gold to red to purple and finally black. It shrank in the molds even more, leaving the wrinkled texture of burned skin. And after that, there was no more separation. I felt water again and looked up to the ceiling. A light rain fell down through the vent soundlessly. It was welcome, but it wouldn't rain much, not enough to seed by. Rain has to be paid for before it comes. It was time to travel toward Heart of the Beast.

30

Wallowa Lake stretched out before us, as we made our way to Heart of the Beast. The sunset lit the water and the clouds from within like temples. Over us they glimmered soft as veils. The sun came out just before it dropped below the rim, and the mountainsides glowed green in the wind, catching a glint of grassbacks and alder leaves. Coming upon a fork in the road marked by an old wagon wheel, we turned away from the lake and climbed up the hill toward the homestead. Telephone poles, which held two wires, followed the road. They still bore the green Depression glass conductors.

I slowed as we arrived at the corrals. They sprawled out like a spiderweb from the old and menacing barn. The windows were boarded up, and the red paint peeled and bubbled down the grained wood.

It made sense to me now, I thought, having heard old man Creech. I parked and the three of us walked slowly over, looking at the thick poles stuck in the middle of the corral. They were for the breaking of horses. My grandfather and great-grandfather had tied the animals there for days, starving and without water, until they were too weak to fight and could barely walk. My relatives weren't horse lovers. They were con men; spent their time at the bars, drinking and playing cards, reeling people in as far as they could.

Years before, in the tack room of Heart of the Beast, I found an old trunk full of needles and running branding irons. A box full of the tricks of the trade glared now as evidence of the family business: running irons to smear brands, needles to bleed horses calm. I should have looked more carefully. Horse trading was as old an art as prostitution, and almost as interesting. When I was little I read about how the Gypsies disguised the Lipizzaners as their cart horses so that the Nazis wouldn't steal them when they invaded Austria. I imagined my own relatives had practiced the same type of dealings.

I looked out in the corral. The corrugated tin roof of the broken-down horse feeder angled up into the dusk air where I had once taught Henry to ride. The gates hung open, long caught by drifting dirt. Now only shadows worked their way down the eaves of the barn, pulling the building under with darkness. It didn't take long up here for the place to revert to its natural state.

"I feel like someone is still here," Tansy said. She trailed behind us as we made our way to the white house. She crossed her arms as if she refused to be contaminated.

The house was still painted white with green trim. Elise and I had treated it five years ago, to protect it from the wind and the rain. The closed blinds visible through the windows shut off the house so passersby couldn't look into our history. Near the top of the house glared an access hole to the attic I had boarded shut.

"Do you want to come in?" Hanna asked, polite as if she had lived there all her life. But I could see how coming home had set her back. Her voice cracked; she held on to the jamb of the front door. She was distracted by everything, the padlock on the door, the dying bushes along the front sidewalk.

Tansy shook her head; she was impatient. She walked over to the dinner bell, cemented to the side of the house, silent and unrung for forty or more years. Grabbing the knotted rope, her small hand flung it to the side. The bell shattered the silence that seemed to conspiratorially hold the place hostage. I unlocked the padlock, and Hanna disappeared inside without a word.

The lights in the house blazed on. Through the window I could see the antennas of our rabbit-eared TV, and the table in the center of the room colored by a gingham cloth. Around it stood stools, covered with flowered contact paper. More of Hanna's paintings hung on the walls where Elise had arranged them years ago. I saw Hanna quickly light candles as if she expected the electricity to go out.

I walked outside aimlessly under the old clothesline, the pins unaligned. I picked one off; the tightly wrapped springs sounded like the winding of a watch. The wood smelled of rain and felt like the shedding horns of a buck. I snapped it on my knuckle, and jumped when I realized Tansy was standing next to me.

The dead trees above us had the gray ink look of an etching, like places where witches hid, where Medusa and her snakes took form, where the wind howled. The branches had given up providing shade and made the landscape hotter in the summer and colder in the winter. They grew particularly crooked, as if they were diseased, not from lightning but neutron bombs. The branches, bent by the wind, had broken off like spiders' arms caught reaching to the sky in their own brittle web.

"Let's get out of here," said Tansy, flicking an unseen bug off the anarchy jacket.

We walked out of the yard toward the sacred site of Heart of the Beast, closing the picket gate. Across the farm site, we entered the shop through the small side door, not the pulley-operated machine entrance.

The air was heavy with oiled dust. The darkness of the dusk obscured the tools, as much as the covering of grease. An old crank drill hung on the wall; several creosoted railroad ties stacked up in a corner, giving off the faint smell of tar. Barrels lined up along the back wall. Some still had dirty spigots for gear oil and engine grease. The corrugated tin of the roof sounded like something cracking to pieces as it settled down into the night. The fine dust from our footsteps gathered in the air, hovering over the dirt-floored shop like a cloud of dry ice. A broken-down forge with bellows had blackened the far wall with its smoke; pitchforks with broken prongs hung on the walls. I thought of Gary at the forge and imagined Hephaestus, lame and chained here, sweat covering his body as he tried to keep the fire lit.

We walked on, out the back door, and stood surveying the land. Behind the leveled ranch site, the property continued up the meadow where Remley had run away from Henry. Years ago, Jake had cut a fire road up the mountain over a centuries-old trail. Tansy and I walked up there to Heart of the Beast. The spring rain had collected fool's gold in rivulets that ran together and apart down the road. It glowed under the sunset sky, but I no longer wanted to pick it up.

We entered a town of trees, protected by the clouds that cottoned them. The pine needles hung in horsetail switches over their scaly bark.

"Should we stop and rest?" I asked after we had climbed for fifteen minutes. I caught a faint scent of flowers, and I recalled having given Tansy some Joy perfume.

"No," she said. "I want to go on. I want to see it while there is still light." She was determined, resolute. She didn't look back at me when I slowed.

"There will be light," I told her. "It's a full moon." Around us, the sound of water cascaded off the mountain and headed to the lake in rhythmic fanning splashes. The wind hit us where it came through the trees.

"My mother once told me," I said, breathing hard, "that a Nez Perce traded my grandfather a horse for the right to come on this property and search for a secret root. The Indian said it could only be found on Heart of the Beast. It was supposedly a medicine that would save a friend's child from dying." I stopped finally to catch my breath.

"Did it work?" she asked, halting.

"I hope so. They killed medicine men who failed to save children."

"Good," she said, tossing her head back. Her black hair swung halfway down Jake's worn coat.

I laughed and reached out to touch her hair.

"Why didn't you know what happened here?" said Tansy, shrugging me off.

"No one wanted to remember," I said, pulling my hand back quickly. The wet grass soaked through my boots, and I held my mother's coat tight around me. Tansy continued ahead, and I followed slowly behind her. Finally we reached the base of the Heart of the Beast. "It's right there," I said, pointing to a breast-shaped hill in the middle of the meadow. "That's it."

Tansy began climbing up, slowly at first, and then hurried on alone. I stood at the bottom and let her go, watching the pant legs of her

Levi's dragging through the grass, dampening upward toward her knees. I wondered if, a few years from now, Tansy would tell me I couldn't come here with her. *You aren't Indian*, I imagined her saying. *You can't come.*

When she reached the top, she stood silently looking across the valley. "The lake looks like it's glowing," she called finally. She stood there a moment alone, and then motioned for me to join her.

It was the view of a sacred place, to be sure. Sunrise at the Pyramids or the Taj Mahal wasn't more beautiful, nor sunset at Machu Picchu or Uluru. Across the valley, the fraternity of mountains surrounded us like a family. Here and there, they fell away like rotted teeth. The infinite sound of water running was magnified into rivers by the gorges and the ravines. The air smelled of smoke, pine trees, and rain. Down into the valley, canes of wild roses harrowed the creeks swollen with dirty milk–colored water. The birthplace of the Nez Perce, and the burial ground of a thousand horses.

"It's peaceful here," she said. "Like hands are holding my head." She sat down, and I sat beside her. "Ghosts," she murmured, looking at the clouds.

I was disgusted with ghosts, disgusted with those things I was unable to put to rest. "If you believe in ghosts, you believe in revenge. Things that walk the earth until they get retribution. I've never known a revenge that didn't take both parties to the grave. It's time to move on," I said, pulling my coat tightly around me again.

She spread her fingers out on the land, touching the grass that was ordered by the walking snow of spring. I watched how her hand came out of Jake's jacket and Pendleton shirt cuffs, how her fingers tapered down to small cold red fingertips. Finally, I understood why the grass was greener here, why the cattle flocked here—all that carbon sinking into the ground making it fertile. "The ghosts soothe me," she said, pursing her small mouth. "They talk, tell me things. I depend on them."

I shook my head. I wanted reality, not fantasy. "I keep thinking I should see something when I come to this place," I said. "A sign. I should see the heart of the beast." The sunlight was disappearing. Crimson silk clouds streamed across the sky and turned the water below scarlet. "But I never see anything."

"I don't see anything," Tansy said, narrowing her eyes. "I feel it."

"I don't believe in ghosts," I told her. I picked a blade of grass and ran my fingers down it until it screamed.

"No," she said. "You wouldn't. Everyone has their own way of making things right. Making sense of things. Of belonging." She looked up at the sky. She was just like me riding Jade out into the fields, hanging on with barely a hank of mane. But Tansy looked to the sky, and I looked to the ground. I realized there was a fundamental difference between us, just as there had been between my father and brother. "I have ghosts," she said, taking a deep breath. "You have the land. And those heads."

Tansy was extraordinary. I wondered if she received her wisdom from her Indian half, her ability to actually think rather than escaping her thoughts with manic work the way my family had always done. At the same time, she seemed too composed, as if she were in some other reality, and I wondered if she was in a kind of trance. I wanted to tell her how much I loved her, needed her. But what I said was, "Don't give me this ghost crap," like some suburban parent telling their kid to clean up their room.

She was silent for a moment. She folded her legs Indian style. "Did you hear him?"

"Who?" I asked.

"The medicine man."

I thought back to the trial, the medicine man standing behind us.

"He said he saw me in a vision."

I started to sweat a little and wondered if she was on drugs. I leaned down to look her in the eye.

She returned my stare. I saw the way her thick lashes went right up against the skin of her eyelids and how her curls came down around her high forehead like question marks. "I thought he was talking to me," I teased.

"He spoke to both of us," she said, blinking rapidly for a moment.

"I didn't hear him say anything to you," I said. "The only thing I heard was . . ." I shook my head.

"What?" she asked.

"'Short Microsoft stock.'"

She erupted into laughter. And I laughed too. "You'd better do it then," she said, smiling.

I looked at the green grass there in front of me, the strange undulation of the land, and marveled at how fast the bones of those horses had disappeared, had caught dirt and sunk beneath the surface. But she couldn't deny the fact that my family and others like us had changed this place forever. I sat there next to her, waiting for what I knew was coming.

"I always thought something would change. That I would know for certain that I wanted to live with you. But," she said, "it never came. And during the trial, I asked myself why I was sitting on your side of the table. Why I wasn't sitting on the side that was defending my people."

Moonbows slung over the mountains. There, low to the ground, they were a golden red color. The clouds were clearing. "Neither you nor I had anything to do with what went on last century," I answered, almost by rote, and then I stopped. I was silent for a long while, staring at the water flickering and gleaming in the cradle of the valley. "Your father was the reason you were sitting on my side." I wasn't mad anymore. I finally began to feel the permanent kind of sadness that matched the weeping granite faces of rock.

"I want to go back to my mother's family in Idaho."

I wanted to say, "That would suit me fine." I wanted to nod down the pain and anger just as Ike had when Jake abandoned him. I was good at loss. "Do you think moving to another place will turn off that noise in your head? Will kill your anger?"

"I'm still going to be a mad Indian," she said wryly, screwing up her face. Finally she had come out of that rapturelike daze. She leaned forward, balling up. "It's just that I will know where I belong. I'm not property, Iris. I'm not like the land. Or the sculpture. You can't make yourself feel better by changing me."

"It's not for me," I said, rubbing my eyes. "It's for both of us. To share the things your father talked about. I want to share the land, my life. Do the things I never did when I was a girl your age, and move on."

"I don't want it," she announced. "Being a Steele is what killed my ancestors. My mother said it's what killed my father."

"He killed himself," I said, slapping my palm on my thigh. It made a soft thud through the thick coat. I looked hard at her; she returned my stare as if to say, *well, it's true.* "He's the only one responsible for his death," I said finally. "You can't pin that on anyone but him. Someone can put a beast inside you, but they can't keep it there."

"My mother never told me how he died," she said.

"You were at the ranch when it happened," I answered. I took a deep breath, and told her of the day.

"Why did Ike shoot my dog?" asked Tansy.

"I think it was because Jake had married an Indian," I said softly.

"So he married my mother and had me just to get back at his father?"

"I don't know," I told her truthfully. "I know he wanted to give what was his to you. All of this," I said.

"He didn't love me enough to stay alive."

"He left you with me. He went down to the creek where we tied our horses that day. And shot himself with the rifle my father had given him. Used a stick shaped like a wishbone to reach the trigger. He made sure Mother found him—he was furious at her for not stopping Ike. Jake knew she would never forgive Ike for what he did to her son."

"And you never forgave him, either," said Tansy, turning toward me.

A gust of wind blew hair into my face, and I tucked it behind my ear. I looked at Tansy sitting next to me. Her jeans had to be completely wet where she sat on the spring grass. But she didn't notice. Funny what she cared about. "Yes," I replied uncomfortably. "I did forgive him."

"I think there are some things that aren't forgivable," she said, looking away.

"Your father thought that too. He never forgave Ike. He blamed everything on him," I said, shaking my head. "Jake never faced himself. He ran away from it. It devoured him. No one helped him. Like I could help you." I started to shake. I held on to the ground, and crossed my legs. I placed my head on one fist, concentrated on breathing.

"What happened to Ike?" she asked slowly.

"There was an accident." I shut my eyes, but the tears came anyway. "We had an accident, the two of us." Finally, I let go. I tried never to cry because I was afraid the tears would never stop.

I felt a weight leaning on my back, pulling my head up out of my hands, and a coolness on my forehead. It was Tansy stroking my hair.

"I killed him," I said, softly.

She continued stroking my hair, running her fingers through it, smoothing the tangles with the salted sweat of her palms.

That was when it came. I wasn't sure it was anything at first. I turned my head to get rid of the slight rustle of the wind. Ever so faintly I heard the crying sound of an infant. It became louder, constantly dragging down the air with its plea.

"It's yapping at the moon," Tansy whispered. "I've never heard a coyote sound like that. Maybe it's in pain."

"Maybe we should just shoot it," I said.

Then the howling stopped. The wind ceased. The moon rose up out of the red-tinged horizon and cast a perfect white light over the Valley of the Wallowa. At last it came again, the incessant whining complaint. A smile drifted across my face as if an old friend had finally come home.

31

Ike HAD BEEN UP FOR HOURS, THE MORNING OF THE LAST cattle drive. "It's H-hour," he shouted, looking at Emma's watch as we rode the LVT, the amphibious landing craft, over to the island. My father paced in the hold where the troops had once stood as they went to war. His cigar burned down to a stub, and anchored in his teeth.

"Beautiful day, beautiful day to jump off a cliff. That's what they did in Okinawa. When we invaded the first home island. The kamikazes came first. There were hundreds."

The sun rose over the river from the east, a magnificent hanging ornament, the color of a snake's eye. That morning it felt as if witchcraft had chased the sun up from the earth and hung it in an unnatural position. The waves of the river caught the yellow tinge on their crests, thousands of candles lighted and magically flowing around the island, east against the tide of the ocean.

I drove the LVT, standing on my chair so that my head thrust out the hatch. The river brought the scent of algae, mud, and fishing trips. Unnatural-looking geese flushed and headed north above me, their bodies like a formation of flying bowling pins. I pulled my bandanna down over my ears, freezing in the spring morning air.

Everything was going according to Ike's program. The cattle had been rounded up, they'd cleaned the island of grass, and once we transported them back across the river, they would be ready to make the long trek to the Bar S.

"Last battle of the war," Ike shouted to no one in particular. "They fought to the last man." Several seagulls blown in from the coast followed the Indian fishing boats downriver. They laid out complaints of the day with their lugubrious caw.

"We have three hundred thirty-seven head of cattle over there," he said, walking back and forth along the side of the hold. My father now talked only campaign language. Ike and I had shoveled gravel onto the floor for the cattle. His cowboy boots ground the rocks into the steel-bottom boat. "That will be fourteen waves," Ike calculated. "Twenty-five boat spaces each wave."

I stepped back down into the driver's seat to turn in to the landing. "Including calves?"

"I counted them," he replied.

"We'll bring Jade back with the last load?" I asked doubtfully. "I don't want her to get kicked and end up lame."

"Nothing'll happen to her," he said as he paced.

I had left Jade on the island overnight because we'd completed the roundup of cattle late the evening before. All of the animals were now held in the small barbed-wire pen on the shores of the island. I could see them kicking up dust and sand as they looked longingly to the green grass of the mainland. The dust rose, as if some bad-smelling riot were going on.

That's what I remember most about the last day with my father—the smell of the neglect and ferment of the cattle. The animals had been left too long—through the end of winter and into spring. As it was, only sparse grass grew out there. It was a rock-covered, windswept six-hundred-acre island. We were barely able to land the LVT because only a small beach proffered any harbor, but that was enough for my father.

Ike Steele had become busier and deadlier since my brother died. My father was a soldier. And when Jake pushed that hate, guilt, and revenge back into all of us, Ike reverted to the only thing he knew for sure, and that was the marines.

I called him "sir." Said, "How you doing, sir?" late at night when he was drinking Early Times bourbon, his feet up on the table, watching war movies. Five years had passed since Jake's death, and since then time had run on the twenty-four-hour clock. Ike began to wear his old military clothing, the way the colonel had done; the only difference was Ike wore fatigues and the colonel had worn uniforms. His dogs lay in their lair under his chair.

He sat up late at night smoking his cigars, tapping the ashes into the tops of those missile shells. He never said a word to me about Henry, but he watched us just the same. And I did likewise to him, biding my time. Ike didn't talk to me about the plans Henry and I had, because my father had plans of his own. That was around the time he bought the island. And the LVT.

Ike had fought in the South Pacific, and that was where he fell in love with LVTs. He cared for those machines more than he ever did any person. They were amphibious landing craft, the most crucial element in conquering the region. Riding in one, Ike must have felt unassailable.

Two summers after Jake died, Ike told Elise he was going to an auction at Bremerton. He took the Kenworth and the lowboy and disappeared for three days up to the biggest naval base in the Northwest, where military surplus vehicles were shipped back to the states from the wars. He brought along his dogs and his checkbook.

I found the Sunday *Oregonian* that he had been poring over. An ad circled from the United States Marine Corps, the Navy, and the Army announced an auction. "Bremerton Naval Base will be holding a public auction Saturday, December 5th. Military surplus equipment includes: excavators, loaders, dozers, forklifts, bomb trucks, skidloaders, Cat D-3, Cat D-2, supply trucks, half tracks, M-4 Sherman tanks, LCTs, LCMs, and LVTs."

Henry had already left for his residency, and Elise and I took leave to Portland for R and R. I bought an extravagant ski outfit. Elise purchased another I. Magnin dress. We ate Dungeness crab at Dan and Louis' and stayed at the Imperial Hotel, standard fare for a trip to Portland. Everyone from eastern Oregon stayed at the Imperial. In the lobby, they displayed a huge photograph of our family's sixteen-mule jerk-line team, reproduced from the Oregon Historical Society. Plus, they arranged photos of the Pendleton Rodeo queen and her court above the check-in counter. We reserved the corner room on the ninth floor, the highest. We felt like royalty ourselves.

When we returned home, the Kenworth was idling in front of the house, and the lowboy lay empty. Elise and I walked out to the shop looking for Ike. Inside, we encountered the most enormous vehicle we had ever seen.

"Ike," yelled Elise. "What the hell? You bought a tank? Have you lost your mind?"

Ike crouched next to the iron tracks and pulled off the extra armor bolted to the side. "It's not a tank," he answered. He spat snoose on the floor; it joined a puddle of grease. "It's for haulin' cattle," he stated, pounding on the ratchet with a sledgehammer to break the bolt free. "It's an amphibious landing craft. An LVT 3. The kind we used on disembarkation in Okinawa."

Elise walked halfway up the gangplank and then backed down. "Christ," she said. "Another one of your brilliant ideas. What you going to do next? Bomb the place?"

I watched my father working like a maniac, harder and harder each day. I wondered why he even bothered to sleep anymore. I sized up the LVT because I knew the task of driving it would eventually fall to me. It did look like a tank, boxy with trapezoid-shaped tracks that went up at splayed angles.

A treaded ramp at the back worked up and down with a crank. The hold where the troops stood was partially covered. Up in the front, by the ignition and gears, a turret swiveled out of the roof for a gunner.

Army-navy surplus wasn't new to me; we had the Monster, the Auto Car, and the water tanker for fire season. Every single one of them was a bitch to drive: the gears ground, the steering slopped out, and the brakes worked only if you had legs of steel. All were colored Marine Corps dark green, a white star prominently placed on the side. In the case of the LVT, it glowed smack in the middle of the tracks.

"This is how we're going to get those cattle out to the island," he said.

I had to admit it was perfect for cattle, just like a stock truck that floated. "There anything the matter with it?" I asked, watching him work deliriously on the tracks. There was always something wrong with the things Ike came home with. "The armor?" I continued, pointing to his ratchet.

"Taking it off," he said, grunting as he pulled the tool. "Too heavy, need to make it lighter to get more cattle in."

I climbed up inside. Two seats filled the front, the driver's seat and a spot for the copilot. No cushions, just the bent iron chairs bolted to a platform. Above the driver's seat opened a hatch for visual navigation.

Two levers operated the steering mechanism: a gas pedal, and a reverse switch. It was much like an old Caterpillar. A tiny square hole directly ahead of the driver gave a slight view, at best, of what we might be running over. Behind that, everything shone green steel and military tread. Handholds covered places where troops needed to crawl—out the top and down the outside. Two long metal bars lined the side of the hold where troops braced themselves as they entered enemy territory and began shooting. When my father and I headed out to the island, I always wondered how many lives had ended on this boat.

It wasn't like entering enemy territory when we took the LVT out to the island, more like Hades. All the islands in the Columbia, separated from the mainland, grew barren—no animals and few trees. A small number of them had been where the Indians buried their dead.

Ike had a copy of Lewis and Clark's journal at the house. I looked up in their ill-spelled writing the part about the Memaloose islands in the Columbia:

> We observed a great number of humane bomes of every description in a pile, scul bomes forming a circle around that. The westerly part appeared to be appropriated for those of more resent death, as many of the bodies of the deceased were raped up in leather robes and lay in rows on boards covered with mats. We saw skeletons of several horses at the crypt, which convinced me that those animals were sacrefised to the deceased.

Our island wasn't one of the burial sites, but those words were all I thought about that morning of the last cattle drive. I couldn't get the idea out of my head that we were joining the dead.

Earlier, Ike and I had driven the motorcycle out to the river. Elise and Carl would follow later with Remley in the stock truck. We headed west toward Portland until just before we hit the Deschutes River. We passed miles of trains, multicolored caravans carrying cars, sawdust, and prefabricated housing. Destitute families were stopped here and there along the highway, moving off the farms to the cities.

Ike slowed the 125, and we left the freeway, bumping onto the dirt road that led down to the river. The LVT was parked there, at the loading dock. I started the boat up. It rapped loud and mean like a machine gun and cruised about seven miles per hour. It took us ten minutes to get across to the island. The cups on the tracks worked like a million dog-paddling hands and left a wake of whirlpools.

I eased the LVT up onto the island's shore where the fence came down into the water. Ike lowered the ramp and strode onto the beach like a general. He always touched land first. He gripped a stock whip in one hand, the cattle prod in the other. His pistol was tied to his right leg. He was a dark blue ghost, covered in Levi's armor. Ike never wore a hat; the deep furrows in his brow ate up cancer rays.

Immediately, he set out to sort the calves from the cattle. The calves were to go in the stock truck, because their small hearts wouldn't be able to make the thirty-mile trip back to the ranch. "You're driving the stock truck with the calves," Ike had instructed Mother.

Elise hadn't argued. She sensed something special about this particular cattle drive, and she had come with us, ready to ferry the calves. Carl and I were prepared to ride horseback, and Ike was armed to gun the motorcycle.

Ike and I cut the calves away from their mothers in less than an hour. The calves stood in their pen, lost, wandering aimlessly. Eventually all of them ended up at the fence, their noses catching whatever last bit of smell came from their mothers as we began to haul the cows away, twenty-five at a time, across the river.

Ike drove the first wave. I pumped bilge. After the first trip of the LVT, the bilge had to be worked constantly because of the leaks that came through the bullet holes. Ike had a set of wooden plugs that he kept in the side shelves where the radio had been secured. He told me that was what they did in the war when they were shot—pounded a plug through the hole and kept on going.

The bawling of the cattle, always loud during a roundup, became unbearable once the calves were separated from their mothers. At least three types of cries ripped through the air: the high continuous calling, the deep ones that started smoothly and ended up in a heave, and the constant lowing of the calves.

On the way over to the mainland, one cow tried to jump out of the boat. She rose up and hooked her front legs over the side. I stopped pumping bilge, climbed through the gunner hole around the boat, and lashed her head with the stock whip until she fell back into the herd, face bloodied.

The cattle milled right behind us, a flimsy wire mesh grate the only thing separating us from their crushing bulk. A bull routed and snorted back with the cows. Bulls listed the boat so badly we could take only one per load. The LVT, covered with excrement from the prior trips to the island, roared along loud and haphazard as the crazed payload. I felt like a stockyard worker, a poor immigrant from the last century.

Once we reached the mainland, some of the mothers wanted to go back. They tried to wade into the water. Others, starving and lean, forgot their calves and immediately began feeding on the thrushes along the riverbanks.

Elise and Carl arrived at the river just before we rode back for the last wave. Elise sat glaring through the windshield in the stock truck as she waited. Carl kept watch over the herd as we left. Above us, oblivious to the cattle drive, the commerce of the freeway made a low drone.

We squeezed all forty-three calves in, and then I led Jade up the ramp, crowding the calf backs ahead of me. Gravel and cow manure showered down on her as I cranked up the ramp for the last time, then I crawled into the copilot's seat. Ike stood there staring out at the edges of his island. "I got a feeling," he muttered, and then climbed down the gunner's hold and pulled those levers back that sent the LVT rolling down the beach. There where the sand shoals dropped off, where the canneries used to catch salmon with seines pulled by great draft horses, we tumbled forward into the river.

Water came through the view hole. Jade pulled back on the halter rope, trying to break it. Her back legs slid on the graveled floor and she fell but immediately righted herself. She reached her head over the side of the LVT and smelled the water; she shook and snorted.

Ike was a MacArthur steering that vehicle for all he was worth. He stood up, looking out the top hatch at the island. I sat next to him, pulling the T bar of the pump until I had one of those slow burns in my back. I stopped once to look out the gunner hatch. Only about two feet of metal stuck out of the water, the rest of us submerged under the glass of the river.

Reaching the mainland, we hit the ground hard and rose instantly. Jade slipped again. The metal of her shoes gained no traction. Ike throttled down and I unwound the ramp.

The lead rope was almost fused at the knot, Jade had pulled it so tight. I pried it loose and scrambled out of the way. Jade placed one front hoof on the ramp and jumped. She landed, blowing hard at the sand and trying to roll as if she had swum across the river. The saddle was on her, which was the way a stock horse always traveled. I hit her with the rope to keep her from rolling and breaking the saddletree.

We unloaded the calves into the stock truck. "Let's move 'em out," Ike said, gunning the bike.

Elise ground the truck into gear, and the cattle began the journey home, hooking under the bridge of the Deschutes across the railroad tracks and onto the small road alongside the freeway that led to Riggs.

Elise wasn't the best driver. And she made it a policy never to do exactly what Ike told her to. When she had the calves in the truck, she decided she would be a flagger for cars more than a pied piper of cattle.

The lead cattle moved to the front, searching for their calves. They were like the first two mules in the jerk-line team. They may as well have had hame bells ringing at their withers keeping the herd in stride. The thunder of calling would have soothed a cowboy's ears and heart, but there were none present. The cattle stretched out over a mile; flies, dust, and a half million dollars of black, brown, and white bovines ambled slowly out onto the road home.

Vehicles passed us, driving right through the herd. The people stared at us, stared at our cattle and horses. Three cars passed, all of them going in the opposite direction. In one of them, I saw a child. No seat belt. He stood up in the front seat, looking at the sea of cattle surrounding him. The spooked cattle ran off to the sides of the road and tried to turn back. Cows were so stupid; returning to find their calves meant swimming across the Columbia to the island. I finally lost them. They split, and one side escaped. The heifers went angrily trotting down the road, bellowing. My failure to hold them enraged me.

Ours was the last cattle drive the city fathers allowed through Riggs. The cattle ruined the town, crumbled sidewalks, left dirt and shit everywhere. The employees of the businesses came to the windows to watch us—Middle Columbia Insurance, the Goose Café, Dedlin Oil—they all gawked. The women shook their heads; the men smiled and made lassoing motions with their hands.

The voice of the herd was cacophonous: cows' bellowing, my yelling, Ike's whistling. There was no missing us. The cattle spread over the street and onto the sidewalks. They streamed around stop signs, mailboxes, and parked cars. We turned the main street of the city into a mess, the road deadened and brown where we cut a swath.

Leaving the riverbanks, we followed the Oregon Trail up to the plateau and on east. From then on, we rode the old trading route, out to the river of the madman, John Day.

The bluffs of the John Day narrowed down in places. Elise drove a thin line, a gravel road that dipped dangerously toward the ravine below. Some cattle followed in the road behind the truck, the dedicated mothers. But most of them obeyed the river and stayed down in the arroyo, following the deer trails.

Sagebrush grew high down in the canyon, which meant I would have to strip naked for Elise that evening and have her examine my body. Sagebrush was loaded full of ticks that, when disturbed, sent minions to hide in the most nefarious places on my body. They sought out head hair because it provided shelter, and they disappeared into underarms. But more times than not, they went for the groin.

I never let Elise look at me down there; I would rather have suffered Lyme disease. Anyway, by the time you found a tick, it was usually already embedded in the skin. They entered the body by chewing into it and sucking blood until they bloated out and became swollen gray devils.

If you tried to extract one with fingers, the head came off and all that poison went into your body. The way to do it was use a match and burn their backs so they would crawl out on their own to try and escape. I never knew why the ticks always seemed to get on me. They had never bothered with Jake or Ike.

Deep in the sagebrush, cow-sense rules held that a person should never crowd them. But that was when they were fresh and ready to bolt. By now, they had tired out and slowed down; they wanted to eat the never-grazed grasses of the John Day. It was hard work forcing them along the canyon. No sooner would I get the cattle on the rock bottom moving than the ones higher up on the ravine would stop and eat. Only when Jade's chest was at their haunches did they move.

I became increasingly worried about the point in the journey where the cattle would cross the John Day and head up Rock Creek. They would have to walk over a bridge. The cattle hated crossing bridges, especially ones that had some type of structure over their heads like the drawbridges spanning the Columbia. When I hauled animals to the vet, I could feel them pulling back when I drove under the girders. Then they surged forward when we came out to the other side.

Stuck in the canyons with the cattle, I ruminated on why Ike had wanted to drive them instead of truck them home. Ike didn't care about anything anymore. He was behind in his seeding; he needed the trucks to haul seed wheat to the seeders. That was why he took a chance on driving the herd. "What the hell," he said. "It's been done before."

Everything was annoying me as the cattle began slowing. It infuriated me that he hadn't fed them some hay before we left so they wouldn't be starving and so hard to move.

Mother reached the bridge across the John Day and started over it. She still had a quarter of the herd following her closely. The rest of them were spread out over a mile and a half. She needed to wait there at the entrance until the rest caught up with her, so they would all follow. But she didn't. She sped across the bridge, hoping to get to the other side to flag people down before they drove on that thin trestle with the cows.

That was when the herd split. Some of them charged farther up the John Day and some tried to turn back, but none of them escaped by me.

Ike and Carl raced forward to try to turn them. Sitting there peering over the disaster, I realized I needed to hold my group there and head the lead cows onto the bridge. The fury boiled up in me, at Elise and Ike. It was impossible to hold one group of cows and at the same time turn the others a half mile ahead of me.

I climbed up the canyon onto the road. I saw Ike up the river through the dust and dirt. He dismounted his motorcycle and walked down in the sage, grinding dirt into nothing with his boots. The higher the heel the better they were for busting broncs and stopping steers. Cinched to his hip rattled his pistol, in his right hand flew his whip. I'd seen it before, how Ike moved things with sheer will. He commanded machinery, people, and animals by force of determination, and rarely did mutiny occur.

The saddle creaked as Jade shifted, and I watched the debacle unfold. I now understood the story of the pioneer woman who threw her baby into the Columbia. I imagined what my father's hands smelled like—gas from the motorcycle, sweat, leather, and manure from the whip. I began thinking back to my childhood and how my favorite pastime was killing rattlesnakes and cutting off their heads and rattles. I had a collection of snake tails. One of them bore twenty-four rattles and a button; I kept it around my neck in a steer-skin pouch so I could enjoy the sound at any time, and I always shook it at a snake before I killed it. What I loved about killing snakes was that frank sound of hatred.

Down in the sagebrush, I saw a bull mount an exhausted cow. I reserved my utmost loathing for the bulls. They were obese and voluminous, like dark ugly sultans. What came out of them was poison. Their hindquarters were covered with green excrement, caked and dried in the fall and winter, shiny and smeared in the spring and summer. They could be smelled from fifty yards away, even though they tried to hide in the canyon underbrush in the mountains and the forest of sage at the Bar S. I didn't need the cattle dogs to find them. Their stench hung in the air, like the smell of roadkill.

When I herded them, I watched the black torpedo-shaped bag of testicles dragging along under their haunches. Sometimes I ran them out of hatred, until their mouths hung open, tongues lolling. I loved to see their fatness become a burden to them. I chased them hard through the sagebrush, hoping that black bag would catch on a branch of sage, split open, and transform them into something that wouldn't devil me.

I stood there rooted in a fury, battling my horse. I saw then that the cattle were coming back; they moved fast at first, still spooked from the immense effort of Ike and Carl's heading. I hoped they would slow down, take their time, turn onto the bridge, and cross it. Ike and Carl held back as they were supposed to. I held my breath, fighting my anger at Elise for crossing the damn bridge. The bridge was where my family fell down.

This day held a wind that stole breath from the heart. It blew through the sad-smelling knotted sagebrush full of bloodsuckers and dead leaves, curled in and out again amongst the baking rocks where it had blown for hundreds of years, immutable to everything but its own freedom. It watched all things turn and disappear as if the deadly caress of its veil marked things of death: the indomitable glaciers that gorged the valley come and gone; the great tribes of the Nez Perce and Cayuse Indians crumbled; the salmon extinct from running its rivers; deer from hunters and frigid winters; the pioneers, shouting in their pitiful voices, gone now too. Only the wind, singing war songs to the hills and cliffs, remained.

The cattle stopped. I held my breath. I even thought about prayer. They nosed around, milled. I could see them smelling the rest of the herd already across. Suddenly a group of five bolted over the bridge. That was how cattle did things when they were unsure: they ran. A couple more followed and then the whole herd began trotting nervously across.

Once we were all over, open wheat fields lay ahead of us. Another five miles, and we came upon the Miller place. The wheat spread out on both sides of Rock Creek, and so did the cattle. By now, there was nothing to do but force them forward until they reached our place. Ike and Carl had come back to trail with me. It was nearing late afternoon, and I was anxious about whether we would make it to the ranch before nightfall. If we didn't, we'd lose the herd.

I ran Jade. Sweeping. Moving the scattered flank back into line. Cattle that were too far out, I just left. I relished this as Ike's punishment—losing things he owned. Jade began wheezing after running the flank twice. I ignored it; if the herd didn't make the ranch by dark, all of them would scatter over Illian and Horrow Counties. I hated having to clean up Ike's problems. And as near as I could tell, this was just that—another of Ike's messes that had ruined the family from the beginning.

I ran Jade, expecting her to fall out from under me dead as I looked down upon the rapidly running haunches of the cows. I loathed the cows, loathed the day, loathed life. After five sweeps, I made a dead run along the uneven side of the herd to the beginning. Halting ahead of the cattle now, I waited while the first few made the correct veer to the right, toward our place, before the sun dropped below the high sides of Rock Creek.

The single most important rule of cow sense when driving cattle is that you must take them to new pasture *and* all the way to their new water source. Otherwise, they are so ignorant they'll walk all the way back where they came from to get to the last water source. But all of the cows had been damaged from this day and looked as if they could go no farther. Their mouths wide open, tongues lolled down, snot and saliva dripped from muzzles, sides heaved from backbones. I goaded Jade; I ran those cattle down, moving them toward the fence and on to water because the river was too far. They'd certainly die trying to return.

My legs and crotch were raw. When I'd dismounted Jade at the bridge, my crotch burned so badly I'd had to hold myself apart to urinate without crying. By now, I wouldn't be able to go to the bathroom or take a bath. The rawness of my thighs and legs would react against the hot water so badly I'd never get in. I imagined myself squatting in the tub, dirt flowing in tiny streams down my feet into the white porcelain and disappearing in the drain. I desperately wanted to wash the animal parts off my body. I began talking to myself as we moved the lost and parched cattle from the canyon bottom to the gate of our place and to water.

Jade was rattling huge barrels of air: blood from her nostrils stuck to her forelegs, making black medieval shields. Her Appaloosa hooves were jagged and shattered; the right front split up the side. I screamed at my hands, the braided reins laced through my bloody third fingers. I held them in front of my eyes in a dialogue with my appendages and blisters. My face was muddied.

It was then that I saw Ike. I started laughing hysterically at the source of this catastrophe, and then I became incoherent from rage. I couldn't ride normally; I unplanted my legs from Jade's sides and flopped backward in the saddle. The stock seat dug into my back. I kicked my raw legs up.

Ike stood, the only one that the drive had not vanquished. His presence aborted the desire to come near him. He walked forward with his bullwhip, forcing the cattle through the last gate, picking them up and moving them with flicks of the black screaming leather. The sun, unable to hold itself aloft any longer, dropped its head below the cliffs.

A larger and larger group of cattle had found the gate. More were grabbing the herd instinct and charging there. Now they smelled it. The cattle were turning by themselves. Once they trotted inside the gate, they headed down looking for the spring and a place to bed down. The cold dusk removed feeling from the body, and things slammed. They were coming and crowding. Smashing and crowding.

I rode Jade over to catch a group of cows backtracking. I stared them down. They turned, and I trailed them alongside the cliffs of Rock Creek, so called because it was mostly dry. What grew along bottom land was fed by underground springs; several bubbled up on our place and made watering holes for cattle.

Jade suddenly stopped. She backed up, dragging her hooves on the now powdered dirt. I froze in the saddle, listening. It was strangely silent. I smelled the remnants of the drive, the manure, the sweat, the broken and bleeding sage. Something back along the cliff walls moved. My horse shied, blew. The hairs on my arms lifted the way they did driving the Caterpillar in a lightning storm. My hands shook. I grabbed Jade's mane and kicked her forward.

Neither one of us saw anything at first. I thought about Ike's pistol strapped to his leg. I had nothing. I noticed something black against the rock wall, where the basalt had cracked away in a crystal-like pattern. It was beautiful, full of white-veined snakeskin rock, tiger's-eye, snowflake obsidian, and thunder eggs.

A faint lamenting sound came from twenty or so yards away. I figured whatever it was, it had fallen on the ground. Maybe an injured animal, maybe a ghost proving to me they existed. I urged Jade forward again, eight yards away from the noise and the cliff. We came upon a black cow. She was down, panting and sweating. I saw her sides heaving in the dusk. It surprised me actually that this was the first cow to die from this trip.

I turned Jade to look the cow over, see if she could be saved. It was then I saw she was giving birth. A red lump glistened at her rear, a chunk, really—nothing coherent. But crouching behind that, haunches tucked under, tail flowing bushlike out and sweeping the ground, was an enormous gray coyote. It took me a moment to realize what it was. The cow had gone down to give birth, and the coyote was eating the calf as it came out of her.

The calf was almost out now. I saw the blood at its head, coming from the ripped flesh under its neck. Once the baby had come out farther, the coyote moved in to eat the soft flesh of the anus and belly. It huddled down now, taking mouthfuls of stomach as if it were a baby sucking on its mother's breast. Its head went forward and back feeding off the flesh. The ears pinned back, it didn't even hear us.

"You bastard," I screamed. "You killed him."

At that moment, the coyote turned its head to look at us. Its nose and throat were covered with red. It licked its jaws the way a dog does after it eats a particularly good piece of steak. I saw the sparkle of its eyes as it squinted at me in the moonlight. I wanted to kill the son of a bitch.

I didn't bother with neck reining. I leaned down and grabbed both reins close to Jade's bit. I forced her back where we had come from. My father was still there, his cheeks cracking, the whip raging against the shit-smeared wall of the moving mass. Ike went on driving them through the barbed wire fence; the gate was nonexistent. They were scarring their way through it. Only the cloven hooves remained intact; clumps of hair pulled off bodies; hides tore; eyes ripped; ears sliced through. A blond Charolais cow had caught her head in the fence and was bellowing as he clubbed her with the butt of the whip. She attempted to kick him; he moved to the side and stabbed at her thin haunches, aiming for the soft udder and anus. The whip penetrated the cow, and he gave it a vicious crank as if he were starting a car.

My raw legs slapped down on Jade with heels dug in. She moved out with a leap, flattened her ears, sank low to the ground, and ran one last time. I screamed at my father, my throat burning. Ike let go of the whip where it was stuck and turned to me. I expected him to take out his pistol. He had the time. He saw the crazed eyes of Jade, the red foam, the meat-colored nostrils. There was silence and coolness as the night set in save for the snap and spark of her hooves. I knew exactly why Jake had done it. The rage, we all had it. It was what had brought my family here in the first place.

My father stood perfectly still and watched me. He must have been amazed by the mutiny. I wanted to tell him to stop; my horse was bleeding; I was screaming. And what I said was, "And he was just like you. Only Jake was better."

That was when Ike placed himself in front of me, and I rode him down.

32

I GRIPPED THE REINS AND TRIED TO USE JADE AS A BAT-
tering ram straight into Ike. The fearlessness of the Nez Perce horse
didn't disappoint me. The saddlehorn dug in and lifted under my ribs
where I leaned over my horse. Through mane tips coated with lather, I
watched Ike go down.

The side of Jade's neck, her shoulder, and her knees knocked into
his belly and chest. It surprised me how hard he was, how solid. Jade
tripped; she fell onto her cannons. Ike rolled up into a ball, but not fast
enough, because I was thrown, too. I headed face first into the cold
dirt, but he broke my fall. My skull bored into his chest; both of us
went down, but only Ike cracked his head on the hard spring ground.

Carl came running the way he always did when I was bucked off a
horse. He would hurry out of the shop when he heard the galloping
hooves on the gravel lot. On the way to pick me up and dust me off, he
would retrieve parts of the saddle the bucking horse had thrown—
stirrups, snapped reins, ropes, once an entire bridle, bits of my clothing. But this time was different; he just came running, and his old dry
face wasn't looking with concern at me.

Ike lay on his side. Carl knelt down and slapped my father's dirty
stubble-coated cheeks. "Ike?" he asked softly. It was completely dark
now and there was no reply.

I was on the ground next to him, with that black suffocating sentiment I always felt when bucked off a horse, the feeling that something completely huge had just kicked the shit out of me.

"I'mna lay you back now," I heard Carl say.

Then Ike moved his legs and slowly rolled over.

Carl made jerky movements as he cradled Ike's head.

"I gotta get back on that horse," I muttered.

No one said anything back to me.

It was amazing how the rage slipped silently away after the violence. When it went away, I was naked and had nothing. I stood up slowly. The inside of my lip bled, and the taste of iron filled my mouth.

"Stay here," said Carl. He gently rested my father's head on the ground. "I'll get the stock truck." He took off on Ike's motorcycle, which was still idling in the darkness. I watched the small beam of light traveling on angled planes away from us as he negotiated the terrain out to the road and down to the chute where Mother had parked the truck and opened the gate for the calves.

The smell of broken juniper and sage clouded the night air. The crickets in the creek sawed. Ike lay before me, the way countless creatures had in the past. The dog, bitten by a rattlesnake; the old eagle buried in a grave of feathers; the broken-footed horse; coyotes peppered red with bullets; the five-point buck, loose, warm, and limbernecked as the rack was pulled up and examined.

I knelt down. I didn't say I was sorry. I didn't say anything. I waited. The moon rose over the cliffs and over the alder trees surrounding the spring. It glowed huge and brimming with red, a harvest moon, the white body still full of blood and the warmth of the earth.

The light cast a shadow over Ike's dirty face, his glasses gone, his eyes closed. In the distance I heard the tightly wound motor of the truck barreling down the gravel road. I walked over to the gate, my knees aching and my skin raw. I pulled the end post around, dragging the loose barbs across the trampled and powdered earth. I occupied myself with work. The cattle had almost disappeared down into the sage and tree forest that crowded the spring lake. Those that had escaped us were gone by now, jogging back to the river for water.

The wire gate sang, pulled taut with the help of the metal bar. I closed it tight and wrapped the tool around that crooked post and left it there. I was the fence mender. Unlike my father and mother, I closed things securely.

Jade stood grazing ten feet away from Ike, her head down, the reins slopped upon her ears. I called to her and made my way up slowly. I knew she was sore, her feet ground down, steam rising from her flanks and belly.

I uncinched her, unbuckled the bucking strap, and pulled the saddle off, a waft of vapor rising as I did. I threw the saddle down in the powdered dirt and laid the pad over it, wet side up, because the day was finished. I unhooked the throat latch and slid the rubber bit out and threw the bridle under the blanket. I turned her loose, figuring Jade would be home in the morning because even in the dark she knew the way.

I waited for the truck, sitting Indian style by my father. Beside me a yarrow plant was ground into the dust. I remembered Ike telling me Achilles used yarrow to heal his soldiers' wounds after battle. I looked back at my father. During those minutes he had turned his head, opened his eyes, and looked at me.

I could tell Carl was driving. The truck screamed over the lip from the gravel road onto the powdered dirt road that led to the gate where Ike had gone down. Carl and Elise came on toward us, halting in a slide that kicked up too much dust. Elise jumped out of the passenger seat and came running. I watched her face in the moonlight, and it was the first time I knew she really loved him. Carl ground the truck into first gear and turned off the engine. He left the headlights on and came running too. Elise took Ike's head, Carl lifted at his waist, and I took his feet. I grabbed his glasses before we lifted and placed them in my heart pocket.

Carl drove the short route to the ranch, up another impossible grade, racing the engine all the way. Elise held Ike, and I rode in the back like the calves. Carl and I transferred him to the red Ford pickup, and we flew down the road to Death Mile Hospital.

Farm accidents. Falling off a tractor and being run over by an implement, thrown from a horse, suffocated in a grain bin, crushed in a truck wreck, electrocuted, eaten by fire. "Farmers have the highest insurance rates in the world," said the gurney-pushing ER nurse, shaking her head as she took a look at the dirty pickup.

Another nurse came out after a half hour and showed Elise, Carl, and me the way to a waiting room. We passed through the hospital, walked by every department, including the nuclear accident wing where Hanford victims were hosed off and operated on from behind lead shields.

The doctor came five hours later. He wore green scrubs, even over his shoes. The mask, pulled down, looked like a second chin.

"The Steele family?" he asked.

Elise and I nodded. Neither of us stood up.

He pulled a chair from the table on the far end of the room. "My name is Dr. Singh. Your husband had a severe head injury. I tried to release some of the pressure during the operation." He grimaced. "But he had a pretty good bleed, and there is swelling."

I practiced holding my breath and swallowing, taking another breath and holding it some more.

"We're hopeful that the inflammation will reduce, and it will drain." He paused and looked at me. "We won't know what shape the brain is in until then. It will be a couple of days. At that time, we'll need to do an EEG. It will show how much activity is happening up there, the electrical signals, et cetera."

"Can we see him?" asked Elise.

The doctor nodded. "He's in Intensive Care." He led us into the ICU.

We stood outside the door. Nurses on the night shift flat-out stared at us. I'd forgotten my sweaty and shit-spattered clothes.

Elise and I moved with as little energy as possible. Everything seemed to be magnified. The smells were harsh, the killers of staph infection. I detected the yellowish odor of putrid wounds. Artificial breathing machines hissed. Ventilators made sucking noises as if water were filling up cavities and then being removed.

"You can see him now," a nurse said, coming out of the room. She made way for us and pulled back the curtain as we entered. Carl waited outside. It was a large room, the bed positioned far away from us. Ike lay heavily in the bed, his head wrapped in bandages. Everything about him was pulled down by blue and green candy-colored tubes and hoses. All but his nose and feet.

I studied Ike, couldn't believe someone as strong and as invincible as my father could be taken down. But still, he lay there. I recognized his eyes, though they were puffed and swollen shut. I saw the shape of his mouth even though tubes injected air, allowing him to breathe. His arms, tanned and covered by curly black hairs, now had needles going into his veins. Nothing in the world is safe, when children are stronger than parents.

"Tell Ike you love him," Elise said, stroking his forearm and holding his hand. "Come on, Ike," she cajoled. We stood on opposite sides of the bed. The bags of air and water hung from the rack above us. My tears dropped onto the light blue box-stitched blanket. I touched Ike tentatively on the chest where I had hit him.

Elise laid her head on Ike's heart, hearing his beat.

"Tell him it's time to get up now," I whispered. "Just like he used to do to us in the mornings."

"Wake up, Ike," Elise said. Everthing was quiet except the sound of air. I watched the monitor's green lines of the heartbeat. It was comforting. The regularity.

The nurse came in after some time. "Maybe you can come back in a little bit?" she asked. It was because she had to empty the catheter, attend to the embarrassing things.

"Let's give him a rest," Elise said, raising her head. Her eyes were rimmed with red but not a tear fell. She was hopeful.

I slunk out of the room, following my mother, and looked at the ground. Outside I dropped down to the floor, sitting cross-legged by his door like a dog waiting for his master. I watched the nurses' feet come and go through water-blurred vision as they served up bits of life. The nurses looked at us with pained expressions, the color drained from their faces. I knew it was because they had seen Ike's chart. They knew how bad things looked.

"Would you like some chairs?" one of them asked.

I shook my head no.

"No, thank you," Elise replied. It was the nurse I liked; she had a kindly face, brown nightingale eyes. Around us, the sounds of gloves snapping on, warning bells, two nurses having a discussion of the preschool classes of their children. Someone said, "Just relax your arm, Mrs. Stout." Then the low buzzing of the air pumps on the legs of a patient went off.

When I finally decided I could move again, I got up off the floor, and Elise and I left the hospital together. We found Carl waiting in the pickup.

We went to see Ike three times a day. We watched him constantly for movement. And he moved. He reached out as if taking hold of something. Bizarre reflexes, they told us. "They don't mean anything," the nurses said. But I didn't believe them. I remembered Henry telling me about a reflex in the foot, and I poked my index finger along his arch to see for myself. His strange foot and thick mannish toenails were cold; they did not move.

I began to hate the sound of the heart-lung machine and the smell of dying repulsed me, fetid and musty. Unhealing wounds were worse. The odor of the body when it has given up is like the smell of a forgotten animal, four weeks dead.

On the third day we called a conference with Dr. Singh. That was when we heard that the EEG was flat; Ike could be brain-dead.

"Can we do another one?" I asked. "To see if he might be making some improvement over time?"

Dr. Singh nodded. "We'll schedule one in six hours," he said. "But if it remains the same, you will have to make the decision," he added gently. "Whether to disconnect him from life support or keep him alive artificially."

I looked down. Tried to make myself think of things completely unrelated to where we were, like how I wanted to rearrange the tack room, put the curries and dandies on shelves instead of thrown in an old bucket.

It happened fast. The intern wheeled the EEG machine in, and we sat on the ground in the hall outside his room, waiting for the results of the test.

As they walked out, the nurses had mouths set like those dolls that when you turn them upside-down they're angry, you turn them right side up they're happy.

Dr. Singh returned with a stack of papers. "The results are negative again," he said. He showed us the photographs in the nurse's station. The film highlighted severe brain swelling.

"You will have to make the decision now, whether to disconnect your husband from life support."

"Yes, disconnect him," Elise replied without hesitation. "I don't want him to live like this."

"I started a special program," said Dr. Singh. "I want to tell you about it."

I wasn't interested in anybody's program.

"I must inform you that your husband is a candidate for harvest."

"What?" asked Elise.

"Harvest. Patients declared brain-dead are prime candidates for organ donation."

"You want to sell off parts of my father?" I asked incredulously.

He shook his head. "Not sell," he said softly. "Your father's eyes, lungs, liver, kidney, bone, heart, and skin can be harvested," he went on. "You could save four people's lives and make life worth living for several others." He looked down at his papers. "We've gone through the tests to determine if he would be appropriate. All movement is due to spinal cord function. There is an absence of hypothermic conditions, depressant drugs. Absent cough, pupillary light response, and two apnea tests have been performed. The EEG shows electrocortical silence, and no intracranial blood flow is evident."

"No," I announced. "No way." I remembered Henry telling me how medical students treated donated bodies. How cadavers received names in lab. Old Ethel, Poor John. They got awards too, blue ribbons, for big dicks. A lesbian got ahold of the blue ribbon member and announced loudly, "I've always wanted to cut one of these off."

It was strange, I thought, how before the accident, I would have loved to cut Ike up, give his body to strangers in revenge for how Ike had never given to anyone when he was alive. But somehow now that he was dead, and it had been my fault, I hated the idea.

"I started the donation program ten years ago," Dr. Singh said. "It came about because of our nurses. You see, at a trauma hospital, this kind of tragedy happens altogether too often," he added with a sigh. "Our nurses weren't able to handle the sadness. The staff psychiatrist was in here counseling the trauma nurses day and night until we started the donation program. I searched long and hard to try to make something positive out of a totally negative, tragic circumstance. It's an option for you to consider."

Elise held her head in her hand.

"You can think about it," he said.

"I don't need to," Mother replied. "Yes. You can go ahead."

Dr. Singh looked at me. I didn't look at him; I glared at my mother. "No," I stated again. "Forget it, Mom." I didn't want to be anyone's hero. I didn't give a shit whether someone I didn't know lived or died. I wasn't giving up any more. I thought of how I had run into my father and felt sick. I imagined the doctors going through Ike's body and eating it piece by piece. "How can they use his body?" I asked angrily. "He's not young. All they want are young donors."

"Actually, that's correct," allowed Singh. "But we need bridge organs for patients that are close to dying. We need your father's body now."

"What, so they can wait for a better one, and then throw my father away?"

Dr. Singh grimaced. "I'll let you two discuss it," he said, moving to get up.

"You can go ahead," said Elise, ignoring me. "It's the right thing to do."

I stood up. I couldn't stand being seated for any more discussions.

Dr. Singh paused another moment before handing Elise a stack of papers. "You'll need to sign these, please," he said. "For consent." And then he left.

After some minutes, they opened Ike's door. We walked in slower than before, with the realization we were encountering a dead person.

"You need to say good-bye to your father," Elise said. At the same time she smiled crazily, as if it were a cheerful and temporary good-bye.

I watched her lean down, tears streaming. She kissed him on the lips, even though there were tubes going into his mouth. "Clear," she said. "It's clear, Ike. You can take off now. Go on. Damn it. Fly." She turned and strode out of the room.

I thought about saying "Good-bye, sir," thinking that's what Ike would have liked—a military good-bye and a salute for a brave soldier. I stood there looking at him. "You bastard," I uttered. But when I leaned down to kiss his cheek, holding his hand, big, strong, and flaccid, what came besides my sobs was, "Good-bye, Dad."

Outside, three helicopters sat waiting, surgeons in all of them. I stayed to watch the doctors go in. I wanted to see what they looked like, the harvesters of the body. A burly, curly-haired man in his sixties; a clean-shaven thirtyish fellow with wire-rim glasses; and the last man, a Sikh with a mustache and beard. Following them were nurses carrying Coleman coolers for his organs, two red, one green, and one blue. I never looked at a Coleman the same way after that.

"They need you to sign these," said another nurse with a clipboard. And then they wheeled Ike into the OR, and that was the last I saw of my father, headed down to harvest.

I stared into the room. The windows were open, and air blew through and onto my face. The hissing snakes of the heart-lung machine had stopped. I wondered if Ike had given the Lazarus response. Years ago Henry had told me about the bizarreness of death; how, when disconnected, the body raises itself and reaches forward, like a baby reaching up to its mother for life.

I remembered back to the night of the accident. Ike had turned his head ever so slightly, opened his eyes, and looked at me. Maybe he thought I was Elise, maybe he was hallucinating, but what he said was, "You are the most beautiful woman in the world." How strange it is, I thought in a hysteric calm, that people wind up loving what kills them.

As we left, they handed us an orange plastic bag with a string that closed the top like a tote. It read, Hanford Regional Health Center. Ike's personal items were in it. The hospital had to do that so that the staff wouldn't steal things off the unconscious or dead patients. The bag looked cheap, as if it might have contained a bottle of whiskey. I rummaged through and pulled out the watch and his wedding ring. I folded the bag down neatly, saving it for later. Ike would have hated waste, but most of all, he would have hated to not keep going, somehow.

I asked them to inform me when it was over. The procedure took a long time, almost five hours. The balding surgeon from Oregon Health Sciences University came out and talked to me because the University of Washington team had already helicoptered away. The doctor told me that when they began to harvest his heart they found scar tissue in the cavity. They were successful but had a difficult time removing it, and the operation took much longer than they expected. He said Ike's heart was just plain tough to cut.

33

WHEN THERE HAS BEEN NO RAIN FOR AN ENTIRE YEAR, the question of when to seed becomes whether to seed. I spent my spring days looking for signs. I walked the fields, digging down in the dirt. I clumped the earth together with my thumb and forefinger. There in my palm, I checked to see if it would hold tight with moisture to produce crop. But every time I tried to mold it into something that would grow wheat, it broke apart into dry dust.

There are plenty of things besides drought that can ruin a crop. Even when the rain wets the top layers of dirt, and the germination cracks the ground asunder, sometimes roots hit hardpan. In times of distress, when the ground has been neglected, the earth has a way of sealing herself over. The barrier is an intensely packed layer of soil that doesn't let anything through. If rain comes, the land needs opening up for it to accept the water, a plowshare to break it. Otherwise, the runoff washes through gullies and ditches, taking the soil with it down and out to the ocean.

I dozed diversion terraces to work with nature, to hold the rainwater on the earth. Long rolling mounds followed the contours of the land as if it were a topographical map. Then when the cloudbursts came, the water seeped into the earth or puddled in troughs. There were no more signs of ugly erosion gouging straight down the sides of the hills into canyons. The flash floods still came, but mostly they carved up the range and destroyed county roads.

And the wind still blew. It wrenched the water right out of the ground. A farmer has to fight the wind same as she does any other bit of weather or insect. I alternated my crops in summer fallow to conserve moisture and to prevent the blows. I'd seen blows before on the Runcid place. It looked like the photos of the Dust Bowl, what sent the Okies out to California. Varying which fields were in crop held the land back from the gales. I always made sure something gripped the ground when the wind came whipping out of the gorge.

There are many heartbreaks along the way. Once planted, the seed fought wireworms, click beetles, aphids, and freezing. I've seen full-grown crops taken out by the black and pastelike advance of aphids. They eat everything the way heroin or alcohol does, leave nothing but the stalks. An early freeze kills too, leaving the most beautiful crop in the world white, limp, and dead.

The seasons are everything to a farmer, they're what a farmer is made of. And that spring was my last chance for a stand. I hurried to prepare the land for spring seeding because the seed has to be in the ground when the cold thaws, when the wind of winter stops and the vernal warmth touches the face of the earth again. I drove the truck to Pendleton to buy spring seed wheat, and fashioned everything ready to place the pink seed into the soil at the exact time.

Spring wheat was not born to endure freeze. Only the old kind of wheat, winter wheat, loved the cold, thrived on winter, and then matured in the scorching heat of summer. It was part of its character. If winter wheat didn't freeze, it didn't go through all of its maturation. Like my parents, it liked the stress on its body, extremes. The coldness and heat brought out the best in it.

The land, worked and fertilized, lay open and prepared to accept the grain. I had pulled the Cultaweeder with the fertilizer tank behind. In the shanks of the implement, nitrogen seeped into the ground with the plowshares. It placed food in the soil the plant would need on its trip down to the deep moisture. Following everything, the turning rods of the weeders burnished the earth. The wands sealed up the ground and held the moisture back from evaporation until the final stage, the seeding.

I understood the soil by heart; it came from growing up on the land.

When I planted my wheat, I knew where the best ground was without the help of a global positioning system. I recognized where the moisture was likely to be, along the fence lines, in the troughs of the erosion terraces. Those were the places to plant more grain. I stayed away from the alkali spots, only lightly dusting the white and shallow sides of those hills. I fancied the white color to have come from bone and figured I could leave it well enough alone.

The seeding time, the ideal time, is when the two types of moisture meet. Eight inches below the surface rests the deep moisture. And this could make a crop. It was a gamble, though, planting a stand when all that remained was deep moisture. A farmer had to hope the wheat plant would survive long enough to send the roots down to drink before it died.

Soil scientists say deep moisture and rainwater never meet, that it is impossible for the deep moisture to rise, to defy the laws of gravity. But a farmer knows water will rise. We've seen it.

Only after a rain does it come. The shower doesn't need to be a deluge, a forty-day flood. It is much simpler. The storm comes down and covers the earth with a soft wet blanket. That's when it happens. It calls the deep moisture up, encourages it to come forth. Because water is a thing that loves life.

Even then I knew I had to do one more thing. The judge handed down his decision; Miles called me on the telephone to tell me the news.

"What is it?" I asked. I had to sit down.

"You won," he said. "He found the land to have been purchased legally."

"Miles," I asked. "If you knew about the mix-up in the executive order, why did you make me go through with the trial?"

"I wasn't sure it would hold up," he replied. "And you never want to run from a fight, Iris. You should know that from your parents."

"What happens next?" I asked, clearing my throat.

"They'll appeal. They'll continue to challenge the judge's ruling. You might be tied up here for a very long time. Because there's one thing the tribe has that you don't."

"What's that?"

"Time. And one lawyer after another."

"I don't think they'll appeal for a while," I replied quietly.

"I'll send you a copy of the decision today," said Miles, not hearing me.

"Miles, there's one more thing I'd like you to do," I interrupted.

"What's that? Anything you want," he answered.

"I want to arrange for Tansy to buy me out of Heart of the Beast when she turns eighteen."

There was silence on the telephone. "You don't have to do that, Iris. You won the lawsuit. Why did you fight the claim if you were going to give it to the Indians all along?"

"I'm not giving it to the Nez Perce, Miles. I'm letting Tansy buy Heart of the Beast for twenty-eight thousand dollars. When she turns eighteen she'll need a place to stay."

"First of all, she doesn't have that kind of money," he said quickly. "Where's she going to come up with that?"

"No, she doesn't. But I know where she can get it," I said.

"Where? The tribe?" he asked, incredulously. "Oh, yes, I'm sure they'd take it off her hands."

"I will help her, if she needs it," I answered.

"Second of all," Miles said, "that place is worth over a million."

"I know that," I told him.

"You don't want to do this, Iris. You'll be losing the hunting fees, and the range fees. That land is going to become invaluable in twenty years. People will pay anything for a place as beautiful as that, with a view, a lake, and hunting."

"She deserves it," I said. "It's the right thing to do." I thought of my mother at the hospital with Ike.

"You think giving them this land will make up for some historical injustice?" Miles asked angrily. "Nothing can make it up, and it's not your fault. You can't buy moral virtue and a just and ethical past. It just keeps reducing the Indians to victims accepting tokens here and there to improve their status insignificantly."

"You're right, Miles," I replied. "What happened in the past was terrible. It is a mess and probably always will be."

"This just means Tansy will have to fight her own tribe in court, all over again. I would advise you, as your lawyer, not to do this. You will be sorry in the end. And we would have to work it out with Tansy and her guardians. You can never get anything straight with Indians. Besides, what if Tansy just turns around and gives the land to the Nez Perce?"

"That'll be all right with me. Do you have her new address in Lapwai?" I said. "I can give it to you if you don't."

"I have it," he replied. The sound of shuffling papers came through the phone. "Care of Albert and Margaret Redhawk."

"That's right."

Miles remained silent on the telephone.

"Let me know when the deed is ready to be signed."

I imagined Miles might be weeping on the other end.

"Thank you," I said finally. "Thank you, Miles, for everything you've done."

After that conversation, I went to work. In the morning, I fed the animals. The dogs, the horses, and the calf came running at seven when I walked down to the barn. Midnight, the calf, had grown strong; already larger than her mother, she looked as if she would live a good deal longer. She followed Jade around the corral, ate by her in the manger, and rested with her at the water trough soaking up the warmth of the sun on cold spring afternoons. She lost her baby coat as the spring came on and emerged a beautiful shade of ebony.

After I fed the animals, I ate breakfast alone because Hanna blew out and down our drive as suddenly as she had come. Once the sculptures were cast and installed into place, she had no more need to be there.

"Where will you go?" I asked her.

"Scotty Jamison said he'd teach me welding," she replied. "The Scots know how to work with a crazy woman."

"But you're not crazy," I said.

There was no arguing with her. I tried, but it didn't work. Scotty came and picked her up the same day she announced her decision to me, leaving me alone with a gallery of bronze family members and land to seed.

I knew then it was time to farm. I felt the sun on my feet again and had the urge to swim in the river until my hair turned green. I loaded the seed wheat into the truck. It came out pink colored in the light of the dawn, like a rosy mound of infant flesh.

I drove out into the field and filled the seeders with the side auger hooked onto the truckbed. The land, when it was ready to receive the grain, glowed black and smooth like dark chocolate icing. Driving the drills was like frosting a cake, swirling the knife back and forth across the surface until it was covered smooth and lush.

My knife was always the old Caterpillar, the D-6, Ike's favorite. It held a straight line better than the other tractors, made turns uniform and true. The old Cats had the steering in floor levers. If I wanted to turn one direction, I pulled back on one side. It cut the power from that track, and I pivoted in the direction I wanted to go. The turns were tight because the crawler could twirl in one spot without even moving forward. I just had to make sure I didn't turn too tight and run over the hitch. And I didn't want to leave any skips. Only people like Runcid left skips in their seeding; the skips were obvious because by summer the weeds grew there like a waving green flag in a sea of golden wheat.

I saw the neighbors driving by. The Runcids, Cunninghams, the Wagonchaffs. They flocked slowly past, shaking their heads at what I was doing. Seeding when there had been no rain. Some of them had planted in winter and had weak crops barely surviving. Others were holding out as long as they could to see if it would rain. They would be behind when it finally came, because after precipitation, farmers have to wait until the field dries out before they can move their tractors in the fields. Otherwise they bog down in mud; the huge ruts made by the tractors will ruin the land, take out the moisture for years.

I drove four swaths through the field before I needed to stop, dismount, and fill up with seed again. It surprised me when I came back around to reload and saw the truck coming toward me. I stopped ahead of the seed road so the International could pull up beside the drills and fill me with grain.

I saw his sandy hair first, and then I saw the white hands on the steering wheel. Henry. The truck pulled up smooth and perfect without my telling him what to do. He walked back and flipped up the tops of the seeders, drew out the silver auger, and filled me completely.

That was the way it went for two weeks until Henry's vacation was over. The United Tribes had hired another doctor. Permanently. So Henry now had someone to share his call. By day I drove the D-6, and Henry ferried the seed in to me. We worked together and watched the sky for signs of rain. At night, we ate dinner together, made love to each other, and slept in the same bed until dawn.

On the last day of seeding, we pushed to finish. The clouds had come. I knew they would. It usually takes death, takes sadness, to bring the rain. But sometimes it arrives with the rightness of things.

The storm came from the Pacific—a big black daughter of Poseidon. The showers flew in as if a goddess was letting down her streaming, swirling purple hair. The smell of rain permeated the air. It was like a full stomach. It was the smell of reinforcements, of aid, of succor. It was the smell of awe.

We left the Cat and the half-empty seeders where we finished, by the fence line we had mended together years before. We drove home, the windshield wipers smearing the dust into mud on the glass.

The house felt full when we walked in. It was always full now that the heads had come home. They didn't jump out at me anymore. Muted and quiet, they blended into the walls as if they were part of my house. I went in and looked at the bronzes in the green room: John Winter, as ugly as he ever was; next to him, his son, complicit in their swindles, the horse trader, the bon vivant; Dagmar, with the truly dark Norwegian look, the skin that was transparent, and the mood that was toxic; the barrister and chronicler, Mark; and his lifeless wife, Emma, whom he hung around my father's neck. They all looked the same.

It was only when I looked at Ike and Elise that I noticed a change. They had become mine; it didn't make me uncomfortable to be in the same room with them anymore. It wasn't that their appearance was any more handsome, beautiful, ugly, or ruthless. They had softened, like rain on our dry land. I saw bits of myself in their faces, and theirs in mine. Finally, I was able to see the best parts of them.

I walked up to my mother and father. Henry stopped behind me; he just stood there, holding me. I knew what he was doing, trying to see what I saw. I don't think Henry noticed that my mother finally acknowledged me. I stood in front of her, there on her pedestal in front of the window that led out to the Columbia River, and she looked at me.

Henry and I waited for the depth of the storm. The rain finally came down. The sound of it covered the house with a floating peacefulness. It wasn't the tone of a grieving rain; it was the timbre of forgiveness. I glanced back at my mother and thought of her words. It's rare when it happens, but it is possible that water will rise. I gazed back down to the river over the freshly seeded land, dark brown and rich. I looked down there with all the hope in the world for the harvest.

This book is dedicated partly to the dead,

Harrison M. Weatherford, 1925–1979
Mark H. Weatherford, 1953–1978
Scott W. Weatherford, 1961–1969

Mostly to the living,

Alice W. Harper
Richard E. Harper
Irene O. Weatherford
Ann O. Martino

And most of all to

James A. Cushing
Carson W. Cushing

Acknowledgments

I want to thank Sarah McGrath for her thoughtful and expert editing, which made my first rewrite a learning experience instead of a panic. Thanks as well to Liz Darhansoff, Nan Graham, and Susan Moldow for investing their minds, hearts, and considerable talent in this book. I would also like to acknowledge Kate Braverman, John M. Daniel, and Chris L. Minnick. I have immense gratitude for their encouragement.

Throughout the course of working on *Heart of the Beast*, I have been graced with the assistance of many wonderful people. I appreciate their kindness—as they say, a bushel of wheat is made up of thousands of kernels. Many thanks to Adrienne Adelman; Justine Amodeo; Margarita Labra de Arellano; Tomas Berglund; John Billingsley; Lavina Blossom; Kathleen Bowman; Ruthanna Bridges-McKay; Michael Cendejas; Anne Cherry; Kevin Culhane, M.D.; Willard and Patricia Cushing; Douglas and Judy Cushing; Caitlin and Meredith Cushing; John deBenedetti; Scott Dorn; Jon Duffy of Duffy and Shanley; Richard Edelson, M.D.; Jean Femling; Janet Fitch; Sandra Giedeman; Gabrielle Glaser; The Grand Ronde Tribe; Lt. Col. Robert C. and Dorothy Harper; Glen Hartley; Allen S. Jio; David Juman; Alicia Kamian; Alex Kanfer; Lt. Col. John and Nancy Keane; Casey Kerrigan, M.D.; Jayme Kerrigan Kusyk; Kristin Lang; William Lydiatt, M.D.; Jo-Ann Mapson; Anne Wallace McAndrews; Caroline R. McCallister; Mission Hospital Regional Medical Center; Robert Monson; Mim Mulford, M.D.; Douglas Nash; Ron Neeley; The Nez Perce National Historical Park; Josiah Pinkham; Lynn Pleshette; Donald Rawley; Mark Ruane; Susan Shattuc; Tatjana Soli; Nina Srejovic; Claudette Teifke; Chuck Verrill and the staff at Darhansoff and Verrill; Charlotte, Margaret, and J. K. Weatherford; Laura Wise; and Edward Wyatt.

HEART OF THE BEAST

DISCUSSION POINTS

1. *Heart of the Beast* opens to Iris's disturbing and bloody dream of the Nez Perce Indians and concludes with her father's violent death. What other violent images and scenes do you remember from the story? What do these scenes tell us about this land, this life, and this family? What does the calving scene illustrate about the relationship between Iris and her mother, and, likewise, what does the branding and castrating scene show about Ike and his children?

2. Farming has often been portrayed in literature as the work of men against an implacable earth. In this novel, the farmland is often portrayed as feminine: on page 7, we learn that the family farmed by the cycles of the moon; on page 8, the ground lies "vulnerable, carvable, and pliant," and later, the "gold grain rushed into the bin the way a mother's milk comes in a while after a baby is born." How do these and similar images shape our perception of the land and the act of farming? What do they say about Iris as a single woman running a farm on her own?

3. The novel revolves around the question of whether Iris and her family are the rightful owners of the property they call Heart of the Beast or whether the land belongs to the Nez Perce. Were you surprised by the way this issue was ultimately resolved? Was the decision fair? Who do you believe the land belongs to, and what would you have done in Iris's position?

4. As her mother approaches death, Iris is charged with caring for her as if she were an infant. Have their roles reversed or stayed the same during this time? How were these two strong women different, and what did they have in common? Given more time, do you think they would have grown to value each other more?

5. Discuss the concept of legacy. Aside from the property itself, what legacies have been passed down in Iris's family? Are family legacies a kind of fate? Can they help Iris—and us—grow, or are they more like weights around our ankles?

6. As she takes in the harvest, Iris reflects, "With each day, I felt the dirt in handfuls landing on top of me. I was disappearing; the land

was taking me over. I began to look like it, my skin turned dull like earth, my fingerprints rubbed out, obscured by dust" (page 52). What is the significance of this statement? Do you think that the land is literally burying her?

7. Iris has always hated the sculpted busts of her family members, and has always wanted to get rid of them. What do these busts symbolize for Iris and for the story as a whole? Do you think she made the right choice about them in the end? What does her decision imply about her future relationship with her family's history? At the end of the book, Iris looks at the sculptures of her parents and sees them in a more positive light. Have they really become better people or is it just that Iris understands them better in her heart and mind?

8. Iris's aunt Hanna is strikingly different from the other members of her family. What makes Hanna unique? What does she have to offer Iris?

9. On page 207, Iris thinks, "Children bothered me. In fact, I loathed them. . . . It was more babies that made me sick. . . . Women and children never worked out." Where do you think this aversion comes from? Do you think her feelings are set in stone, or are they likely to change? Do you think Iris actually hates babies or hates and fears a vulnerable, small, immature part of her own self?

10. Tansy's arrival breathes fresh life into the farm. How does she change Iris, and what does her presence signal about the family's future? Were you surprised that she chooses to remain on the reservation? What is the importance, if any, of Tansy, who is both white and Indian, ending up owning Heart of the Beast?

11. Do you agree with Iris's decision to stay on the farm, even after the successive deaths of her brother, father, and mother? Is she trapped by her family's land? Empowered by it? Neither? While helping Tansy settle in, Iris realizes that "everything of my dead family was still in the house" (page 271). How is this true of more than just their personal effects? Why hasn't Iris cleaned house?

12. On page 296, Iris tells Henry, "I'm not bleeding. But I'm dying as much as anyone." What do you think she means?

13. Reread the story (pages 305–6) that gave Heart of the Beast its name. What does this legend mean to you? What can the story tell us about the Nez Perce, about Iris, and about America?

14. In the beginning of the novel, Elise tells her daughter that water will never rise above its source. It is only at the end of the book that we finally see the first image of rain and moisture rising. What message does this image leave us with?

Printed in the United States
149437LV00002B/7/A